BY FAITH DIVIDED

Recent Titles by Margaret Allan

THE MAMMOTH STONE
KEEPER OF THE STONE
THE LAST MAMMOTH

THE DOCTOR AT PARTRIDGE HILL
HIGHLAND DOCTOR
THE MAN FROM LAMB HILL
RETURN TO EDEN
SPIRITS WALKING WOMAN

BY FAITH DIVIDED

Margaret Allan

This first world edition published in Great Britain 2001 by
SEVERN HOUSE PUBLISHERS LTD of
9–15 High Street, Sutton, Surrey SM1 1DF.
This first world edition published in the USA 2001 by
SEVERN HOUSE PUBLISHERS INC of
595 Madison Avenue, New York, N.Y. 10022.

British Library Cataloguing in Publication Data

Allan, Margaret, 1922–
  By faith divided
  1. Women clergy – England – Yorkshire – Fiction
  I. Title
  823.9'14 [F]

ISBN 0-7278-5771-1

Except where actual historical events and characters are being
described for the storyline of this novel, all situations in this
publication are fictitious and any resemblance to living persons
is purely coincidental.

Typeset by Palimpsest Book Production Ltd.,
Polmont, Stirlingshire, Scotland.
Printed and bound in Great Britain by
MPG Books Ltd., Bodmin, Cornwall.

To Heather and Charlie
with thanks for the
great blessing of their love

One

It was a glorious morning. Already the sun was gilding the stone of the pack-horse bridge which spanned the beck and colouring the walls of Nyddbeck Church a soft rose. Andrea pushed her bedroom window wide open and gazed down on the village, empty and silent at this early hour. Silent except for the ever-present murmur of the hundreds of sheep that were scattered all over the craggy hillsides in this area of North Yorkshire.

For the next few years, at least, this village was to be her home. Her home and Ian's, once Ian moved out of the house in Durham and came to join her here in the manse. She had hoped he would have been with her last night, holding her in his arms in the big white-covered bed to kiss and caress her, to make love to her until both her mind and body were at ease. If Ian had been there she would not have still been wide awake at three a.m. listening to those sheep.

Now it was six thirty, and time for her morning prayers. Time to give thanks that her years of study and work at her placement churches were over. Time to give thanks that on this day, 6 July 1999, she was to be ordained and inducted as Minister of Nyddford with Nyddbeck. Joy surged through her at this last thought. Then she was impatient to be showered, dressed, and on her way to the small church here in Nyddbeck to prepare herself for the service of induction and ordination which was to take place in the larger church of Nyddford later in the day.

1

There was no one about in the village as she walked, tall and graceful, with her long dark hair loose about her shoulders, over the bridge, round the village green and into the little church which had, after only a few days here, already become dear to her.

'What a wonderful day this must be for you, my dear! I hope you'll be happy here, and find true fulfilment in your work.' Her predecessor, Mr Bickerdike, took her hands in his as he spoke to her in the porch of Nyddford Church shortly after the service of ordination came to an end. He now lived in a nursing home on the edge of the market town of Nyddford.

'Thank you, Mr Bickerdike.' She smiled into his gentle eyes, and promised to visit him soon, before turning to the next member of the congregation who was waiting to greet her.

'I'm really glad you decided to come to us, Andrea. If there's anything I can do to help you settle in don't hesitate to give me a ring. Dorothy Bramley, Abbot's Fold Farm,' the pleasant middle-aged woman reminded her. Andrea remembered that Dorothy was one of the church elders who had interviewed her when she had come to 'preach with a view' at the two churches earlier in the year.

'Thanks a lot, Dorothy,' she murmured, knowing already that here was someone she would enjoy getting to know better.

Then there was another woman reaching out for her hand, a tall, thin woman whose refined accent was informing her that they hoped she would not be making too many changes. 'I'm sure you'll bear in mind that we have a great liking for the Charles Wesley hymns at this church. They are part of our history, after all,' she could not resist adding.

Surely the contemporary Christian songs written by Graham Kendrick would become part of history in the next century,

Andrea longed to say, though she kept that thought to herself as the woman moved on to follow the crowd now moving in the direction of the church hall for refreshments.

'You'll not find things easy here, lass,' a burly red-faced man warned her. 'Folk don't send their children to Sunday school these days like they used to. They take 'em shopping instead. You'll have your work cut out keeping your church half full, but I wish you well all the same.'

'Thank you, I'll do my best,' Andrea managed to respond before the next handshake came.

'Don't take over much notice of Josh,' said the owner of a firm, work-worn hand. 'He's just a bit flummoxed at the idea of us choosing a woman this time. We never had the chance of a woman before, with Mr Bickerdike stopping here all these years. Good luck and God bless you, love! Anything a man can do, a woman can do just as well, I say!' This brought a chuckle from the people around her and a swift smile to Andrea.

So it went on, the greetings and good wishes from those who knew her and those who did not, once the solemn service during which she had promised to faithfully serve these people was over. The church door was propped wide open to allow the people from Nyddbeck, Nyddmoor and Nyddford, the members of her family, her fellow mature students from college and the friends she had made in Durham since her marriage to Ian to stream out into the church garden. The strong, heady scent of a huge arrangement of lilies that towered above Andrea in the church porch brought back to her sharp memories of that other service when Ian had stood beside her at the funeral of their adored only child. Pain pierced her, as it had done every day since wee Andrew had become a victim of meningitis. She fought the pain, and was giving silent thanks for the two short years of joy brought to her by the boy when Ian's mother came to speak to her.

'Have you seen Ian yet, Andrea? I thought he must have

arrived late and be staying at the back of the church, but he's not here, is he?'

'No.'

'Perhaps he's gone over to the church hall for some tea, if he's had a bad journey,' Marion, her own mother, suggested.

'I don't think he'd do that, but we'll soon find out. Shall we go over there?' Andrea saw that the church was empty now of everyone except the organist, who was still filling the air with the sound of Handel's *Water Music*. She led her parents and Ian's mother through the church garden to the hall. As they entered the building she turned to look back at the church, at the high arched windows and the graceful spire. A great sense of achievement filled her then, a feeling of pride that out of the depths of the grief and despair she had experienced a few years ago had come this new opportunity. This new life . . .

Inside the church hall her eyes widened with amazement when she caught her first glimpse of the huge table which was laden to overflowing with good Yorkshire fare provided by the ladies, and a few of the men, from her parishes. Pies, quiches and savouries fought for space with cakes, scones, teabreads, fruit flans and trifles.

'Oh, my! Just look at that!' she heard her mother gasp to her doctor father, Robert.

'They've certainly done you proud,' he exclaimed.

Then someone was putting a cup of tea in her hand and urging her to 'set to' and help herself to the food.

'It's been a big day for you, minister,' a male voice was saying as she gulped down the tea gratefully and waited for her cup to be replenished. 'Your husband must be very proud of you, and your parents of course,' he added. Then, 'Was your husband not able to be here today after all? I understood he had his own business, so there wasn't a problem about getting away for the day?'

'No, there wasn't,' she hastened to assure the man. 'I don't know why he's not arrived yet.'

'He had an early morning appointment somewhere, but he was expecting to be here before lunch,' Ian's mother began. 'I hope he hasn't . . .' She broke off then, not wishing to embarrass Andrea by making her own anxiety too obvious.

'Maybe he's had trouble with the car and had to stop off at a garage?' That was Marion speaking. 'How far away was his appointment, Andrea?'

Andrea hesitated. She really didn't know. Was it that she had been too busy to take enough notice of what Ian had said? Or was it that he hadn't told her exactly what his plans were? It was a couple of days since she had seen him, up at their house in Durham. She had urged him then to make his mind up about selling that house, but he had evaded the issue again and told her it might be better if they kept it so he could stay there overnight when he had to work late in the family antique business, established for many years in the city, or when the weather was bad.

'If he's got car trouble why hasn't he rung to tell us what's happening? He'll have his mobile with him, won't he?' Andrea's father frowned as he said that.

'He usually does.' Andrea was beginning to feel uneasy.

'I don't like it. I can't help worrying,' Ian's mother confessed. 'I wanted Ian to drive down with me this morning, only he said—'

Andrea's father turned towards her. 'What exactly did he say, Nancy? Where was he going that was so important that it couldn't be left for another day?'

'I don't know. I did ask, because I was so surprised at him making an appointment for today, but all he said was that it was too important to be postponed.'

The questions were brought to a halt by the first guests, some of whom had travelled a long distance to be at Andrea's ordination service, coming to take their leave. There were more good wishes, and more friendly exchanges to push the mystery of Ian's non-appearance to the back of Andrea's mind for the time being. Though more than once as she moved around the church hall she overheard people speculating about what had kept her husband away from the service and the celebration tea. Soon she became impatient to get back to the manse, where she was certain there would be a message from Ian on the answer-phone explaining why he hadn't turned up. Or he could be there in their new home waiting for her. Her spirits lifted at the thought. She wanted to be with him, to share with him all that had happened to her on this momentous day: the things people had said to her, the many kind thoughts they had expressed, the beauty of the flower-decked church and the glory of the music – even her sense of amazement that the people of her churches should have produced the lavish spread of food which was now being cleared away by a dedicated band of ladies from the two churches.

'What a marvellous tea!' she told them. 'I really can't thank you enough for all the trouble you've taken. Can I give you a hand with the washing up?'

'Oh no, my dear! Not today of all days. There'll be plenty for you to do here at other times. Go home now to the manse and put your feet up. You've been on them for a long time today.' That was Dorothy Bramley, balancing a full tray of used cups and saucers on her arm as she spoke. 'I'll see you in church tomorrow.'

As her father pulled his car into the drive of the manse, Andrea felt unease stir in her again. She had been hoping that Ian's car would be already parked there in the open garage beside her own small vehicle, but there was only an empty space. There could be a message though. There had to be. She jumped out of her seat and hurried to unlock the front door, leaving it open while she crossed the hall swiftly to check the answer-phone. Disappointment hit her when she found there were no messages at all.

'Isn't there a message from Ian?' his mother wanted to know.

Andrea shook her head. 'I can't understand it,' she muttered. 'Where is he? Why isn't he here?'

'Do you think there's been an accident?' Nancy Cameron was voicing her fears openly now.

'If there had been, we'd have heard by now,' Robert put in quietly but firmly.

'I expect he'll turn up soon with an explanation.' That was Marion trying to calm Ian's mother.

What sort of an explanation would it be though when Ian knew how much Andrea had wanted him to be there with her today? Why hadn't Ian come down from Durham yesterday after the business closed? Surely this business appointment could not have been more important to him than being beside her as she became Minister of Nyddbeck with Nyddford? Bewilderment grew stronger in Andrea's mind all the time.

Perhaps Ian had not really taken on board, even now, how much it had meant to her when her strongly felt call to serve her church had replaced the grief and depression that had soured her life after the death of their child? Certainly he had not discouraged her, but neither had he shown any real enthusiasm for the idea. Maybe he was grieving too deeply still for Andrew to be aware of the way he had allowed his life to become overfull of business meetings or sessions on the golf course, as he tried to fill the empty spaces that had once belonged to her and Andrew? They'd have to talk about it when he did get here, because he was spending more and more time away from her now. Andrea pushed that thought away from her as Ian's mother asked if she might use the phone to find out whether he was at the business premises in the city or at her home on the outskirts of Durham.

'Of course you can, Nancy, though I don't suppose he'll be up there,' Andrea said with a frown. She was at a loss now about what to do next. All she could think of was to go

7

into the kitchen and set the kettle to boil while she waited for Ian's mother to make the calls.

'There's no answer from either of them, so he's not there,' Nancy said as she joined Andrea in the kitchen.

For what remained of the day they all tried not to keep looking out of the window every time they heard a vehicle drawing near to the manse or straining their ears for the ringing of the telephone, which stayed ominously silent while Ian's mother watched television and Andrea's parents took a stroll around the village. For Andrea there was the solace of her study and the sermon for tomorrow that she needed to check once again. She wanted to have that finished before Ian arrived.

Nancy Cameron stared unseeingly at the TV screen. She wondered, yet again, why Ian had arranged an important business meeting for this morning, and who he could have been meeting. There had always been days spent away at large country house sales, but not these recent longer absences from his home in Durham. So what was going on? Was it all to do with Andrea's decision to train for the ministry rather than to return to teaching after the loss of baby Andrew? Whatever the reason for Ian's absence today, Nancy was disappointed with her son for not being beside Andrea when she needed his support. It must have looked bad to all those people who had filled the church and the hall where the celebration tea was held. It was not the best start for Andrea in her new life.

Yet Ian had certainly given her the impression that he would be here today, even though he had said he would not be able to drive down to Nyddbeck with her.

'You go ahead so you can give Andrea a hand with the lunch, then I'll join you all in plenty of time for the service in the afternoon,' he had promised.

So where was he now? Why had there been no word from him? Nancy could not rid herself of the feeling that something had happened to him.

*   *   *

'Where is Ian then? What's happened to him?' Marion Craig asked when she and Robert were alone in their room.

'I suppose there could be a good reason why he's not here. Perhaps he's underestimated the importance of this day for her: I'm not sure that he shares her strong faith.'

'That doesn't excuse his absence today. He was away on their anniversary too.'

Robert Craig sighed. 'I don't know what's happened any more than you do, but there's nothing we can do except be here for her if she needs us.'

'I felt so sorry for her when people were asking where her husband was. I think Nancy was feeling uncomfortable too, and quite worried about Ian. You don't think there could have been an accident, do you?'

'We'd have heard by now if there had been.' Robert frowned, unable to push aside his own uneasiness yet not wishing to alarm his wife.

'Ian's never been the same since the boy died. He seemed to shut Andrea out then and I don't think they've been quite as close since,' Marion Craig said thoughtfully.

'I've watched it happen that way sometimes with patients. One parent can find a way of coping with the grief and another can't. They often try to blank it out by overwork, or drink or drugs. Not that I've seen any evidence of that with Ian, though he could have been working too hard I suppose.'

'I can't bear to think about what might have happened. Andrea's been through so much already. I wish we lived nearer. Somewhere we could see her more often, as Ian's mother does,' Marion worried.

'Perhaps when I retire we'll move closer to Nyddbeck, if that will make you happier. This worry will be behind us then. Now, let's try to get some sleep because we've a long journey ahead of us tomorrow.'

Though her husband switched off the lamp and appeared

to slip into sleep easily Marion was unable to do the same. Her mind was too full of concern for her daughter's marriage. Would Ian manage to settle down here in this tranquil village away from the city where his business and most of his friends were? Would Andrea find the fulfilment here that she needed to make up for the loss of her child, and the fact that Ian refused to contemplate them having another baby? He had made no secret of the fact that he would not take the risk of having another child after losing Andrew.

'Don't worry about me, Mum,' Andrea had told her mother. 'I have my faith to lean on.'

Would that faith be enough for her in the days to come?

There was a bell ringing somewhere close at hand. Andrea woke from a troubled sleep and leapt out of bed to race down the stairs, pulling her robe about her as she went. How long had it been ringing? It could be someone in need of her help. Or it could be Ian, who had forgotten the key she had given him for the manse. She was breathless as she pulled open the door and peered out into the darkness.

There was a man standing there, but it was not Ian.

'Yes. Who is it?' She switched on the outside lamp as she asked the question, and saw that her caller wore a dark uniform.

'Sergeant Murgatroyd, Nyddford Police. Are you Mrs Andrea Cameron?'

'Yes.'

'May I come in please?' the man asked quietly.

'Yes, of course.'

Her heart seemed to stop for a long moment, then to thud loudly in her own ears as she opened the door wider and stepped to one side so that the uniformed man could enter the square hall.

'Shall we go somewhere where we can sit down?' he suggested.

His voice was quieter still now. He was a burly middle-aged man with iron-grey hair and troubled eyes. As she looked into those eyes Andrea knew that he had brought her bad news, very bad news. She clenched her hands tightly as she led him into the living room.

'I think you should sit down before I talk to you,' she heard him say.

Now she knew for certain that it was bad news, as she lowered herself to the sofa and waited for him to tell her what was plainly making him so ill at ease.

'Is your husband's name Ian Cameron?'

'Yes. Has there been an accident?' She had to know, could not bear to wait any longer trying to pretend that all was well.

'I'm afraid so.' He gave her time to absorb that before going on. 'A bad one.'

She took a deep breath, trying to quell the sickness that was invading her stomach, making an immense effort to hang on to her self control. 'How bad?' she heard herself ask.

'Your husband was dead when the rescue service arrived. They were there quickly so he would not have suffered.'

'Where? Where did it happen? I wondered why he didn't come . . .' Her voice trailed off, but it still sounded calm to her own ears.

'On a country road near Ravensdale.'

'Ravensdale! I'm not sure where that is . . .' She began to tremble violently.

'Is there anyone else living here with you? Someone who can come and help you?' He was on his feet again, a big gentle man who had never come to terms with this, the worst part of his job.

'My parents are staying, and my husband's mother,' she managed to tell him through chattering teeth.

It was then Andrea became aware of Ian's mother standing at the open door that led into the hall. Nancy was grey-faced as she stared with anguished eyes at the policeman. Andrea got to her feet and stumbled across the room to put her arms about the older woman.

'I guessed there had been an accident; I knew he'd be on his way here. Ian was on his way here, wasn't he, Andrea?'

'I suppose so. It happened at a place called Ravensdale, but I don't know where that is.'

Nancy shook her head. 'There must be some mistake. He wouldn't be there if he was on his way here for your service. There must be some mistake.'

'I'm afraid not. There were documents in his wallet with this address as well as some business cards for an antique dealer's business in Durham, and a photograph of Mrs Cameron.'

'I asked him to travel down with me . . .' Nancy began. 'If he had done he would still be . . .' The rest was lost in a storm of weeping.

'I'll make some tea for you,' the policeman said then. 'It might be a good idea to call your doctor too; you've both had a terrible shock.'

Andrea led Nancy to the sofa, biting hard on her lips as she struggled to contain her own shock. 'We won't need a doctor,' she managed at last. 'My father's a doctor and he's staying here at the moment.'

'I'll make that tea, then perhaps we should wake your father. You may need his help.'

The remainder of the night took on an unreal quality for Andrea as her parents came downstairs and the police sergeant left them to console one another, telling them that he would be in touch with them later. When morning light filtered into the room they were still sitting there with the curtains drawn and the fire switched on. Robert had wanted to give Nancy and Andrea a sedative and send them to bed but neither of them would have that. Instead they had taken in endless cups of sweet tea which neither of them wanted.

'I'll have a shower and get dressed,' Andrea told them when the curtains had been drawn back to let in a misty light. 'There's the nine thirty service at Nyddford,' she reminded them.

'You'll have to ask someone else to take that, won't you?' her mother said as she was on her way to the door.

'There is no one else. I'll have to be there.'

'You could cancel it. They'll understand, I'm sure,' her mother persisted.

'I want to be there. I need to be there. So don't fuss, Mum, please.' With that Andrea made her escape up the stairs to shower and dress.

When she went down again her father was waiting for her in the hall, looking immaculate in a dark suit and tie.

'I'll come with you,' he told her.

'There's no need, I can cope, but thanks, Dad.'

'I know you can cope, but I'd still like to come with you, if you'll have me.'

Her eyes filled with moisture as he took her hand firmly in his and went with her through the back door of the manse to where his car waited.

'We'll go in my car this morning,' he said.

This time she offered no protest but took her place beside him, ready for the journey through the mist-shrouded morning along the winding road that followed the beck from Nyddbeck to the larger village of Nyddford. They did not speak on the way. Robert knew an overwhelming love and compassion for his daughter. She was going to need so much courage, and so much faith, in the weeks and months and years ahead of her. He could not help wishing she had chosen an easier way of life, one which would not have placed such a heavy burden on her, but he knew that the choice had been made for her and that she could meet the challenge even on this most terrible day. Andrea had plenty of courage. He was proud of her.

Somehow Andrea got through the next couple of hours,

thankful for the weeks of careful preparation which enabled her to lead the service as calmly as though there had been no visit from the police and no such terrible news. She was aware at times of the almost tangible love flowing into her from the figure sitting in the front pew, and of that other love which had so often sustained her in days of acute anxiety and grief.

This time the grief was going to be so much worse, once the numbness of shock wore off. This time there would be no loving husband and family surrounding her with their care and concern. She would need that other love as she had never needed it so badly before. For now, all she could do was lift her gaze from the rows of people sitting before her listening intently to what she had to say and concentrate on the beauty of the east window.

As yet those people did not know what had happened to her husband. When they did know it would be much more difficult for her to face them.

Two

It was finished now, that terrible week in which Andrea had been told of Ian's death, been present at the inquest and then at the funeral in Durham. She was on her way back to Nyddbeck Manse to take up again the new life she had been forced to leave behind while she dealt with all the formalities and the sad little things that sudden death forced upon the next of kin.

Was it really less than two weeks since she had driven along this same road to begin her new life as minister to the parishes of Nyddbeck with Nyddford? The sun had been shining then and her mind had been filled with joyful anticipation of the work that lay ahead of her. She had known just how fortunate she was to have been offered the chance to live and work in such a beautiful place. The only thing to cast a shadow over her happiness had been the knowledge that Ian seemed to be spending more and more time away from her and becoming less and less interested in her work. He had been so relieved when she started to throw off the depression which had descended on her after the loss of their little son and began to talk about going back to her work as a primary school teacher until they had another child.

Then, when she was really well again and back at her job, he had told her that he did not want another child. She had been appalled, unable to believe that he meant what he said. When she had questioned him about it he had been adamant that he was not willing after losing Andrew to take such a

15

risk again. It had been a temptation to her at first to become pregnant against his wishes but she could not bring herself to do that.

Her longing for another child gradually fuelled her resentment against Ian. When the subject came up they would have arguments which usually ended with him walking out of the house. When she became afraid that Ian would one day leave her for good she knew she would have to learn to live with her disappointment. Gradually, imperceptibly, she found solace in her strong faith. When, unexpectedly, she had a breakdown in health and went to stay with her parents in Scotland she found herself with more time to think about how she was going to cope with never having another child. Sometimes she would go alone into the little kirk and ask for guidance. It was there one day that the answer came to her.

She could not change the way things had gone for her in the past but she could certainly change her future and find a way of life that would be more satisfying and fulfilling. Her strong faith seemed to be compelling her to make such a decision.

At first Ian did not believe she meant to make such a drastic change in their lives, but gradually he seemed to get used to the idea and perhaps even to be pleased that she no longer hankered after having another child. So she left teaching and began her years of training and study while he spent more and more time expanding the family business. It was in her final year that she began to wonder how things would be between them when her training was finished and her work and his might be in different places. Would it put more stress on their relationship?

'We don't have to live in Durham, even though the business is here,' she had reasoned. 'If we move to a place which is close enough for you to drive to work every day things will work out fine.'

Ian had not been so sure. 'Will they? Let's wait and see.'

'I'll have to live on the job,' she had pointed out. 'It's different for you, and the fact that your mother lives so close to the business will be a help, won't it?'

'I don't know. I just don't know how it will work out, for either of us.'

'You do know I have to do this, don't you, Ian?'

He had not answered her, had simply picked up his golf clubs and walked out of the house, not stopping to kiss her as once he would have done or to call out a goodbye.

Why was she going over all that in her mind now that she had left the motorway and was taking the single track road that led across the moors to her new home in Nyddbeck? There was no point in her going over all that again, as she had done so often every time she had been alone during the last few days. She would never know, now, whether the gulf which had widened between them would have been healed once they settled down together to life in Nyddbeck.

Neither would she ever know whether Ian had been on his way to join her in Nyddbeck when his car had smashed into a stone wall at Ravensdale, miles from the direct route between Durham and this area of North Yorkshire. It was one more mystery in a life which had been suddenly ended on that July day when she had been ordained . . .

Because the winding road which ran over the heather-covered moors was brilliant with sunshine and was not yet familiar to her, Andrea did not see the dog until it was too late. The dog leapt through a gap in the drystone wall ahead of her, intent on chasing a sheep that got away, and hit the side of her car with a thud that sickened Andrea. She slammed on the brakes, skidded slightly off the road and came to a halt with her front wheels resting on the heather. For a moment fright paralysed her, then the sound of the dog whimpering sent a wave of relief washing over her. It was alive! A moment later she was out of the vehicle and bending over the creature.

'Oh, you poor thing!' she murmured when she saw the

17

blood oozing from the damaged foreleg. 'I wonder who you belong to? I'll have to let them know you're hurt.' The dog, a handsome black and white collie, yelped when she touched it and found the identity disc hanging from a leather collar with the words 'Bramley, Abbot's Fold Farm, Nyddmoor'. 'I wonder where that is?' she murmured to herself. 'I'd better get the first aid box and try to bandage you up before I start looking for your owners.'

She turned back to the car and reached into the glove compartment, then swung round again as she heard a male voice speaking from just behind her.

'There's no need for that. I'll see to him when I get him home. You'd best take more care on these roads or it could be you that gets hurt next time.'

Her eyebrows rose. 'I was taking care. It wasn't my fault that he was running free—' She spoke more sharply than she intended, not yet over the shock of what had just happened.

'He was doing what he's meant to do, fetching the sheep for me.'

'Perhaps you should be taking better care of him when he's working then?' She could not resist adding that, even though it only resulted in the frown on the man's long, narrow face becoming even deeper.

'I didn't know the wall needed repairing again. I only fixed it a month or so ago after the last lot of visitors damaged it, and now my best dog's damaged as well. Sometimes I wonder why I bother to go on,' he remarked morosely.

Andrea did not know what to say. The man was so obviously sick to his back teeth. She knew that the farmers had been hard hit by the beef crisis and the long spell of bad weather but she had not expected so young a man to be giving in to despair because of a hurt dog and a damaged wall. She searched her mind for something to say that would not sound either stupid or patronising, but could think of nothing that would not be likely to cause offence. Not that the man would

linger now that the dog was on its feet and giving a weak
wag of a plumed white-tipped tail as he bent to stroke the
thick white ruff that circled its smooth black head. The dog
licked his hand and did not whimper as he lifted it carefully
under his arm and prepared to walk away.

'I could give you a lift if it would help,' she heard herself
offer. 'He'll be quite a weight to carry if you have far to go,
won't he?'

She was not surprised when he refused. 'You won't want
his blood all over your car. I've a tractor on the other side
of the wall that I can use.'

'You will get him to a vet?' she called as he crossed
the road.

'If I think it's necessary. Vets cost money.'

Andrea watched as he clambered over the damaged drystone
wall, carrying the dog under one arm as easily as if it had
been a little terrier rather than a large collie. Then the tractor
roared into life and carried man and dog over the heather until
they were out of her sight.

She turned back to her car then, but as she moved to open
the driver's door she found her eyes burning as moisture
gushed into them. Her shoulders began to shake and her
hands trembled so much that she was unable to get into the
car. Fighting now to regain self control she put both arms
up on the roof and allowed her head to fall on them, but the
tears which were never far away when she was alone engulfed
her. For some time she was unaware of everything about her,
unaware of the beauty of the rugged scenery, unaware of the
soft murmuring of the hundreds of grazing sheep or the hoarse
croaking of the pheasants. All she was aware of was her own
sense of guilt.

Was it her fault that the dog had been injured? Had her
thoughts been too much centred on her own troubles rather
than on the narrow, winding, unfamiliar road? Had it been her
fault that she could not settle for the childless marriage that

Ian had decided on? Had Ian become aware of the resentment she had harboured against him because of that?

'Dear Lord, forgive me,' she murmured as she ran out of tears at last and accepted her own shortcomings. 'I'll have to do better than this, won't I?'

She lifted her head and began to take deep breaths of the fresh moorland air, allowing her body to relax with her back resting on the side of the vehicle. It was then she saw the figure striding towards her along one of the many sheeptracks which dissected the moor. She began to fumble with the door handle and found it difficult because of the dampness on her hands where her tears had overflowed her small hankie.

'Are you all right?'

The man, tall and athletic in build, seemed to cover the distance between them much quicker than Andrea anticipated. She had hoped to be back in the car and driving away before he was near enough to be able to see that she had been weeping. By the time she had managed to open the door he was within touching distance of her, close enough to cause her acute embarrassment.

'I'm fine,' she mumbled, wishing he would walk on.

He was frowning as he spoke to her again. 'You don't look fine. In fact you look rather upset.' His glance was challenging, inquisitive.

Andrea sighed audibly. He was standing right in her way. She would have to wait for him to move before it would be safe for her to get back on to the road, and he seemed to have no intention of moving. Her eyes took in the haversack which sat easily on square shoulders clad in a checked shirt, but she avoided looking into his face again. All she wanted was for him to go, to move off before he could be certain that she had been crying.

'I'm fine, really,' she insisted, unaware that her voice betrayed her.

'I was afraid when I first spotted you that there was

something wrong; that perhaps you were hurt. Or maybe feeling ill and needing help. You were leaning over your car and you seemed to be in some distress.'

'Your eyes must have been deceiving you.'

'There's nothing wrong with my eyes.'

'And there's nothing wrong with me!' She was becoming angry now, and terribly afraid that if he did not go she might break down again at any time and embarrass both of them. Then she saw the expression on his face and knew that she had offended him. He did not deserve that, after showing such concern for a stranger.

'Then I won't detain you any longer.' He took a couple of steps backward, allowing her enough space to move the car.

'I'm sorry! It was rude of me to speak to you like that when you only meant to be kind.'

'I made a mistake. I shouldn't have intruded,' he said harshly.

So he knew that there was something wrong, but he did not know all of it.

'I hit a dog as it came over the wall there,' she said by way of explanation. 'It left me rather shocked.'

'This isn't the easiest of roads to use when you're a stranger to the area.'

He must have seen her suitcase on the back seat.

'No,' she agreed. Perhaps he would move on now she had given him an explanation for her distress. Then she could be on her way too.

He seemed in no hurry to move on. 'What about the dog? How badly hurt was it?'

'A damaged paw. It's owner took it away. He had a tractor on the other side of that damaged wall.' She indicated the place where the dog had come from.

'Sounds like Dave Bramley. Some of his land comes as far as this.'

21

'I wanted him to take the dog to a vet, but he didn't seem to think it necessary.'

'Perhaps he was thinking about the expense. He's having a tough time on the farm.'

'I would have paid the bill, as I was the one who caused the injury.'

'I doubt very much whether Dave Bramley would have let you do that. He's certainly pushed for money but he's also very proud.'

'Surely the welfare of his dog is more important than the man's pride?'

'You needn't worry about the welfare of Tyke, if it was Tyke you hit. Dave's a good man; he cares more for his animals than he does for himself.'

'Obviously he's a friend of yours.' Had she put her foot in it with her criticism of the farmer? She seemed to be getting things all wrong today. 'I'm sorry if I spoke out of turn.'

'He's my landlord. Or rather his mother is. I'm staying in her cottage at present. So we might meet again while you are here. I hope so anyway.'

Obviously, after seeing her luggage on the back seat and learning of her unfamiliarity with the moorland road, the man had assumed she was on holiday in the area. Andrea decided she was too tired to put him right about that. If he was a holidaymaker himself they would be unlikely to meet again. All she wanted now was to get safely back to Nyddbeck and spend some time alone in the manse preparing for tomorrow.

'I'll have to be going. Thanks a lot for your concern,' she said, forcing a smile. 'It was very kind of you to bother.'

'As I said, you had me worried for a moment.' The long glance from dark brown eyes that met her own blue stare made her look away to where several sheep were gathering at the rear of her car. 'Take care now, and don't worry too much about the dog. Dave will make sure he's all right,' he told her with a smile.

'Can I give you a lift back to your cottage, as I've delayed you?' She felt bound to offer.

'I'm only out for a walk so I won't take you out of your way, but thanks all the same. By the way, I'm Bill Wyndham.' He extended a hand and shook her own with warm, strong fingers.

'Goodbye now,' she said as she switched on the engine and set the car in motion.

He lifted a hand to wave briefly as she drove past him. She wondered whether she would ever see him again, then put him out of her mind as she came to the place where a couple of hairpin bends needed extra careful negotiation.

Bill Wyndham watched her car from his vantage point high above the village of Nyddbeck until it turned into a side road and disappeared from his view, but he could not dismiss the woman herself from his thoughts as easily. She had explained her recent tears by telling him she had hit Dave's dog, but the puffy skin around her eyes and the dark half-moon shadows beneath them spoke of a much more profound sorrow. Her attitude towards him had been defensive too, as though in some way she resented his concern for her. When he had introduced himself just before her departure he had expected her to do likewise but she had avoided doing that, deliberately perhaps?

Who was she, and where was she staying? With a bit of luck, and judging by her unfamiliarity with the road, she was just arriving for her holiday. So maybe he would meet her again on one of his afternoon walks? Whoever she was, she was certainly beautiful in a way that did not require make-up to enhance it. Her voice was lovely too, in spite of the huskiness left over from her weeping, with that faint hint of Scots which no amount of education would ever quite manage to eradicate.

It was a long time since Bill had given so much thought to a living woman. His women nowadays were all creatures of his imagination, except for the one who lived still in his memory, and it was better that way. The black-haired woman with the amazing blue eyes and the remote air would be soon forgotten once he was back in his studio and working again. It was only his unexpected encounter with her at a time when she was so obviously trying to come to terms with some recent trauma that made him unable to forget her as he strode across the broken wall. He stopped there to replace the stones to a height where the sheep would not be able to trespass as far as the road before making his way up the rough track that led to Jacob's Cottage.

Three

There was no one about in the village as Andrea drove slowly alongside the beck until she reached the manse and got out of the car to open the gates. Early chrysanthemums bloomed against the drystone boundary wall. Closer to the house there were roses whose scent wafted towards her as she took a look around. Someone had cut the lawns while she had been away in Durham. She must find out who, and thank them for their kindness.

Most of the villagers would know by now that she was no longer a wife but a widow. They would not know what to say to her when she met them, as she was bound to do during the next few days. She would probably find it difficult to know what to say to them too. During her long training she had been involved with so many different situations which would test her to the limit, but not this. Her father had said she would cope with it, that her faith would support her; and she was quite determined that it would.

She reached the porch before she caught sight of the flowers leaning against the broad front door, a huge sheaf of apricot and white gladioli and tall carnations. Her first thought was that they must have been sent by her parents, or by Ian's mother. Their thoughtfulness and love brought a lump to her throat as she picked up the flowers and carried them into the house.

Once inside the hall, she seemed to be surrounded by letters that had arrived during the days she had spent in her old home in Durham; the home she had shared with Ian. There were several envelopes scattered around which had overflowed from the letter cage attached to the front door and were now spread in a wide arc of white and pastel colours on the carpet. More cards of condolence, she guessed. When would it all end, these messages from friends and acquaintances some of whom she had almost forgotten? They would all have to be answered, sooner or later.

Because the place seemed stuffy and airless she hurried about opening windows before finding a vase to put the flowers in. As she removed the outer covering of flower-printed paper she discovered an envelope with her name on it. Inside, on a single sheet of thick notepaper, a few words expressing sympathy from the church members were written above the signature of Dorothy Bramley. A PS from the woman Andrea knew to be the most senior elder at the village church invited her to ring Nyddbeck 5345 if Dorothy could help her in any way. She would ring Dorothy Bramley to thank her as soon as she had drunk the mug of tea she was longing for.

She took the tea into the back garden when it was ready, and found there on the garden seat a basket of eggs and some tomatoes which smelled still of the local greenhouse where they had been grown. There was no note with these, just a tiny card bearing only two words, 'So sorry'.

How kind these strangers were. They would never know just how much their tokens of compassion meant to her. For a while she sat sipping the tea and allowing the silence that was broken only by birdsong to bring her a few moments of tranquillity after a week in which she had rarely been alone until she went to her bedroom at night, with sleeping tablets already beginning to take effect.

This would be her life from now on: coming back to an empty house where there was no longer even the chance of her husband joining her, where there was no longer his passionate love and companionship to look forward to. So that other deep spiritual love which had brought her to this place would have to be enough for her from now on. It *would* be enough, she vowed, for the rest of her life.

Later, she rang Dorothy Bramley's number to thank her for the flowers.

'They are so lovely, I can't tell you how much they cheered me up when I saw them propped against the front door,' she said warmly.

'Against the front door?' Dorothy Bramley sounded surprised. 'I asked my son to bring them down for me this morning when he was delivering some potatoes to the Nyddford Inn, but I told him to bring them round to the back garden so it wouldn't be obvious to anyone that you were still away. David can't have remembered. Though I mustn't be too hard on him because he's a lot on his mind just now.'

'All was well, anyway,' Andrea hastened to reassure her. 'In fact when I opened the back door some other kind person had left me a basket of eggs and some tomatoes. I don't know who to thank for those because there was no name on the little card.'

'That was probably Ben Harper. He lives at Ford House, on this side of Nyddford, and he grows his own tomatoes. You would have met him at your ordination service, but I don't suppose you'll remember now, after what happened that day. I'm so sorry, my dear, about all you've had to go through since I last saw you. I know how terrible it must have been for you . . .'

'Yes. I need to try and get on with things here, now that I've done everything I can in Durham. There's the service at Nyddford tomorrow, I'll have to talk to you about the music for that, and about readers.'

'I was hoping to come down and see you about that tonight, but David's dog has been hurt and he needs to take it to the vet, so I'll have to stay here with the children till he gets back,' Dorothy Bramley explained worriedly.

'Shall I come and see you then?' Andrea offered.

'If you're sure you feel up to it, my dear.'

'I'll be much better doing something, keeping busy.' She had been doing that through all her waking hours these last few days, keeping busy clearing the Durham house, trying not to think too deeply about what had happened to Ian.

'Then come up as soon as you like. Follow the beck until you reach the main road, cross that and drive up Abbot's Hill until you see the abbey ruins ahead of you. Take the right turn and you'll find us at Abbot's Fold Farm.'

'I'll see you in an hour or so then, and thanks again, Dorothy.'

Was it the dog which had run into her car, Andrea wondered as she put down the phone. It could be, even though Dorothy had called her son David rather than Dave, as Bill Wyndham had named him. If it was the same farmer Andrea hoped she would not meet him when she went to Abbot's Fold Farm to discuss the details of tomorrow's service. The impression had remained with her that he held her responsible for the accident to his dog.

She was in a for a surprise when she reached Abbot's Fold Farm, an hour or so later, after driving there on one of the roads she had not encountered on her previous visits to the area, the long, winding uphill road that was called Abbot's Hill. Her reading of the history of Nyddbeck with Nyddford had supplied her with the information that in centuries past the monks had travelled on foot or on horseback down this hill from the now-ruined abbey to minister to the people of those villages in a small building close to the bridge in Nyddbeck. All that remained now of that building were a few scattered blocks of stone. Much of the rest had been used in the construction of some of the farmhouses and cottages to be found in the area.

Because Bill Wyndham had told her that the Bramleys were experiencing hard times she had half expected to find a small run-down dwelling when she turned into the side road as directed by Dorothy Bramley. Instead, as she parked her car outside the sturdy gates and got out to open them, she was amazed to see across a concrete-surfaced yard a large and absolutely lovely building which more closely resembled a small manor house than a farmhouse.

In the mellow evening light the huge blocks of grey stone from which it was built glowed pale golden beneath a blue slate roof, the many windows reflecting back the rose colour of the dying sun. There was no evidence to be seen of poverty or neglect.

'What a beautiful house!' she exclaimed as Dorothy Bramley came through the open back door to meet her half-way across the yard.

Dorothy's face lit up with a gentle smile of pleasure. 'Yes. We're lucky to still have it when so many farmers are being forced out of business. It's been in the family for over two hundred years, so of course we'd like to see it handed on to young Jack one day. That's unless he decides he doesn't want to be a farmer like his dad or his grandad. At the moment that's all he does want, to be working alongside David as soon as he's old enough.'

'Jack is your grandson, I suppose?'

'Yes, he's ten and just like David was at the same age. Carla is fifteen and more like Jill. Come along into the house and we'll sort things out for tomorrow while we have the place to ourselves. Then perhaps you'd like to stay and have supper with us if you've nothing else planned.'

She did not wait for Andrea to answer but led the way through the back door into a back hall where there was plenty of evidence of family and country life, with raincoats hanging on pegs above a rack of stout shoes and wellington boots, and a few walking sticks stacked in a corner.

As they moved on through the centre of the house Andrea caught glimpses of a spacious kitchen which housed an

Aga cooker, a disused pantry which had been turned into a playroom and a dining room furnished with table, chairs and a dresser of dark oak. The room they settled in to discuss the music for the next day's service faced over the front garden of Abbot's Fold Farm and had a wide view of rolling moorland and craggy hills. In the distance the remains of the old abbey which gave the farm its name could be plainly seen.

'I suppose that's the abbey, or what remains of it,' Andrea mused.

'Yes. It attracts quite a lot of tourists at this time of the year, which is a help to us now that the farm isn't earning enough. We're able to let off the cottage and take a few bed and breakfast bookings,' Dorothy told her.

'I met one of your tourists this afternoon, I think. A man called Bill Wyndham.'

Dorothy smiled. 'Bill is hardly a tourist any more. He's been here for months now.'

'A long holiday!' Andrea's voice expressed her surprise.

'Not really. Not now. Bill came here last winter for a rest and liked it so much that he's now looking for a home to buy somewhere around here.' Dorothy sounded pleased about that.

They settled down then to the business of choosing hymns, which did not take very long since Dorothy had already given some thought to it. When that was done Andrea became aware that the older woman was anxious to say something to her but didn't quite know how to begin. Of course, she guessed, this woman who had so much more experience of the life of the two local churches must be worrying about how she was going to cope with things tomorrow. She would have to find a way to reassure her.

'Please don't worry too much about how I'll manage, Dorothy,' she said quietly. 'I was able to cope on the morning after I heard about the accident, and I've had over a week since then to come to terms with things. I'll be all right.'

'I was afraid the shock might not have fully registered with you yet,' Dorothy confessed. 'It can take some time when it happens very suddenly. It certainly did for David.' She paused, her eyes suddenly full of sadness, then added, 'In fact I don't think he has really come to terms with what happened yet.'

'Do you mean when your husband died?'

The older woman shook her head. 'Oh no, Jacob's death was a merciful release, since there was no cure available. I mean when Jill died.'

'Was Jill your daughter-in-law?'

Dorothy sighed. 'Yes, and I still miss her a lot. She was a dear girl. Everyone loved her. David was devastated.'

The silence that followed her remark was broken by the arrival of a Land Rover at the gate of the farm and the excited barking of more than one collie. Dorothy got to her feet at once and made for the door. 'That'll be David back with Tyke. He'll be ready for something to eat. You will stay, won't you, Andrea?'

'I really ought to get back and finish my sermon . . .'

'I don't suppose you've had a meal yet, have you? You won't have had time.'

'No,' Andrea confessed. 'I haven't unpacked or anything. I was later getting away from Durham than I expected to be.'

'So you might as well eat here. It will save you time.'

Andrea bit her lip with frustration. How was she going to avoid staying now without hurting the other woman's feelings? Dorothy seemed so keen for her to stay, but Andrea was not looking forward to having to meet David Bramley again. She knew she would have to meet up with him again sooner or later but she was not ready yet. How could she get out of it without offending Dorothy? She followed Dorothy out of the room and through the hall to the kitchen still searching for the right words.

The big farmhouse kitchen which had been empty half

31

an hour ago when she had caught a glimpse of it seemed to be full now of people and animals. There was David Bramley, his face secretive and unsmiling, stroking the head of the collie, which had a bandaged paw. There was a small dark-haired boy who had to be David's son because of the likeness in mannerisms as well as looks, and there too was Bill Wyndham. He was the one who spoke to her first.

'I didn't think we'd meet again so soon,' he said, obviously pleased. 'Don't tell me you are staying here too?'

'No, I just called to see Dorothy.'

Andrea was conscious of the eyes of David Bramley resting curiously on her while she was talking. He was probably waiting to tell her how badly she had injured his dog. How could she possibly stay for a meal, with him judging her so harshly for something which had not been entirely her fault?

'I told you the dog probably belonged to Dave, didn't I?' Bill Wyndham said. 'I told you not to worry so much, too, and here's Tyke all patched up and almost as good as new.'

'What happened to Tyke?' The small boy hurled himself across the kitchen to fling himself on the floor at the feet of the dog and gaze with enormous eyes at the bandaged paw.

'He's had a bit of an accident, Jack,' Bill Wyndham said before David Bramley could speak. 'You know, like you did last week when you fell off your bike.'

'Why has he got a bandage on? Is it because his foot's falling off?'

Bill laughed. 'No, of course not! It's just to keep the cut clean.'

Jack scowled. 'But I only had a plaster on my cut leg.'

'But you didn't go to the vet, did you? Your gran sorted you out,' Bill told him with another laugh.

'Why did Tyke get his leg cut?' Jack persisted. His frown made him look more like his father then ever, Andrea noticed.

'Because he didn't look where he was going before he crossed the road,' Bill answered.

'Why didn't he look?'

'Because he was chasing a sheep.' It was David Bramley who spoke this time and his voice was curt as he spoke. 'Now shall we close the subject?'

As if to make certain that the subject was closed he walked out of the kitchen and into a smaller room which opened off it. Andrea could hear water running as he washed his hands at a sink there. She was unable to dismiss the injury to the collie from her own mind because a memory lingered there of the comment David had made when she suggested him taking the dog to a vet. 'Vets cost money,' he had said. So she was going to have to offer to pay the vet's bill, wasn't she, and making that offer to a man like David Bramley was not going to be easy.

The meal to be shared with the farmer and his family was something she could have done without, but it was too late now because Dorothy was drawing out one of the chairs set about the large oblong table which dominated the kitchen and waiting for her to take her place there. A couple of minutes later David Bramley came back into the room and slid into the empty chair right opposite to her. He was unsmiling and silent. Plainly he was not pleased to have her as a guest in his home.

Four

Had she done the right thing in asking the new minister to stay and have supper with them, Dorothy Bramley wondered uneasily as she caught the expression on her son's face. It had seemed like a good idea at the time, since the poor girl was on her own now without the support of either her parents or her mother-in-law to help her come to terms with her loss. Now another long survey of David's set face was helping the doubts to pile up fast.

'Whereabouts in Scotland are you from, Mrs Cameron?' Bill was asking, trying to ease the heavy atmosphere which had descended on them all.

'Freochmore. It's a small town, or large village, in the north-west Highlands. My father is a doctor there and my mother a nurse.' Andrea smiled as she answered.

'Mum was a nurse!' Carla Bramley broke in eagerly. 'She was—'

'Eat your meal before it's cold, Carla,' her father ordered. 'Your gran needs you to finish the ironing she didn't manage to do this afternoon.'

He still couldn't bear to hear anyone mention Jill, not even her own children, and it was more than time he helped them to come to terms with their grief by talking about her. Dorothy felt the familiar knot of worry tighten inside her. She knew that David carried a burden of guilt about what had happened to Jill. That, and what was happening to the farm profits these days, kept him awake and pacing the floor of the room above her head for hours most nights. The letting of her own spacious cottage and the money she earned from doing bed and breakfasts was just about keeping the farm going. Even that seemed to upset David. He kept telling her she ought to keep the money herself rather than putting it towards the housekeeping or bill-paying.

'I don't think I've been to Freochmore, though I've seen a lot of Scotland both on holidays and on working trips,' Bill began again. 'It's a beautiful country.'

'Yes, if you like mountain scenery.'

'I certainly do. Are you a climber, or a walker? If so, you must miss the mountains.' Bill was determined to keep the conversation going. David's unfriendly attitude to the new minister was probably making him feel uncomfortable. It had been a blessing having Bill here in Jacob's Cottage these last few months. Dorothy knew she would miss him when he found a place of his own to buy.

Bill was such good company, so interesting to talk to over a mug of tea or coffee, and easy for the children to talk to too. He ought to have children of his own, she mused, not for the first time. He was talking now to Andrea about some of the places in Scotland where his work as an artist had taken him, and Carla was hanging on to his every word. Carla and Jack would certainly miss Bill when he left, but David was beginning to resent his presence in the house.

'If you've finished, Carla, you can leave the table and get on with the ironing.' David spoke sharply to his daughter.

'But I wanted to hear more about Scotland,' Carla protested. 'We've just got a new girl at school from up there. I can't understand everything she says about where she used to live because she's got such a funny accent.'

'That can wait. The ironing can't. There are the school shirts to be done. I don't want your gran doing those tomorrow as well as cooking the dinner. Or she might not have time to go to church, and we don't want that, do we?'

The final remark was made with such heavy sarcasm that Dorothy felt a tide of hot colour flooding up from her neck to her cheeks. How could he, and with Andrea Cameron sitting only a short distance away from him? She would speak to him about it as soon as they were alone, she decided. No matter how miserable David was there was no excuse for such unkind behaviour to a young woman who had not even had the time yet to adjust to the loss of her own partner. Dorothy held her breath as she waited to hear how Andrea Cameron would respond.

'I'd love to help you with the ironing, Dorothy,' Andrea said quietly. 'It's one of the things I most enjoy doing.'

'I hate it! It's really, really a pain!' Carla told her, pulling a face which made Andrea laugh.

'It can be fun. I had a holiday job once during my college days, working as a wardrobe mistress at one of the theatres in Edinburgh. There were rehearsals going on all the mornings and actors and actresses coming and going all the time. I got to see some of the shows as well.'

'I want to be an actress,' Carla declared, striking a dramatic pose with one hand beneath her chin and the other on the back of her head.

Jack spluttered with laughter. 'Pigs might fly, our Carla!' was his comment.

They all smiled at this, except for David who rarely smiled these days. He got to his feet ready to set about the next task on the farm, but turned back to speak to his daughter.

'Don't forget what I said, Carla.'

Carla scowled at him but did not answer.

'Can I help you, Dad?' Jack was already on his feet and half-way to the door.

David nodded. 'All right, till your bedtime.'

'Could I have a word with you, please, before you go?'

Dorothy felt unease stir in her again as Andrea made her request. If it was anything to do with the church David would not want to know. He might even refuse to talk to her. Perhaps she ought to have warned Andrea about why neither of the children took part in any of the Sunday school or church activities with their friends from the village, but it was too late now. All she could do was offer a silent prayer that her son would not be rude again to this poor young woman who had already suffered such a bad beginning to her life here.

Andrea guessed that David Bramley was eager to get back to his work on the farm, and she certainly was not looking forward to detaining him. She had experienced enough of his surly behaviour over the supper table to last her for some time, but since the services of a vet had been required for his dog she felt obliged to offer to pay the bill, even if the injury to the animal had not been entirely her fault.

He was waiting for her by the back door, scuffing his feet impatiently. The dog, which had been lying on the mat just inside the door with the bandaged paw outstretched while he licked at it busily, began to wag a plumed tail in welcome and at the same time struggle to his feet.

'Lie down, Tyke! You're on the sick list today,' came the command from his master, but softly.

'I won't detain you for long,' Andrea began. 'I just wanted to say that I'm quite prepared to pay the vet's bill when it comes.'

'That won't be necessary,' he replied curtly.

'If it was my fault,' she protested. 'You did seem to blame me at the time.'

'I didn't know who you were then. I took you to be a tourist.'

'What difference would that make?'

'I'd rather not go into that.'

'I don't understand why.'

'I should have made allowances. I like to be fair.'

She was beginning to understand now. He was putting the

accident down to her state of mind. Assuming she had still not got over the shock of Ian's death.

'I like to be fair too. If I caused an injury to your dog I should be responsible for paying for his treatment.'

He sighed, and suddenly she saw beneath the anger and frustration a man who had plumbed such depths of loss and grief himself that he was able to fully comprehend a world where everything, even matters of safety, had no meaning. He was not to know that for her, because of her faith, life would always still have meaning.

'My mother will be very upset with me if I allow you to pay the vet's bill,' he said at last when she had begun to wonder whether the silence between them would ever be broken.

'There's no need for her to know, is there, if you just send the bill on to me and I post a cheque back to you?'

'I'd rather you forgot about it,' he said harshly. 'I'm sure you have plenty of other things to worry about just now.'

With that he strode away across the yard to where Jack waited for him.

Back in the kitchen Andrea found Carla setting up the ironing board while Dorothy washed the china and cutlery they had used for their meal at the sink unit beneath the window.

'Why don't we have a dishwasher like everyone else has, Gran?' the girl wanted to know.

'Because we can't afford one just now. There are things we need more for the farm.'

'The farm! It's always the farm every time we need things everyone else has!'

'I don't think everyone has a dishwasher. It's only some people,' Dorothy reasoned.

'Have you got one, Mrs Cameron?' Carla asked.

'Not in the manse. I had one in my house in Durham.'

'Why didn't you bring it with you?'

That wasn't easy to answer. Andrea found that she did not

want to have to tell the girl, and the older woman, that Ian had argued that he wanted to keep on the house in Durham. She had suggested that they let the house to holidaymakers, or to people from the university, but he refused to consider that either. So she had been forced to leave behind quite a lot of things that would have been useful in the manse.

Now the thought came to her that she would be able to do as she liked with the house in Durham because Ian had left everything there to her, though for some reason much less money than either she or his mother had expected. She pushed that thought away from her with a shudder and concentrated on answering the girl's question.

'Because we hadn't quite decided what to do about the house in Durham, whether to sell it or let it to someone from the university. If we let it we would need to leave things like the dishwasher. Now, if you'll find the iron for me I'll give your gran a hand with ironing some of those shirts.'

'There's really no need for you to do this. I'm sure you've got a lot to do down in the manse,' Dorothy protested.

Andrea shook her head. 'There's only my sermon to finish off. I wrote most of it very early this morning when I woke up too early and couldn't get back to sleep.'

'What did you do before you were a minister?' Carla asked as she banged the steam iron down on the ironing board.

'I was a teacher, a primary school teacher.'

'Why did you stop doing that? I mean, teachers have lots of holidays and they don't often have to work on Sundays like ministers do. Mr Bickerdike hardly ever went on holiday and he always had to work on Sundays,' Carla told her.

'You ask too many questions, Carla.'

'I don't mind, Dorothy. I enjoyed teaching very much but . . .' Andrea hesitated and decided not to go on and tell the girl about the lovely little son who had not lived, and how she had felt afterwards that she could not go back to teaching small children when there was no longer any prospect of her having a child of her own. 'You see gradually I came to realise that there was something I wanted to do far more than I had ever wanted to teach.'

'You mean you actually wanted to be a minister more than you wanted to be a teacher?' Carla could hardly believe what she was hearing.

'Yes, that's right.'

'Of course part of your work now will involve teaching, won't it?' Dorothy put in. 'With there being a church school at Nyddford and the Sunday schools at both of the churches.'

'We don't go to Sunday school or church any more,' Carla said loudly, almost aggressively.

'Don't you?' Andrea turned to Dorothy with surprise in her expressive eyes. As their grandmother was an elder at Nyddbeck Church, Andrea had assumed that they would also go there on Sundays.

Dorothy looked uncomfortable as she confirmed what Carla had just said. 'No, not now. Not for the last year or so.'

Andrea frowned. 'Perhaps you'll start going again when we get some of the new projects that I'm planning under way?'

'I don't think so. Dad wouldn't let us,' the girl said decisively.

Andrea was about to say something else when she saw Dorothy shaking her head, warning her perhaps to leave the subject alone. So she would, for the time being anyway. 'Where are these shirts, Carla?' she said instead.

She was leaving the farm an hour later, having finished the ironing, when Dorothy Bramley raised the subject again as they walked together to the gate.

'I . . . I hope you'll be able to understand about the children, Andrea,' she began hesitantly. 'I feel very badly about them not going to church as they always used to do. I know Mr Bickerdike was quite upset when they didn't come with me after their mother died. It's difficult for me to explain the reason without sounding disloyal to my son.'

Plainly the older woman was embarrassed and finding it difficult to go on. Andrea guessed at her distress and wanted to help her but she knew she must proceed with caution. So she smiled and touched her on the shoulder, knowing it would be all too easy to say the wrong thing.

'We'll have plenty of time to talk later, Dorothy,' she assured her. 'I must be going now or I won't get my unpacking done before I go to bed. Thanks so much for asking me to supper, I really enjoyed it.'

'Thanks for ironing the shirts, my dear. You're much quicker, and better, at that than I am. I hope you'll come and see us again one day.'

'I hope so too, though I expect we'll meet down in Nyddbeck before long.' It was Bill Wyndham who spoke now as he left the farmhouse and looked across the yard to where wide gates were open to reveal a rose-filled garden and a stone-built single-storey dwelling. 'I'd better go and finish the work I abandoned for a long hike,' he remarked to the older woman.

Andrea left then as the colours in the evening sky changed from blue and white to crimson and gold. When she reached her car out in the lane she stood for a long moment looking back at Abbot's Fold Farm. The scene was so peaceful, with the lovely old farmhouse coloured deep gold by the dying sun and the late song of a blackbird bringing an aching sweetness to the moorland air. It was all so tranquil.

Yet beneath the tranquillity she was certain there was so much anguish, so much discord, so much bitterness that was already infiltrating the lives of Carla and Jack, and bringing worry and pain to their grandmother. It was a good thing Dorothy had those children for company, and Bill Wyndham close at hand. She was going to need all the help she could get, with her son in such a morose state of mind.

Dorothy Bramley moved across the yard to lean over the drystone wall and give Andrea a farewell wave as she drove slowly along the narrow lane on her way back to the village below. She had a suspicion that David had upset the new minister about something during the few minutes he had spoken to her alone out here in the yard. What had it all been about, she wondered.

Surely David had not already been telling Andrea in his sometimes too forthright manner why Carla and Jack would not be at Sunday school or church? Surely he would not be so cruel as to pour out all his own bitterness and disbelief to this young woman who had just as much to be angry about, but who was behaving with such courage and dignity? Certainly she had got the impression as she watched through the window of the utility room that there was some tension between her son and the new minister.

What was happening to David these days? It was eighteen months now since the tree had fallen on Jill as she got out of her car on that storm-filled winter night and still he had not come to terms with what had happened. In fact he seemed to her to be more shut into himself now than he had been in the early days of his bereavement. Then he had been quiet and withdrawn with her but had managed to speak kindly to his children. Now he was permanently on a short fuse with his children, with her and with himself.

It had not helped that there were such hard times these days for all farmers because of the beef crisis and that the sheep prices had been at an all-time low, but he had the blessing of his children to be thankful for, his good health and the fact that he was the owner of Abbot's Fold Farm and not a tenant farmer as some in these parts were. Yes, David had so much to be thankful for yet he was thankful for nothing these days. Worse still, he believed in nothing. There was a total lack of faith in him now which he was attempting to pass on to his children.

Dear God, please help us all, Dorothy found herself praying.

Five

During the days that followed, as she immersed herself totally in her work in the two Dales villages of Nyddbeck and Nyddford, Andrea found herself thinking back at times to her first visit to Abbot's Fold Farm. There was nothing to take her up to Nyddmoor again during that first week, yet memories of words that had been spoken at the farm, or a feeling about things that remained unsaid kept coming back to trouble her. She knew that one day she would have to go to the farm again. Dorothy Bramley had already invited her to do that and she could not hurt Dorothy's feelings by refusing.

'Come as soon as you've had time to get settled in, my dear,' Dorothy had urged when they met after the morning service the day after Andrea's first visit to her home.

'It won't be for a while, Dorothy. As well as my work here I'll need to keep going back up to Durham to clear the house there and see my solicitor,' had been Andrea's answer. 'I'm not looking forward to doing that but it has to be done before I can really settle in here.'

'Come when you can, my dear. We'll look forward to that,' Dorothy had answered.

Even as Dorothy Bramley uttered the words Andrea knew that one person at least would not be looking forward to her next visit to the farm. At least the drives up to Durham would help to delay her next visit to Abbot's Fold Farm. There was a lot to be done before she need face up to meeting David

Bramley again. She was not yet feeling strong enough to encounter his thinly veiled antagonism. When she was feeling stronger and had come to terms with the way things were it would be different. Then she would not find herself either angry or upset by his attitude, she would be able to cope with the man and his prejudice.

After all, there was still a fair amount of prejudice around about women becoming church ministers. In some places it was necessary for a woman to prove she was up to the job. Maybe Nyddbeck with Nyddford came into that category. It would be interesting to find out . . .

Though Andrea managed to evade meeting David Bramley again during that first couple of weeks she seemed unable to miss the other young man who lived up at Nyddmoor. Bill Wyndham was house hunting, and he was determined to find a suitable property somewhere in Nyddbeck. So, as Andrea walked across the village green early one morning from the manse to the church she met Bill parking his car outside a substantial stone-built house positioned close to the beck. He greeted her with a smile as he held out a large hand.

'Mrs Cameron! How are you?'

'I'm very well, thanks.' She withdrew her hand. 'Are you going walking again?' She lifted a hand to indicate the narrow flight of steep stone steps which led up from behind the house. The wooden waymarker at the foot of the steps indicated that there was a public footpath of one and a half miles leading to Nyddmoor.

'No, I'm going to look at a couple of properties today. This is one of them,' he replied.

'It looks quite large. Do you have a family?' She asked the question more to be sociable than out of curiosity.

'No, but I would like to have, one day. I don't intend to spend the rest of my life on my own.'

His words gave Andrea a stark reminder that this would be the way things were for her from now on; that she would have to spend the rest of her life on her own. The smile died from her mouth and her eyes became bleak.

Instantly Bill was aware of the hurt he had inflicted with his thoughtless remark. His hand came out again to her. 'How clumsy of me! Do forgive me, Mrs Cameron, please?'

'Yes, yes, of course.'

She turned away from him then and hurried over to the church, pushing open the heavy oak door and stepping into the dim coolness with a sigh. There would be more such innocently uttered words to bring hurt to her in the days to come, she guessed, and she would have to get used to coping with them without showing her distress as she must have done to Bill Wyndham. For now though the pain was too raw, the grief was too recent. She needed to be alone with it, to find solace in the only place there was any help to be found now. Slipping into the nearest seat she bowed her head and allowed the tears to flow over her folded hands.

Bill Wyndham stood for a long time with his hands on the latch of the wrought-iron gate watching the tall, slim woman whose cloud of black hair reached her shoulders as she walked with swift grace into the little church. At first he was still cursing himself for his clumsiness, his lack of thought in speaking to her as he had done. God, he was no better than Dave Bramley, and that was saying something after the anger he had felt against Dave for his rudeness to the girl last week. Her eyes, those wonderful deep blue, dark-lashed eyes, had mirrored her anguish so plainly in the few seconds before she turned away from him and walked into the church.

What had made a girl like her take on such a way of life? It was a life few women like Andrea Cameron would choose, though more women were taking to it these days. His curiosity was still working overtime for long after the woman who had provoked his speculation had entered the church. She was beautiful in a remote way that was perhaps intended to keep a man at a distance. Yet up there in the kitchen at Abbot's

Fold Farm as she had talked to young Carla there had been warmth in her face and laughter in her voice.

Bill had thought about her often since then and wondered about the husband who had been killed so soon after her arrival in Nyddbeck. How long had they been married? Were there any children of the marriage? If so, were they away at school? Bill knew he would find the answers to his questions sooner or later, but it troubled him quite a lot that he should be so impatient to find those answers. It disturbed him even more to have to acknowledge to himself that he was unable to keep Andrea Cameron out of his thoughts for long.

His eagerness to find a house in this village where both the manse and one of Andrea's churches were situated had brought him down today to look at two properties which might be suitable for his purpose. Beckside, right in the heart of the village, was spacious enough to provide him with both a home and a studio. It was also within sight of the church, and Andrea would have to pass it on her way from the centuries-old packhorse bridge which led to the manse.

As his tour of inspection came to an end back in the front-facing sitting room of Beckside he saw Andrea emerge from the church with her head held high and her slim shoulders straight. She wore a long cotton skirt and a pale blue cotton shirt open at the neck, with sandals on her feet. The sight of her made his heart give a jolt and sent his feet instinctively heading for the door so he could meet up with her again.

Then he stopped and told himself not to be such a fool. Because she was not his sort of woman, and he would not be her sort of man. So he must put her out of his mind at once.

Andrea felt calmer and more at peace with herself after her half-hour spent in the church. There were no urgent parish meetings or visits to be done today as this was the day of the week that she had decided would be her day off. So she would pack herself a picnic lunch, then drive up to Durham to collect some more of the things she had left in the house there. It would also be necessary for her to pay a visit to her solicitor to sign some documents. Later she would call and spend a couple of hours with Ian's mother before coming back to Nyddbeck.

As she drove northwards Andrea tried to decide whether she ought to leave the house she had shared with Ian furnished and let it to holidaymakers until she found a buyer for it. One thing she was quite certain of was that she would not ever live in that house again. There were too many memories there, and not all of them were happy ones.

If she kept the place she would need to keep going back to it to check that it was clean and tidy for each new booking. Unless she asked Ian's mother to do that for her. That idea was soon discarded because Nancy had remained involved with the family antique business after the death of her husband a few years ago and would need to give even more time to it now that Ian was no longer there. So it might be better to just wait until a buyer for the house came along. She would ask the advice of her solicitor, she decided as she neared the city.

When she reached his office in one of the streets of tall old houses close to the cathedral she was surprised to discover that this might not be such a long wait as she had anticipated. After they had exchanged a few words about her health and how she was coping with life down in the Yorkshire Dales the elderly partner moved tactfully to the question of what was to happen to the home she and Ian had shared for eight years.

'I've decided to put it up for sale, though of course it could be some time before I find a buyer,' she told him. 'We had talked about doing that before I was ordained, but Ian seemed to want to keep the house on so he would have somewhere to stay up here whenever he was working late or the weather was bad.' The thought came to Andrea then that

Ian could easily have stayed overnight with his mother, who lived only a mile or so outside the city.

The solicitor cleared his throat, then gave her a smile before speaking. 'Then you may be pleased to hear that we have already received an enquiry about the house, Mrs Cameron.'

'Really? So soon?'

He cleared his throat again before explaining as delicately as he could how this came about. 'It was because of the report of the funeral service in the newspaper. There was quite a big piece about it. You may have seen it?'

Andrea shook her head. She could recall little of those early days after Ian's death. They had passed in a kind of thick fog built up of shock, grief and bewilderment.

'One of the professors from the university who is about to retire has close friends living very near to your old home. He heard from them that your work was in Yorkshire now, so he made enquiries about the house in a roundabout way through a mutual friend. He insisted I was not to mention his interest in the place unless you decided to sell it. Of course you must think very carefully, my dear, before you come to a firm decision about such an important matter.'

Of course he was thinking of her still as the young bride who had made her will here soon after her marriage to Ian Cameron. Or as the bewildered young widow who had listened to him talking about her husband's estate soon after the funeral. He did not realise that she was no longer so young, or so terribly bewildered now. He was trying to help her as kindly as he could, so she smiled at him

'Yes, I'll certainly do that. I'll be in Durham for the rest of the day so if I come to a decision before I go back I'll give you a ring and then you can let this man know what is happening.'

It seemed like an answer to a prayer, it hardly needed any thinking about. If the man's offer was a reasonable one she would take it and then be free of at least some of those hauntingly sad memories. Once the house was no longer part of her life she would be able to concentrate on the future and let go of the past.

The past was waiting to engulf her from the moment she opened the elegant black-painted door beneath the half-circle of leaded lights and stepped into the hall of her old home. It was there in the cloying scent that seemed to linger still from the funeral flowers, the lilies and carnations that had arrived in van loads from friends and business colleagues. It was there in the pile of cards taken from the sprays and wreaths by Ian's mother, cards which she had read without really seeing them. It was there in the newspapers still lying neatly folded on the hall table beside the cards.

Turning away from them with a shudder, Andrea found herself facing the letter cage behind the front door where a pile of correspondence had built up since her last visit a fortnight ago. She would deal with those after she had opened some windows to let in the fresh air she needed so badly. It might be a good idea to have her picnic lunch out in the back garden before she did anything else because the atmosphere inside this house, which only weeks ago had been shared with Ian, was oppressive to her.

As she went from room to room opening windows wide it struck her that it was like being in someone else's house now, rather than the home she and Ian had created with such love in the first few years of their life together. The kitchen she had once been so proud of looked clinically clean and far too tidy, with no baskets of vegetables or bowls of fruit to be seen; no recipe books scattered about because she had been in too much of a hurry to tidy them away. Even the dish cloths and tea towels had been neatly folded by her parents, or Ian's mother, before they left to go back to their own homes. She would never cook in here again, she thought, as she filled the jug kettle and switched it on to make coffee to go with the sandwiches she had brought with her.

Her quick survey of the bow-windowed sitting room confirmed that to be in the same state of unnatural tidiness, with
no fresh flowers or green plants to be found. The dining room
had patio doors leading to the back garden, so she opened
these to allow in fresh air to banish the unlived-in smell of
the place. There were only the downstairs cloakroom and the
tiny study where Ian had sometimes done paperwork brought
home from the showroom. She would leave those for now
and go upstairs until the kettle boiled.

The master bedroom was immaculate, as left by her mother
and father who had slept there for a few nights before the
funeral while she herself stayed with Ian's mother. She had
kept out of that room since Ian's death because it had been
the scene of a disagreement with him during the week before
she moved down to Nyddbeck. She had hoped Ian would ring
her and say he was sorry, but he had not done so. Now he
never would. Andrea pushed open the window, then hurried
out of the room blinking away tears.

The guest room had not been used for a long time. She
gave that a brief inspection and decided that later she would
dust it in case the prospective purchaser wanted to come and
view the house soon. There was only one more bedroom now
to be looked at, and she had left that to the last because of the
dread she felt growing inside her. It was across the landing.
Did she really need to go in there? Wouldn't it be better to
ask Ian's mother to take a look round before any prospective
purchasers came to view the property?

No, it would hurt Nancy just as much to go again into the
room where her adored little grandson had once slept. It was
not fair to ask her to do that. The past had to be faced up to
and dealt with before she could put it behind her and get on
with her life. Not that she could ever forget Andrew, or want
to forget him. He had been a special gift given to her for such a
few years on this earth, but he would be in her heart always.

There was a ceramic plate showing a picture of a robin

on the door. Inside the room all the animal and bird pictures Andrew had loved still hung on the pale yellow walls. His teddy bear lay still on the pillows which matched a Thomas the Tank Engine quilt cover. Everything else, all the picture books and toys, had gone to the Oxfam shop. Andrea picked up the teddy bear and rested her cheek against it. 'You're going with me now, Eddy,' she whispered, using the name Andrew had chosen to call his beloved bear. The pictures would go too, they were all she had left of her son in worldly things. No tears were shed as she left this small room; they had all been used up long ago.

It was cool and peaceful, soothing to her spirit, as she sat on the patio seat to drink a mug of coffee and eat her sandwiches. There were traffic noises but they were muted in this quieter part of the city. She ought to cut the grass again, it had grown since her father put the lawn mower over it before going back to Scotland. With that thought in her mind she went indoors and found the key to the garden shed where the mower was housed.

Her heart sank when she saw the clutter that was inside the shed. How on earth had they managed to gather so many useless-looking bits and pieces without her being aware of them? Of course she never went into the wooden building which was tacked on to the rear of the garage. Ian was the gardener, so she had no need to go in there. Before she sold the house she would have to go through all this stuff and get rid of most of it, though she had better keep a few garden tools for use in the manse garden since she would now either have to take to gardening or pay someone else to do it for her.

She sighed as she reached to move a large cardboard carton out of the way so that she could haul out the lawn mower. Why had Ian kept that in here instead of taking it to the recycling tip outside the city? For a long moment she stared down at the letters stamped on the side of the carton. They formed the name of one of the city toy shops. What had been inside the carton?

51

Or, more to the point, what was still inside the carton? She lifted two of the flaps and stared down at golden brown fur fabric. A moment later she was lifting out one of the largest teddy bears she had ever seen.

Had Ian bought this for their little boy before Andrew died? If he had done she would surely have known about it and sent it to the Oxfam shop along with all the other stuffed toys. Maybe he had bought the big bear for an employee's child? She frowned as she cast her mind over elderly Mr Staindrop who would soon be retiring, middle-aged Mrs Stanley who was a widow without children, and young Lee Lofthouse who had just joined the firm straight from college. No, the bear could not have been bought for any of them.

Next she turned her thoughts to their friends, most of whom certainly had children, but could not recall any birthdays which were imminent. Had the bear been bought as a raffle prize for one of the local charity events? Maybe, since there could be no other explanation for it being here in the shed. Why had Ian not brought it into the house to store until it was required?

She was sliding it carefully back into the carton so as not to crumple the deep blue ribbon band which encircled the neck of the bear when her fingers encountered the tiny folded square of card set beneath the ribbon bow. With fingers that were unsteady she lifted the expensive toy out of the cardboard box again so she could take a closer look at the gift card. There was a single red rose on the front of it. Her heart began to thud as she opened it out and began to read what was written there.

Only a few words, but they made her feel giddy. 'Happy Birthday, my darling. All my love to you and Jamie. Ian'.

Who was Ian's 'darling'? Why had he bought her this expensive gift? Why did he send this unknown woman all his love?

Six

A ndrea felt sick as she closed the lid of the carton and
moved it out on to the paved square next to the shed
so that she could get at the lawn mower. That card could not
really mean what she thought it meant, could it? Had there
been another woman in Ian's life that she had known nothing
about? Someone he had been seeing all the time she had been
trying so hard to save their marriage, trying to see his point
of view on the differences which had grown between them?
If so, why hadn't Ian told her? Why hadn't he been honest
with her?

The harsh whine of the lawn-mower engine should have
silenced the questions in her mind as she pushed it back and
forth over the long narrow strip of lawn at the back of the
house, but it did not. When the job was done Andrea emptied
the grass box and put the machine away. Then she was left to
wonder what to do about the big cardboard carton containing
the teddy bear, that mystery present which had brought such
disquiet to her. Maybe there would be an address on the box
to indicate where it was destined to be delivered. She turned
it this way and that, but could find no address other than that
of the toy shop where it had come from.

As she stowed it back where she had found it and closed
the door of the shed the thought came to her that somewhere
there must be a woman who would probably be expecting
a gift from Ian. Someone who might not even be aware of
his death. Before she did anything else she would take a

look inside the desk in Ian's study. There might just be the information she needed in there.

It was not easy, going through all those papers, which were mainly to do with the business, in search of the sort of information which in her heart she did not want to find. There was nothing to be found there in Ian's desk, no clue to indicate who this woman was or where she lived or worked. All the documents related to the Cameron Gallery, or to the house. Apart from those there were just a number of business cards tucked into one corner of the leather-bound blotter she had bought for Ian a few years ago. Acting on an impulse, she bundled all the papers into the large travel bag Ian had been in the habit of using if he found it necessary to stay away when going to a house auction or a trade fair. For some reason she decided not to include the business cards. Instead, she bundled these together and tucked them into her handbag. Everything else could go to Ian's mother when she visited her this evening, since they were all concerned with the business.

The next thing to do was to go upstairs and sort out the clothes in her wardrobe which she had left behind when moving to Nyddbeck. Things she had known she would not need until the colder weather that winter would bring to the dale. There had seemed at the time of her last visit to Durham to be plenty of time to collect those. Now there was not, because now she knew beyond doubt that she was not going to keep this house for much longer; that she wanted to be rid of it as soon as possible.

She knew she ought to go through all Ian's clothes too, ready to send them to one of the charity shops. It came to her then that there could be a clue in those clothes, in a pocket perhaps, to the identity of the other woman in his life. Her whole being felt revolted by the idea of going through those clothes. She could avoid the task because Ian's mother had offered to help her with it, yet she would not ask for that help in case anything did come to light. Nancy would be so distressed if anything like that was revealed, and Andrea did not want her to suffer any more hurt than she had already endured with her son's death.

Ian's clothes were all of good quality and immaculately kept, dark business suits and tweed or cord slacks and jackets which had been worn at weekends or on holidays. There was the aroma of expensive aftershave about them as Andrea began to slide them across the rails in the big built-in wardrobe. Suddenly she knew she could not go on with this. It was too soon and too deeply personal, this searching of garments which she guessed might have been touched by some other woman, clothes which could even have hung in another woman's bedroom.

She would have to get away from here before her composure broke and she gave way to all the shock and bitterness which had been growing inside her ever since she had opened the cardboard box and discovered the teddy bear and the message of love from her husband. All she wanted now, all she desperately needed at this moment, was to get away from this house where during the last couple of hours her few remaining happy memories had been destroyed.

Within minutes the cases she had packed were inside her car, the windows she had opened earlier were closed and the doors of the house were all locked. Before leaving she telephoned her solicitor again and told him of her decision to sell. She also arranged to call at his office to leave a set of keys with him.

'You are quite sure you want to do this, my dear? It isn't a decision you've come to a bit too hastily, perhaps, because you are upset?' he asked gently.

'I'm absolutely certain I'll never want to live in that house again. My home is in Yorkshire now, where my work is.'

'Then I'll be pleased to act for you as regards the property, which I seem to recall was in your joint names?'

'Yes, with the mortgage insurance ensuring it would belong entirely to me if anything happened to my husband,' she confirmed.

'That will make things a little more straightforward. There will still be no hurry though, no need to rush the sale through.'

'I'd like it all to go through as quickly as possible. I don't want to have to keep coming up here.'

'It's natural you should feel like that, in the circumstances, Mrs Cameron.'

You don't know what the circumstances really are, she found herself thinking as she shook hands with him and made her escape. You don't know that my husband was cheating on me.

As she walked away from the solicitor's office Andrea realised that it was too early as yet for her to go to Nancy's house. Ian's mother would still be at the showroom, which did not close until five thirty. So she drove to the cathedral and parked her car as close as she could get to the magnificent towering building which drew tourists from all over the world. The air inside was pleasantly cool after the heat outside.

Soon she had left behind the people clad in jeans and T-shirts, cotton skirts or shorts, who were sauntering about the historic building staring up at the great arches of the roof and the glory of the stained-glass windows, and was making her way to a small chapel which had been set aside for private prayer. She needed so much what she knew she would find there. In that quiet place she would encounter the assurance of a love which would never fail her as the human love to which she had devoted so many years of her life had failed her. Peace of mind would be waiting for her, and she needed that as she had never needed it before.

'Are you sure you've made the right decision, dear?' Nancy Cameron asked her daughter-in-law as they sipped dry white wine out in the beautiful garden Nancy had created behind her little Georgian house. 'Isn't it a bit soon to make your mind up? After the shock of the accident, and with you not having time yet to know whether you are going to like Yorkshire enough to want to settle there permanently?'

Andrea met her anxious gaze frankly. 'It doesn't matter whether I like Yorkshire or not, Nancy. That's where my life and my work will be from now on. I've taken on a commitment there, and I intend to keep it,' she added firmly.

Nancy bit her lip, afraid that she had spoken out of turn, and hurried to make amends. 'I'm sure you do. I only meant that you might be wiser to keep your old home in case things don't work out. Because the manse goes with the job, doesn't it?'

'Yes, but things will work out. Please try to understand, Nancy, I really don't ever want to live in the Durham house again. That part of my life is over. I have to make a new life for myself now, and that life will be in Yorkshire.'

The older woman reached across and took her hand. 'Forgive me, I suppose I was being rather selfish, wanting to be sure you kept coming back here so that I wouldn't lose touch with you. I've become very fond of you, and you are all I have left now.'

Andrea felt warmed and touched by her words. It was so much worse for Nancy than it was for her because Ian had been her only child and there were no grandchildren to follow after him. No one to inherit the flourishing antique business which earlier generations of Camerons had built up over so many years with their hard work and skill. She was saddened to think that Nancy had no deep and abiding faith to help her through these terrible days of loss and grief.

'I wish I had your faith to lean on, my dear,' the older woman was confessing now. 'All I have left are doubts and fears for the future. It's a bit like looking down a long, long tunnel which has no light at the end of it.'

'You will find some light, if you keep searching for it. So

many people do, once the earliest, blackest days are behind them,' Andrea murmured.

As she uttered the words a face came into her mind. Not the face of her dead husband but the face of David Bramley, the man who had not yet found the light that was there to help him but who was lost still in a world of bitterness and pain. She pushed the thought of him away from her, as she had done so often since her visit to Abbot's Fold Farm.

'I'll have to be on my way now, Nancy, because I've got a few things to do when I get back, but we won't lose touch, I promise. I'll be here again in a week or two to collect some more things, and then we'll arrange for you to come down to Nyddbeck for a few days' break. You'll like it there. The people are very kind, and the scenery is wonderful.'

'I hope you'll be happy there,' her mother-in-law said wistfully as they went together out to where Andrea had parked her car.

Dusk was falling softly over the village as Andrea turned the car out of the main road and into the lane that ran alongside the beck. The scent of honeysuckle and rambler roses drifted in through the open windows. Swallows swooped and dived over fields of grain that glowed pale gold in the evening light. After the miles of noisy monotonous driving she had left behind her it was bliss to be able to slow right down and drink in the sight and scents of late summer in this Yorkshire village.

This was her village now, this was her home. The people dwelling in the cottages that bordered the winding lane and in the larger more expensive properties beyond them were her flock. She was there to serve them, and there was a great thankfulness inside her that she had been called to do that.

As soon as she opened the front door of the manse and stepped into the hall she felt herself enveloped by an almost tangible feeling of welcome. Yes, this was where her life would be lived from now on. All around her were her own pieces of furniture which she had chosen for this house, old things and new things which went harmoniously together in the old stone-built building. On the hall table beside the telephone were flowers, gold and white chrysanthemums which had graced the altar of Nyddford Church last Sunday and which the church member who had donated and arranged them had insisted Andrea must take home with her after the evening service. They were another reminder to her of how warmly she had been welcomed into Yorkshire by the people of Nyddford and Nyddbeck. Or by most of them, she thought ruefully as the image of David Bramley and the echo of his sarcastic words came unbidden into her mind again. There were sure to be others like him, she knew, so she must not allow his face and his voice to keep intruding into her thoughts.

She set the kettle to boil for a late cup of tea while she went into the garage to bring indoors the cases of clothes she had brought back with her. There was no need for her to unpack the cases tonight, that task would keep till tomorrow, but there were a couple of sympathy letters from old college friends which she had found waiting for her at the Durham house which must be replied to. She would answer those while she drank her tea, then have an early night.

When the mug of tea was resting on her desk in the small room she was to use as a study she paused to reflect on how wonderfully quiet it was after the traffic noise she had endured on the A1 motorway. From this room at the back of the manse the only sounds to be heard were the late song of a blackbird coming from the great trees which bordered the beck and the sighing of a soft summer breeze. A familiar prayer of thanksgiving slipped in and out of her mind as she sipped the refreshing brew before starting on the task of answering the letters from Laura and Jake, who had been friends since her teacher training college days.

Because she had no heart for the task it was easy enough

to postpone it while she watched a thrush digging in her back lawn for a worm, and then stared intently at the shape of a hedgehog emerging from beneath one of the flowering shrubs close to the retaining wall. Beyond the wall the land sloped gently uphill, covered with a carpet of golden grain. At the lower edge of the field a figure came into sight, that of a man walking slowly with a dog at his heel. It was the man she had so recently been thinking about. Even as the fact registered in her mind, the dog took off in pursuit of a rabbit and seconds later was clearing the drystone wall to continue the chase in the back garden of the manse.

With a startled exclamation Andrea ran out of the open french window and across the grass to attempt to catch the dog before it could get at the rabbit. Moments later the farmer leapt over the wall after him. It was all just a game to the young black and white collie, who allowed the rabbit to go and proceeded to start a boisterous friendship with Andrea by licking her hands and circling round her legs till she found herself laughing at his antics. His owner was not amused.

'Lie down, Brack, damn you!' he cried furiously.

This was a signal to the dog to pull free of Andrea and take off round the side of the house with her pursuing him. David Bramley stood quite still and rent the air with a piercing whistle that Andrea thought could probably be heard in the next village. The dog stopped in its tracks, plainly puzzled by the noise and uncertain what to do. The animal's eyes were alight with laughter and one ear was comically raised, giving it a rakish look.

'Lie down, damn you!' came the next command, which brought the other ear up for a second or two before the dog flopped down on the gravel path at Andrea's feet.

'You're a bad boy!' admonished Andrea, who was fond of dogs.

'It's not he, it's she, as you might have guessed,' the farmer said grimly.

Andrea suppressed a smile. 'Would a young male have been any more obedient at this age?' she asked gravely.

He scowled as he answered. 'I usually use dogs, not bitches, and they are usually responding well to training by this age. Only I allowed my children to influence me in the choice of this one when I ought to have known better.'

'How are your children? I haven't seen them since I was at your farm,' she found herself asking, even though she guessed he would not wish to linger in her company. His dog seemed in no hurry to leave her though.

He took a long time to answer that. So long, that she began to wonder whether he had not heard her question. 'I suppose Jack's happy enough as long as he's helping me with things about the farm, but Carla's becoming a problem. My mother does her best but she doesn't have time to get the girl out and about as my wife used to do, and the farm is some distance away from all her school friends.'

'We'll be starting up the church youth club again soon. That might be a help,' she told him.

'I don't see what help that could be to her.' His response was curt. The frown which furrowed the brow between arched black eyebrows deepened.

'It's a place to meet other young people and to become involved with new skills and activities. I'm planning a course there for the girls which will help them gain in confidence and poise.'

'If you're hoping to get her back to church that way you'll be disappointed,' he broke in. 'None of us has time for that now.'

'Your mother has, that's why I thought—'

'My mother pleases herself. *I* tell my children what they are allowed to do.'

'So you won't allow Carla to come to the youth club even if she doesn't come to church?' This was unbelievably bigoted of him, Andrea thought.

'We've nothing to thank the church for.' He hunched his slim shoulders as he said the words.

'Surely you can't mean what you've just said when you've got such a marvellous mother and two lovely children? I'd have said you had a lot to thank God for.'

'Don't tell me I should be thanking God for taking my wife away from me at such a young age!'

'Of course not! But you shouldn't be punishing your children, or your mother, because of what happened to your wife.'

'You'd be best to keep that sort of talk for those who haven't been through what I'm going through, Mrs Cameron. They might be able to believe it. I can't!'

Did this man really believe that he had the right to pour scorn on her belief like that? Had he forgotten that she had also lost someone she loved at far too early an age, and only a very short time ago? Her brilliant blue eyes blazed with anger as she stared into his face, that long, narrow sun-browned face which wore such a cold expression. Then quite suddenly the anger died and only her grief was left, grief for herself that love had ended so cruelly and grief for him that he had closed his mind to the source of her own comfort and strength. Grief brought tears to sparkle and increase the beauty of her eyes, then sent her stumbling away from him across the grass and back through the open window into the house before he could witness her distress.

Seven

There had been tears beginning to sparkle in the new minister's eyes in the second or so before she had turned so abruptly away from him and hurried through the french window into the manse, and they had been brought there by his own stupid, thoughtless words! David Bramley felt sick inside as he acknowledged that, but it was too late now to take the words back. The new minister would never forgive him for them. Why should she?

He was a bloody fool to have allowed his black mood to overflow in her direction. It wasn't her fault that he had been so disturbed by something in the proud way she had challenged his foul-tempered attitude. The long, cool glance that came from her brilliant eyes had made him feel uncomfortable enough to anwer back even more rudely. It wasn't her fault that something in the way she had stood up to him reminded him so forcibly of Jill. It wasn't her fault that Jill's life had ended so suddenly on that February night eighteen months ago. It was his fault.

Since he knew the blame was his alone why did he punish everybody he came into contact with by speaking out of turn? Why didn't he reserve the punishment for himself? He was the guilty one. He was the one who deserved to suffer, not this young woman who had so recently and shockingly lost her own partner.

When was he going to come to terms with what had happened to Jill, as his mother had said he must do for the sake of his children? When was he going to stop looking inward at his own misery and put some effort into getting on with his life without Jill? Everything he did these days, everything he had done since the night of the storm, was done on automatic pilot and done with no heart for the task. So that these days he did not look at his fields of grain, or at his flock of sheep, with pride and thanksgiving.

Thanksgiving had died when Jill died. Bitterness and intolerance had taken the place of all the things that had once been so good in his life. Now he often spoke curtly to those he met, and far too often spoke harshly to his children and his mother. Since he was aware of that, and of the hurt it caused to those he loved, why did he go on behaving in such an intolerable way?

David shook his head helplessly as he faced the truth about himself. He had been dealt a savage blow by fate, and was trying to make everyone he came into contact with pay the price for his own suffering. His mother had tried gently to make him aware of that several times in recent weeks but he had always cut short her efforts. Sometimes he had been cruel in his dismissal of her concern for him, and had known shame afterwards.

His mother just did not seem able to understand. How could she understand his feelings when she had never had to experience anything like them? Because his father's life had ended peacefully in his own home, made easier by the family doctor, she did not know how great was the agony of having your partner snatched without warning from your life. It had been like that for him because Jill had been young and fit. Jill had been going out to do her job as a nurse when the tree fell and ended her life.

She had been a devoted wife and mother, a church member and a Sunday school teacher. There was no way Jill could have deserved what happened to her that day. David's mother did not seem to understand how bitterly angry he still was about the unfairness of it all, about the injustice of being robbed of the wife he had adored. Nor did she realise how great was the burden of guilt he carried in his heart. If she were to know how he had poured his bitterness on the new minister tonight she would be shocked and angry with him. Shame stirred in him again as he thought of what she would say.

When was he going to be able to feel hope in his life again? When was he going to be able to look at his children without pain because they reminded him so forcibly of Jill and the love which had created them? Only the land gave him a reason for living now, and even that brought more worry than joy. The sight of this field of barley, rich, golden and almost ready for cutting, would once have filled him with pride. Now the harvesting was just another task to be done so that money would come into the farm to set against the loss they would make on the animals when they went to market.

Suddenly, and to his horror, he felt despair overwhelm him. His shoulders began to shake as he bent his head and began to beat his fists against the top rail of the five-barred gate. Blood flowed from his knuckles and went unheeded. The young dog whined as it sensed his distress, and began to nudge his knee. David Bramley ignored it. All that filled his mind now was the decision he might soon have to take, whether it would be better for his children if he drove to where the river ran deep and fast and put an end to his misery once and for all.

Andrea stumbled over the threshold as she hurried through the patio door and into the study, bringing pain to her toes and more tears to her eyes. At least, though, David Bramley had not seen her tears. She had managed to get away from him quickly enough to conceal them. It appeared that he could not come face to face with her without being sarcastic at her expense. Well, she would not allow him to upset her because she was here to do a job and she would do it whether he liked it or not. This was where she had been called to be, and here she would stay.

Right now there were those two letters waiting to be answered, so she would put David Bramley out of her mind and get on with them. First though she must switch on her computer. The letters were not easy to answer, but then they would not have been easy for her friends to write, because what can you say to a woman not yet thirty years old whose husband has been killed?

When she read her replies through, two almost identical documents which were short and too formal, she took up her pen to sign them and found it was empty. There was another pen in her handbag so she began to fish about in one of the organiser sections for it. In doing so she encountered the dozen or so visiting cards she had picked up from Ian's desk in case they gave any clue to the woman he had bought the teddy bear for. The search for the pen was forgotten then. Suddenly it was much more important that she should scan those little oblongs of card instead.

Mostly they gave the business names and addresses of people connected with the Cameron antique business: firms and individuals Ian would need to contact from time to time. There was a card from the London hotel where he sometimes stayed, and ones from places in Edinburgh or Glasgow that he also used. The odd one out was a card for a hotel which was obviously much smaller than the city hotels since it boasted only five en-suite bedrooms. The Raven Falls Hotel, near Ravensbridge, certainly was not known to her. It was not a place where they had both stayed. She frowned as she stared down at the address, trying to decide whether or not it was important. 'Jeff and Beth Barclay, proprietors of this old coaching inn in the heart of the Cumbrian fell country assure you of a warm welcome and excellent home-cooked food' was the promise made. Her spine began to tingle. Was this the clue to that mystery gift she had discovered earlier today? Had Ian booked a meal there, or a room there, to be shared by the other woman in his life? That woman she had known nothing about until today?

Before she realised what she was doing, Andrea found her North of England road map and set about looking up the location of Ravensbridge. It was not a place she had ever visited, yet there was something vaguely familiar about the name. Something she tried to push out of her mind but was unable to do so. Something she did not want to remember. She closed the map abruptly and walked to the window of the study with her heart hammering against her ribs.

What she saw from there gave her such a jolt that everything else was pushed into the back of her mind. David Bramley was some distance away from the manse, half-way up the path that ran round the edge of his field of ripe grain. His Land Rover was parked there on the other side of the five-barred gate which gave access to the lane, but he was not opening the gate. He was slumped over it. Something in the total stillness of his attitude brought a frisson of alarm to Andrea. Was the man ill? Had he collapsed there, and was the heavy gate his only means of support?

Andrea did not hesitate. She ran straight out of the open french door and raced over the back lawn till she came to the drystone wall which separated the back garden of the manse from the field belonging to Abbot's Fold Farm. Then she was scrambling over that wall and making her way swiftly uphill, using the narrow footpath which skirted the field of barley.

Because she was wearing only soft-soled sandals, and because the man was utterly lost in his own misery, David Bramley was unaware of her approach until his young collie stopped whimpering and gave Andrea a welcoming bark. Even then he did not move, hoping she would ignore him and walk on to wherever she was going.

'Are you ill, Mr Bramley?' she asked breathlessly as she came close to him.

67

He did not answer. Did not even lift his head to look at her. His dog whimpered again.

'I asked if you were ill, Mr Bramley?' Andrea spoke sharply this time. Her alarm was deepening because she was unable to tell whether he had fallen unconscious over the gate. She put out a hand nervously, wondering whether her touch might bring him crashing down at her feet.

'No,' came the muttered response, which was barely audible.

Andrea bit her lip, at a loss what to do next, since there was so obviously something very wrong with the man. Even his dog was worried, looking up at him with distressed eyes and whimpering softly.

'I saw you from my window. You appeared to have collapsed. I thought you might need help—'

'There is no help you or anyone else can give me,' he muttered without looking up.

'Why do you say that? Do you really think you're beyond medical help? Are you dying?' she asked quietly, feeling calmer now that she knew the farmer was at least conscious.

'No, but I wish I were!'

The force behind his words startled her.

'You can't possibly mean that when you've got two lovely children to live for!' She was angry with him now and did not trouble to conceal this from him. 'In fact you don't know how lucky you are to have those children!'

'You don't know what you're talking about,' he broke in. 'If you did, you wouldn't be wasting your time on me. Because there's no way you are going to convince me that there's a loving God, and there's no way you're going to get at me through my children. You're just wasting your time, and mine.'

As David Bramley hurled the words at her, he glared at her so ferociously that for a few seconds Andrea felt fear stir in the pit of her stomach. There was a strong impulse urging her to turn her back on him and run back to the safety of the manse before he could vent any more of his bitterness on her. She took a step back, ready to escape. As she did so her view of the scene altered and instead of the figure of the farmer standing stiffly upright now against the gate she caught a glimpse of the spire of Nyddbeck Church, her church. Her reason for being here. Fear left her and calmness took over. She was in control, and she would show it.

'I'm not trying to get at you, Mr Bramley. I'm not wasting my time either. All I'm doing is to remind you that you've got Jack and Carla and that they are your good reason for living. I just wish I had children to live for.'

She heard the sharp intake of his breath, and knew she had got through to him. That she had given him a jolt he had not been prepared for. There was no reason now for her to stay here. For a long moment their eyes met and her brilliant blue gaze challenged the hopelessness revealed in his dark stare. During that time she found herself praying silently that she had got it right and that now David Bramley would not do anything desperate to hurt his children more than they had already been hurt. Then she knew she must get away from him before either of them said anything else. She turned her back on him so swiftly that the young dog became excited by her movement and began to leap up at her, barking loudly.

A swift rebuke from the man stopped the animal from following her as she strode swiftly along the narrow path downwards. She did not once look back at the farmer, but his eyes narrowed as he stared after her until she reached the stone wall and clambered over it to reach the safety of her own garden. Then he began to curse himself aloud with such vigour that the dog stared at him with puzzled eyes, wondering what she had done to deserve such black-sounding reproof.

When he saw the lights come on in the manse David

Bramley climbed over the stile next to the padlocked gate, with the dog following, and clambered into his vehicle. In the moment before he switched on the engine he heard an owl hooting from the great oak tree which spread wide branches over the boundary wall at the foot of his barley field. It seemed to be mocking him for his stupidity, his bigotry. 'More fool you! More fool you!' came its haunting call into the scented silence of the night.

He slammed the door of the vehicle with such force that the young dog yelped a protest as she slid off her seat beside him. Then he put the engine into gear and roared away along the road that led out of the village and up the hill towards his farm.

Andrea stood for a moment or so just inside the open door, taking deep breaths of the cool night air in order to calm herself. Into the silence came the hooting of an owl from somewhere fairly close, perhaps the big oak tree near to the bottom corner of the grain field. She knew she ought not to have allowed David Bramley to rattle her so much that she spoke out of turn to him. It had not been her intention to speak so strongly, the words seemed to have come out of her mouth before she could stop them. Then she had been forced to escape before she was required to explain or apologise.

Yet if her hasty words stopped him from doing something terrible she would be glad she had uttered them. Tomorrow, after the morning service, she must try to have a quiet word with Dorothy and find out if there was any way she could give help to the family without having to come into contact with David. For now though there were the letters to finish and sign before she prepared for bed.

Dropping into the chair at her desk, she looked down at the small squares of card scattered on the blotter. She found herself staring at the card which had raised so many questions in her mind she had gone to the window to get away from the disquiet they brought to her. Those questions must be faced though at some time, and the sooner the better. Because if Ian had been unfaithful to her she had a right to know. Knowing the truth was always a good thing, however bad that truth might be. She picked up the card and read again the few words printed on it, sure that they were of significance.

The Raven Falls Hotel, Ravensbridge, Cumbria. No wonder the place name was vaguely familiar to her. It was on the Ravensbridge road, near Ravensdale, that the accident had occurred. It was there that Ian had died. She did not need to look at any documents to confirm that. Why had she not become aware of the significance of that particular card at once?

She got to her feet and began to pace about the room, searching her mind now for any reason why Ian should have been travelling on that road, so far out of his way between the city of Durham and the village of Nyddbeck in North Yorkshire. He had promised her he would be at her ordination service. His mother had been certain he had intended to be there, even though he would not agree to travel down with her. His reason for that had been an early morning meeting with an important client. Was that client someone at the Raven Falls Hotel?

Thoughts, ideas, reasons for her husband's absence all crowded into Andrea's mind but she could make no sense of them and find no answers to the questions which teased her brain. When it was late and the two unsigned letters still lay where she had left them she admitted to herself that if she was ever to find out the truth about Ian's death in that unfamiliar place she must go to Ravensbridge and search until she found it.

Eight

Having decided to waste no time in discovering the truth about Ian's gift for a mystery woman, Andrea soon found herself having to put the plan on hold because of pressure of work in her parish. All the various groups connected with the churches were now preparing to start up again after the summer holidays, which meant many meetings with leaders and committees. At the same time the sale of her house in Durham was moving much faster than she had anticipated, so that she was forced to spend her days off travelling up to Durham with a car full of empty suitcases and cardboard boxes and returning to the manse with them full of clothes and the sort of things she did not want to leave to the removal men to pack. So the weeks just seemed to rush past, and still she had done nothing about her plan to visit the Raven Falls Hotel and try to discover why Ian had met his death on the road to Ravensbridge.

Another vow she had made, to try and keep out of the way of David Bramley since they could not meet without crossing swords, also did not work out the way she had expected. This was because of a phone call which came one Saturday morning in early September as she was stacking suitcases and cardboard boxes into her car ready for yet another trip to Durham. The caller was Dorothy Bramley, who sounded both flustered and a little annoyed. After listening to her saying that she would be unable to read the lessons at the family service to be held in Nyddbeck Church the following morning Andrea waited for her to explain. Surely David Bramley would not try to stop his mother coming to church as he had his two children? Surely Dorothy would not allow him to do that?

'I feel a bit of a fraud, Andrea,' Dorothy confessed with an attempt at a laugh which did not quite come off. 'You see I've been ordered by Dr Appleby to stay in bed for a couple of days.'

'That sounds as if you're not very well, Dorothy?'

Dorothy sighed. 'I felt a bit off colour when I first got up but it passed off. Then when David came in for his ten o'clock break I flaked out and before I knew it he had Dr Appleby here.'

'What did he say? Dr Appleby I mean.'

'He said my blood pressure was well up, and that if I didn't put my feet up for a few days he'd have me in hospital.'

'You'll need to do as he says then, won't you?' Andrea suggested gently.

'Yes. That's why I'm backing out of what I had promised to do tomorrow. I'm terribly sorry, Andrea, to let you down like this.'

'You mustn't worry about that,' Andrea assured her. 'What you have to do now is get some rest. What can I do to help you? There must be something. What about the cooking?'

Dorothy sighed again. 'David says Carla must do that, but she's only fifteen and only just starting to learn how to cook. She's not even very interested in it, as I was at her age. It wouldn't be so bad if there were just the three of us to cook for, we could muddle through, but Bill has his main meal here most days. That was the arrangement when he took Jacob's Cottage.'

Andrea made her mind up quickly. 'I'll be with you in twenty minutes, Dorothy. So please stop worrying and go back to bed.'

'But you've got so much to do already. Weren't you

planning to go up to Durham today? I'm sure you said so when we were at the meeting yesterday.'

'No, that wasn't today,' Andrea lied cheerfully. 'It was next Saturday.'

'Well I can't deny I'll be glad to see you. I'm not sure Carla will be able to cope, and my friend Joyce Grantley is away just now at her niece's wedding so I can't ask her to help.'

'I'll be pleased to help you, Dorothy. So do go to bed now.'

Andrea put the phone down and went at once to unload the suitcases and boxes which she would not now need until next week. Dorothy Bramley had been a tower of strength to her in the weeks since she arrived at Nyddbeck to start her ministry, always ready to fill in at services when other people were away on holiday or tied up with harvesting. There was little wonder that she was so unwell now, what with coping up at the farm with her grandchildren and her dour, difficult son. Andrea knew that she might have to deal with David Bramley herself today, but she would face that challenge when she had to, and not before. What mattered most was being there to help Dorothy as soon as possible.

Driving up the long winding hill to Abbot's Fold Farm a few minutes later Andrea was struck once again by the beauty of her surroundings. Used as she had been for most of her life to the grandeur of the Scottish mountain scenery, then to the splendour of the ancient buildings in the cathedral city of Durham, something about this landscape of rugged moorland, peaceful stone-built villages and huge fields of green and gold enclosed by drystone walls had made an instant appeal to her and already she loved it. The view from the top of the hill as she switched off the car engine and parked in the lane outside the farm was breathtaking. Purple heather-clad moorland stretched away into the distance as far as the silver stonework of the abbey ruins, while down below there were fields of harvest-ready grain glowing gold in the sunshine with the spire of her little church at Nyddbeck plainly visible above the trees that lined the banks of the beck.

She was so absorbed in her contemplation of the village that was now her home that she did not at once realise that another vehicle was drawing to a halt behind her own. She turned round to face the driver as he went to open the farm gate for her, half-expecting to see the black hair and secretive dark grey eyes of David Bramley. Her heartbeats steadied when she saw that it was not him. It was the tenant of Jacob's Cottage.

'Hello, Mrs Cameron! I haven't seen you lately.' Bill Wyndham's face was handsome beneath a thick thatch of bronze hair which matched his short beard as he smiled his pleasure at meeting her again. He wore an open-necked cotton shirt and light coloured slacks.

'That's not so surprising as you live up here and I live down in Nyddbeck,' she told him as she moved ahead of him through the farm gate then waited for him to close it again.

'I've been down in Nyddbeck several times to look at a couple of properties that are up for sale. I might have seen you then, but I didn't.'

'You'd have seen me at my church, of course,' she reminded him with a wry smile.

'Why are you here today instead of on your way to Durham?'

She frowned. 'I'm here because Dorothy is unwell and has to rest. How do you know I ought to be going to Durham?'

He shook his head. 'That doesn't matter. What does matter is that Dorothy is ill. When did that happen? She seemed her usual self at breakfast this morning.' He paused, then added. 'Or almost her usual self. Maybe she was a bit more stressed than usual . . .'

'She rang me less than half an hour ago to say that she had flaked out when her son came in for his mid-morning drink, and that when the doctor came he said she was to rest. Please don't mention the fact that if she hadn't rung just then I'd have been on my way to Durham by now. I told her she was mistaken and it was next Saturday I was planning to go up there again.'

Bill said, quietly, 'Of course I won't. I hope she's going to be all right. I've become quite fond of her since I've been living in the house, and quite sorry for her too.'

Andrea did not have to ask him why he was sorry for Dorothy. She could guess. They were going into the house now by the open back door and being welcomed by the young collie, Brack. The noise made by the dog alerted Carla to their arrival.

'Oh, am I glad to see you!' she told Bill, quite unaware that her pretty, flushed face was splashed with mud from the potatoes she was washing at the sink, as was her white T-shirt. 'Do you know anything about cooking meat? I heard you telling Gran that you liked cooking.'

'It depends what sort of meat you're cooking. I'm quite good with a wok and Chinese, and I'm not bad at bacon and eggs. Mrs Cameron will be the best one to help you, I think.'

'What are you cooking, Carla? Whatever it is, it's beginning to smell good.'

'It's roast lamb, but it doesn't seem to be cooking fast enough for us to eat at half-past twelve like Dad said.' Carla was looking worried.

'Would you like me to take a look at it?' Andrea offered.

'Yes, please. Dad said I wasn't to worry Gran about it.'

'Your gran needs to rest. That's why I'm here, so I can give you a hand.'

'What can I do to help?' Bill Wyndham wanted to know as Andrea took a look at the joint of lamb and decided that the oven was not hot enough.

'You could help with the vegetables perhaps. Carla will show you where they are.'

So it was that when David Bramley brought the Land Rover to a roaring halt in the yard and came striding into his home he found Bill Wyndham shelling garden peas at the kitchen table and chatting to Carla who was slicing carrots into a pan. Andrea by then was chopping mint for the sauce at one of the worktops. Her fingers became clumsy with tension when she heard first the engine stopping then the footsteps striding across the concrete yard. She did not look up from the task she had taken on but gave added concentration to it.

'What's going on?' David Bramley said sharply as his glance moved around the kitchen.

'Andrea came to give us a hand, and Bill said he'd like to help as well.' It was Carla who rushed to explain. Andrea noted the anxiety in her voice.

'Bill is a paying guest here, and I'm sure Mrs Cameron has plenty to do down in the village. I told you to get on with making the dinner, Carla, and I didn't expect you to start shouting for help as soon as my back was turned.'

Andrea felt sorry for the girl, to be rebuked in such a way during this family crisis and in the presence of outsiders. Hot colour was running up into Carla's cheeks. She waited for the clash that she knew was inevitable.

'I didn't shout for help as soon as you were gone!' The young voice rose as the vegetable knife fell with a clatter from the girl's fingers on to the tiled kitchen floor. 'I didn't, did I, Andrea?'

'No, of course not,' Andrea began, sending a comforting glance at the girl which she hoped would be enough to stop more angry words escaping from her.

'Then why is Mrs Cameron here when she ought to be about her own business down in the village? Tell me that, girl!'

No one could tell this man anything and expect a sympathetic hearing. Andrea could not wait to put him right on this one. With something of a clatter, which betrayed her rising fury, she tossed her own sharp knife aside and faced the farmer.

'I'm here because your mother telephoned me to let me know she would be unable to read the lessons at church tomorrow as she was unwell and had been ordered to rest by her doctor. So I decided to come and see what I could do to help her.' She was dismayed to find that her voice sounded so loud, so aggressive.

'She has Carla to help her.'

'It takes some years of experience to cope with cooking a roast meal for several people, and your daughter hasn't had time enough yet to get that sort of experience,' Andrea pointed out.

'Her head is too full of other things. Things that won't be much use to her when she has to run a home of her own.'

'I didn't think she was doing too badly. The meal was already started when I got here.'

'Well, we needn't detain you any longer now I'm here,' the farmer threw back at her, along with yet another scowling glance.

Andrea knew if she stayed she would unleash more of her resentment against him for treating both her and his daughter in such a surly fashion, and that she might later regret this. So she closed her lips firmly to repress the words that were bursting to come out and, turning her back on David Bramley, made for the door.

'Aren't you going to see my gran, Andrea?' Carla called after her.

She hesitated for a few seconds, then made up her mind that it would be better for her to get away from Abbot's Fold Farm as quickly as possible.

'Not just now, Carla,' she answered. 'I'll come another day, when it's more convenient.'

Bill Wyndham caught her up as she started to unfasten the heavy farm gate. 'I'm sorry about that, Mrs Cameron. Really sorry. You must be feeling very upset at such treatment.'

She smiled ruefully at him. 'I'm afraid it was what I half expected.'

'Yet you still came?'

'Yes, of course. His mother is my friend. She made me feel so welcome from my first day here that when I heard she was ill I wanted to give something back, some practical help.'

'Dave's treatment of you was unpardonable.'

'But not surprising. Not to me at any rate.'

'Why did you let him get away with it?'

She laughed. 'Perhaps it's all part of my job, the work I came here to do. The work I'm here to do isn't for the faint-hearted,' she added quietly.

'I was tempted to have a go at Dave myself when I heard him speak to you in such a way,' Bill confessed. 'Then I realised I might only make things worse for the family.'

'I'm glad you didn't. After all, you have to live there for the time being, don't you?'

'Not for much longer, if my offer for the house down in the village is accepted.'

'So you've made your mind up about staying here?' Andrea was glad to steer the conversation away from the subject of David Bramley's antagonistic attitude towards her.

'Yes. I should know by tomorrow whether my offer has been accepted.'

'Which house have you decided on? I know there are two or three on the market.'

'Beckside.'

She frowned. 'Which one is that? I haven't had time yet to do much walking around the village, although I will when I get a dog.'

'It's the house in Church Lane. So we'll soon be neighbours, I hope.'

'Yes.'

Andrea had a sudden feeling of disquiet as she met the warm regard of his unusual hazel-coloured eyes. There was something in the look he sent her which made her want to take a step away from him, to back off, to distance herself from him. It was a look she had seen before in the eyes of other men; a look she had been used to seeing in Ian's eyes until the change came into their relationship. She did not want to dwell on that look so she gave him a hurried word of farewell and made her way back to her car.

Bill Wyndham watched her go with regret, because the flush which had crept into her ivory skin had made her look even more desirable than she had been when the brightness of anger had taken over her features. It could prove to be a mistake for him to go and live so close to her. Yet he knew an irresistible compulsion to get to know this woman such as he had never experienced before.

David Bramley stared moodily out of the back window in his farmhouse at the couple who were engaged in such deep conversation and felt the first stirring of shame come to life inside him. Bill Wyndham would be trying to apologise to Andrea Cameron for the scene which had just taken place in this kitchen, in spite of the fact that the apology should have come from him. Why did he have to take out his foul temper on her every time they met? She had come to his home to give help to his family and must now be wondering just what sort of savages she had encountered in this remote farming community.

His mother would be furious with him when she heard of his rudeness to Andrea, as she surely would soon hear from Carla. How was he going to explain himself to her? How was he ever going to make her understand, without using words, the pain which engulfed him every time he was forced to come face to face with this new young woman minister?

Nine

W hen she arrived back at the manse, a few minutes after leaving Abbot's Fold Farm, Andrea found herself still angry and upset about the way David Bramley had treated her efforts at helping his mother. She knew that she must be prepared for the sort of treatment he had given her. As she had told Bill Wyndham a few minutes ago, the job she had taken on was not for the faint-hearted. Yet the memory of what David had said to her, and the way he had looked when he uttered those scornful words, would not easily be cast from her mind.

A glance at her watch showed her that it really was far too late for her to set off for Durham as planned. Before she did anything else she would need to find someone to replace Dorothy Bramley at the service tomorrow. Her Filofax provided a possible replacement in Ben Harper, a man of about Dorothy's age who lived on the edge of Nyddford but preferred for some reason to attend the little church in Nyddbeck rather than the larger and newer one in the small market town of Nyddford. She would ring him at once.

'Hello, Mr Harper! It's Andrea Cameron here. I wondered whether I could ask you to take Mrs Bramley's place as a reader tomorrow?'

There was only a short pause before her answer came in a strong masculine voice that held more than a hint of Yorkshire accent.

'No problem, Mrs Cameron. I'll be glad to help.'

82

'Oh thanks a lot, Mr Harper, I'm sorry to ask you at such short notice but I've only just heard that Dorothy isn't well enough to be with us tomorrow.'

'What's wrong with her then?' he broke in, almost before Andrea had finished speaking.

'It seems she flaked out this morning while her son was in the house for his coffee break. He sent for the doctor, who ordered her to stay in bed for a day or two.'

'I knew she was doing too much! I've been telling her so for months now, but she just kept on saying she was all right and able to cope with the house and the children and that sour-tempered son of hers. Obviously she can't, so I must get in touch with her at once and see what I can do.'

Andrea was surprised at the concern she recognised in Ben Harper's voice. Were they related, Ben Harper and Dorothy Bramley? She had not been here long enough yet to discover who was kin to whom in the neighbouring villages or up on the moorland dwellings above them.

'I doubt if her son will let you do anything. He soon sent me packing when I went to the farm to help Carla cook the dinner,' Andrea told him.

'He won't send me packing in a hurry or I'll have something to say that he won't like,' Ben Harper said forcefully. 'If I'd had my way Dorothy would have been away from there long before now. I knew she would overdo things! I tried to tell her but she wouldn't listen to me.'

'You'll need to be careful what you say, Mr Harper,' Andrea felt compelled to warm him. 'I don't think you realise what sort of state David Bramley is in just now. He won't take easily to what he might think is interference from outsiders. He left me in absolutely no doubt about that.'

'I'm not an outsider, Mrs Cameron,' Ben Harper informed her. 'If Jill Bramley had not been killed at that time I would have been married to Dorothy by now, and she would have been living at Ford House with me to look after her and make sure she didn't work herself to death.'

'Oh, I see! Now I can understand your feelings, your anxiety about Dorothy. I didn't mean to talk out of turn, Mr Harper. I'm a newcomer here and have a lot to learn about the people from my churches. I do hope you'll forgive me,' Andrea finished hastily.

'Of course I will! You meant it for the best, I'm sure. My name is Ben, by the way, and if you're a friend of Dorothy's you'll be a friend of mine. I'll go up to the farm right away and see how things are.'

Andrea felt happier in her mind when she heard that, reassured enough to make herself some coffee and a sandwich to eat while she considered what to do with the rest of her day. Should she go up to Durham after all, but just concentrate on packing more of her clothes and some of the fragile items instead of fitting in a visit to Nancy as well? Thoughts of her mother-in-law also brought Ian sharply back into her mind, and the now-familiar aching sense of loss which seemed to descend on her every time she considered she was coming to terms with what had happened to him and to their marriage. Would those feelings be any less painful if she were to discover just what had gone wrong with their arrangements for that day and found out why Ian had died in a traffic accident on a road where he should not have been at that time? She would have to find out, one day. If she didn't there would never be any peace for her, never any hope of losing the bitter memories and retaining only the happier remembrances of their time together.

Perhaps the time to find out was now, before she said goodbye to the home they had shared in Durham. Because it could be that somewhere in that house were clues to the secret life she had become more and more certain Ian had been living when he was apart from her. Except for the name of the place where he had met his death, and the finding of that expensive gift-wrapped teddy bear, she had nothing to go on. Since the teddy bear had yielded no clue she was left only with Ravensbridge road and the Raven Falls Hotel. So that was where she must start her search, and she would waste no more time. She would go there at once.

Tension was mounting inside her as she drove out of the village and headed for the main road that led her half an hour later to the motorway. From there a left exit brought her to country that was new to her. Here the fells were vast and awe-inspiring, even clad in the warm gold of their autumn garb. A huge viaduct dominated the landscape as she reached endless acres of rough grazing land inhabited by thousands of sheep.

Through the heart of this area, which appeared almost empty of dwellings, ran a narrow winding road enclosed on both sides by rough stone walls. This then was Ravensbridge road. Somewhere along here, before the next market town came into view, her husband had met his death. Why? Why had Ian been here in this remote place so far from Nyddbeck?

Ahead of her on the side of the road, which was so narrow that she was forced to drive very slowly, she caught a glimpse of a patch of bright colour. Golden yellow and white flowers, but not the sort of flowers which would grow wild in this or any other place. Her heart began to race. Her breath was painful as it struggled to escape from her lungs. She brought the car to a halt just short of the flowers and sat there for some time just staring at them; at the huge spray of gold and white chrysanthemums which were so fresh that they could not possibly have been there ever since the accident. An attack of violent shivers beset her as she acknowledged that. Since neither she nor Ian's mother had at any time asked for flowers to be placed at the scene of his death, this could be the clue she needed to find out whether Ian really had been living a secret life . . .

It seemed a long time to her before she was able to force

herself to open the door of the car and get to take a closer look at the flowers. As she did so she was to experience another shock as she read the small card fastened to one of the stems. 'With all our love, always. Beth & Jamie' was the simple message written in bold clear script.

Who were they, Beth and Jamie? Was the message intended for Ian? She would have to find out. There would be no rest for her mind until she did so. Pain engulfed her as she stood there staring at those flowers which might, or might not, have been left in tribute and love for the man who had been her husband. Pain and grief must surely have also ravished the woman called Beth if she had sent her love to the person who had died here. Andrea bent her head and prayed for the strength not to judge that woman too harshly.

The sound of a vehiclé approaching made her turn quickly away from the flowers, but not quickly enough to miss seeing the scars cut into the drystone wall by the car which had run off the road and collided with it. She shuddered as she groped for the door handle of her own vehicle and collapsed into the driving seat seconds before an estate car drew level with her, slowing down for a moment before gathering speed to move away into a slightly wider section of the highway. When it was out of sight she allowed her head to fall over the steering wheel while she fought to regain control of her feelings so that she might drive on and see if she could find the Raven Falls Hotel.

'Dear Lord, please help me!' she found herself praying desperately, as she had done so often during the weeks since she had been widowed.

The hotel did not take much finding. Less than half a mile further along the Ravensbridge road, but set back a little from it, the building stood square and solid-looking, constructed of the same dark grey stone as the walls which encompassed the moorland grazing. There were bright boxes of geraniums set on the window-sills and sturdy-looking seats set below them.

On this day of autumn sunshine there were several walkers occupying the benches while enjoying food and drink. A board indicated that there was car parking behind the hotel, so Andrea followed the arrow, brought her vehicle to a halt beside a few others, and made her way to the sign that led to the lounge bar.

Before she reached the open door she looked behind her, alerted by the sound of fast-moving water, and caught her first sight of the waterfalls which could be plainly seen from this vantage point. They were a magnificent sight, those torrents of water glittering in the sunlight as they fell from a great rocky height into a deep pool far below. Andrea wanted to take a closer look at them, but not until she had satisfied her curiosity about the connection between the man she had been married to for eight years and this place. So she turned her back on the beauty and went instead through the door from which came the aroma of good food being cooked and the pleasing sound of leisured talk.

The lounge bar was traditional in style, with an air of being well cared for as light caught the gleam of brass and polished dark wooden surfaces. Comfortable-looking chairs and settles were cushioned with floral chintz. Copper jugs held tall sprays of chrysanthemums that were gold and white. The same colours as the ones she had found beneath the damaged drystone wall, she noticed with a lurch of her heart.

Behind the small half-circle of dark polished wood which was the bar area a middle-aged man waited to take her order after greeting her courteously. She ordered cider and a sandwich that she did not have any appetite for, then took a corner seat from which she could survey most of the room. The people sitting around sipping drinks or eating bar meals appeared to be mostly holiday-makers clad in jeans, shorts or cotton skirts with brightly hued T-shirts. They were mostly couples, since the family parties were eating and drinking out in the garden, which was set to one side of the Raven

Falls Hotel. Had Ian spent time here eating and drinking, time she had known nothing about? What had brought him here? Had it been some sort of business done in the area, a house-contents sale perhaps? Or had he come here to this place so far away from both his home and his business to spend time with someone whose presence with him might cause gossip in the places where he was well known?

'Was your order a prawn sandwich?'

Andrea turned her head to meet the enquiring glance of smiling green eyes set in a heart-shaped face with a dimple in the pointed chin.

'Yes. Thank you. That was very quick!' she responded.

'Well our busiest time is over now so we're not trying to serve everyone at once like in the peak holiday season,' the girl told her.

'Are most of your customers tourists then? Or do you get some business people too?' Andrea found herself asking.

'Oh, we have accommodation for a few business people which is used all the year round by reps and area managers and such, but during the summer months we get more tourist trade and the walkers out for the day to explore the fells. Enjoy your sandwich!'

The girl moved away, her prettily rounded figure drawing a few admiring glances from some of the male customers as she made for the door marked 'Private'. She was in her early twenties with golden blonde hair curling about the shoulders of her open-necked white cotton shirt. Andrea continued to gaze at her until she disappeared behind the door with a trayful of empty glasses. Then she took a long drink of the ice-cold cider before making a start on the prawn sandwich, which was tastefully garnished enough to whet her appetite.

The place was almost empty by the time she had finished her meal but still she lingered, her mind occupied again with the sight of that bright spray of fresh flowers and the damaged wall where her husband might, or might not, have met his death a few weeks ago. She would need to find out who had died there, but was the Raven Falls Hotel the place to ask? Or should she seek the help of the local police? If she did that they might wonder why it had taken her so long to become curious about her husband's actual place of death. The truth was that neither she nor Ian's mother had felt able to look at the place which had brought such tragedy to them. Now she was quite desperate to know everything that there was to know about the accident.

As these thoughts flitted in and out of her mind she became aware that the middle-aged man and the attractive young waitress were sharing a joke behind the bar area. Their shared laughter indicated that they were good friends as well as colleagues. Dare she risk breaking into their conversation to seek the information she had come here to find? She was on the point of rising from her seat to approach the bar when something the man said caused her to drop down into her chair again.

'I can manage now, Beth. You can go and get Jamie ready for his trip to the doctor if you like, then it won't be such a rush for you.'

Andrea froze. So the pretty, curvy blonde was called Beth, and she had someone called Jamie who needed to be taken to see the doctor! She began to feel sick. It was impossible for her now to get up and go to the bar to ask her question about the accident, especially when she heard the girl's reply.

'Thanks a lot, Dad. Is there anything I can get for you while we're in Ravensbridge?'

'I don't think so, love. Mind how you go. Take care!' he replied.

'I will, Dad. Don't worry. I'm fine.'

The girl smiled up at her father, her expression soft. He put a hand on her shoulder, briefly, and spoke again. 'I can't help but worry now. You and Jamie are all I've got.'

'And you are all we've got, Dad. I don't know what we'd

do without you, now.' She reached up to kiss him lightly on his cheek before disappearing through the door which led from the bar to the kitchen.

Beth Barclay had been the name of one of the proprietors of the hotel. Was her father Jeff Barclay? Andrea knew she would have to move soon, that she could not remain in the now-empty lounge bar of the Raven Falls Hotel for much longer, but her legs seemed to have turned to jelly. Was she being foolish to assume that Ian's secret life had been somehow involved with the girl called Beth? Two names on a card that was tied to a bunch of flowers left in memory of someone did not prove anything.

'Can I get you anything else? Some coffee perhaps?' Beth's father asked as he came out from behind the bar to stand closer to her.

Andrea forced a smile. 'Nothing, thank you. I've stayed here longer than I intended to, and I really wanted to have a look at the waterfalls,' she ended on a burst of inspiration.

He smiled back at her. 'They are certainly worth a visit, but perhaps you've seen them before?'

She shook her head. 'No, this is my first visit to this area. It was a relative who suggested I came here for lunch.' It was easy enough to lie, once you got started.

'I'm pleased to hear that. We do get quite a lot of customers coming back on return visits,' he told her.

'It was someone from Durham,' she heard herself say in a low voice.

'Someone from Durham? From the city, or the county?'

There was something guarded in the man's face, something which had wiped away the pleasant expression which had been there earlier.

'From the city,' she managed to answer.

The man shook his head. 'I'm trying to remember who it might be. Perhaps I'll remember next time he, or she, comes here again?' He seemed to be watching her intently as he said that.

'He won't be coming here again,' she said very quietly. 'He was killed a few weeks ago in a road accident somewhere around here.'

She heard his swift intake of breath in the moment before panic descended on her. Then she was on her way out of the room, stumbling in her haste to escape from the truth that waited to be told. The truth that she could not yet face up to.

Ten

T here was a huge lump in her throat which was making it hard for Andrea to breathe even when she found herself outside the Raven Falls Hotel. She gripped her hands tightly to her sides as she fought to control her emotions while she stumbled towards where she had parked her car. As she reached it she heard footsteps behind her and a male voice addressing her.

'Are you all right?'

It was the man she had just spoken to. He had followed her out to the car park because he was concerned about her abrupt departure. She must calm herself and answer him.

'Yes, I'm fine now. I just . . . just had to get outside into the fresh air,' she made herself mutter.

'Are you quite sure? There's no need for you to hurry away from here,' he began, his eyes showing his concern for her.

'You are very kind, but I really am fine again now. I'll need to hurry if I'm to visit the waterfalls before it's time for me to go back,' she said quickly.

'Have you far to drive?' There was curiosity in his eyes again now.

Was he wondering again about why she had turned her back on him so abruptly and dashed out here? She swallowed and made herself answer. 'Quite some distance.'

'I'll leave you to have your walk then. Perhaps we'll see you again some time?' he added.

'I don't know. I have a very busy life,' she hedged.

'Don't let yourself be too busy. Everyone needs to relax sometimes.'

He meant well, Jeff Barclay. It wasn't his fault that her visit to his hotel had brought her such pain. Maybe she ought not to have come here. Perhaps it would have been better if she had pushed away her doubts and suspicions about what Ian had been doing while she had been studying so hard for her degree and her calling to ministry?

She managed to smile at him as she answered. 'I'll go and relax by finding the waterfalls.'

The path to the falls wandered up the craggy side of the fell which towered behind the Raven Falls Hotel. It was bordered on either side by gorse bushes which glowed golden in the sunlight. As she walked, Andrea found herself praying silently that she had done the right thing by coming here to find out what she could about the accident which had made her a widow.

Long before she reached the Raven Falls she heard the thunder of fast-flowing water drowning out the birdsong as it poured down a deep cleft in the ravine. Closer at hand, as she stood on the narrow wooden bridge which gave a downward view of them, the waterfalls were awe-inspiring. Were these wonders of nature the reason why Ian had come here? If so, she could not recall him ever mentioning them to her.

For some time she stared down into the swirling foam, reflecting as she did so that if Ian had died so suddenly during the very early years of their marriage, before their baby had been born or just after he had died from meningitis, she would have felt a strong temptation to throw herself into the torrent which a nearby notice warned was very dangerous. Not now though, certainly not now. Now she had her faith to live for, and a job to do in Nyddbeck and Nyddford.

With the thought of her work in those places, and the sermon that was not yet complete on her computer to spur her on, she turned her back on the falls and made her way down the steep track that led back to the hotel car park.

Her homeward journey took her again past the place where she believed Ian had been killed. This time she did not stop but gave only a brief glance at the spray of flowers which was propped against the damaged wall where his car had come to grief. Life had to go on, and it would go on for her now in Nyddbeck and Nyddford.

At Abbot's Fold Farm, the row which was taking place between Dave Bramley and the man his mother was planning to marry had sent both Jack and Carla Bramley out of the farmhouse. Dave had ordered his son to a task which he knew well enough that the boy could not manage on his own, and sent his daughter down to the village shop to buy bread which they did not need. He was white-hot with anger at what he felt was unjustified interference in his family affairs by Ben Harper.

Dave was on a short fuse all the time these days. Ben Harper had made allowances for that often enough during the eighteen months that Dave had been on his own, but today his anxiety about Dorothy Bramley's health had caused him to forget all about tolerance and understanding and pour out a few home truths to her son.

'I still don't know why you couldn't have let me know as soon as you realised your mother was so unwell,' he said for the third time since his arrival at the farm.

'Because she didn't want you to know. I've already told you that!' Dave exploded.

'I don't believe that. Of course she would want me to know she was not well.'

'Ask her then! Ask her if you don't believe me!' Dave hit back.

'I don't want to upset her when she's not well enough to cope. I blame you for the way she is, young man. It's time you came to terms with the way things are now and got someone to come and help you here with the house and the children. You ought to have done that months ago, then Dorothy and I would have been married now and she would have been properly looked after instead of worked to death as she is.'

'You don't know what you're talking about, and you've no right to interfere anyway,' Dave broke in furiously.

'I know only too well what I'm talking about. Have you forgotten that I was left to cope on my own too, some years ago?'

Dave let go of a harsh laugh. 'Your "left to cope" was hardly the same as mine. Your son was older, and you had plenty of cash available to pay for help in the house. A full-time housekeeper, at that. I can't afford even a part-time one, the way things are in farming these days.'

'I offered to help you, didn't I? Only you turned my offer down.' Ben knew why his offer had been turned down. He had thought at the time when he made the offer, so that his marriage to Dorothy could go ahead as planned, that Dave was simply trying to keep his mother with him at the family farm because he resented having another man take his father's place. Now he wondered if he had been wrong about that. Maybe David Bramley was as proud as his father, Jacob, had been? Too proud in fact to accept a loan from a friend of his parents.

'My offer still stands,' he said quietly. 'Obviously you'll need to think again now.'

'It's no good thinking about taking a loan I might never be able to repay.'

'Don't be so stupid, man! I'll be part of your family soon, just as soon as your mother is well enough to go on with the wedding arrangements.' Ben saw the other man's face darken even more when he said that.

'She might not be wanting to do that. Don't be too sure!' Dave hurled at him.

Ben uttered a growl that expressed all his frustration before turning his back on the farmer and making for the door which led from the kitchen into the hall.

'Where do you think you are going?' Dave asked tersely.

'To see Dorothy.' Ben's reply was harsh. His fingers were already turning the door handle.

'I won't allow that. This is my house and I don't want her upset.'

Ben shrugged that off by opening the door. He was able to see then that Dorothy was on her way down the stairs, clad in a long blue dressing-robe and moving very carefully.

'My dear!' he hurried to meet her, afraid she would fall down the last few steps even though she was hanging on to the banister for support. 'I thought you were supposed to be resting in bed?'

'There's not much chance of resting with all the shouting coming from down here. My room is over the kitchen so I couldn't help but hear you.' Obviously Dorothy was distressed.

'I'm sorry.' Ben put his arm about her shoulders and drew her close. 'I'm afraid my concern for you made me say more than I should have done.'

'How did you know I was ill, anyway?' Dorothy asked wearily. 'I didn't want any fuss.'

'Andrea Cameron rang me to ask if I'd be the reader in your place at the morning service tomorrow. So of course I asked her why you wouldn't be doing it, and she told me.'

'Meddling again in other people's affairs,' Dave muttered. 'I thought she'd have had enough to do without getting involved with us. Why can't she leave us alone?'

'Because you are part of her flock. Your parents have been involved with Nyddbeck Church for as long as I have,' Ben reminded him.

'That doesn't give her the right—' Dave began.

'It's nothing to do with rights!' Ben broke in. 'It's to do

with caring about people. She's that sort of person. In fact she's very like your wife used to be.'

'Leave Jill out of it. I don't want to hear her compared with anyone else.'

'Andrea came up here this morning to see what she could do to help us, but I'm afraid David was rude to her. I don't know what she must think of us.' Dorothy Bramley bit her lip as she told Ben about Andrea's visit earlier that day.

'Don't you worry about that, my love,' Ben tried to comfort her. 'She'll understand that it wasn't *your* fault.'

The emphasis he gave to the word 'your' was not lost on Dave Bramley. 'I didn't ask her to come here. We can manage without her help,' he spat out.

'There was no need for you to upset her. She's had a bad enough time since she came here without that, poor girl.'

Both men were alarmed then to see Dorothy's face crumple and a couple of tears begin to slide down her pale cheeks.

'You are going back to bed right now, Dorothy,' Ben ordered. 'Come along, I'll help you up the stairs. And you can make some tea!' he barked over his shoulder at her son.

To the relief of them both, David turned away and strode in the direction of the kitchen sink to fill the kettle. Ben almost carried Dorothy back to her room, his whole being concentrating now on his worry about her health. The idea of losing Dorothy now that she was free at last to marry him appalled him. For as long as he could remember he had loved her, right from their schooldays, but she had chosen to marry Jacob Bramley while Ben was away at university. It had taken him some years to come to terms with losing her to Jacob. Until, eventually, he had married the woman who had been his secretary. Now Ben was on his own again, and so was Dorothy . . .

'I'm really concerned about the way David is these days,' Dorothy confessed as Ben sat beside her bed holding her hand. 'He seems to flare up at nothing, and he's so bitter.

97

Especially about the church and everything to do with it. The children are not allowed to go to anything connected with the church nowadays.'

Ben had not been aware of that. He frowned. 'It isn't just the services then?'

'No. It's everything else as well. Youth club, choir, Scouts and Guides.'

'They must resent that.'

'Of course they do. Especially the youth club.'

'Why? What reason does he give?'

'He says they've plenty to keep them occupied here, but I think it's because David has lost his own faith since Jill died.'

Ben sighed. 'I can understand that, in a way, with Jill being so young. It isn't fair to the children though. They've suffered as well, losing their mother, and they need things to help them come to terms with it.'

'I've tried telling David that but he just refuses to listen.' Dorothy shook her head despairingly. 'I don't know what's going to happen to them all.'

The arrival of Dorothy's son with two large mugs of tea put an end to the discussion but later, before he left the farm, Dorothy asked Ben if he would try to explain the reason for her son's attitude to the new minister.

'I feel so bad about the way David treated Andrea when she came here to help us this morning. Carla was upset about it, too. She was almost in tears when she came up here after Andrea had gone and asked me why her father was always in such a bad temper these days. I said it was because of all the trouble he was having keeping the farm going now that prices have dropped so drastically, but I don't think she believed me. In fact she said it wasn't Andrea's fault, so why was her Dad being so rotten to her every time they met.'

'Carla has a point there. I don't believe it's anything to do with farm prices either. I can't help but wonder whether it has more to do with the fact that Andrea Cameron has something about her that reminds Dave of Jill,' Ben said thoughtfully.

Dorothy sighed. 'Whatever it is, I don't want Andrea upset by his attitude. The poor girl has had enough to bear already since she came here without having to endure rudeness from my son. So will you try and explain to her please, Ben?'

'I'll call on her on my way home if that will make you feel any better, my dear. Now, why don't you have another sleep while everyone is out of the house?'

As he drove down the long hill that led from Nyddmoor to Nyddbeck, Ben's mind was full of concern for Dorothy and her family. They had come through a bad time since the sudden death of Jill Bramley but the children were coming to terms with what had happened, thanks to the extra love and care their grandmother had given them.

Dorothy had moved out of the lovely cottage which she and Jacob had built for themselves when Dave had married Jill and gone back to live in the farmhouse to care for her son and his children not long before she and Ben were to have been married. The marriage had been postponed. It was only for a few months, Dorothy had promised Ben, but the few months had become a year and looked like going on for a second year if he did not insist on their marriage going ahead soon. How was he going to persuade her to leave Dave to make his own arrangements for the care of his home and his children? He must try to do that without delay or her health would suffer even more and she would never come to share his home. Deciding to do that was one thing, actually doing it would be something different, and much harder, he knew, as he slowed his speed and came to a stop outside Nyddbeck Manse. First he must keep his promise to the woman he loved and try to explain away her son's bad behaviour to the new minister. He was not looking forward to doing that!

*   *   *

Andrea put her car into the garage but did not go at once into the house. Instead she wandered into the back garden, welcoming the tranquillity that she needed so desperately after the turmoil of emotions she had experienced during her visit to the Raven Falls Hotel. There were still so many unanswered questions in her mind. She wished with all her heart that she could get rid of those questions which seemed to nag so ceaselessly at her and just get on with her life here, but something was urging her to get at the truth, however unwelcome that truth turned out to be. As always when she was troubled or perplexed, she turned to where her help always came from and made her way to the little stone church which was on the other side of the beck from Nyddbeck Manse.

It gave her a small shock to find someone already inside the building. A woman of about her own age was putting the finishing touches to a stunning flower arrangement of starburst lilies and pink and white carnations. She spun round as she heard Andrea enter. Her face registered shock.

'Sorry, I didn't mean to startle you,' Andrea told her with a smile. 'I hadn't realised anyone was here.' The young woman was not known to her. It was mostly the older ladies of the church who were responsible for providing and arranging the flowers, and taking them afterwards to members of the congregation who were unwell or bereaved. The flower arranging was usually done on Saturday mornings rather than in the evening.

'Do I know you?' she asked. 'I can't seem to remember meeting you, but it has been so hectic since I came here that I'm afraid I sometimes have difficulty remembering names and faces.'

'You won't know mine because we haven't met before. I'm Julie Craven, a schoolfriend of Jill Bramley. That's why I'm here, because it would have been her birthday tomorrow and until she married Dave we always celebrated together. I was going to ask you if you would see that the flowers went to Dave's mother after the service tomorrow. Jill was very fond of Dorothy,' the small, brown-haired girl added.

'Wouldn't you like to take them to her yourself?' Andrea suggested.

Julie Craven shook her head. 'I don't think that would be a good idea. Dave Bramley can't bear to be reminded of anyone or anything to do with Jill, so he certainly won't want to see me. Unless there's been a change in his attitude recently. If there has his mother didn't say anything about it when I rang her last week to say I was coming over today to do the flowers for Jill's birthday.'

'I'll be pleased to take the flowers for you, and Dorothy will be glad to get them because she's ill at the moment and won't be able to come to church,' Andrea told her.

'Oh, I'm sorry to hear that. I know she's had a difficult time since Jill died.'

'It must have been hard for you, too, if she was your best friend,' Andrea began tentatively.

'Yes. I miss her terribly.'

Suddenly, Andrea made her mind up that her own problems could take a back seat: Julie was biting hard on her lips to stop her tears from overflowing.

'Would you like to come across to the manse for a coffee?' she suggested. 'It sometimes helps to share memories with someone on days like this.'

Julie sighed, then nodded. 'Yes. Thanks a lot. I do need to talk to someone.'

Eleven

When she and Julie Craven were sitting on the seat in the back garden of the manse, each sipping from a mug of coffee, Andrea gave the other woman time to voice what was troubling her. It was always easiest to do that rather than to put pressure on someone who was under stress to pour out their heart to you. Instead, while Julie remained silent, Andrea pointed out the robin who was hopping from branch to branch of the rowan tree on his way down to the lawn in search of crumbs.

'We've become quite friendly since I came here,' she murmured.

'You can't have been here long,' Julie responded. 'There was someone else here when Jill died, an elderly man.'

'That would be Mr Bickerdike. He'd been here for many years. He's in a nursing home now. I only came here in June.'

Julie stared at her reflectively. 'It can't have been easy for you, replacing someone who had been in charge for a long time. People round here don't take easily to changes.'

Andrea smiled. 'I didn't expect it to be easy. Mr Bickerdike is a lovely man, so people were reluctant to part with him. In fact lots of them visit him in his nursing home.'

Julie bit her lip, then sighed. 'I'll never forget the way he spoke about Jill at her funeral service. It was as if he really understood how she felt about her nursing, how she believed it was a waste to go all through the long training to qualify then

102

to stop doing it when you were married simply to become a housewife. Dave never did understand that,' she added.

'I suppose there is rather more for a wife to do in a farm-house than in other households,' Andrea said thoughtfully. 'Especially when there are children.'

'Oh, Jill enjoyed being at home with Carla and Jack when they were small. It was when they had been at school for a couple of years that she decided to work part-time from the village health centre. Dave blamed me for that. You see I'm a nurse too, I trained with Jill and when I came to see her here I suppose it was inevitable that we'd talk about my job, and that sooner or later Jill would want to go back to nursing too. Only Dave didn't understand about that. When she was killed going out to work on a stormy evening he blamed me for encouraging her to go back to work. I suppose he had to blame someone. Maybe it helped him at the time to be angry with me, but it didn't help me. I had to stand there, after the funeral service, and listen to him telling me that if I hadn't urged Jill to take the job at the health centre she would have been indoors with her children that night instead of on the road when the storm brought a tree down on to her car.' Julie shuddered, visibly upset still by the memory. 'It was so awful, so absolutely awful, being blamed for the death of my best friend immediately after her funeral service. I'll never be able to forget it. It's spoilt my life.'

Andrea searched her mind for something to say that might comfort her, but there was nothing readily available. Only a deep feeling of compassion, a longing to help this woman or any other person in distress which was bound up with her own deep faith and her calling to ministry. All she could do was reach out to take the hand nearest to her in a firm handclasp until Julie Craven's storm of weeping began to subside.

'I'm so sorry,' Julie said then in a muffled voice. 'I didn't mean to burden you like this. I only wanted to share it with someone I didn't know. Someone who would not be prejudiced, because they wouldn't know Dave Bramley. You haven't been here long enough to know Dave, have you?'

Andrea gave a rueful chuckle. 'I've been here long enough to know he's not an easy man to deal with, though I do get on well with his mother.'

'Oh yes, Dorothy is lovely. I feel sorry for her because Jill's death seems to have upset her plans to get married again to that nice man who owns the transport business.'

It was at that moment the front door bell sounded, bringing both women to their feet. 'I must go,' Julie said. 'Someone else needs you.'

'I'm not expecting anyone, so please don't hurry away. I'll just see who it is then we can talk again.'

When she opened the front door Andrea was surprised to find the man Julie had just been speaking of, Ben Harper. She stepped back into the hall to allow him to enter.

'I won't keep you long, Mrs Cameron,' he began. 'I've just come from Abbot's Fold Farm and I'm on my way home to Ford House, but I promised Dorothy I would call and give her apologies to you for the way you were treated by her son this morning. She was very upset that David should speak to you so rudely when you had been kind enough to offer help.'

'Please don't worry about that, Mr Harper,' Andrea broke in. 'I do understand.'

'Then you are the only one of us who does understand that young man,' he said forthrightly. 'I think it's time David Bramley came to terms with the way things are now and got on with his life for the sake of his children, and his mother. Dorothy's tired out, and at her wits' end with worry about him.'

Andrea frowned. 'I wish I knew how to help all of them, because they do all need help, David as well as his mother and the children. Only I don't seem to be the right person to give that help. For some reason, every time he sets eyes on me his bitterness seems to boil over. Which makes it impossible for me to even start to help. Is it me he dislikes, Mr Harper? Or is it what I represent that upsets him?'

Ben Harper sighed, wondering whether he ought to be polite and say Dave Bramley was on a short fuse with everyone, or whether he should give the new minister the truth. He had summed her up as a woman who would be able to face the truth, however unpleasant, but of course he could be wrong about that on such a short acquaintance with her. In the end, as she waited for him to answer, with her frank gaze meeting his concerned eyes, he decided on the truth.

'It's something of both, I'm afraid, Mrs Cameron. The Bramleys have always been supporters of the church, not just this generation but Dave's grandparents too, but from the time the accident happened and Jill was killed Dave completely lost his faith. Any mention of the church now within his hearing puts him into a mood of bitterness and anger. There's no reasoning with him. He just can't see beyond his present situation.'

Andrea nodded. 'Yes, I've already discovered that for myself, and it's going to make it very hard for me to help Dorothy as much as I'd like to. Though I'm sure I'll find a way round it,' she added firmly.

Ben felt his instinctive liking for her deepen into respect. He knew she meant what she had just said, but he felt bound to caution her. 'There is something else I ought to mention, Mrs Cameron. Something you won't be aware of.' He hesitated, wondering just how to go on.

Andrea frowned. 'Well, you'd better tell me then. I might as well know it all before I risk another visit to Abbot's Fold Farm.'

'It's just that there's something about you that reminds me of Jill Bramley, and I was wondering whether perhaps that was aggravating Dave, making it harder for him to be civil to you.'

Andrea was startled into silence.

105

'It isn't that you're a Jill Bramley look-alike,' Ben went on. 'It's something else, a certain confidence and warmth of personality, and a sort of radiance that Jill had. Dave must find it hard to be reminded of what a wonderful wife he lost.'

She nodded. 'Yes, of course. It does partly help to explain his attitude towards me. So what do you suggest I do, Mr Harper? Ought I to keep away from the farm just now and wait until David Bramley gets used to me being here? I don't like the idea of not being able to help someone who's been very kind to me, but I want to do what is best for Dorothy.'

Ben Harper took a moment to consider her words, then gave his answer. 'Yes, I think it might be best if you kept away from there for a while. I'll be going there every day, whether Dave likes it or not, so I'll keep you informed. Now I'll be on my way.'

He shook hands with her and strode away, a sturdy upright man with a thick thatch of silver hair. Andrea thought how lucky Dorothy Bramley was to have someone who cared so much for her. Once Ian had cared for her like that, especially in the weeks immediately after they had lost their baby. When had he begun to stop caring for her like that? She pushed the painful thought away from her and went back to where Julie Craven was standing staring out into her garden.

'I'm sorry about that. It was Dorothy Bramley's fiancé, Ben Harper, bringing an apology for the way her son spoke to me this morning when I went up to Abbot's Fold to offer my help.'

'Couldn't Dave have apologised himself for his bad manners?' Julie said.

'Apparently not. I don't suppose it even occurred to him to say he was sorry. I'm sure he does't realise how much his behaviour upsets his mother.'

'Then it's time he did. Jill wouldn't have wanted him to be like this, no matter how much he loved her.'

'We don't know how any of us would react to such a tragedy,' Andrea murmured.

'From what Dorothy told me, you've had to cope with something like it yourself, haven't you?' Julie said frankly. 'It didn't change your personality, did it, when your husband was killed and you had to cope without him?'

Andrea took her time about answering this unexpected remark. Most people seemed to avoid any mention of the way she had been widowed. They just didn't know what to say to her so they avoided the subject and said nothing. Obviously Julie Craven was not one of them. Perhaps it was her nursing experience that caused Julie to be so outspoken. Whatever it was, Andrea appreciated her straightforward attitude.

'Maybe it's easier for me because I still have my faith to support me,' she said slowly. 'Since the accident to his wife it seems that David Bramley has lost his faith.'

'I wondered whether that was part of the problem. If it is, I know Jill would not have been happy about it. She was a great supporter of the church, she was involved with the youth work right up to the time she died. It was one of the things I admired about her, the way she lived out her faith without preaching at people.' Julie swallowed as emotion choked her again.

Andrea came to her rescue. 'I'm sure I'd have liked Jill. I like everything I've heard about her.'

'I miss her so much. She was always there for me; someone I could talk to when I made a mess of things. Which I very often do,' Julie Craven confessed.

'I can't believe that.' Andrea smiled at the idea of this pleasant, attractive young woman constantly making a hash of her work or her life.

'I don't mean with my work, at least not often. I mean with my emotional life. I always seem to fall for the wrong guys, then I get hurt. Or I hurt them. Jill understood about that. She said one day I wouldn't pick the wrong man, or he wouldn't pick me; that one day I'd find the right man for me as she had done with Dave.'

'So it was a happy marriage in spite of their difference of opinions about her working?'

'Oh yes! She adored him and he felt the same about her. I envied her that happy marriage and her lovely children, and her nice mother too. You see I have no one of my own now. No one close that is. I'm an only child and my parents divorced while I was at boarding school. Mum lives in Australia now and my father travels all over the world working for an airline. I hardly ever see either of them. That's why Jill was so special to me. She was always here for me at Nyddmoor, on the other end of a telephone, or we'd meet up in York or Harrogate sometimes. Mostly I stayed at the farm for weekends when I was off duty.'

'No wonder you miss her.'

Julie forced a smile. 'Sorry, I didn't mean to moan. I don't know what got into me, pouring out my troubles like this.'

'Don't worry, Julie. I'm glad you felt able to talk to me. If you'd like to come and see me again fairly soon I'll be pleased to see you.'

The frown lifted from above the sad brown eyes. 'Do you really mean that? You're not just being polite?'

Now Andrea laughed softly. 'Of course not! If I didn't want to see you I could always have told you how busy I am, couldn't I?'

'Yes, I suppose so. Now I must go. I've got a dinner date tonight in York with a good-looking Army guy who'll probably turn out to be another one of my mistakes.'

'Don't be such a pessimist!' Andrea told her with a laugh as they walked to the door.

'I'll tell you whether I'm right or not next time I come,' Julie promised.

'Leave me your phone number, then I can ring you and

invite you to supper next time,' Andrea suggested. 'I'll be able to let you know how Dorothy is too.'

As she watched the small, slim nurse walk back to her car which was parked in the church car park Andrea sent up a prayer that the burden of grief and loneliness that hung over Julie Craven would soon lift and she would find other friendships to enrich her life. How fortunate she was herself that she had such loving parents to keep in touch with her, and Ian's nice mother only an hour or so's drive away. Her life would be the poorer without them.

Even though that thought and thanksgiving stayed in her mind as she sat at her desk giving her sermon for the next day a final polish on her computer, when she went up to her bedroom late that night the memory of her journey to Ravensbridge and the Raven Falls Hotel came drifting back into her mind. All desire for sleep left her then and she went to the window to stare out into the star-filled sky while the questions to which she had not been able to find any answers seemed to hammer into her brain.

Had she become so involved with her studies during her years of training that she had been unaware of this other woman who had become part of Ian's life? Had he felt neglected? If so there had never been any indication of that. His business and his passion for golf had appeared to fill all his evenings as well as his days. In fact she had been the one who felt disappointment quite often when Ian had arranged to play golf on a day that they could have spent together. If she had voiced her disappointment he had brushed this aside by saying how many useful business contacts he was able to make at the golf club. Now she found herself wondering whether all that time *had* been spent on the golf course, or whether some of it had been spent at the Raven Falls Hotel with Beth Barclay.

The thought tortured her for long after she had slipped into bed. Lying there, she faced the fact that until she knew for sure whether he had been unfaithful to her she would not be able to find any comfort in her memories of his lovemaking, and memories were all she would ever have now of Ian. There were tears on her cheeks as she said her final prayers of the day.

At Abbot's Fold Farm, Dave Bramley sat in the sparsely furnished little room which served as the farm office with his head in his hands and paperwork scattered all over the top of the old desk which had belonged to his father and his grandfather. The farm had been through rough times before, he knew that. There had been the years when his grandfather had kept the place going by leading stone from the quarries to where the new reservoir was being built because the income from the sheep and the dairy herd was insufficient to keep bankruptcy from the door. Then there had been the time when an outbreak of animal disease had brought heavy bills from the vet and no sales at Nyddford cattle market.

This time it was problems brought by appallingly low prices for the lambs which went to market; prices so low that they did not even cover the feeding of the animals so that it was uneconomic to sell them and impossible to go on keeping them. In some areas farmers were taking lambs to the animal welfare organisations and leaving them there to whatever fate awaited them. Dave could not do that. Years spent following the family tradition of caring for your animals to the best of your ability would not allow him to even contemplate doing that. Yet what was he to do instead? It was a nightmare, and now there was no Jill to help him decide what was best to do for both the farm and the family.

A few days ago he could have talked things over with his mother, but not now. Not since Dr Appleby had warned him that his mother must take life more easily or her health would suffer even more than it had done already. The doctor had been very blunt with him today, so blunt that Dave had felt uncomfortable. 'You've got used to having your mother take on all the burdens of this household in the last eighteen months, Dave, but it's time you made other arrangements now and gave her the chance to have an easier life by getting married again. I know other people have offered to help you and you've turned them down, but you are going to have to change your attitude, and soon,' had been the elderly doctor's warning.

Dave didn't want anyone else here in Jill's home, taking Jill's place. It had been hard having his mother doing that but he had allowed it to happen because there was no alternative since he could not afford to pay anyone for help. Most of all, he didn't want the new woman minister coming here to his home. It was unbearable having to come face to face with her anywhere. Here in his own home, the place where Jill's ghost had a habit of turning up just when he was at his most vulnerable, it was unendurable.

He knew that he had been outrageously rude to Andrea Cameron that morning when she came to offer her help. He also knew that his rudeness to the new minister had deeply upset his mother. She had told him so, and he had felt like a small boy again trying to find excuses for his bad behaviour. Only he was not a small boy now, he was not even a teenage boy who could be excused because his hormones were working overtime. He was a mature man, an adult who ought to have been able to contain his bitterness against God for robbing him of his wife. It was not the new minister's fault that he had lost the faith which had been with him for as long as he could remember. The faith which had died when Jill had been crushed by the falling tree.

His mother had not only been upset with him for the way he had spoken to Andrea Cameron, she had been angry with him too. Ben Harper had been more than angry when he challenged Dave about the episode, he had been absolutely furious. Dave felt ashamed of the words he had used to tell

Ben to mind his own business. They were the sort of words he didn't make a habit of using, foul words, disgusting language. He felt sick inside about that when he knew his mother had been able to overhear up in her bedroom.

Ben had reacted by retorting that it certainly was his business when Dave was causing such distress to his sick mother. 'I shall take Dorothy away from here as soon as she's fit to go,' he had declared.

Dave had retaliated that his mother would not leave him and the children. He was quite certain that she would not leave them.

'I'll make sure that she does,' the older man had promised. 'If I don't get her away from here soon it will be too late. Get your act together, man! Get real, if only for the sake of your children!'

He had stormed out of the farmhouse then, but not before throwing over his shoulder the remark that he would go to the manse on his way home to apologise to Mrs Cameron for the way she had been spoken to by Dave.

'It's what you should be doing, but you're too pig-headed to admit how much you are in the wrong,' had been his final shot.

Of course Ben was right. Dave knew he was right. Ben Harper was a fair-minded man, a man he had always liked and respected until he had begun to speak his mind too often for Dave's comfort. Only Ben just didn't understand why it was not possible for Dave to go down himself to the manse and face Mrs Cameron with his apology.

Perhaps he should phone her and apologise for his rudeness, if only to appease his mother and Ben. That way he would not have to look at her, would not have to feel that gut-wrenching pain because of the resemblance Andrea Cameron bore to Jill. Oh God! Why did she have to come here of all places to do the work that he no longer believed in? Why?

Twelve

A ndrea, who had struggled so hard to find sleep the night before, would have overslept the next morning if the ringing of her bedside phone had not brought her to awareness at seven a.m. It was probably someone needing help, she decided, as she lifted the instrument with one hand while she rubbed her eyes with the other.

'Andrea Cameron speaking,' she managed, stifling a yawn.

There was a long moment of silence, broken by the high-pitched barking of a dog, before the caller revealed his identity. 'David Bramley here.'

Instantly then Andrea became wide awake, and conscious of alarm. 'Is it Dorothy? Your mother, is she worse?'

'No, at least I don't think so.'

His voice was harsh, uncompromising. So why had he telephoned? Andrea held her breath as she waited for him to go on.

'She was worrying. About the way I spoke to you yesterday, I mean.'

Andrea remained silent as uneasiness built up inside her. Was she about to be subjected to another barely concealed expression of this man's obvious dislike for her?

'She thought I had no right to speak to you like that.' David paused, sighed, then went on. 'I suppose she was right. It was inexcusable of me. Please accept my apology.'

How ungracious he sounded. Had Dorothy pleaded with him to apologise to her? That was what it sounded like.

'Are you still there?' He sounded uneasy now.

'Yes. Is there something else you have to say to me?' she asked crisply.

'Only . . .' he began. 'Please don't blame my mother for what happened. It was entirely my fault.'

'I wasn't blaming Dorothy. I knew she was pleased to see me.'

'She was afraid, after the way I spoke to you, that you wouldn't come to see her again.' He spoke stiffly, reluctantly, as though not wanting to utter the words at all.

'If Dorothy asks me to visit her again, I will.'

'I'll try to keep out of your way next time you come,' he said, and hung up on her before she could respond.

Had it been Dorothy's idea that he should ring her to make the apology or had Dave's own conscience forced him to call her? Did it matter to her whose idea it had been? Andrea found herself unable to answer that.

David Bramley swallowed the remains of the huge mug of black coffee which had now gone cold, but did not move at once to where his collie waited to accompany him on the early morning tasks about the farm. Why had he added that final surly comment about keeping out of Andrea Cameron's way next time she came to Abbot's Fold? There had been no need for him to say that, even though the thought had been in his mind as he imagined her tall, graceful figure walking across the yard, her black hair falling in a cloud about her slim shoulders. As he recalled the way Andrea had raised her eyes from the table where she was preparing food for his family, and given him a long stare of astonishment as the rudeness of what he had just said to her penetrated her mind, the pain hit him again. The agonising pain of grief.

There had been something in that challenging stare which reminded him far too forcibly of the way Jill used to look at him when they reached an impasse in important family discussions. It was the way Jill had stared him down so many

114

times when he was voicing his objections to her going back to nursing.

'You won't even consider anyone else's point of view but your own! You're still living in the past, Dave. Nursing is my profession just as much as farming is yours,' Jill had declared. 'Besides, we need the money now that the farm income is going downhill.' He seemed to hear Jill's voice still, as though the echo of it remained here in the untidy little office where they had had that last row before Jill took the part-time job in the village health centre.

That was the worst bit, always. Remembering how Jill had told him that they needed the money that she would earn with her nursing to help keep the farm going. It made him feel guilty, as if his failure to keep Abbot's Fold Farm in a profit-making situation had forced her to go back to nursing instead of spending all her time on her home and family. Yes, he was as guilty as hell, and nothing would ever take that sense of guilt away from him. It was his failure as a farmer which had deprived him of a wife, and his children of their mother.

If there had really been a God, a loving God, as David had grown up believing, things would not have gone as disastrously wrong for those whose living depended on the land. There would have been no need for his wife to supplement their income. Jill would have been at home then on the night of the storm, spending the evening with him and the children instead of driving out to answer a call from the health centre. If there had really been a God, Jill would have been the one to stand in his kitchen preparing food for the family.

There would have been no need then for that other woman to take her place, to lift her calm blue-eyed gaze to his as though she could not believe what she was hearing him say. Why could he not get that woman out of his mind? She seemed to pose a threat to him just by her presence in the area. Surely Andrea Cameron should not still be here in these Yorkshire Dales villages going calmly about her work, when her own life had fallen apart? How could she still believe in a loving God when her own young husband had been killed on the day of her ordination? How could she possibly go on believing in God now?

The thought came into his mind then that perhaps Andrea Cameron was also no longer able to believe in a God who allowed such tragedies to happen. That she was only still working as a church minister because she did not know what else to do. This last thought was strangely comforting to David Bramley as he strode out with his dog into the early morning mist.

As she entered Nyddbeck Church that morning, the scent of the flowers Julie Craven had placed there in memory of her friend brought a smile to Andrea's face. How had Julie's date with her Army guy gone, she wondered. No doubt she would find out when she rang Julie to invite her to supper. While she was alone there in the little church which had already become a place she loved, Andrea offered silent prayers for Julie Craven, for Dorothy Bramley, Jack and Carla Bramley and for David Bramley. It was David who needed her prayers most, she felt certain. For how could he ever hope to come to terms with the loss of his wife, and make a good life for his children, without a strong faith to help him?

Her own deep faith had been of immense help to her in coping with the shock of her sudden bereavement, and the days of despair which had followed. Her faith had not protected her from the pain of loss, or the physical longing for the husband who was no longer there and never would be again, but the words of comfort to be found in the Bible were a constant source of hope for the future to her.

She knew she would need those words of comfort and hope often in the days to come, once she set out to unravel the mystery of why Ian had met his death in Ravensdale at a time when he ought to have been here with her.

'Good morning, Mrs Cameron! How are you today?'

The deep, firm voice of Ben Harper broke into her thoughts and scattered them. She turned with a smile to answer his greeting. 'I'm fine, thanks, Ben. You don't mind me calling you Ben, do you? If you'd rather have your formal title—'

'I wouldn't,' he broke in. 'If you are Dorothy's friend we ought to be on first-name terms. I hope it won't be long now before you are marrying us here in this lovely little church.'

'I hope so too. It would make me very happy to do that.'

'You haven't had much to make you happy since you came here, have you?' he said quietly.

What could she say in answer to that? She swallowed, and cast about in her mind for words. There were none available.

Ben came to put a hand on her shoulder. 'I shouldn't have said that, my dear. You won't need any reminding of how different it must have been from what you expected. I'm sorry.'

She was touched by his concern. 'Please don't worry about me, Ben. Other people have bad times to go through. At least I have my faith and my work to help me get through the bad times.'

'You'll do well here, once people get to know you. There's a kindness in you, a warmth, that will help you make friends here,' he told her.

'I think I've already made one, as well as Dorothy that is. Her name is Julie Craven. She came to do the flowers yesterday in memory of Jill Bramley. She told me that she and Jill were nursing together before Jill married, and that the flowers were for Jill's birthday today.'

Ben sighed. 'I suppose that's why Dave was in such a black mood yesterday. I don't know what we are going to do about him, but we're going to have to do something if I'm ever to get Dorothy away from there. I'd like to persuade her to just leave him to it and come to me, but I really think she's afraid of what Dave might do if she isn't there to keep an eye on him.'

Alarm surfaced in Andrea. 'You don't mean he might . . .'

'Might take his own life? Who knows? He's been a man in torment since Jill died, and now that the farm is going downhill he might think he has nothing left to live for.'

'He has his children to live for,' she pointed out.

'They might not be enough for him,' was Ben's sombre comment.

Andrea shuddered. The thought of those two lively children, Carla and Jack, being robbed of their father as well as their mother put fear into her mind. It must not be allowed to happen. She must see that it did not happen. Though right now she could not think how she would be able to prevent such a terrible thing.

'We have to do something, Ben,' she began. 'For all their sakes.'

'Do you think I haven't been trying to do something?'

'No, of course not. I only meant—'

'We'll talk about it later, after the service.'

People were drifting into the building now: the organist, the stewards, and those people who had been picked up in cars from their isolated homes. The air began to buzz with their conversation. Andrea decided it was time she retired to the vestry and prepared herself.

When the family service was over, and she was feeling hopeful that she had perhaps got the right mixture of what would go down well with the young children and their parents without antagonising older members of the congregation, she stood at the open door of the church ready to shake hands with people as they left. This was when they would tell her if she hadn't got it right, she guessed, and of course it probably would not have suited everyone. The breeze lifted her hair from her shoulders as she waited in the porch, listening to the organist bringing the morning worship to a close with a well-loved piece of Handel.

'Grand service, lass. Just reet!' said a burly, red-faced man whom Andrea took to be a farmer, but who later turned out to be a shopkeeper.

'Very nice, minister,' murmured the next voice, sweet and rather genteel, belonging to a long-retired schoolmistress. 'I do like the old hymns best though. You really can't beat Wesley for a good sing, but I expect you'll get it right next time.'

Oh dear, Andrea thought, so much for letting my own preference for Graham Kendrick win. She smiled at the woman and promised to remember about Wesley next time, then went on to the next pair of hands and the next comment on the service, her sermon, and the music. Overall, they seemed pleased with her, but of course they would still be showing sympathy and kindness to her because she was so recently widowed. As the last of the congregation departed, making their way to the church hall to share coffee before going home, she saw someone coming the other way, through the gate and to the church door. He was holding out a hand to her.

'Mrs Cameron, how are you?'

Andrea felt his fingers gripping hers, strong and warm. They were holding on for just a little longer than was necessary. Their owner wore a fleece and cords, with walking boots. His bronze hair glowed as the sun caught it and it struck her anew what a handsome man Bill Wyndham was.

'I'm fine, thanks. How are you? Did you manage to get the house you wanted?'

He nodded. 'Yes, I did. So I'll soon be seeing more of you. I'm looking forward to that.'

Something in the way he said it, and in the look which went with the words, alerted Andrea to the possibility that

119

here was a man who could become a nuisance to her if he was living almost on her doorstep. Was Bill Wyndham just naturally flirtatious with every woman under pension age? A sort of professional charmer. Or was he more than that? She'd soon find out.

'Does that mean I can expect to see you in church then, Mr Wyndham? Once you're in residence, I mean.' Her voice was serious as she asked the question, even though she was finding it difficult to restrain a smile.

He was studying her thoughtfully, and taking his time about answering so that Andrea began to wonder whether her invitation to her church had embarrassed him.

'That depends on you, Mrs Cameron,' he said at last. His face was sober but his eyes gleamed with amusement. 'On what sort of neighbour you turn out to be.'

Now she found herself laughing. 'I suppose you mean whether I play loud music late at night to disturb your sleep?'

'No. I doubt very much that I'll ever have that sort of problem from you. I was thinking more of whether you would turn out to be a friendly neighbour.'

Andrea hesitated before replying to that, unsure of exactly what Bill Wyndham would mean by a friendly neighbour. Her hand went to the band of white set about her slender neck, the collar which proclaimed her calling. 'I'll be there if you need my friendship or help, of course. I'm here for everyone who needs me, whether they come to one of my churches or not.'

'That wasn't quite what I meant. I was really wondering whether you would be friendly enough to have lunch, or dinner, with me one day?'

She was taken aback, and about to refuse him on the grounds that she was too busy with her parish work and the removal of her things from the house in Durham, but while she hesitated, wondering how to turn him down kindly, he spoke again.

'As a matter of fact I do need your help, your advice, as well as your friendship. I need to talk to you fairly soon.'

The amusement had been banished from his eyes now and they were full of something very different, something she was almost certain was anxiety.

'We'd better arrange a time then,' she told him quietly. 'I'm rather tied up today, with a baby to christen this afternoon and an early evening service at Nyddford Church tonight. Will you be around tomorrow or are you away working somewhere else?' Dorothy Bramley had told her that Bill Wyndham was an artist who specialised in painting landscapes.

'I'll be here because I have to let workmen into the house at nine o'clock. If you have any time to spare for me then?'

He looked anxious, pleading almost, so that her curiosity was aroused. 'What about ten o'clock? At the manse,' she decided.

'I'm really grateful to you, Mrs Cameron. I didn't know who to turn to, as things are now.'

Suddenly she was beset by doubts. 'I just hope I'm the right person. I haven't been here very long and don't know everyone yet.'

'You're the only one who can help me, and you do know the people concerned.'

She frowned. 'Do I?'

'Yes. I wish now that I hadn't become involved. I came here to get away from problems, to make a new start. It doesn't seem to be working out like that though.'

'Perhaps you haven't given it time yet?' she suggested.

'I thought I had, but now I don't know.'

Just what was it all about, this problem he felt she could help him sort out? Plainly, whatever it was had turned him from being the sort of person she thought she would have little in common with into a human being in need.

Someone was locking the church door, the organ music had long since stopped and people were beginning to leave the church hall in small groups. A woman in one of the groups called out to her, 'Don't you want any coffee, Andrea? They're keeping it warm for you.'

Instantly Bill Wyndham moved away from her, apologising. 'I'm sorry! I ought not to have kept you so long.'

'Please don't worry. This is what I'm here for. This, and other things,' she told him.

'All the same, it's not as if . . .'

'Not as if what?'

'As if I were one of you.' He pointed in the direction of her church.

'Do you think that matters to me?' she challenged.

'It might.'

'I can assure you it doesn't. I'll see you at ten tomorrow,' she said crisply, before moving in the direction of the church hall.

Thirteen

Eating a hasty breakfast the next morning while she ploughed through a pile of letters, Andrea came to one which informed her that the sale of the house in Durham was now nearing completion and requested her to make an appointment for the final signing. The letter added that the buyers were anxious to have vacant possession as soon as possible.

For some time she sat holding the letter, painfully aware that the signing away of the house would be the final severing of the link between her and Ian. They had been so happy in that house during the early years of their marriage, and even happier after Andrew was born. It was only when they had lost their baby to meningitis that the joy had gone from the home and the marriage.

Was it then that Ian had met Beth? Had he found her own state of utter desolation too much to bear and instead turned to the brightness and sparkle of a girl who was not living under a cloud of sorrow? She would probably never know the whole story, but she had to find out as soon as possible whether Jamie, Beth's baby, was Ian's son. It could be that when she finally emptied the Durham house she would uncover more evidence about this other life her husband had been leading. She would try and get back there today, she decided.

Before then there was her meeting with Bill Wyndham, and it was almost nine o'clock now. She rushed through the rest of her breakfast so that she could take a brisk walk before he arrived. There was a bite to the wind this morning strong enough to have brought more leaves to rustle about her feet as she took the footpath that led away from the church and the manse in the opposite direction to where the house was that Bill Wyndham had bought. She had no wish to run into Bill until he arrived at the manse. First she needed time to clear from her mind all her own worries and anxieties, all her suspicions that she had been betrayed by Ian, and all her fears that she might not yet have the experience to be able to cope with whatever it was that Bill Wyndham was so anxious to share with her.

She would also need to banish from her thoughts the man who had been so much in her mind ever since her visit to Abbot's Fold Farm. Somehow she was going to have to get help for David Bramley before it was too late. So far all she had been able to do was offer up her prayers for David and his family, but how would those prayers be answered? When the help was there for him, would David accept it? Or would his stubborn pride win again and the help be turned away?

Within half an hour the fresh air and brisk walk had worked their usual magic for Andrea and she was walking back towards the manse, having watched a heron catching his breakfast, seen a couple of squirrels moving fast as lightning up the trunk of a tall tree and listened while a robin sang from his perch on a drystone wall.

As she climbed the stile which would bring her to the field path that led to the back gate of the manse she paused and surveyed the village of Nyddbeck from this raised vantage point. How beautiful it was, with the beck glinting silver in the morning light as it wound past a row of stone cottages built two centuries ago, wandered on to reach the square stone house belonging to the doctor and on again until it reached the ancient pack-horse bridge and the village green.

There was a car parked close to the bridge, an elegant silver saloon whose front doors were opening. Bill Wyndham was emerging from one of them, then turning back to speak to someone who was still inside the vehicle. A glance at her watch showed Andrea that Bill was several minutes early for his appointment with her. She dropped down from the top of the stile in case he caught sight of her and thought she was watching him. It was necessary, she thought, to keep some space between them until she knew just what it was that he so urgently needed to talk to her about.

While she waited for him to ring the doorbell she gave her hair a quick brush, then put some coffee on to brew. The provision of tea or coffee seemed to help relieve the tension in people who were burdened with anxieties, she had found. It would help her when she spent time with some of the seriously ill patients and their families or carers later in the day. It was ten o'clock now, the chiming grandmother clock which her own Scottish grandmother had given her on her marriage was reminding her as the aroma of the coffee began to invade her senses. Bill Wyndham would be on the doorstep, since he had already reached the village.

So why wasn't he ringing the bell? Was the doorbell not working? It had certainly been working earlier that morning when the postman had delivered a packet of leaflets for her. A glance through one of the side windows of the front bay which gave a view of her porch failed to reveal the tall upright figure of the artist. Perhaps Bill had forgotten something and gone back to the house he was buying, or to Jacob's Cottage where he was still living, to collect it? Andrea sat down in a low chair where the sunshine poured into the room and began to read the front page of the *Yorkshire Post*.

Almost half an hour later, as she was beginning to feel annoyed with Bill for not having the courtesy to let her know that he would not be coming to see her, her phone began to ring. It was no surprise to her when she heard his voice.

'Bill Wyndham here, Mrs Cameron,' he began. 'You must be wondering—'

'What happened to you?' Andrea broke in. 'You were here. I saw you. Then you went away.'

'I'm sorry about that.' She heard him give a long sigh then an exclamation of irritation. 'It was that bloody girl!'

'What did you say?' Had he really meant to say that? Or had the words just slipped out?

'I'm sorry about that too. She's got me so I don't know which way to turn.'

'Hadn't you better turn in my direction then and tell me all about it?'

This time his sigh was definitely one of profound relief. 'I was hoping you would say that, but I know how busy you must be so I didn't dare to expect it. Can I come right away, please?'

'Yes. And don't change your mind this time,' she warned.

'I won't. I've got rid of the girl now, thank God.'

What an extraordinary thing to say. Andrea shook her head in disbelief as she put down the phone and went back to check on the coffee percolator. Five minutes later, Bill was on her doorstep. He was frowning, and still visibly put out. Her curiosity was stirred anew.

'Come in, Bill,' she invited. 'I expect you'd like some coffee?' She did not wait for his answer but led the way into the large pleasant sitting room, where she seated herself on the sofa and waited for him to drop into one of the armchairs.

'I really am terribly sorry to keep you hanging about like this,' he began as she poured his coffee, strong and black.

Andrea smiled. 'Forget it. At least you're here now.' She gave him time to relax by remarking how much she had enjoyed her walk that morning. 'That's when I saw you get out of your car, as I was coming back over the stile from the riverside footpath. Then when I looked again you'd gone. So I thought you might have changed your mind about talking to me.'

'Oh no, I certainly hadn't done that. In fact what happened

126

this morning made me more anxious than ever to talk to you.' His frown deepened, banishing the good humour which was habitually reflected in his features.

'So what happened this morning?' she prompted.

'The girl was waiting at the house, at my new house, when I got there.'

'Which girl?' Now Andrea was frowning.

'Carla. Carla Bramley, Dave's daughter.'

'Why should she be there? Surely she ought to have been in school?'

Now there was a dark flush invading Bill's bronzed cheeks. He was embarrassed, Andrea realised. Too embarrassed to go on, perhaps? She waited, exploring as she did so the possibility that she was about to hear something disturbing. Surely he hadn't allowed himself to become emotionally, or physically, involved with such a young girl?

'Yes, of course Carla should have been in school. She certainly left the farm at the usual time to get the bus as she always does. Then, when I arrived at the house, there she was chatting away to the workmen.'

'Why would she do that?'

Now Bill was visibly uncomfortable. In fact he appeared to be having difficulty in finding the words with which to answer Andrea's question as he continued to stir the sugarless coffee while he stared down into it.

'That's what I wanted to talk to you about,' he said, lifting his glance to hers at last. 'She seems to imagine that she loves me.'

'Oh, I see,' Andrea murmured. Poor Carla, so vulnerable, even more vulnerable than most young girls because of her troubled home life.

'You don't see! Not really. How can you, when you've never been in such a situation yourself?'

'I know it's something young girls are prone to, especially if their fathers don't have much time for them,' she pointed out.

127

'It isn't a fatherly relationship Carla's wanting with me,' he told her bluntly.

Andrea had already guessed that, but she'd needed to hear it from Bill.

'You haven't . . . ?' she began quietly. 'Done anything to encourage her, I mean?' She had to ask that, had to give him the chance to tell her the worst. If there was a worst to hear.

'Of course not!' he exploded. 'Good God! What do you take me for, a bloody paedophile?'

'I had to ask. You need to be frank with me if I'm to help you.'

Suddenly the anger left him. 'I'm sorry about that. About my language, I mean.'

'I've heard it all before. That and much worse, during my student years at an inner-city placement church.'

'All the same, you shouldn't have to hear it in your own home.'

'Shall we get back to what you came here to talk about? Tell me how it started, and how you've managed to cope with it so far,' she suggested.

So he began at the beginning: the time early in the year when he had found Jacob's Cottage while he was walking around this area of North Yorkshire to find the right locations for some illustrations he had undertaken to do for a travel book.

'I thought it would do me for the few weeks I expected to be here. Then, when I heard that Dorothy Bramley was going to marry Ben and move in with him at Ford House I considered making an offer for the place. That was before Carla began to make such a nuisance of herself.'

'How did that start?' she wanted to know.

'Well, of course I felt sorry for the kids, left without their mother at such a young age and with their father in a permanently sour mood. You see I like children. I had hoped to have some of my own before now, only . . .' He came to an abrupt halt. Andrea waited, watching his features show a range of different expressions.

'That's another story,' he said at last. 'Nothing that would be of interest to you. When Carla discovered that I was an artist she began to ask my advice about her school artwork, I suppose because neither Dave nor his mother had time to help her. I found she was quite good, good enough to deserve encouragement. Because I helped her she kept bringing things to show me, and then one day . . .' Bill found himself unable to go on. The look he gave Andrea was appealing.

'Go on,' she prompted.

'I discovered that she was not as interested in painting and drawing as she was in me. I tried to discourage her then from coming to the cottage. I didn't want Dave or Dorothy getting any wrong ideas. Neither of them seemed to notice how Carla kept haunting me. How she was always on the lookout for me when I arrived back at the cottage, and always making excuses to come over there and talk to me. I changed my mind then about making an offer for Jacob's Cottage and began to look for something a bit further away from the farm. When I bought the house in Nyddbeck I didn't expect Carla to start following me down here. I was really shocked when I found her at my new house this morning. In fact I got very angry with her and told her I was taking her to school at once and if she played traunt again I'd go and speak to her headteacher.'

'How did she react to that?'

He sighed. 'She started to cry and to tell me how unhappy she was at home. There was no one she could talk to now that her gran was ill, she said. She seemed to be terribly afraid of what would happen to her and Jack if her gran died.'

'Poor Carla,' Andrea murmured. 'We have to try and do something to help her.'

'What she ought to be doing is spending more time away

from her home, with young people of her own age. Isn't there anything at your churches for the kids to become involved with?'

Andrea hesitated. 'It isn't quite as simple as that, Bill,' she said slowly. 'You see Dave is not willing for either of his children to come to anything connected with the church.'

Bill frowned. 'Why not? I mean, there's nothing up there at Nyddmoor for them, is there?'

Now it was Andrea who frowned. 'I don't really know. I haven't been here long enough yet to be able to find out everything about the three villages of my parish. Not that there's a church at Nyddmoor. There isn't. The people from the farms and the few big houses up there seem to come down to Nyddbeck Church.'

'So why don't Carla and Jack do that? Come to Guides or Scouts or youth club I mean.'

Andrea shrugged her slim shoulders. 'How long have you been living up at Nyddmoor, Bill?'

'Several months now.'

'And you've no idea why the children don't come to any of the young people's activities?'

'Is it because their father hasn't time to bring them down here and collect them again?'

'I don't think it's anything to do with transport,' she began carefully. 'Because their grandmother has her own car and is living with them. She couldn't do anything to help now that she's ill, of course . . .' Andrea's voice tailed off as she considered whether or not to share with Bill Wyndham the reason why Dave Bramley would not allow his children to join in church youth or any other activities. She did not know him well. Yet he seemed very concerned about the isolation of the Bramley children.

'What is it to do with then? Or is that something you are not prepared to share with me?' There was challenge in the

130

hazel eyes that met her own troubled glance, although the words had been spoken quietly.

'I can share it with you, but you may not be able to understand.'

'Try me,' he suggested.

'It seems that when Dave's wife was killed he lost his faith as well as his wife.'

Bill sighed softly. 'I'm beginning to understand now. Of course it shakes you when something like that happens. I suppose it's all part of the shock. It takes time to come to terms with what has happened and adjust to it.'

'Yes.'

'Your own loss must have dented your faith quite severely?'

'I could not have coped with it, with any of it, without my faith,' she told him.

'I think you must be a most remarkable woman.' There was admiration in his steady regard now. She found herself forced to look away from him and stare instead through the window at the roof of her little church which was just visible.

'I'm just a woman who has a job to do. Part of that job is to try and help people like Carla. How I'm going to do that I don't yet know, but I will do it somehow or other. Thank you for telling me about her, Bill.'

She was on her feet, indicating that the interview was coming to a close.

Bill also got to his feet, holding out a hand to her. 'Thanks a lot for listening to me. It has helped a lot just being able to unburden myself to someone. You see I'm rather a loner now, so I don't have anyone to talk to.'

With her hand still in his she smiled. 'We all have someone we can talk to, Bill.'

His bronze eyebrows lifted as he questioned this.

'It's called prayer,' she said. 'You could try it.'

He did not answer her but released her hand so that she could walk to the door with him.

'Would you mind if I called again some time?' he turned to ask as he strode away.

'Of course not.'

Andrea watched him go, wondering as she did so whether she would have put him off by advising him to try prayer. Only time would tell.

Fourteen

This new minister was someone special, Bill thought, as he walked away from the manse. Not that he had a great deal of experience of ministers these days, he reflected with a wry grin. He had sensed a genuine concern in Andrea Cameron for that sour-natured guy Dave Bramley, and an even greater concern for Dave's young daughter. She would find it hard going to tackle the problem of Carla Bramley, he guessed, because Carla was a very wilful young girl who was more than determined to get her own way.

A wave of embarrassment swept over him as his thoughts returned to the part of his problem with Carla that he had not yet shared with Andrea Cameron. He halted to lean over the parapet of the old stone footbridge which crossed the beck, as his mind, which had veered away in panic from sharing with Andrea the latest experience he had been forced into with Carla, now leapt back into sharp focus. What would Andrea have said if he had told her that Carla was quite prepared to come and sleep with him when he moved into his new home at Beckside?

'I'll tell Dad I have to stay on at school because of the rehearsal for the school play, then I'll get off the bus at the usual place and come down here after the work-men have gone. You'd like that, wouldn't you, Bill?' Carla had said when he had hurried her out of the garden at Beckside.

'No! I damn well wouldn't!' Bill had broken in explosively.

'You're only a schoolgirl. I don't go in for that sort of thing. You know I don't!'

'But you're not gay, are you? You can't be. I'd know if you were.'

'Of course I'm not gay,' he had snapped.

'Well you don't have a partner do you?'

'Not now.'

'Why not?'

'That's nothing to do with you, Carla, and it's time we ended this conversation.'

'I could be your partner.'

'I'm far too old for you,' he snapped. 'You'll find someone of your own age, when you're ready.'

'I'm ready now, and I'm in love with you.'

It had all been said this morning after he had found Carla waiting for him at Beckside when he went to give instructions to the decorators. He had been furious with the girl, angry and alarmed too. So alarmed that he had shouted at her and then remained silent all the way to the High School at Nyddford where he had bundled her out of the car and told her to keep out of his way in future. Why hadn't he told Andrea Cameron how afraid he had been?

He had been on the point of telling Andrea when a ray of sunlight had touched her face and made him aware once again of how beautiful she was, and how strongly he was drawn to her. So the words about his fear of Carla's pursuit of him had remained unspoken, pushed aside by his desire for this cool, calm woman whose appearance in his life had cracked the shell of isolation which he had built around himself . . .

As soon as she had closed the door behind Bill Wyndham, Andrea began to rush around the manse gathering together the suitcases, bags and boxes she would need to hold the remainder of the smaller personal items she intended to bring back with her from the house in Durham. While she was in the city she would meet Nancy and ask her to collect any of

Ian's things that she wanted to keep. Nancy seemed to have assumed that Andrea would want to keep everything which had ever belonged to Ian but this was not now the case. It would be necessary though for Andrea to go through all Ian's things to make certain that his mother did not discover that there had been a woman called Beth in her son's life, and possibly a child called Jamie. Andrea knew that such a discovery would hurt and embarrass her mother-in-law and she liked her too much to want that.

This was the only day she would be able to go to Durham this week because there were meetings, school visits and sick visiting to be fitted in on all the other days. Even today there was a visit to be made to the retirement home where her predecessor now lived because she was anxious to ask the advice of Mr Bickerdike about how she could best give the sort of help to the Bramley family that Dave Bramley would permit them to accept. She would make that visit on her way to Durham, she decided.

Mr Bickerdike welcomed her warmly and asked if she would rather talk to him in his own room than in one of the communal sitting rooms. 'I know some of the other residents enjoy having a chat with you, my dear, but you might have things you would prefer to discuss with me in private,' he remarked.

'Yes, I do have something I'd like to talk about confidentially, Mr Bickerdike.'

'Then we'll go to my room where we're not likely to be disturbed.' Leaning heavily on his walking stick the retired minister led the way along a wide corridor, through a spacious conservatory and to his ground-floor room which had a french door leading into the garden. Once there he drew forward a comfortable chair for Andrea and waited for her to be seated before lowering himself into his own leather wing chair.

'It's a pleasure to see you. I was wondering how you were getting on. Especially after all you have had to endure

135

since you came to live in Yorkshire,' the old man began. 'I have been doing the only thing I could do to help you by remembering you in my prayers. You can be sure I'll continue to do that, and that I'm here for you to call on whenever you need me.'

'Thank you, Mr Bickerdike. At first, when I heard someone tell me they had a difficult situation that they needed to talk to me about, I wondered how I was going to deal with it since the person concerned had rejected everything that the church or anyone connected with it could offer. Then I remembered you, and I knew I must share this one with you as you've known the people concerned for far longer than I have. I'm talking about Dave Bramley and his family.' She came to a halt, waiting for the old minister's response.

His gentle face took on a troubled look. 'I might have guessed it. Things have been steadily getting worse up at Abbot's Fold Farm ever since the tragedy. It's put a very great strain on poor Dorothy Bramley, who ought to have been married by now to Ben Harper. I had been rather looking forward to conducting the ceremony but I'm beginning to wonder if it will ever take place now.'

'Did you know that Dorothy was taken ill a few days ago?' she asked him.

He shook his head. 'I've been expecting that to happen. How ill is she?'

'Ill enough to have Ben Harper worried out of his wits, I'm afraid.'

'So you want to know what you might be able to do to help?' Mr Bickerdike suggested.

'I don't think Dave will allow me to do anything to help. He made that quite clear when I went up there to give Carla a hand with the cooking on the day Dorothy collapsed.'

Mr Bickerdike shook his head sadly. 'Poor David! So afraid to become beholden to anybody, and not realising that he's asking too much of his mother.'

'It isn't just his mother. I think Ben Harper will take care
of Dorothy. As soon as she's well enough to leave Abbot's
Fold he'll have her away from there. He's made that quite
clear to me, and probably to Dave as well. It's Carla I'm
very worried about.'

'Carla? Is she ill as well?'

'She isn't ill, but she is causing a problem. That's what I
wanted to talk to you about.'

'What sort of problem? She's a very bright child, so it can't
be her school work that is suffering.'

'No, it isn't her school work. It's what she's doing when
she's out of school that's creating a lot of concern,' Andrea
told him.

A faint smile creased the parchment-tinted face of the old
man. 'Oh, I see now. Boy trouble! I suppose it's only to be
expected at her age.'

'It isn't exactly boys, Mr Bickerdike. It's a man. A man
who's much older than Carla.'

'Is it someone I'll know?' he asked then.

Andrea hesitated. 'I'm not sure about that. It's the man
who's renting Jacob's Cottage from Dorothy Bramley.'

'The artist? Is that who you mean?'

'Yes, Bill Wyndham. Do you know him, Mr Bickerdike?'

'I've certainly met him once or twice when I've been
visiting Dorothy. I wouldn't say that I know him, though I
do know that he's a very successful and gifted artist. Quite
a handsome fellow too.'

'Evidently Carla Bramley thinks so too. She's begun to
make rather a nuisance of herself by chasing Bill Wyndham,'
Andrea explained.

'Oh dear, that's very unfortunate.'

'Bill says he's tried to discourage her, but she just won't
listen to him.'

'Are you sure he hasn't encouraged her? Carla is a very
pretty young woman.'

'Bill assures me that he has not encouraged her attentions in any way.'

'Are you sure that is quite true? That he hasn't been tempted into acting unwisely with the girl when he knows she is under age?'

Andrea shrugged her shoulders. 'Well of course I don't know Bill well enough to be certain of that. I only know that he's desperate to discourage her now.'

'Then why doesn't the fellow move from Jacob's Cottage and put some distance between them?'

'He's just about to do that. In fact he's bought a house down in the village, the old cottage called Beckside, but Carla has taken to following him down there. When I spoke to him earlier this morning he had just been taking her back to school because she had gone down to his new home instead of going there. He said he had threatened to talk to her headteacher if she went absent again to follow him.'

Mr Bickerdike sighed. 'Dear me, as if they didn't have enough trouble at Abbot's Fold without all this!'

'Bill seems to think it's because her father doesn't care much about her any more that Carla is running after him.'

'That's nonsense! Of course Dave cares about his daughter. He's always been a very good father, just as he was a devoted husband to Jill.'

Andrea bit on her lip as she heard this. 'Have you seen Dave Bramley lately, Mr Bickerdike?'

'I haven't seen him for a few months, not since I came here to live.'

'Then you won't realise how difficult he's become. How bitter. So bitter that he won't even allow the children to come anywhere near the church now; not to church or youth club or badminton or Scouts and Guides. Bill thinks it's the isolation Carla is enduring after school that is making her imagine she's in love with him.'

'I didn't realise things were as bad as that with David. I

knew he had been hit hard by the tragedy but I thought by now he would have been coming to terms with it.'

'He isn't. When I went up to the farm after I heard Dorothy had been taken ill he was quite rude to me. In fact he was very rude indeed, which upset Dorothy and made me feel very uncomfortable. I couldn't see any reason why he should treat me like that.'

Mr Bickerdike sighed again. 'Don't take it personally, my dear. He's a very worried man, and a desperately unhappy one. It would be very hard for him to have you in his home, harder perhaps than you realise.'

'I had only gone there to help, not to interfere, but he made me feel so . . .' Andrea broke off. 'So unwelcome. It was almost as if he hated me.'

There was a long moment of silence, as if the old minister did not know what to say. In that moment Andrea heard a bird begin to sing out in the garden of the home. Then Mr Bickerdike spoke again. His voice was gentle.

'It isn't so surprising that David found it hard to accept your presence in his home, Andrea. You see there's something about you that strongly resembles Jill, so he would be shocked perhaps at finding you there in the kitchen of his home.'

'Someone else told me that I reminded them of Jill,' she said slowly. 'So would your advice be to keep away from Abbot's Fold?'

He nodded. 'Yes, I think it would be wiser to do that as things are at present. Though there's no reason why you shouldn't keep in touch with Dorothy by telephone.'

'How am I going to be able to help Bill sort out the problem of Carla? What can I do that won't antagonise her father even more? I must do something.'

Again there was a long silence while the old man who had spent so many years serving the small free churches of the Yorkshire Dales considered what could be done without causing more friction than already existed. This time the silence was broken by the sounding of a gong out in the hall to signal it was time for the residents to get ready for their lunch.

'What you could do is to try and talk to Carla somewhere away from her home. I take it that you got on all right with her?'

'Oh yes. We were doing fine sorting out the food between us until her father came in.'

'Then try to meet her, as if by accident. Start talking to her, woman to woman, as Jill would have done.'

'She probably won't like it.'

'I know it won't be easy for you, but I also know that you're not afraid of a challenge. That's the reason I was so glad when you decided to come here. Things have become rather static in the two churches in recent years, partly because of my own health going downhill. You need energy as well as commitment in order to bring about the sort of changes that are needed if we are to move forward into an exciting new century. New ways of worship are needed as well as new social events and new ways of raising money. I feel sure you'll be able to handle that challenge, and I'm sure you'll be able to find a way of meeting up by accident with Carla Bramley and helping her to understand why she must not put temptation in the way of Bill Wyndham.'

Andrea smiled. 'Meeting up by accident with her? It sounds as though you've done things like that yourself, Mr Bickerdike?' She rose to her feet, preparing to leave.

'Of course I have! I've learned a trick or two during my forty years in the Dales,' he confessed.

She laughed. 'Where would you suggest is the most likely place to meet a schoolgirl, other than her home?'

He was on his feet too, and holding out a hand to her. 'The school bus stops at the top of Abbot's Hill. There's space up there to park a couple of cars, and a wonderful view. The bus stops there at about a quarter-past four every school day.

Good luck, my dear. My prayers will be with you. Come and let me know how you get on.'

'Yes, I'll do that when there's something to report. Enjoy your lunch, Mr Bickerdike!'

Andrea was still smiling as she walked back to the car park and headed for the A1 and Durham.

Mr Bickerdike watched her go thoughtfully. Andrea Cameron had a rare courage, a sense of purpose that would certainly be needed at times as she struggled to build up the two churches which were not these days as full as they had been during his own early days in Nyddbeck. Now Sunday shopping was the new religion and many children were strangers to Sunday school. Perhaps Andrea Cameron would reverse that trend. He hoped so.

As to what she would be able to do to help the Bramley family, he had grave doubts about that, though he had not voiced them to her. It had disturbed him deeply to hear from her how David Bramley was becoming totally immersed in his own bitterness. After the tragedy which had robbed David of his wife the old minister had made some attempts at trying to help him come to terms with his loss, until his own health had begun to break down and he had been forced to abandon his efforts. He had begun to suspect then that David had lost his faith as well as his wife.

For Andrea the great stumbling block would be her own likeness to the wife David had adored. The very sight of her would be like a knife in his heart. Yet he needed the help Andrea had to offer if he was not to wreck the home life of his children. It might not have been so difficult if she had been following any other profession. Meeting Andrea could have changed David's life for the better, and the life of his children too.

David Bramley needed to find another partner before it was too late and he had wrecked the lives of everyone living at Abbot's Fold Farm. It was obviously too soon for Andrea to look at anyone else, with the death of her handsome young husband only a few short months behind her, but she had the consolation of her faith and the challenge of her work to live for. For her, faith would be there when all else was gone. For David there was no faith left now, and so no hope for the future.

Dear God, why did you not give me the strength to go on working for a little while longer so I could help David when he needed me most? Or was it that I didn't try hard enough when I had the chance to help him? The old minister felt tears prickle behind his eyes as he confronted what he felt were his own failings.

'Come along, Mr Bickerdike, it's time for lunch,' said the woman who managed the retirement home, giving his shoulder a pat to urge him away from the window.

Carla drew another doodle in her notebook as the history teacher droned on about the events which had led up to the Great War. She had no interest in history, it was one of her worst subjects and would be of no use to her when she left school, she decided. What mattered to her was the present and the future. The present was looking a bit grim, with another twenty minutes of Miss Lanchester to be endured and no prospect of seeing Bill again today. He was furious with her so she would have to ease off for a day or two and give him time to forget that she had rushed things a bit this morning.

Carla knew she had been crazy to tell Bill then that she would live with him when he moved into his new house. She had spoken without thinking. Now Bill would really believe she was just a slag, when all she wanted him to do was to fall in love with her as she had done with him. If it bothered him that she was so young she would wait for him until she was sixteen. Then she would be able to do as she liked. Bill would not be able to say then that she was too young for him and should find someone of her own age to fall in love with.

Boys of her own age were so wet. Carla was not interested in getting involved with any of them. What she wanted was to become an artist, like Bill. She knew she had the talent. Bill had told her that her painting showed promise.

If she teamed up with Bill he would be able to help her. She knew he would. Teaming up with Bill would get her away from home too, and she couldn't get away from there fast enough. Home wasn't home any more since Mum had died. It was just a place where she went to sleep, and to do her homework and be shouted at by Dad. It was a place where she was forced to do more and more housework and cooking too, now that Gran was ill. It just wasn't fair! She hated having to spend time at Abbot's Fold Farm, and she would get away from it as soon as she could. Even if she had to run away. Yes, she just might have to run away.

Fifteen

S he would not think any more about the problems of the Bramley family, or Bill Wyndham, until she was back home in the manse tonight, Andrea decided as she reached the point where she would join the A1 road which would take her to Durham. It was easy enough to stick to that resolve while she was giving intense concentration to driving on the crowded motorway with lorries thundering alongside her and speeding cars overtaking her. When she was alone in the quiet house which had once been her home it was not so easy.

There was an air of neglect about the house now that so many things which she and Ian had bought together, or which had been given to them as wedding gifts, had already gone from it. It smelled faintly musty and there was an accumulation of dust on the mantelpieces in the dining room and sitting room. Andrea shivered as the forlorn atmosphere enveloped her. It struck her then that this was what it must be like for David Bramley every time he entered his home, now that his mother was not well enough to care for it.

How was she to help the family at Abbot's Fold Farm when David would not even permit her to go there to visit his mother? This would not have been much of a problem if David had not been a farmer. If he had followed any other means of earning a living he would probably have been away from home for most of the day, but as it was he was always working close to home and liable to call into the house for food or to use the phone. So it was going to be difficult for her, if not impossible, to go to Abbot's Fold Farm without running the risk of meeting David . . .

She would not allow it to be impossible, she decided, otherwise she had taken on the wrong job in becoming a minister. David Bramley's young daughter chasing after Bill Wyndham was the first major problem she had been asked to help with since her arrival at Nyddbeck. Perhaps other people in her two churches also had worrying situations they were needing her help with but they were being kind enough to give her time to adjust to Ian's death before sharing them with her.

Bill Wyndham could not afford to wait to share his own hazardous situation with her. She was glad he had done so because she must not allow the growing suspicion that she had been betrayed by Ian to take control of all her waking thoughts. If she did that she would not be able to function properly as a minister of the church. She would not even be able to function properly as a committed Christian. The best thing she could do now was to immerse herself in her duty and push the question of whether or not Ian had been unfaithful to her with Beth to the back of her mind.

First there was the small utility room which Ian had used as a home office to be cleared of any remaining items connected to the family business. When she had phoned Nancy last evening to arrange a meeting today Nancy had told her that she now had everything she needed from that room and that there were only a few odds and ends, plus Ian's desk, left.

'Will you be taking the desk to use in your study, my dear?' Nancy had asked. 'We can sell it in the business if you don't want it because it really is rather nice.'

'I'll think about it and let you know tomorrow when I see you,' Andrea had decided. Her own desk, brought from her study in this house, was plain and well used but large enough to hold her computer. Ian's desk was a beautiful piece of antique furniture which would look well in the sitting room of the manse. Ought she to keep it, she wondered, as she ran her hand over the smooth tooled leather which was revealed now that all the paperwork had gone.

She was still considering this as she moved away from it to open the window and let some air in. It was as she turned back to check that all the drawers had been emptied that she spotted the oblong of thin card which had fallen down between the desk and the wall. An old photograph which Ian's mother must have dropped as she sorted through the various business papers, she guessed.

It was not an old photograph, she discovered with a sense of shock as she picked it up and turned it over. It was a fairly recent picture of the girl called Beth and her baby son. More than that, the clear, coloured close-up, taken on a bright day against a background of the fell scenery, showed that the baby called Jamie bore a distinct resemblance to Ian. The baby's smile was Ian's smile, the shape of the chubby face was Ian's too. So it was true, not only had Ian been unfaithful to her but there was a child to prove it. Anguish pierced her as she stared down at the woman and the child Ian had given her even though he had refused to consider having another child with Andrea . . .

'I just can't bear to go through all that again,' he had declared. 'I won't go through it again, and I'm amazed that you are even considering it.'

'Other people go through the trauma of losing a child but it doesn't stop them from having another one,' she had reminded him.

'That's up to them. I'm not prepared to chance it. Or even to talk about it,' he had insisted.

The subject had been closed as far as Ian was concerned, and not just as a matter for discussion. Lovemaking became a thing of the past, and something else that they did not discuss. On the surface, Andrea and Ian were still the happily married couple. In private, there was an ever-widening gulf between them which they both began to fill with their own interests: Ian's involvement with the antique business and golf, and Andrea's life as a mature theology student.

Perhaps it would be different when they moved to a different place where there were no memories to haunt them, Andrea had thought. Maybe they would have another child then, she had hoped. Though she never voiced that hope to Ian. It was in God's hands now. So she would not worry about the way things would work out when her training was finished and they moved into a manse close to whichever church she was called to.

It hadn't worked out like that because Ian had postponed his move into the manse at Nyddbeck until after her ordination, saying he needed to be at the house in Durham. Now she was here in that house for the last time with the proof that Ian had been quite ready to have another child with someone else. A fierce burst of anger replaced her sorrow, a sense of outrage. She beat her knuckles so hard on the top of the desk that the skin split and blood began to trickle on to the fine green leather. Why? Why? Why? The question beat into her brain relentlessly as she sucked at the blood then wiped the surface of the desk clean with her handkerchief.

Would she ever know the answer to that question? Not now, she knew, as she felt the first tears beginning to smart behind her eyes. Now she would have the rest of her life to wonder why Ian had not loved her enough to give her that other child she had so much longed for. It had seemed to her that the time of weeping was over, that she had come to terms with her grief, but now it overwhelmed her. Grief for the loss of her husband, and for the loss of their child. Grief even for the child they might have had. The child this other woman had given birth to. She flung the photo on the desk and gave way to a spasm of weeping so intense that it exhausted her.

*   *   *

147

Nancy Cameron, waiting for Andrea to arrive at the prestigious antique gallery which had been in the family for almost seventy years, wondered how she was going to face her daughter-in-law today. At one time she would have been looking forward to this meeting and the meal they would share, because she was very fond of Andrea. From the first time Ian had brought home the tall, slender Scottish girl with her intensely blue eyes and cloud of dark hair Nancy had liked her. After the death of baby Andrew five years ago they had been drawn closer by their shared grief. When Andrea had revealed her intention of training to become a minister Nancy had understood and given her support to the idea.

Of course she had hoped that Andrea and Ian would have other children one day. She had been shocked and disappointed when Andrea told her Ian was determined they would not because he could not go through the trauma of losing another child. It was not fair on Andrea, Nancy had decided, but it was not for her to interfere in this very private area of their lives. Maybe time would change Ian's mind. In the meantime Andrea had the consolation of her faith and her training for work in the church. Surely God would grant her another child one day? Nancy began to pray regularly that this would happen soon.

It had not happened though. Instead Ian had been killed and now Nancy knew that she had nothing left to live for. Nothing left to work for or hope for. Not even any faith left to help her. She was lost in grief and desolation. How was she going to face Andrea, talk to her about the future, when there was no future left for her without her son and her grandson?

They would have to talk about the future because Nancy's solicitor had advised her that with the death of the son who was to have inherited the business, and with no grandchildren to follow after him, she would need to make a new will. She would leave everything to Andrea, apart from a few bequests to old employees, because she was very fond of her daughter-in-law.

Andrea would be deeply hurt if she guessed that the death of Ian had brought about the loss of her mother-in-law's faith. She would find it hard to understand; perhaps impossible to understand. So it would be best if she did not know that for Nancy attendance at the Sunday services held in the cathedral had ceased, and that praying belonged to the past.

'Nancy, how nice to see you!' Andrea kissed her mother-in-law warmly then turned to walk into the rear of the showroom where the lighting was more subdued, so that the other woman would perhaps not notice how red and swollen her eyelids were.

'How are you, my dear?' Nancy followed her into the office, which was tastefully furnished with some fine pieces of antique furniture.

'Quite well, and terribly busy,' Andrea told her, keeping her eyes averted from Nancy's gaze.

'Things will be easier for you, perhaps, when you no longer have to keep going back to the house.'

'Maybe. I never realised just how much stuff we had accumulated in our years there. I've decided to keep the desk. It will look nice in the sitting room of the manse.'

'I can see to the delivery of it, and anything else that you want to keep, in one of the firm's vans, if that will help you?' Nancy offered.

'It will, thanks, Nancy. I want to have the house empty by next week because the buyers are anxious to be settled in before Christmas.'

'It's going to be a difficult Christmas for us both this year,' Nancy said with a sigh. 'I'm really dreading it.'

'Why don't you come down to Nyddbeck and spend it with me? I'd love to have you.'

Nancy's face brightened. 'I would like to do that. Perhaps I could help you with the cooking? It certainly will be nicer than going to a hotel, as I was thinking of doing, if you're sure it won't be too much for you having me as well as your parents?'

'There's plenty of room in the manse. Four bedrooms. A real family house.' Andrea bit on her lips to stop them trembling as she said that. The thought crept into her mind then that baby Jamie would be enjoying his first Christmas. 'Mum and Dad aren't coming for Christmas because Dad's new partner has young children and Dad has offered to be on duty then so he can be with them. I'm going up to them for New Year,' she added hastily.

Later, as she drove back to Nyddbeck through a murky late October evening, there was a deep feeling of relief inside her that she was going home to Nyddbeck Manse, and that she did not have to go back any more to the house in Durham because that part of her life was over. From now on she would spend all her time and energy in Nyddbeck becoming more and more involved with the communities of her two churches. That would be something worth living for.

There was a bunch of flowers propped up against her garage door when she reached the manse. Long-stemmed carnations of a deep peach colour tipped with crimson. Their scent enveloped her as she carried them into the house. What a kind thought on someone's part! A small white square of card bore a few words of explanation. 'Many thanks for listening to me. Bill.'

She would meet the school bus at the stop on the summit of Abbot's Hill tomorrow and see if she could talk some sense into Carla Bramley, she decided, as she began to arrange the flowers in one of the crystal vases which had been a wedding present to her and Ian.

What was Mrs Cameron doing waiting at the bus stop? Carla felt her heart begin to pound madly as she recognised the woman who was standing beside the parked car in the bay

150

where the bus always dropped her on her way home from Nyddford High School. Had something happened to Gran? Or to Dad or Jack? Carla was so worried that she did not even hear the calls of her fellow students as she jumped down the steps to land on the gritted surface of the parking bay. Already the bus was chugging on noisily towards the next moorland hamlet as Carla stared at Andrea, dreading to hear what she was here to say.

'Is it Gran?' she heard herself burst out before Andrea had time to say anything. 'Has something happened to her?'

'Oh no, Carla. It's nothing like that. I'm sorry if my being here to meet you gave you a fright.'

The shock slipped away from the girl's features to be replaced by a scowl. 'Why did you come then?'

'Because I wanted to talk to you in private,' Andrea told her quietly.

'What about?' Carla's smooth young features were marred by downturned lips, and hostile eyes.

All the words Andrea had rehearsed beforehand suddenly left her as she was overwhelmed with pity for the girl. Obviously her own unexpected presence here had given Carla a fright. It was something she had not bargained for when she had spent time last night and again this morning thinking, and praying, about how to tactfully make Carla understand that she must leave Bill Wyndham alone, both for her own sake and his.

She took a deep breath. 'About something I think your mum would have talked about if she had still been here.'

Carla gave a harsh laugh. Mrs Cameron hadn't a clue about the way things were these days if she thought she needed to start on the biology lessons!

'I don't need that Mrs Cameron. I'm clued up on all that stuff. We all are by the time we're about twelve. What has it got to do with you, anyway?'

Andrea smiled. 'I'm not here to give you biology lessons,

Carla. I'm sure your Mum went through all that stuff with you ages ago. What I'm here for is because I've got a problem I need to talk to you about, if you are willing to listen?'

Carla shrugged her shoulders. 'Oh, you mean about Dad not wanting you to come to the house, or us to come to anything at church?'

'No, I don't mean that. It's about your friendship with Mr Wyndham.'

'What do you mean?' Carla's voice was offhand. Her glance moved away from Andrea's face and came to rest on the mist-shrouded moors.

'I mean that you are causing Mr Wyndham some embarrassment, Carla, by following him around. It could cause problems for him, and for you as well.'

'Have you been spying on me?' Now Carla's voice was rising. Her stare was challenging.

'No! Of course not!'

'How do you know then?'

Andrea took her time about answering that. 'How do you think I know, Carla?'

'It won't be because Dad told you. He won't even have noticed. He doesn't care what I do, as long as I don't come to your church or the youth club.'

'I'm sure he does care, Carla. It's just that he has so much grief to bear these days that he can't cope with it any more.'

'If he cared he'd take more interest in my school work, like Bill does. That's why I see so much of Bill.'

This last sentence was said with such assurance that Andrea knew the girl had been rehearsing it ready for delivery when needed. 'Are you quite certain about that, Carla?' she asked carefully.

'Why shouldn't I be?' Carla was on the defensive now.

'I don't think Bill, or your dad, would think it a good idea for you to miss out on school so you can follow Bill to his new house. Do you?'

Hot colour rushed into the girl's face. 'How do you know about that? You *have* been spying on me, haven't you?'

'No, I certainly haven't been spying on you, Carla. I'm far too busy to go in for that sort of thing. I only know about it because Bill came to ask for my advice about what he should do. He was worried about you missing school, and even more worried because you didn't seem to think it mattered when he tried to talk to you about it.'

'I don't believe you. You're just trying to interfere in something that's nothing to do with you. You should stick to your your praying and your meetings, the things you came here to do, and not get involved with people like us.'

Andrea took a deep breath while she damped down her urge to tell the girl not to be so childish. 'I came here because I wanted to be involved with people like you, Carla. Because I wanted to be able to help you. That's part of what my work is all about.'

Carla opened her mouth to say something but before the words could come out there was the sound of a powerful vehicle roaring up the hill and screeching to a halt very close to her. Her eyes grew wide with dismay as her father wound down the window and began to fling his angry words at her.

'So this is where you are! You should have been home long since to give your gran a hand with the food instead of having her worrying about why you were so late.'

'I can't help it if the bus was late!' Carla flared.

'You can help standing here gossiping when you've things to do at home!'

David Bramley was on an even shorter fuse than the last time they had met, Andrea realised. 'It was my fault,' she told him. 'I should have realised you'd be worried about her.'

'That's one thing he isn't! It's the food he's worrying about,' Carla cried, close to tears at being ticked off like a small child when she was almost an adult.

David Bramley reached across to open the passenger door for his daughter. 'Get in!' he ordered.

A moment later the Land Rover was carrying them both away across the moor.

Sixteen

Andrea watched the Land Rover disappear from view with a mixture of frustration and anger against herself for the mess she had made of her meeting with Carla. She hadn't got this one right, she knew that. In fact she had if anything made matters much worse as far as Carla and her father were concerned, and had not managed to do anything that would help Bill Wyndham to discourage Carla from pursuing him.

On her visit to the farm to offer help to the family Carla had seemed ready to like and trust her. Now quite obviously she did neither. The only thing left to do right now was to admit defeat, for the time being, then go home and think up a new strategy. Because she could not give up on this one. She had to make Carla see sense before her father discovered that she was chasing Bill Wyndham, or the situation would become totally out of control.

It was almost dark when she reached the manse. As she climbed out of her car Andrea took a moment to look beyond the garden to where a single lamp shone over the stone bridge which crossed the beck. Mist shrouded the area but lights were piercing the gloom from the few large houses and the row of cottages which stood alongside the church. There were no lights showing in the square stone-built house that Bill Wyndham would soon be moving into so he must be back at Jacob's Cottage. She ought to phone him and thank him for his flowers, because it would be too late to do that when she got back from her meeting with the elders at Nyddford.

'I'm glad you like them,' Bill responded after hearing her words of thanks. 'It was such a relief for me to be able to talk to you as I did. I was becoming desperate, once I realised the risks Carla was taking, and I didn't know who to turn to for help.'

'I'm afraid I haven't been able to do anything to help you, as yet,' Andrea told him. She could not bring herself to tell him of her attempt to reason with Carla which had been brought to such an abrupt end by the arrival on the scene of her father. Her sense of failure was still too acute and discouraging, so she must keep it to herself.

'I don't suppose you've had time. You must have a very busy life,' he remarked.

'Yes, I do. So many meetings and so much visiting to do.' Would that sound too much like making excuses to him? 'I'll probably have a bit more time now that I've finished clearing my house in Durham. I've had to make a lot of trips up there during the last month or so.'

'Oh, I didn't realise you were still involved with things like that,' he broke in. 'I assumed that you had already finished your moving when you took over the manse in Nyddbeck.'

'No, my husband needed to stay on in Durham for a while because of the family business there,' she told him. 'The house we had there has only recently been sold.'

'So that's why—' He stopped, suddenly aware that he had been going to voice his curiosity about why Andrea's husband had not been with her at the church for her service of ordination. Or at the celebration tea for the parishioners of her two churches and her family and friends which had followed it. Dorothy Bramley had seemed to be puzzled about that when she told him of the accident to Andrea's husband the day after it occurred. For some reason, Bill was able to recall quite clearly the words Dorothy had used.

'What on earth was her husband doing so far away from here on what was such an important day in Andrea's life?'

A startling flash of honesty made Bill admit to himself that he wanted to know the truth because Andrea Cameron had become very important to him.

Andrea took a deep breath during the long moment of silence that followed. 'Why Ian wasn't here for my ordination, I suppose you mean?' she said at last.

'Forgive me, please? I shouldn't have spoken my thoughts aloud.'

'I suppose a lot of people will have been wondering about that. About why Ian was not here with me that day. I still don't know the reason for that myself,' she confessed.

What a relief it was to admit at last to someone that she also had been puzzled about Ian's failure to arrive for her service, as he had promised. Even now, when she was almost certain that Ian had been living a secret life of which she had no knowledge, she did not know why he had been killed on the Ravensbridge road at a time when he had promised to be here with her in Nyddbeck for the ordination service and celebration tea. Perhaps she never would know why. Perhaps, in time, it would not matter to her.

'Sometimes it's best not to know,' Bill said quietly.

'Do you really believe that?' Her voice was full of surprise.

'I used not to. I used to believe that it was always most important to discover the truth and reveal it. Now I'm not so sure that it is.'

This last remark stirred her interest in the man. Before it had been uttered, all her interest in Bill Wyndham had been in the problem he had discussed with her, Carla Bramley's unwelcome attachment to him and the trouble it could cause for the family at Abbot's Fold Farm. Now she wondered what went on in the mind of this man who seemed on the surface to be so self-assured.

157

'Why do you say that?' she heard herself ask.

At first she thought he was not going to answer. The silence began to lengthen. Then he gave a short laugh that ended in a sigh.

'Let's just say that age and experience have changed my perspective on life.'

Suddenly she was able to picture him striding through the village with his bright hair glowing and his reddish beard out-thrust. A man in control of his life, a man who was a success at his job. A man who enjoyed his life hugely, as was demonstrated by the way he would stop to make friends with a dog or cat, or to exchange greetings with an elderly person or a young mother taking a toddler to playschool.

'You're hardly in your dotage yet!' she reminded him with a laugh in her voice.

'Sometimes I feel as if I am. As if my life is already half over and I haven't yet achieved what I most wanted to achieve,' he confessed.

'Oh, but surely that can't be true,' Andrea began. 'I mean, you are obviously successful in your career?'

Bill's reply came swiftly. 'That was certainly not what I expected you to say, Mrs Cameron. You, of all people!'

Now she was perplexed. 'I don't understand you, Bill. What did you expect me to say?'

'I thought you might have put a happy personal life, family life, before monetary success.'

'Of course I do, but maybe we are not meant to have it all?'

'I don't see why not,' he answered sharply.

This conversation could easily lead to the sort of theological discussion that Bill Wyndham might not yet be prepared to share with her. She must take things slowly if she wanted to hold on to his trust, and she certainly wanted to do that. Perhaps it was time to bring the conversation to an end as politely as she could.

'I'd love to talk more about that but there's someone at my door,' she told him.

'We will talk about it again, one day,' Bill assured her. 'Goodnight now, Andrea.'

Bill laid down the phone but remained staring down at it with his mind still full of the talk he had shared with Andrea Cameron. He could picture her walking to the door of her manse to admit her caller, that's if there really had been a caller to interrupt her conversation with him. Perhaps he had upset her by asking that question about her husband. He had been a fool to allow his curiosity to escape in that way because he was certain there was something about the absence of Andrea Cameron's husband on the day of her ordination that must have raised questions in her mind.

Why did it matter so much to him that he should know the answers to those questions? Especially when he had told Andrea he no longer believed it was always important to discover the truth. How different his own life might have been if he had not discovered the truth about what Gina had been doing while she was away in America. He had been devastated when Gina told him she was not coming back to the life they had planned together, the family life that was to include children and pets. He had been furious when she told him that her career prospects were better in America, and that she had met someone who would be able to help her. He had been bitter when she asked him to send all her belongings to her parents. Yet none of it mattered now. It was his future that mattered. His future here in this village.

A sullen silence hung over the kitchen at Abbot's Fold Farm now that all the angry words had been said by Dave Bramley to his daughter, and a number of furious accusations thrown back at him by Carla. Dave knew that he'd gone over the top a bit. More than a bit, to be honest, but he had been getting anxious about why Carla was so late home from school. She

159

was growing up fast, too fast for his liking. There was a lurking fear inside him sometimes that somewhere in her life when she was away from the farm there was a serious boyfriend. Maybe a boy of about her own age. Or perhaps someone older who would catapult Carla into a relationship that she was not able to cope with.

What if Carla became pregnant? Dave felt his heart pounding with fear as he faced that possibility. He tried to push the thought out of his mind as he stalked out of the kitchen to give Jack a shout that the evening meal was about ready. If Carla became pregnant it would be the final disaster for them all, the thing his mother would not be able to live with. Her doctor had already given Dave a stark warning that his mother must take life much more easily or she would finish up in hospital.

He must find some way to get more help in the house for her, even if he could not really afford to pay for it. Otherwise she would try again to do some of the things Carla was doing, because she kept telling him that Carla ought to be concentrating more on her homework now that her important exams would be coming up in a few months. The only way he had any chance to find money to pay for domestic help would be by selling something, because the horrendously low prices the sheep had been bringing at auction meant he had an overdraft that he could not ever hope to decrease. What was there he could sell? The only really valuable piece of jewellery Jill had owned was the engagement ring he had bought her, and he had been set on keeping that to give Carla on her eighteenth birthday.

What was he going to do? Where could he turn for help? He stared out of the kitchen window at the dark shape of the hills, which were only just visible now. A few words came into his mind then. Words that he thought he had forgotten. Or was it that he did not want to remember them?

'I will lift up my eyes unto the hills; from whence cometh my help.'

They were the words chosen by his mother to be part of the funeral service for his father. She had told him that those words gave her the courage to go on alone. Did they mean what they said? Or were they only of help to church people? If so, there was no chance of help for him. The church would not help him. Why should it, when he had turned away the young minister who had come to offer her help to his mother?

Dave moved away from the window, and found himself recalling the way the minister had been standing at the kitchen table with a knife in her hand, preparing vegetables for the family meal. He remembered the look there had been in her eyes when he spoke to her so rudely. First disbelief, then hurt, then anger. Why had he spoken to her like that? Why? Why?

It was not Andrea Cameron's fault that she so closely resembled Jill, he knew, when the answer to his bewilderment came to him. No wonder his mother had been so annoyed with him. She had not spared him her reproach after the minister had been driven away by his churlishness. She knew Andrea had only wanted to help, and that they needed that help. Andrea Cameron knew they needed the help too, just as she would have known when he telephoned to apologise to her that he was only doing so because his mother had insisted on it.

He had been a fool then, and he had been a bloody fool again today to blame Andrea for keeping Carla talking when the girl got off the school bus. There had been no need for him to go on like that. All it had done was to spark off another row with Carla which had sent her to her room in floods of tears; and it must have convinced Andrea Cameron that he was unfit to be a parent.

Dear God, what's wrong with me? When will I be in my right mind again? His clenched fists struck the kitchen table

161

with such force that the mugs standing on it toppled over . . . The noise brought a whine from the collie that lay on a rug close to the Aga. The dog came padding to his side to nudge his knee and reach up with a warm tongue to lick his wrist.

'Why did she have to die, Tyke?' Dave whispered. 'Why?'

'Have you hurt your hand, Dad?' Jack asked as he walked into the kitchen and saw the overturned mugs and the traces of blood on Dave's knuckles.

'No, lad,' Dave muttered, scrubbing his eyes with his fingers. 'I'm all right. There's nothing for you to worry about. Just give Tyke a drink while I get your dinner.'

Seventeen

S he would have to try again to talk sense into Carla, Andrea
decided when she caught a glimpse of the girl hurrying in
the direction of Bill's new home the following afternoon as the
school bus chugged away from the stop it had made at the end
of Church Lane. Earlier in the day it had been in her mind to
drive up to the top of the hill again to meet Carla at the stop
nearest to the farm, even though that could mean the risk of
encountering David Bramley also, but her afternoon with the
Ladies' Fellowship at Nyddford Church had lasted for longer
than she had anticipated so she had been forced to change her
mind. It would have been a wasted journey anyway because
Carla had ignored her warning and was even now going to
Beckside in search of Bill.

How was the girl going to get back home to the farm after
Bill sent her packing, as he certainly would do? Was Carla
relying on him not doing that? If so she could be in for a shock,
and a long uphill walk home to Abbot's Fold in the rapidly
falling dusk. At the end of that walk there could be another
ticking off for her from her father for being late home again.
Andrea shook her head at the foolishness of the teenager, who
could not see the worry she was causing. It struck her then how
dangerous the walk up the hill would be in such poor visibility,
especially where the sharp bends were. Perhaps she ought to
keep an eye out for the girl leaving Beckside, as she would
very soon, and offer her a lift home?

So it was that as Carla stumbled away from Bill's new

163

home, where the workmen who were on the point of finishing for the day told her Mr Wyndham was not around, Andrea just happened to be walking back from the church to where her car was parked close to the bridge.

'Hi, Carla! What are you doing here?' she greeted the girl.

'Walking home from school, of course,' came the surly response.

'It's a long walk from here, surely? I mean, doesn't the bus go on to the top of the hill?'

Carla scowled. 'I had something to show Bill. Some work I wanted him to help me with. Only he's not there.'

'Can't you show it to him at Jacob's Cottage when you get home?' Andrea suggested.

'Not if Dad has anything to do with it! Once I'm back home I'll have to do the cooking and housework or there'll be another row, and I just can't cope with that.'

'Is your gran no better then?'

'She is a bit, but Dad gets really angry with me if she even tries to help me. It's not fair!'

'I expect your father is still terribly worried about your gran.'

'Why doesn't he get someone in to help then, like Mr Harper wants him to do?' the girl said resentfully, beginning to walk away from Andrea as though there was nothing more to be said.

'Perhaps he can't afford to do that. This is a very bad time for farmers you know,' Andrea pointed out, walking alongside her.

'There are people who would help us without being paid, only Dad won't let them. He wouldn't let you help us, would he? He wouldn't even let Mum's friend Julie come and help us on her day off when she wanted to. Gran was upset about that,' Carla added.

Andrea smiled. 'I met your mum's friend Julie when she

came to put some flowers in the church. I liked her very much. She's coming to have supper with me one evening.'

'Dad doesn't like her. He says, if she hadn't interfered, Mum wouldn't have gone back to work at the health centre and she wouldn't have been going out on call when the tree came down on her car. I think it was just an accident and Dad shouldn't blame Julie for it,' Carla declared. 'If I'd been her I wouldn't have even offered to come and help after some of the things Dad said to her. He really upset her.'

'I expect Julie understands why he's so upset.'

'He ought to be getting over it now. I mean, people do, don't they? They meet someone else and they get married again, don't they?'

Andrea sighed. 'Some of them do, but it isn't so easy when you have children, especially children of your age.'

'I'm not a child now. I'm grown up. Old enough to do what I want.' This last was said defiantly, with a toss of Carla's long blonde hair.

'Would you really want to do things that could bring worry to your father or your gran? Or to Mr Wyndham,' Andrea added.

'I don't know what you're talking about,' the girl hit back.

'I think you do, Carla. You're a bright girl so you must know what I'm talking about. To keep following Mr Wyndham about as you are doing will be likely to cause the sort of gossip that could harm his reputation, since you are under age. So you need to be more careful, don't you?'

The girl laughed scornfully. 'Bill wouldn't care what people said about him.'

'He'll care very much if the gossip gets back to your father,' Andrea pointed out. 'It could cause bad feeling between them.'

'That won't matter once Bill's moved into his new house. He'll be away from Abbot's Fold then and Dad or Gran won't know what he's doing.'

Andrea sighed. 'Your father will still know when you're very late home from school, Carla. He'll probably already be worrying about you now. I think you'd better let me take you home.'

'There's no need!' The answer came swiftly. 'I can walk.'

'It's almost dark, and your clothes are so dark you won't be easily seen as you go up the hill.' Andrea paused, then went on. 'I can't believe you really want to risk bringing another tragedy to your family. One is enough for most families, as I know from my own experience.'

They were standing beneath the Victorian lamp that illuminated the stone pack-horse bridge as Andrea uttered those last few words in a low voice. She waited for another outburst from the girl, but it did not come. Instead there was silence, except for the gurgling of the water as it ran beneath the centuries-old bridge. The silence went on. Andrea held her breath as she dragged her thoughts away from her own tragedies and began to pray silently that she had got through to the girl who stood so close to her.

There was a muffled sound, half gasp, half stifled sob, then a rush of words.

'I'm sorry, Andrea. About your husband, I mean. Really, really sorry. He must have been quite young, younger than Dad, because you don't have any children.'

Andrea let out her own breath on a long sigh. 'We did have, once. We had a wee boy called Andrew.'

'What happened to him? Was it an accident?'

'No, it was meningitis. When he was almost three.'

There was another period of silence before the girl spoke again. This time her words were slow, puzzled, reluctantly uttered.

'I don't know how you can still believe in God, after that. My Dad doesn't any more, after what happened to Mum.'

Andrea took her time about answering, gathering together as she did so all that she had heard about Carla's mother. What

Mr Bickerdike had told her, what Dorothy Bramley had said about her daughter-in-law, and the admiration Ben Harper had expressed for the way Jill had gone about her work. Jill Bramley had been a dedicated nurse who gave of her best to those who needed her. Where did she get the strength from to do that? Where did she get the courage from to risk going out to tend a patient on a night of such severe weather?

'I've been told that your mum was a very special person, Carla. That she was very caring and very brave.'

'She was. It said on TV that the gale was severe and people should stay in, but Mum said that didn't apply to people like her who had patients depending on them. So she went and gave old Mrs Robinson her pain-killing injection. Then the tree came down on her car as she turned into our lane coming home.' Carla's voice trembled as she told Andrea that.

'Did your mum ever tell you why she was able to do the work she did, go out in all kinds of bad weather, even when she was feeling grotty herself?'

'She did once, just before she was killed. She said it was because nursing was the work she felt called to do, and that was why she had to give it her best.' Carla smothered another sob as she shared this with Andrea.

'That's the way I feel about the work I've been called to do, Carla. I used to be an infant teacher but after I lost Andrew, while I was still feeling devastated and not knowing how to go on without him, I became involved with some people who had all been through similar experiences to mine. One of them was much older than me so she had no chance to have other children. She told me how she had almost ended her life one day, and why she hadn't done that.'

Carla hiccupped back another sob. 'What did she say?'

Andrea smiled, remembering her friendship with Sophie St John. 'She said that as she was about to jump into a river she saw a puppy there struggling to get out of a sack that someone had thrown into the water. Sophie rescued the puppy,

167

then realised that it would need looking after because it was exhausted. She said she felt very angry at first with God for making her find that little dog which needed to be cared for. Later, when the puppy had helped to heal her pain by giving her so much love, she came to believe that it had been a sign to her that God had some particular work for her to do. So she did it.'

'What sort of work?' Carla whispered.

'Caring for abandoned dogs. Sophie had a big house and a big garden, and quite a bit of money. So she opened an animal sanctuary and made that her work.'

'How did that help you? I don't understand . . .'

'As I became more friendly with Sophie and visited her at her home I saw how her life had been changed by the love she had found for that little dog, and how in turn she was helping lonely people to find companionship with some of her rescued dogs. It seemed like a kind of miracle to me. I began to wonder if there could be anything like that waiting for me.'

'Was there?' Carla asked.

'Yes, but not immediately, and not so dramatically. Because I became ill I went to stay with my parents until I was fit enough to go back to my teaching job in Durham. While I was there they asked me to help out one Sunday with the children at the little church where I went when I was small. I didn't really want to do it. I thought it would hurt too much. Only I was wrong, it didn't hurt at all. As I read the Bible stories to the children I began to heal inside. By the time I was fit enough to go back to teaching I knew what I really wanted was to become a minister.'

There was another long silence, during which Andrea began to worry about what David Bramley would have to say to his daughter when she arrived home late yet again. It would probably provoke another argument between them so she must persuade Carla to go home.

'Aren't you sorry you came here?' Carla asked. 'I mean

because of your husband, and the way my dad was so rude to you and everything.'

'No, Carla. I came here because I wanted to, and I already love it here. Now, are you going to let me give you that lift home?'

'If you really, really want to,' came the grudging reply.

'Yes, I really, really do,' Andrea told her with a smile.

When she stopped her car in the lane that led to the farmhouse Andrea saw that as well as the lights shining out from the house there were also lights glowing in the windows of Jacob's Cottage, which was closer to the farm gate. It struck her then that if Carla decided to go to the cottage first to see Bill she would be even later home. So she must head her off by going to have a word with Bill herself. Carla would not follow her, she guessed, because she would want to see Bill on her own.

'I think I'll have a word with Mr Wyndham while I'm here,' she said as Carla slipped out of her seat and reached into the back of the vehicle for her schoolbag.

'Oh, I was going to—' Carla began.

'Your dad seems to be looking for you. He's in the porch. You'd better hurry.'

Andrea could feel tension building inside her at the sight of David Bramley. Was he about to accuse her of making his daughter late home again? She'd better hurry to Bill's cottage before he could do that. He was already out of the porch and making his way towards them across the pool of darkness that was the farmyard, so she decided against locking her car door in favour of getting to Bill's front door before David reached her.

She could feel her fingers trembling as she grabbed her handbag and slammed the driver's door. Carla had gone ahead of her and was already racing across the yard, giving her father a wide berth. Yes, David Bramley was letting his daughter pass him and making straight for Andrea. She knew she would be lucky to reach Jacob's Cottage before he caught up with her. Panic gave speed to her feet as she made a swift turn left and in her haste fell headlong, face first on to the cobbled surface, and lay there stunned and shaking.

For what seemed to her to be an age, she remained spreadeagled in the mud, praying once the moment of shock had passed that the farmer would go back into his house and vent his anger on his daughter while she managed to pick herself up and get back into her car. Because obviously she was in no fit state now to call on Bill. Only David Bramley was still standing there, and he was far too close for her to be able to get to her feet without bumping into him. Not that she was in any hurry to get up, with her knees stinging and her face smarting. Dear God, please make him go away, she found herself silently praying.

'Are you hurt?' he was asking, not attempting to move away from her.

'No, I don't think so.' Only my pride, she thought, as her eyes began to sting.

'Let me help you.'

His voice was rough. Andrea prayed again that he would go away before he noticed that she was crying.

'I don't need help,' she muttered.

'I'd say that you do. Come on, let me lift you. Don't be daft!' he added as she tried to utter more words of protest.

She knew then that it was too late for her to escape, because her bruised hands could not get a firm enough grip on the cobbles to support her while she got to her feet. Humiliation engulfed her as she felt his hands lifting her as easily as if she had been one of his lambs. Having lifted her to her feet he did not let her go but kept an arm firmly about her shoulders.

'Do you think you can walk as far as the house, or shall I carry you?' he was asking.

Andrea swallowed. 'I'll be able to manage as far as my car.' She'd get there, even if she could not cope with driving yet.

'What makes you think you're fit to drive?'

'I have to get back—'

'Not yet. Let's get you into the house.'

Even as he said it she knew she could not make it as far as the door of the farmhouse. She was aware now that there was blood trickling down from her damaged knees, and that her legs felt curiously weak and unsteady. Also that there were a couple of tears sliding down her muddy cheeks. She took a deep breath while she fought to regain control of herself.

'We'll take it slowly.'

His voice was almost gentle as he half carried her carefully across the treacherous cobbles in the direction of the house.

'Are you feeling better now?' she heard him ask when they reached the porch.

She tried to say yes, only the words would not come out because her lips were shaking too badly. Both his arms came around her then, steadying her when she seemed about to fall and drawing her head close to the softness of his padded jacket. It was easy then for her to relax and forget everything except the kindness of him, the gentleness of him. It was easy for her to cry quietly against his shoulder. She found that she did not want him to move away from her. All she wanted was for him to stay with her, keeping her safe from further harm.

'It's all right, you're safe now. You'll feel better soon.' He was stroking her hair, talking softly to her as he would have done to his children or to a frightened animal.

Andrea did not want him to stop doing that so she kept her head down and began to relax enough to almost enjoy these moments of tenderness. She did not want to lose this gentle side of the man she had only previously known as someone full of bitterness and hate. This David Bramley was so different that he was slowly but certainly reminding her of just how lacking her life was now of the sort of love she had once shared with Ian.

They seemed to be cut off here in the porch of the farmhouse

171

from everything in the outside world, and she did not care. All she cared about was prolonging the precious moments of being held close to the heart of a man, held within the strong arms of a man. It was madness, and she ought to bring it to an end at once. Yet she could not bear to do that.

'It's been so long,' he murmured, echoing her own feelings as he drew her so close that her breath caught in her throat.

She must stop him before he became aware of who she was. It would spare him, and herself, embarrassment later. 'You must let me go,' she muttered.

'Why?'

'Because I'm not who you think I am. Look at me!' She raised her face so that he could look into it, and waited for shock to register in his eyes as he recognised her.

'I'm looking,' he said so quietly that she could only just hear the words.

There was no shock to be seen on his face, but there were tears. Tears, just a few, which slid slowly down from the grey eyes, which looked so different from when Andrea had last seen them. He did not attempt to hide the tears from her. She lifted her fingers and gently caught the tears before they reached his chin. Her own throat was tight with sorrow as she waited for him to release her. He seemed in no hurry to do that, not even now when he knew who she was.

'I'm sorry,' he murmured. 'More sorry than you'll ever know.'

'I'm sorry too. That I'm not who you thought I was,' she managed to utter. Because she now guessed that he had been expecting someone else to arrive at the farm. Perhaps some woman he had a relationship with. Only she had been the one to arrive and fall at his feet. No wonder he was apologising for those tender words and gentle touches. There was a frown dawning on his brow, bewilderment in his gaze, though he did not release her.

'But you are,' he began.

Andrea felt sick with apprehension. He must think she was Jill, who had died almost two years ago. Grief and bitterness had taken a much greater toll than either she or anyone else had realised. How was she going to deal with it? Compassion for him overwhelmed her. Dear God, please help me! Tell me what to do. Because I have to do something, and quickly.

'Dave, you need help! You must let me get help for you—' she began.

He shook his head fiercely. 'You've got it wrong, Mrs Cameron,' he said.

She was too surprised to say anything as she waited for him to drop his arms from around her. He seemed to have forgotten that he was still holding her. The silence that enfolded them, shutting out the sound of the murmuring sheep and the bellowing cows, lengthened. Andrea knew she ought to shake off his arms and move away from him but she seemed powerless to do either.

'What I was trying to say to you was that I'm more sorry than I can say for the way I've been treating you. For my rudeness and disregard for your feelings. I don't deserve it, but I'm asking you to try and forgive me? Will you ever be able to do that?'

In the moments which followed, immeasurably long moments when their glances met and held, Andrea felt a sudden and quite unexpected wave of joy overwhelm her. It was a long time since she had experienced such a feeling. Far too long.

'Yes, David, I'll do that. I'll be glad to do that,' she told him.

He touched her cheek with muddy fingers. 'This morning I thought I had nothing much left to live for,' he said. 'Now, I'm not so sure. Come inside and I'll make you a cup of tea, Andrea.'

Eighteen

'Andrea, my dear, whatever happened to you?' Dorothy Bramley rose from the rocking chair she had been sitting in as she mended a sock and turned a concerned stare in Andrea's direction.

'I stumbled as I was going to have a word with Mr Wyndham and fell flat on my face out in the yard. I'm afraid I'm not a very pretty sight.' Andrea felt confused, wondering now whether she ought to have gone back to her car instead of allowing David to bring her into his home.

'I'll make you some tea. You look as if you need it.' Dorothy took a step towards the kettle already singing on the Aga, but David was there before her.

'I'll make the tea, Mother, if you'll show Andrea where the shower-room is. I expect she'd like to have a wash before we see to her cuts and bruises.'

'Oh yes, I would.' Andrea followed Dorothy out into the spacious hall, where one of the former pantries had been converted into a cloakroom with a shower cubicle. She noticed that Dave's mother moved carefully and was much slower than when she had first met her back in the early summer.

'How are you feeling now, Dorothy?' she asked.

'Much better these days, thank you. In fact I'm probably feeling better than you must be at this moment, after your fall.' This was said with a smile that made Dave's mother look quite young and pretty. 'I'll leave you to get rid of all the blood, then I'll practise my first aid on you.'

'There's really no need. I'm not much hurt. I look worse than I feel,' Andrea assured her even though her heart was still thumping away.

'I'm so glad to see you. I've missed your visits,' the older woman told her quietly.

'I've been thinking of you, and praying for you. Hoping that things would work out for you and Mr Harper.'

'Ben's been such a tower of strength for me while I've been ill. I don't know what I'd have done without him these last few weeks. I'm going to leave you now to clean yourself up then you'll be ready for some tea.'

The hot water stung as Andrea bathed her badly grazed knees. Her face did not look as bad as she had anticipated once she had cleaned the mud from it and stared at herself through the film of steam on the mirror. She must go and face David Bramley again now. Though she found herself reluctant to do that.

What had made her abandon her usual reserve, as she had done with Dave tonight? It was as though she had never been at odds with him; never been upset by him, hurt by him, angered by him. In fact it had been almost as though—. This last thought was so alarming in its intensity that she pushed it hurriedly away from her and set about tidying the cloakroom in order to calm herself before she had to face David again.

With her hand gripping the handle of the kitchen door she paused to take a deep breath. It could all be quite different by now, she told herself. David Bramley could be his old self again, bitter and unkind. Ready to be rude to her and send her packing. Did she want to risk that? There was only one way to find out. She opened the door and went into the warmth of the kitchen.

'Do you feel better now?' she heard him ask quietly.

Andrea stared at him, in fact she seemed unable to look away from the concern in the grey eyes which she had only ever seen before expressing his dislike for her. Since she was so taken aback by what she was seeing in his face she found difficulty in answering him. So she nodded.

'Come and sit here.' He was drawing a chair closer to the Aga for her.

How ridiculous it was for her to feel all at once out of her depth. Yet that was certainly how she felt at this moment, as she lowered herself into the Windsor chair and placed her hands on the time-smoothed oak arms for support. She found herself glad of that support, thankful too for the large mug of tea placed beside her by Dorothy.

'You are both very kind,' she managed at last, after gulping down some of the hot liquid.

There did not seem, just then, any need for her to say anything else. No explanations had been asked for as to why she had been there in the yard of Abbot's Fold Farm when she tripped and fell. It was even possible that David was unaware that his daughter had come home in Andrea's car. She knew she might need to come up with a reason for why she had been there, but for now it was good to just sit there sipping tea and feeling the warmth of the Aga help her relax. It could not go on indefinitely, this peaceful interlude, but she found herself wishing that it could.

Even as the thought lingered in her mind, the door into the yard was opening and Jack was bursting in with a collie dog at his heels. The boy's spiky blonde hair was untidy. His fair-skinned face was flushed bright with exertion. His breath came in laboured gasps. Without seeming to be aware of either his grandmother or Andrea he called urgently to his father.

'Dad, there's a ewe in trouble up at Far End! I've had a look at her, but I think you'd better go and see to her yourself.'

'Right, son. Are you coming with me to help me find her?'

'Sure!'

A moment later they were away. As they left the house

Andrea heard David call to his own collie, Tyke. Then the Land Rover roared away and Andrea was left alone with Dorothy.

'I hope it's nothing serious with the ewe,' Andrea began, thinking of the vet's bills.

'So do I! David has enough to worry about these days,' Dorothy said with a sigh. 'There seems to be no end to the problems.'

'At least you are on your feet again, Dorothy. That must be a relief to him.'

'In one respect, yes. Though he keeps on worrying now about me doing too much, and Carla not doing enough in the house. It's a constant source of friction between them, and of course Carla is just at that age when she's hard to reason with. She only has to be a bit late coming back from school and David's down on her like a ton of bricks. It's hard on her really, just when she needs to spend more time on her homework. She was late again tonight, only David didn't get round to ticking her off because of your fall,' Dorothy confided.

So there certainly would have been trouble for Carla as she went racing across the yard if she herself had not come to grief there first, Andrea reflected. It was worrying. So worrying that if she had not got through to the girl with her words of warning about the folly of chasing Bill Wyndham in the village tonight she would have to try again as soon as possible.

'What brought you up here tonight, Andrea, my dear?' Dorothy was asking now.

Andrea hesitated. Should she admit to having brought Carla home and risk this getting back to David? Or would it be safer to use Bill as an excuse for her appearance at the farm? On reflection, it would be best to do the latter, since no explanation would be called for then.

'I wanted to have a word with Bill,' she said. 'That's

where I was heading when I went down face first out in the yard.'

'Oh, I see. Would you like me to ask Bill to come over here to see you?' Dorothy offered.

'Oh no! It was nothing very urgent. I certainly don't intend going to see him now. Some other time will do.'

'He won't be here for much longer. He's moving into his new home at the end of the week.'

'So soon? I hadn't realised that the alterations to the house he's bought were finished.'

'They're not finished yet. He wasn't going to move into Beckside till the end of the month but he says he wants to be on the spot now to keep a closer eye on things. So you won't have to go so far to see him, will you? He'll be one of your neighbours.'

'Yes,' Andrea answered. 'So he will.' Probably Bill had brought his move forward to put more distance between him and Carla. Though maybe Carla would keep turning up at Beckside looking for him, as she had done after school today. If she did, it would certainly stir up gossip in such a small village where almost everyone seemed to know everyone else.

To her relief, Dorothy Bramley changed the subject then and said how good it was to have her company, and how much she had missed being able to go to church.

'I could come to you, bring Communion to you, Dorothy, if you wish,' Andrea offered when she saw the wistful look on the older woman's face.

'Yes, I would like that, if you are prepared to risk it my dear. To risk running into David, I mean,' his mother said with a smile. 'I know he's not usually very welcoming!'

Andrea laughed softly. 'Yes, I am prepared to risk it.' A frisson of anticipation ran up her spine at the thought of running into David Bramley again.

Now his mother chuckled. 'If you come on market day

the risk will not be so great,' she pointed out. 'He's away soon after breakfast and not back again until almost time for afternoon milking.'

'Which is market day? Is it Wednesday or Thursday?'

'Thursday for Nyddford.'

'I'll come then, and I'll bring an apron as well as the bread and wine so I can do some cooking or cleaning for you.' With that Andrea rose to her feet, eager to depart before David came back, because she wanted to remember him as he had been tonight, so gentle and concerned about her, and not as she knew he could be at other times.

'Are you sure you're fit to drive home, Andrea? Wouldn't you rather wait until David comes back so he can take you?' his mother said then.

'He might be some time, and I've a meeting tonight. So I'll be on my way.'

She was on her way to the back door when Dorothy spoke to her again. The words halted her in her tracks.

'Please try to forgive David, my dear. The way you've seen him tonight is the way he always used to be a couple of years ago. Before things started to go wrong. Before he lost his faith and became so bitter. He does need your forgiveness, and your prayers, so much.'

Andrea turned round. 'Yes, I know he does. Goodnight, Dorothy, I'll see you on Thursday.'

Then she was out in the porch again, and remembering the moments when she had been held so close to David. She could hear his voice asking for her forgiveness, feel his fingers gentle on her face. She could even experience again the sudden flame of hope which had so unexpectedly burst into life inside her. What did it all mean? It was probably best not to think about it because she did not want any more complications in her life. She just wanted to get on with doing the job she had come here to do. Which was why she must get back into her car and drive down to the manse where she would change into some fresh clothes and hope to get to the elders' meeting at Nyddford only a little late.

A glance at her watch as she got carefully, and quite painfully, out of her car a few minutes later told her she would certainly not be on time for the meeting, and that she had no time for anything to eat. That would have to be left for later. It turned out to be very much later, because the main purpose of the meeting – what should be done to improve the shabby exterior of the church building – resulted in long and involved discussion between two of the elders who had very different ideas on the subject.

One of them, a teacher, was all in favour of having a clean sweep and taking out an old overgrown hedge and a large lawned area and converting this space into a much-needed car park, then floodlighting the building to show the community that the church was there and that they were welcome to make use of it.

The other man put up a strong argument in favour of keeping things the way they had been for the best part of a century. 'I can't see any sense in spending all that brass on getting rid of a good old-fashioned hedge what's been there since I were a lad,' he kept reiterating. 'Folk round here know as there's a church here if they want it.'

'I'm not thinking about the people who've always lived here,' insisted the teacher, who had moved from a city a few years earlier. 'I'm thinking about all the people like Helen and me who had to ask where there was a church because even though we must have passed this one several times the hedge had hidden it. There are more and more people moving in now that the Nydd Gardens estate is getting bigger and bigger.'

'Just because they've come to live here it doesn't mean they'll come to this church, or any other church,' the senior citizen pointed out.

'That's a defeatist attitude, if you don't mind me saying so,' argued the teacher.

So it went on, while Andrea felt the pain from her cuts, bruises and grazes getting harder to bear. She had apologised for her lateness but not given any explanation other than that she had been delayed while sick visiting. Now, as those present grew bored with the over-long discussion she was aware of their attention becoming focused on her damaged face. So much so that she became embarrassed. The discussion had gone on for long enough and was far from reaching a conclusion but she did not think she could sit in silence for much longer. It was time for her to speak out or these two would go on all night.

'We've all listened carefully to what you've both said, so shall we now hear from one or two other people before we take a vote? Then we must bring the meeting to a close with a prayer that the right decisions are made.'

As Andrea spoke, she put a hand up to where the worst graze, on her right cheek, was throbbing painfully. She ought to have taken some paracetamol before she left the manse. The pain was making it difficult for her to concentrate.

Ben Harper was on his feet, shoulders back, voice firm, manner authoritative. 'I'm in favour of getting rid of the hedge and the lawn and letting everyone see the church. Showing them we're here. Let's have some bigger notice-boards too, and some good modern slogans in large letters on them. Don't let the supermarkets get all the people from the new estate on Sundays! Let's see if we can get some of them in here with us! Our new young minister here has already managed to get permission to take assembly on some mornings in the school, so let's see if we can get some of those children into our Sunday school.'

A chorus of approval greeted this stirring speech, followed by a buzz of excitement that made Andrea forget her throbbing face for a few minutes. The vote was taken, in favour of banishing the hedge, and a closing prayer was said by Andrea. A moment later she felt herself swaying on her feet while the

181

walls of the room grew dim. She would have fallen if Ben Harper had not rushed to her aid.

'What's happened to you, Andrea?' he wanted to know. 'Have you had an accident in your car?'

She laughed shakily as the room came back into focus. 'No, the car's fine, which is more than can be said for me. I tripped and fell face first on to the cobbled yard at Abbot's Fold when I was up there earlier this evening. It's nothing to worry about, Ben.'

'I'm not so sure about that. Your face is injured, and you're all of a shake, lass.'

'I'll be fine, once I've had something to eat. I know it was stupid of me but because the fall made me late back and I didn't want to keep you all waiting, I didn't have any supper. That's probably why I felt faint.'

Ben shook his head. 'You're right, it *was* foolish of you. In fact I think you ought to have sent your apologies to us and left us to get on with it instead of sitting through all that waffle when you obviously weren't feeling very well. Now are you going to be sensible and come home with me for something to eat before I take you back to the manse?'

'Oh, I couldn't possibly do that!' she protested. 'It's nearly ten o'clock, Ben.'

He laughed. 'So what? That's the time I usually have a bit of supper. Come along with me, then you can give me the latest news from Abbot's Fold. We'll leave George to put out the lights and lock up. I didn't bring my car as it's such a short walk from here to Ford House, so we'll have to go in yours, and it might be as well if you let me drive.'

It was no good arguing with Ben, Andrea decided. She might just as well do as he wished, but she would have to think up a reason why she had been to Abbot's Fold. A reason which would satisfy this astute businessman, who would be very angry if he learned of the problem Carla was causing. It would not do to say that she had been visiting Bill Wyndham either, because she had gained the impression that Ben did not altogether approve of Bill.

Soon they were pulling into the drive of Ford House, Ben's large Victorian home, which was beautifully situated on rising ground close to the ford which straddled the stream that also ran through Nyddbeck. The spacious grounds ran down to the edge of the water, which was much shallower here. A couple of carriage lamps shed circles of light on to the wide drive.

'Let me help you out, Andrea,' Ben was saying with a chuckle. 'I don't want you flaking out again, because I'm not much good at first aid.'

'I'm fine again now,' she insisted, even though this was not strictly speaking true. 'I'm sure I can manage to drive home. It's only four miles to Nyddbeck from here.'

'You're going to have something to eat before you do that, or Dorothy will never forgive me. So come along in, my dear.'

With his hand on her arm to guide her up the short flight of steps to the front door Andrea did as she was told. Once inside Ford House she was shown into a spacious room which was warm and well lit. An elderly golden labrador came to greet them and was given instructions by his master to look after her. Andrea sank gratefully into a big chair, and was asleep with her hand on the dog's head before Ben came back with coffee and sandwiches.

They might manage to save the ewe, and the lambs she was carrying, without having to call out the vet, David decided as he lifted the animal into the back of the Land Rover.

'Will she be all right, Dad?' Jack wanted to know as the vehicle went bumping down from Far End Field towards the house.

'Oh yes, it was only bad bruising and a few cuts. A bit of shock from the fall as well I expect,' David answered. His thoughts were already returning to Andrea Cameron.

'I didn't know she'd fallen, Dad. How do you know that?' Jack asked in a puzzled voice.

'I saw her trip, as I went into the yard to look for Carla. I didn't recognise her at first. It wasn't till I'd got her into the back porch that I saw who she was.' That was when the great rush of pity had engulfed him, as he saw the pain and bewilderment in those unforgettable blue eyes. He had forgotten who she was as he had cradled her in his arms and experienced some powerful moments of tenderness. It was a long time since he had known such feelings for a woman.

'You're not talking about the ewe, are you, Dad?' Jack reminded him in an accusing voice.

'No, son,' David replied after a long moment of stunned surprise. What the hell was the matter with him, forgetting about the ailing animal because his mind was so full of the injured woman? He had no right to be thinking about that woman. No right at all, especially considering who she was. 'I was thinking about Mrs Cameron, who fell and injured herself in our yard tonight.'

'You don't like her, do you, Dad?'

He found himself unable to answer that truthfully. It would have been easier to answer yesterday, or even earlier today, but not now.

'Why don't you like her? Gran says she's nice. She can't be so bad if she came to help us when Gran was poorly, can she?'

David hesitated, then agreed. 'No, son. Perhaps I'm the one who's not very nice.'

'You weren't very nice to her last time she came to see Gran,' his son reminded him as he brought the Land Rover to a halt in the yard.

So why had Andrea come back to Abbot's Fold tonight? Why had she risked encountering his bitter comments and his unjustified anger again? There was only one way to find out. He jumped down from the driving seat, eager to get into the house, flung open the back door and strode into the kitchen, his glance going straight to the chair where he had last seen her.

'Where is she?' he asked his mother.

'She's gone. She had a meeting to go to.'

The force of his disappointment hit David like a body blow.

Nineteen

'Oh Ben, I'm so sorry!' Andrea woke with a start as she became aware of the golden labrador pushing a cool nose into her hand.

'Don't worry, my dear. You've had a trying time tonight. First with your fall, then having to sit through all that waffle about something which should have been decided during Mr Bickerdike's time with us. Have some coffee and a sandwich.'

Andrea sipped the hot freshly brewed coffee gratefully and smiled at the lovely old dog who was gazing longingly at the plate of biscuits which Ben had placed close to her on a small table.

'Do you think our plan to let people see the church in all its glory will be voted in at the full church meeting next month?' she asked, knowing that Ben Harper would have heard the subject discussed many times, and perhaps more heatedly than at tonight's meeting.

'It's got to be, because we can't afford to employ anyone to keep the hedge tidy, and most of the church members are either elderly or working unsociable hours so we can't rely on volunteers to do the job for us. Anyway, enough of that, Andrea. How did you think Dorothy was looking when you saw her today? I suppose you did see her while you were up at Abbot's Fold?'

Andrea smiled. She felt a bit better after the hot coffee and a couple of well-filled ham sandwiches. 'I thought she was looking much better, Ben. In fact, because of the state I was in after my fall, she remarked that I was looking worse than she was. I certainly felt very rough,' she added ruefully. Not too rough to enjoy being comforted by David Bramley though. This last thought sent warm colour into her cheeks.

'What took you up to the farm? Or shouldn't I ask?' Ben's eyes were intent on her face as he waited for her to answer.

Doubt about what to say kept Andrea silent for so long that Ben began to think he had spoken out of turn. He ought to have kept his curiosity about her visit to the farm to himself; he must try to put things right.

'Sorry, Andrea, I know I shouldn't have asked. It's just that I know Dorothy felt that Dave had been so rude to you you wouldn't want to go there again. Has there been a change in his attitude? Dorothy hasn't mentioned it.'

Had there been a change in Dave's attitude? Certainly the way he had been tonight indicated that this might be the case. Yet she could not be sure, because she hadn't waited to see how he would behave when he came back from seeing to the sick sheep. She had wanted to wait, but there had been the meeting to go to. Now she found she did not want to speculate about whether David's attitude had changed towards her. She just wanted to change the subject. In fact she could hardly wait to do that.

'I didn't go to the farm,' she began with a rush. 'I mean, I didn't intend to go to the farm. I met Carla when she was on her way home from school and gave her a lift because I wanted to have a few words with Bill Wyndham. Only I never got as far as Bill's place because I tripped and fell over in the yard, so I finished up in Abbot's Fold.'

Ben was frowning now. 'Dorothy tells me Bill's moving out at the weekend. Going into his new place even though it isn't quite ready.'

'Yes. So I've heard.'

'The sooner he's away from there the better. He's been there too long already.'

So she had guessed correctly. Ben Harper did not like Bill Wyndham. Why?

'I suppose it took him longer to find the right property than he expected.'

'Or perhaps he wasn't trying hard enough.'

What did he mean by that?

'I should think the Bramleys would be glad to have him there, under the circumstances.' She was thinking about the rent for the cottage.

'One of the Bramleys was certainly glad to have him there. A bit too glad, I'd say.'

What did that remark mean? Did Ben Harper know that Carla Bramley was throwing herself at Bill? Did he imagine that Bill was encouraging the girl? If so, why had he not spoken to Carla about it? Or to Bill?

'I'm not sure I understand just what you're saying, Ben.'

Now his square, ruddy face began to look uncomfortable. 'I'm not sure I should have made that last remark, my dear. You'll think me a silly old fool, I know, but I've come to really resent the way Dorothy has been asking Bill into the house for meals. Sometimes when I've asked her to go out with me for a meal, or to come here, she's turned me down because Bill was going there. She says it's because Bill is such good company, such an interesting talker, but I can't help but wonder whether it's because he's such a good-looker, and a bit famous into the bargain.'

Mirth began to rise inside Andrea as she listened, but she managed to conceal it. 'Bill is much younger than Dorothy, isn't he?' she remarked gravely.

'What's that got to do with it? Dorothy's very young-looking for her age, and I'm ten years older than her,' Ben ended morosely.

'Oh, Ben, you don't look anything like that! I'm sure you're worrying about nothing. I think the reason Dorothy enjoys Bill's company is because he talks about things other than farming, which is all bad news these days. After all, David isn't very cheerful company for her, is he?'

'No, he doesn't get any better. The sooner I can get Dorothy away from there and into this house the happier I'll be. My housekeeper won't be needed as much here after we are married, so she's agreed to go and help at Abbot's Fold two days a week. Whether Dave will agree to that I don't know, but he'll have to have help from somewhere when Dorothy leaves.'

'I'll be going there to help her on Thursday while he's away at the market,' Andrea told him. 'I'm going to take Communion to Dorothy then, and while I'm there I'll give her a hand.' She rose to her feet, ready now to go home to the manse. 'Thanks a lot for the coffee and the food, Ben. I feel a lot better now.'

'Are you sure you're fit to drive?' he worried.

'Yes, perfectly. I've already kept you up rather late.'

They saw her to the door, the man and the dog, then she took the winding tree-lined road that led from Nyddford to Nyddbeck, driving slowly, with her mind lingering on her conversation with Ben Harper. She was still thinking of her coming visit to Abbot's Fold when she slowed down to enter the open gates of the manse. That was when she saw a vehicle parked alongside the drystone wall of the front garden.

The vehicle was a Land Rover, elderly and caked with mud. Her headlights picked out the figure of a man sitting back in the driving seat. She recognised him with a sense of shock. The man was David Bramley, and he was sound asleep.

A moment later she was out of her car, which she had parked in front of the manse instead of driving it into the garage. Because there had to be a reason why David had come down here, and why he had obviously decided since she was not at home to wait until she came back from her meeting. On the point of closing the car door, as she stepped out on to the gravel drive, she made a hasty decision. The easiest way to wake Dave would be to slam her door shut. This she did with more than usual force. Then she went up the steps and opened her front door.

It seemed like only a few seconds before David was out of the Land Rover and walking slowly through the gates of the manse. She waited there in the porch for him to climb wearily up the four stone steps until they were only a yard apart, staring at one another beneath the brilliant light cast by the porch lantern set beside the front door.

'Is something wrong?' she asked him quietly.

His face was haggard enough to set alarm bells ringing in Andrea's mind. Was it Dorothy? Had she been taken ill again, even though she had appeared to be so much better when Andrea had seen her only a few hours earlier?

'Is it your mother, David?' she asked, as he seemed unable to say anything.

He shook his head. 'No.' The single word was only just audible.

A new thought came to her then, one that was equally worrying. 'Is it Carla?'

'No.'

'What is it then? What brought you here?'

'You,' he admitted at last.

'Me! I don't understand—' Bewilderment filled her now that the worry had been brushed aside.

'I came to see if you were . . . to make sure you were all right.'

'Oh, I see. Is that why you were waiting for me?'

'Yes. My mother told me you'd left our place to go to a meeting. I was a bit worried because I didn't think you were fit for anything like that after what happened to you tonight.'

Andrea was conscious of a lump forming in her throat as she heard that. Here he was, tired out after a long day working

190

on the farm, coming to the manse to make sure she was all right. It didn't sound much like the David Bramley she had come to know as a bitter, morose, uncaring man who never missed an opportunity to be rude to her.

'That was kind of you, David, but why didn't you just phone me when you were so tired?'

He shrugged his powerful shoulders. 'Because you'd have said you were fine even if you weren't, wouldn't you?'

This brought a soft laugh into her throat. 'I don't think so, not tonight.'

'Mother seemed to think your meeting would probably be all over by about half past nine, and I knew it would only take you a few minutes to drive home from Nyddford. I came down about quarter to ten, but I got very worried when you didn't arrive. So I decided to wait until I knew you were safely home.'

She stared at him, filled with wonder at the change in his attitude, filled with pity for the utter weariness so plain to be seen on his face.

'I'm so sorry you've had such a long wait. Because I looked so ghastly when I got to the meeting, what with my injuries and the fact that I didn't have time to get anything to eat, Ben Harper insisted on taking me to his home and giving me some coffee and sandwiches before I drove back. That's why I'm so late. Now, do go home, David, and get some proper rest or your mother will be worrying about you.'

He managed a rueful grin. How different he looked when he was smiling. 'She doesn't know where I am. I told her I was going to take another look at the sheep up on the top grazing.'

Andrea laughed. 'I think she'd be quite surprised if she knew where you really were. How is the ewe Jack was so concerned about?'

'I think I'll manage to save her, with a bit of tender loving care.'

'I'm glad to hear that. I know you're having a bad time just now, and I'm very sorry. Go home now and get some sleep.'

Still he stood there, seemingly unable to move. Was he waiting for her to ask him into the house? Even as she wondered, and began to debate with herself whether that would be wise, she heard the sound of a dog barking. Then there were footsteps coming nearer as the owner of the dog caught up with it and spoke sharply to it. It was old Mr Gardner from the end cottage with his noisy little terrier. So Andrea made her decision.

'Goodnight, and thanks for coming,' she said clearly enough for the old man to hear.

'Goodnight, Mrs Cameron,' Dave replied as he turned away. A moment later she heard the engine of the Land Rover stir into life. She watched while it turned round close to the bridge, then slowed almost to a standstill while the driver wound down the window and looked back at her for what seemed to her to be a very long time.

Was he thinking of coming back to speak to her again? Her heart beat uncomfortably fast as she waited to see what he would do. Did she want him to come back? The man with the dog had disappeared, so there would be no one to see if he did. She found herself holding her breath, listening for the sound of the motor being switched off. When she heard it spring into powerful life again and the vehicle went speeding away in the direction of Abbot's Hill she let out her breath on a sigh.

The village was utterly silent again then except for the gurgle of the stream as it ran beneath the bridge. A few lights shone out from the cottages which were strung out along the lane that ran alongside the water. In the few seconds before she went down the steps to garage her car Andrea felt relieved because David had not come back. When she went into the house she experienced an unfamiliar feeling of loneliness.

Of course she was lonely, she argued with herself as she

got ready for bed. She had only been a widow for less than six months, not long enough to become accustomed to that state. Yet she knew as she set about brushing her hair that she had been lonely for far longer than that. Her loneliness probably dated from the time when Ian had begun to meet that other woman, the woman called Beth. Only she had been too busy with her studies to become aware of it then.

This feeling that there was something missing in her life would not last, she assured herself as she slid beneath the duvet on the double bed and reached for her prayer book. It was just something which had been kindled by those few moments when she had been held close by David Bramley in the porch of his home. By tomorrow it would be behind her, banished by her full life of work, study and prayer. That was the way it must be, from now on.

The sooner he moved out of Jacob's Cottage the better, Bill knew, as he drove down to his new home. Carla had waited until her father had gone out in the Land Rover and had then come knocking on his door with a handful of drawings for him to look at. At least, that was what she had told him. He wouldn't have minded if it had been as straightforward as that, but once inside the cottage she had come to perch on the arm of his chair, enveloping him in a cloud of perfume and leaning over him in a blouse which was unbuttoned low enough for alarm bells to begin sounding inside him. The only way he had been able to get rid of her, and then with some difficulty, was by telling her that he had to drive down to Nyddford to meet some people who had commissioned several watercolours of local scenes to be hung in their prestigious new offices.

'I could come with you,' Carla suggested.

'No! No you couldn't, the discussions will go on until very late.'

'That wouldn't matter. Gran will have gone to bed and Dad'll be asleep on the sofa as he always is late at night.

193

He won't hear me if I go in through the door leading into the old dairy and up the little back stair to my room. I've done it before and he hasn't heard me.'

'You'll be in real trouble if he finds out you're doing that,' Bill warned her. 'You'd soon be bored out of your mind listening to us talking shop all that time.'

'I wouldn't! You know I want to be an artist when I leave school and you've said my work is promising. So why can't I come with you?'

Bill got to his feet abruptly, eager to put space between the perfume, the low cleavage and Carla's warm flesh. It was playing with fire letting her stay here. Yes, she was attractive, but he didn't go for girls as young as she was. He was going to have to be cruel to get rid of her, and the sooner the better.

'I need to turn you out now or I'll be late for my appointment.'

He strode through the open door of the big living room and into the hall. Carla followed more slowly, but came to a halt when she was facing Bill in the square hall close to the front door. Her lovely face was scowling as she pushed a strand of thick blonde hair away from her eyes.

'I don't believe you are going to meet any business people, Bill. I think you're going to meet her. That's why you want to get rid of me. You are going to meet her, aren't you?'

Bill's frown deepened. 'Meet who?'

'That woman, the new minister. Andrea Cameron.'

'Don't be so ridiculous, Carla!' Bill snapped. He was on a short fuse now, a state of mind he did not often reach, and was having difficulty in remaining calm.

'I'm not! You have been seeing her. I know you have.'

'You're letting your imagination run away with you.' He flung the front door wide open and waited for the girl to flounce out.

'I'm not. I saw you leaving some flowers for her, and I know you've been talking to her.'

'There's no reason why I shouldn't give her flowers, or talk to her. That's why she's here, so that people can talk to her about their problems.' Bill stepped out into the porch of the cottage and waited for Carla to follow him.

She stayed where she was. 'You were talking to her about me, weren't you?' she accused.

Now he was losing what was left of his patience. 'I wouldn't have to talk to her about you if you'd act more sensibly. I don't want to see you get hurt, Carla, and neither does Andrea.'

'It isn't just that though, is it? You're going to live nearer to her because you fancy her, don't you, Bill?'

He opened his mouth to tell her not to be ridiculous again, that she was wrong. The girl was not wrong though, was she? Because he did fancy Andrea Cameron. He more than fancied her, he simply could not get her out of his mind these days. Wherever he was, working in Jacob's Cottage or painting in one of the villages or out on the moor, Andrea's brilliantly blue eyes and beautiful, serene face seemed to haunt him.

'I'm going to live down in Nyddbeck so that you won't always be on my doorstep waiting to pester me, Carla!' he said harshly, with a cruelty which was foreign to his nature.

'Oh, Bill!' It was a cry of anguish. 'I thought you really liked me.'

The light from over his porch showed that tears were there waiting to fall from the girl's eyes. That the soft young mouth was quivering as she struggled for control of herself. Instantly then Bill regretted his outburst. He should not have spoken so frankly, so hurtfully, but Carla had caught him on the raw when she declared that she knew he fancied Andrea Cameron.

Until he had heard it said out loud he had not faced up to what was happening himself. Not admitted that one of the reasons why he had decided on buying Beckside, rather than the more conveniently situated house in Nyddford, was that living there he would be likely to meet Andrea as she walked across the bridge to her church. He had even, in one rare moment of contemplation, wondered whether it might be a good idea to put in an appearance at one of her services once he was installed in Beckside. Christmas was very close so perhaps Andrea would not think it strange if he were to be there among the crowd on Christmas Eve? Oh God, what was he thinking of, allowing his thoughts to stray in that direction!

'Of course I really like you, Carla,' he said after he had succeeded in forcing his thoughts away from Andrea.

'Do you? Can I come and see you sometimes when you move to your new place? Please say I can,' she pleaded. 'It's not much fun these days living up here, with Dad the way he is, and when Gran goes it'll be even worse.'

'Your gran won't be moving out just yet, Carla.'

'She will! Ben Harper's got it all planned for them to get married soon and for Gran to go and live with him in Nyddford. It'll be awful then. I won't have time for anything except cooking and housework and school. It's not fair! It's just not fair!'

Pity for the girl stirred inside Bill. She was probably right about what sort of life would be ahead of her when her grandmother left Abbot's Fold. Yet what could he say that would give her hope for the future? Even as he racked his brain to come up with something Carla was speaking again.

'I'll be away from here as soon as I'm sixteen, next April. There'll be no point in staying because I won't pass my exams anyway. So I'll get a live-in job somewhere working in a bar or a restaurant and Dad won't be able to stop me. If he doesn't care about me, and you don't, there'll be nothing to stay here for. I look older than my age so if things get really bad I might go before then. So you won't need to worry about me pestering you any more.'

As her voice rose, Bill began to feel out of his depth. He

took a step towards her, but she backed away from him and a moment later was on her way across the yard. The sound of her shoes clattering on the cobbled surface startled the collies into a frenzy of high-pitched barking. Bill shuddered as he watched her disappear round the side of the house. His move down to the village could not come soon enough for him.

Twenty

A ndrea was determined, now that there was no longer
any need to keep travelling to Durham, to make another
visit to the Raven Falls Hotel. It proved to be more difficult
than she had anticipated because so many other things took
up what was supposed to be her free time. Her days off
were Thursdays, but having promised to take Communion
to Dorothy Bramley on that day while David was away at the
Nyddford cattle market, and then stay on to give her a hand
with some cooking and housework, she knew there would
not be sufficient time left afterwards to go to the hotel and
find out more about Beth Barclay's involvement with Ian.

Dorothy was so grateful to see her that the feeling of
frustration Andrea had experienced about having to postpone
her visit to the Raven Falls Hotel was soon forgotten. The
hours she spent at Abbot's Fold Farm that day turned out
to be rewarding in more ways than one. First there was
the warmth of Dorothy's welcome, the kiss bestowed on
her cheek by the older woman, who then said that if she
agreed they would share the bread and wine in the small
parlour.

'It's a special place for me, my dear, and you'll see why.'
She led the way to a room at the front of the farmhouse which
was only a few feet square. It had a window looking out of
the side of the house over a landscape which on this day of
winter sunshine was breathtakingly beautiful. Frost glittered
on the branches of the walnut tree which grew close to the

window and lent starkly brilliant colour to the bronze-clad distant fells.

'Yes, the view is wonderful, Dorothy.' Andrea's glance then moved to the huge battered desk that occupied most of the available floor space. 'It must be hard to keep your mind on work in here when the view is so tempting.' She was thinking as she spoke of David Bramley sitting at this well-used old desk struggling to balance the farm accounts. Yet something else was nagging at the back of her mind. Why should Dorothy ask her to offer the Communion here in this tiny overcrowded room where books and papers were piled high on the desk and there was the faintest air of neglect showing on the dusty windows?

'This room was never used for the farm paperwork, Andrea, at least not in our time here.' David's mother enlightened her. 'It's the place my Jacob set aside for his lay-preaching work, for preparing his services and sermons. That's why I particularly wanted to have Communion here. It was here that Mr Bickerdike came regularly to bring the sacrament to Jacob when he was too ill to be able to go to church.'

'Oh, now I understand. I hadn't realised that your husband was a lay-preacher, Dorothy.'

'Yes, Jacob was invited to lead services all over the dale. His faith was very important to him, right until the end of his life. So I feel specially close to him here. We would have moved all the things in here across to the cottage, but Jacob died only a few days before we were due to move out of here and I never got round to clearing everything out. It will have to be cleared though when I move out and marry Ben, but we'll talk about that later. Now, I'm ready to start when you are.'

With that, Dorothy seated herself in the shabby carver chair which stood behind the desk and waited while Andrea opened her briefcase and took out the communion set and the small wooden cross which her parents had given her on her

199

ordination. The sharing of the next few minutes, the speaking of the familiar words and the giving and receiving of bread and wine, were precious to both of them.

Afterwards Dorothy took Andrea's hands in her own and spoke quietly to her. 'This is my goodbye to Jacob's study, Andrea. I'm going to ask you if you'll go through all the books that are in this room and take anything that's likely to be useful to you, then everything else will be disposed of. When I marry Ben I'll be making a new start in a new home.'

Andrea smiled at her. 'Of course I'll be happy to do that. Am I to take it that the wedding will be soon?'

Dorothy smiled back. 'Yes, very soon. Ben and I were talking about it last night. If you are free, we'd like you to marry us on New Year's Eve.'

'As soon as that!' Andrea could not hide her surprise.

'We've waited longer now than we intended to. Ben has been very patient, but he's determined that we won't delay any more, now that I'm on the mend.'

'I'll need to check my diary, but I don't think there's anything that will stop me from helping you to become Mrs Harper.' It would mean her postponing by a day her departure for Scotland, where she had planned to celebrate Hogmanay with her parents, but she knew they would understand. 'It's wonderful news, Dorothy. I'm so glad for you,' she added.

'Yes, isn't it! I'll tell you more while we have some coffee in the kitchen.'

Ben had it all planned out to the last detail, Andrea was to discover, as they enjoyed the warmth of the Aga while drinking their coffee and eating the scones Dorothy had made that morning. There would be a quiet wedding in Nyddbeck Church with only close friends and family present, followed by a wedding breakfast at the Nyddford Inn, which was renowned for the excellence of the food on offer. Immediately afterwards they would start their life together at Ford House, leaving the honeymoon until April.

How would David cope with life after his mother left Abbot's Fold? Would he be able to manage without her help? Andrea found herself worrying about that. Strangely, Dorothy did not appear to be worrying about that at all. At least she was not voicing any concern about it, not over coffee or later over the lunch of soup and cheese which they shared after preparing a huge chicken casserole and an apple crumble for the evening meal.

Even when they were working together giving the farm-house kitchen the most thorough clean it had had since Dorothy had been taken ill, they did not talk about Dorothy's son and what he would do after the wedding. Andrea felt so mystified by Dorothy's silence on the subject that she tried to introduce it herself by asking whether David would want to give his mother away at her wedding.

'Well, I haven't got round to asking him that yet, but I will when the time is right,' Dorothy told her. 'There was so much to be discussed when Ben took me over to Ford House for dinner last night that it was late when we came back and David was in bed.'

Andrea began to wonder what David would say when he heard that a date had been set for his mother's marriage. All she could hope was that he would not spoil Dorothy's happiness by refusing to escort her down the aisle on her special day. If he did it would certainly cause a rift between him and Ben Harper. A glance at her watch showed her that it was time to leave the farm if she wanted to be away before he returned from Nyddford cattle market.

'Have a quick cup of tea before you go, dear,' Dorothy insisted. 'You could be sorting out some of Jacob's books to take with you while I make it.'

Andrea went back to the little room and occupied herself in doing that for the next ten minutes, by which time she had enough books to fill the cardboard carton Dorothy provided. Because Jacob's study was situated at the front of the large farmhouse and she was so immersed in her selection of books, she failed to hear the return of the Land Rover to the farmyard. She was staggering through the kitchen door with the box of books when David spoke to her.

'I'll take those to your car,' he said, and took the box from her before she could utter a word of protest. 'I'll put them straight into the boot.'

Obviously, he was anxious for her to be gone from Abbot's Fold as soon as possible. She felt anger kindle inside her. This was not the David Bramley who had come down to the manse to make sure she had got home safely after her fall. Or the one who had cradled her in his arms out there in the porch. This was that bitter, arrogant man she had done her best to avoid ever since her arrival at Nyddbeck. Suddenly anger left her and she was aware of an immense feeling of loss.

'The tea's ready, my dear. Do sit down near the Aga, you must be quite cold now, there's no heating in Jacob's study,' Dorothy was saying.

Andrea hesitated, but only for a few seconds. Another swift glance at her watch, a glance that did not even allow the time to register properly, brought the words she needed into her mind.

'It's later than I realised, Dorothy, so I'm afraid I'll have to be off. I've enjoyed my day with you very much, and thanks a lot for the books. I'll treasure them.'

'Oh, do you really have to go so soon?' Dorothy protested.

'I still have my letter to finish for the parish magazine, so I really must go,' Andrea said hurriedly. The letter could have waited until tomorrow, but she had to find a reason for her hasty departure and that was as good as any. 'I'll be in touch.'

She was on her way with all possible speed across the yard to where her car was parked out in the lane when Bill opened the front door of Jacob's Cottage and called her name. Startled, she tore her glance away from where Dave was waiting near to her car and looked round instead at the other man.

'Can you spare me a few minutes, Andrea? I've been trying to contact you at the manse, but your answer-phone doesn't seem to be working.'

'I've been here for most of . . .' she broke off there as she realised that David would be able to hear quite clearly what she was saying. She had not wanted him to know how long she had been at Abbot's Fold today. Not now that she knew he was annoyed with her again and eager to see her off his premises. 'I'll just collect my car keys then I'll be with you, Bill,' she ended, making her mind up swiftly that if Bill was waiting to speak to her she would not need to listen to what David had to say to her.

As it happened he had little to say to her. When she joined him he was still standing close to her car with the keys swinging from his right hand. Dusk was falling so rapidly that she could hardly distinguish the expression on his features, though she thought he was frowning with disapproval. Silent disapproval, she was to discover during the long moment when they faced one another out there in the sharp November air, with only the sound of the nearby sheep from the other side of the drystone wall. There was a longing inside her to encounter once again the warmth and tenderness she now knew was buried deep inside the shell of hurt and bitterness that held him a prisoner, but it was not going to happen. Not tonight. Perhaps not ever again.

'Thanks for your help,' she murmured.

'Thank you for helping my mother,' he responded coolly. 'I won't keep you now.' With that he strode off, not across the yard towards the house but away towards the summit of the hill where the grazing land was littered with fragments of limestone rock and hundreds of murmuring sheep. The dog which had been at his heel stayed close to him, with white-tipped tail moving gracefully until the pair of them were out of sight.

Andrea let out the breath she had been holding on a long sigh as she watched them go. The prayer that was forming in her mind was centred on the man whose only comfort these days seemed to be his dog.

Dave Bramley and his dog moved swiftly upwards to the lonely place which had been part of his life for as long as he could remember. The place which had known the richness of his joy with Jill and their children, then later the wilderness of his sorrow when he lost Jill. He had come here often to weep alone, to hide from his mother and his children the despair that overwhelmed him. Now he took with him to that place his bewilderment, his fear and his anger. Because he simply could not come to terms with what was happening to him, could not accept where his thoughts and feelings were leading him.

From the top of that barren, windswept hill he could look down over the village where Andrea Cameron lived. The place was in darkness now except for the pinpoints of light shining out from the few big houses and the long straggle of cottages. He could only just distinguish the spire of the church rising above the other buildings. It was much easier to find the lights that shone out from Abbot's Fold some distance below him, and to recognise those other lights that were coming from Jacob's Cottage.

She was there, inside Jacob's Cottage with Bill Wyndham. He knew she was because Bill had called to her and she had gone to him. What did Bill want to talk to Andrea about? It could not be church business because Bill Wyndham did not go to church. So it must have been something more personal. Another thought came to him, an idea that struck him like a blow. He did not want to let his mind linger over it, but it was too late, the thought would not leave him. Could they be . . . ? Why shouldn't they be? Andrea was a widow, and

Bill was unattached. She was young, and beautiful enough to make any man forget her calling. Even he had forgotten that, he of all people! He, who had lost his faith when he lost the woman he loved.

Dave dragged his gaze away from Jacob's Cottage and told himself not to be a bloody fool. There were the ewes to be checked over before it got any darker. It was nothing to do with him if the woman minister was getting involved with Bill Wyndham. He had enough to worry about with the problems generated by his farm and his children. There was no place in his life for a woman now. Not even a woman whose serenely beautiful face and warmth of spirit was beginning to haunt all his waking hours.

'I wanted to let you know that I'm moving into Beckside tomorrow, Andrea,' Bill said, when they were standing in the hall of Jacob's Cottage.

'Dorothy mentioned it to me this morning. I thought there was still a lot of work to be done there.'

'So there is, but it seemed wiser for me to get away from Abbot's Fold as soon as possible.'

'My little talk with Carla didn't help then?'

He gave her a wry grin as he shook his head. 'It seems not. She was here again last night, asking me if she could come and see me when I move down to Nyddbeck. I had to be quite firm with her and she was very upset. She ran away in tears because I told her a white lie about having to go down to meet some people in Nyddford. I had to do it so I could get rid of her.'

'Would it help if I contrived to bump into her again and had another word with her?' Andrea did not want to do that but nor did she want the situation to go on unchecked until either David or his mother became aware of it. There must be nothing now to undermine Dorothy's recovery and delay yet again her marriage to Ben.

Bill sighed. 'I don't think it would because . . .' He broke off there.

Andrea frowned. 'Because?' she prompted.

'Because she's a very self-willed little madam who just won't listen to sense.'

Perhaps he had gone over the top a bit talking about Carla like that but he certainly could not allow Andrea to risk trying to warn the girl off now that Carla had latched on to the idea that he had a fancy for Andrea. It would be too embarrassing by far, for both of them. Carla was right, he certainly did have a fancy for Andrea Cameron but he was not about to act hastily. He would take his time with Andrea, make sure that what he felt for her was what he believed it to be. There would be so many adjustments for him to make if it was. Things to give up, and maybe things to take on board that he had never even considered before. Most importantly of all, Andrea must not be hurt, because she had already had too much hurt in her life. So he would go slowly, very slowly, but the move to Beckside would be his first move towards friendship with her.

'I hope you'll be happy at Beckside, Bill,' Andrea was saying as his thoughts led him on to whether she would agree to have dinner with him. 'It's a nice house and a lovely village. I feel as if I've lived there for far longer than six months.'

'Are you happy there in your manse, Andrea?' he found himself asking her. 'Perhaps I should not have said that, in the circumstances. Forgive me, please?'

'I don't need to forgive you because I *am* happy there. Very happy. Which reminds me that when I get back to the manse I have my letter for the parish magazine to finish, so I must be on my way.'

'I'll walk you to your car and see you get there safely. I believe you had rather a bad fall out in the yard the other day.'

She laughed. 'Yes, the bruises are only just fading, but I'll be fine, Bill. You don't need to worry about me.'

'I don't have anyone else to worry about, Andrea,' he found himself telling her.

Andrea gazed at him, her eyes soft with sympathy. 'Do you really have no one at all, Bill? No relatives or close friends?'

'Oh, I have friends, quite a lot of them, and a couple of aunts and uncles, but my parents are in Australia now, living close to my two sisters and their families. I meant I had no immediate family, no wife or children to worry about.'

'I expect you will have, one day. At least I hope you will,' she said with a smile as she set off to walk across the yard to her car.

'I wish I could feel as sure of that. I thought I was close to it a couple of years ago, but I seem to have got things wrong. Either expected too much of her or simply made the wrong choice.'

'It's so easy to make a mistake. Not so easy to put it right,' she said with a sigh.

Bill found her words stayed with him for long after she had driven away from the farm. They raised questions in his mind yet again about why her husband had been killed so far away from the place where he surely ought to have been on that day. Perhaps Andrea would answer those questions for him one day. Or perhaps not. Yet as he leaned on the drystone wall and listened to the sound of her car engine fading away as it descended the steep hill, he had a feeling that the answer to the question of why Andrea's husband had not moved into the manse with her could be as important to him as it was to her.

Twenty-One

As Christmas drew nearer, the days became even busier for Andrea, leaving her with less and less spare time. There were special services to be planned, not only for her own two churches but for the schools and some of the nursing or retirement homes in her area. There was also the marriage service for Dorothy Bramley and Ben Harper to be arranged. On her next visit to the farm, again on a Thursday, she discussed this with Dorothy.

'Are you and Ben going to walk to the altar together, as some people do today? Or will you have David beside you when you come into the church, Dorothy?' she asked, determined to get things sorted out now that there were only a few weeks left before New Year's Eve and the wedding.

Dorothy hesitated, the brightness of her eyes dimming slightly. 'I still don't really know, Andrea, because although I asked David almost a fortnight ago whether he would walk beside me on the day, he hasn't said either yes or no as yet. Ben's getting quite annoyed about it,' she added.

'Will it matter terribly to you if David doesn't feel able to do as you want him to?' Andrea could guess the answer to that even as she asked the question, because hadn't the mother and son been through a great deal together during the last few years? Of course it would matter terribly to her.

Dorothy however was determined to put a brave face on it. 'Of course I'd like David to be with me but I know what an ordeal it would be for him so I'll do my best to understand

208

if he feels he simply can't do it. After all, there are so many sad memories for him to face in Nyddbeck Church.'

'There must be some for you too, Dorothy,' Andrea began carefully. 'So if you'd rather have the ceremony at Nyddford Church that can easily be arranged.'

Now Dorothy was smiling again. 'Oh no, I'd much rather have the service at Nyddbeck. I have so many happy memories bound up in that little church, right from the time I came here to teach in the village school that used to be there at one time. I met Jacob at Nyddbeck Church and married him there a couple of years later. It was a very happy marriage right to the end. Then the children were christened there and went to Sunday school there until . . .'

'Until their mother died?' Andrea intervened.

'Yes.' Dorothy agreed with a sigh. 'I'm very sad that they don't have anything to do with the church now. I believe it would have helped them come to terms with the way things are, only David doesn't agree with me about that.'

'Perhaps he will, one day?' Andrea suggested.

The older woman's face brightened. 'I had begun to think, a couple of weeks back, that he was beginning to come out of the worst of his depression. He seemed more like his old self, much more gentle and cheerful, but now I don't know if I just imagined it.'

'I don't think you did. I remember how kind he was to me when I fell in the yard,' Andrea told her. David had been more than kind that day, he had shown her a warm and loving side to his nature that she had not realised existed.

'Yes, that's the sort of man he really is. It's been so awful watching him become more and more shut into himself and becoming so uncaring about Carla and Jack. Although he's never been too bad with Jack, it's Carla he has no patience with. He seems to expect her to be able to cope with all her homework and at the same time take on more and more of the cooking and cleaning. It just can't be done, Andrea. Carla resents it so much that there are sparks flying between them far too often. I know she's at a difficult age, but far too much is being expected of her and it will be worse when I'm living at Ford House with Ben. I can't help being worried about what will happen then.'

'I thought Ben's housekeeper was going to come over here a couple of times a week to help with the cooking and housework?'

'That's what Ben has arranged with her, and he wants to pay her wages as usual so that David won't have the expense to cope with, but so far David has been against the idea. He says it's up to Carla to do the cleaning and cooking. They had another row about it last night. She's easily upset these days, and always worrying about her homework. I think she misses having Bill at hand to advise her with it.'

Andrea knew it was time to change the subject. Of course Carla would be missing Bill. He represented excitement for her, a man older than her schoolfriends, a clever man who was a well-known artist. Most of all, a man she imagined herself in love with.

'I met Bill as I was going across to the church yesterday,' she said. 'He asked me what sort of wedding gift I thought you and Ben would like. I wondered whether you would like anything for the garden at Ford House?'

'Oh yes, we would! There's a workshop for the disabled at Nyddford that Ben has an interest in. They make some very nice planters and bird-baths. Something like that would be lovely.'

When they met, as Bill was working at his easel close to the bridge on one of the watercolours for the Nyddford business commission, Bill had suggested that they have a meal together some time to discuss what he could buy for Dorothy and Ben. They had not arranged a date for this because their conversation had been interrupted by the young mum who ran the church playgroup. Andrea had left rather glad about that because she could not decide whether it would be wise for her to go out for a meal with Bill.

Once again, she spent a good part of the day with Dorothy enjoying the company of the older woman as they baked pies and cakes and caught up with the housework. She would not stay as long today as she had done last time, Andrea decided, then there would be no chance of her meeting David when he returned from Nyddford. This time she almost made it. She was already in the lane beyond the farm and on the point of getting into her car when she heard the sound of a powerful motor engine drawing near. So she knew she must get moving before it was too late for her to escape a confrontation with the farmer.

It was already too late, she discovered, when David parked his elderly Land Rover across the closed gate to the farm at a place where the lane was too narrow for her to be able to drive past him without tipping her car into the ditch. Andrea waited tensely in the driving seat for him to climb out of his vehicle, open the farm gate and drive into the yard, leaving the way clear for her. She kept her eyes firmly fixed on the summit of the craggy hill which towered above the surrounding scenery, where the bronze of bracken was taking on a purple tint as the daylight faded.

Behind her she could hear David's collies giving him a boisterous welcome home, and catch his voice speaking quietly to them. In her mind she knew how he would look. She had seen the fondness he had for his dogs and been touched by it, because there seemed always to be a softness in his face when his hand made contact with the rough black coat of Tyke or Brack. He would be gone in another minute or so, then she could put him out of her mind.

Yet how could she do that when he was there on the other side of her window, waiting for her to open it so he could talk to her? Her hands gripped the steering wheel, as though by doing so she could convince him that she was determined to be away from the farm as soon as possible. Still the two wildly excited dogs circled round him, until a sharply spoken word from him sent them to lie with heads on outstretched paws beside the Land Rover. Then the air was silent and all she could do was wait to hear what David had to say to her.

'I'm glad I caught you, Mrs Cameron,' he was saying. 'I left Nyddford early so I could do that.'

'How did you know I'd be here? It's my day off.' Her voice sounded aggressive to her own ears. There was a nervous tingle moving up her spine.

'Do you always spend your days off working unpaid for other people?' he challenged.

She took a deep breath, and answered firmly. 'If I think it necessary.'

'What makes you think it's necessary here, Mrs Cameron?' His reply came swiftly, sounding sharp on the crisp cold air that drifted in through the open window.

'Because your mother is my friend. Because she made me welcome here when I first came and I needed help, and because I want her to stay well enough to marry Ben on New Year's Eve.'

'I have a daughter who is quite old enough to do what you'll have been doing!'

'You have a daughter who needs to spend more time on homework rather than housework. Who needs help with the homework, not reasons to leave it undone.' She had probably spoken out of turn there, Andrea guessed almost before she had finished speaking.

'I can't imagine why that should be any concern of yours, Mrs Cameron. I understood you were here to work for the church, not the school.'

'I'm here to be of help to anyone who needs me, adults or children,' she began, staring intently into his hostile face as her temper mounted.

'You should leave the children to those who are responsible for them. Those who know what they are doing,' he
hit back.

'I do know what I'm doing! I have been a teacher.' She
took a deep breath in order to go on. 'And I was a . . .'

It was attempting to make herself utter the final word,
the word 'parent', that brought the grief which was usually
pushed to the back of her mind by her work to the surface
again. She needed to say the word to this man who thought
he had the monopoly of suffering. The man who did not know
what it was like to lose a child and have no hope of another.
Only she could not get the word out because of the lump that
choked up her throat.

She could not bear to have him witness her distress. So
she did not wait to see what effect her outburst had on him.
Instead she thrust the car door open so violently that he was
forced to leap out of the way to avoid being crushed against
the drystone wall. Then she ran away from him, stumbling
as fast as her legs would carry her, up the track that led to
the top of the hill.

David felt as though Andrea Cameron had just delivered
a hefty blow that struck him hard on his chest. What did she
mean? Saying that she had been a teacher, and a . . . ? Had
she been going to say she had been a good teacher? Or had
she been about to say she was a parent too? If so, where were
her children? What was she doing living alone in the manse?
Were her children away at school? They could hardly be old
enough for boarding school, surely? Or had her children been
sacrificed to her ambition to take over not just a couple of
churches but the lives of some of those who were members
of the churches?

His gaze was still following her rapidly moving figure as
it moved up and up towards the summit of the craggy fell.
She was furious with him, he knew that. Those brilliantly blue
eyes had flashed with an icy anger that he had not seen before,

and in doing so had stirred something inside him which he was trying hard to believe was not happening.

He must crush that feeling and regain control of himself before he went after her, because there was no way he could leave her to face alone the danger that taking a false step in the gathering darkness could bring. The outcrops of limestone rock were everywhere, waiting to trip a careless walker. They were already taking on the sparkle of frost so he must catch up with her before it was too late and she had an accident. In the mood she was in anything could happen. Calling the dogs to his side with a piercing whistle he started on the steep uphill sheep track, cursing himself for not having set off at once, as soon as he realised where she was heading.

The woman was a bloody nuisance with her interference in his life. He had had more than enough of her turning up at his home to occupy for a time the place in his kitchen that had belonged to Jill, and would always belong to Jill. He would not tolerate her handing out advice about the way he should be bringing up his children. She had no right to do that, even if she had once been a teacher. He would bring her safely down from the fell and then make it perfectly clear to her that she was to stay away from Abbot's Fold in future.

Andrea's breath was coming in great painful gasps as she strode up and up the long slope that would take her far away from David Bramley. He would be on his way back to the farmhouse now because she had heard him whistle to the two dogs. She would give him time to get indoors then get herself back to her car and drive home to Nyddbeck. Only she would have to regain control of her emotions before she got behind the wheel – she was still shaking with the distress that had sent her dashing up here to get away from him.

Her eyes were accustomed to the darkness now and she was unafraid of it. The limestone outcrops that were everywhere needed to be negotiated with care. She paused to allow the stitch in her side to ease. From much further away she was able to glimpse the lights that shone out from the farmhouse where David would be greeting his mother. Perhaps reprimanding her for accepting the help Andrea had offered.

A spasm of rage against David Bramley shook her whole being. What sort of man was he that he could not, or would not, understand that his mother needed help, and his daughter needed help? He was a moron! He was an uncaring brute! He was a—

Another ragged breath, another sharp stab of pain, another rush of moisture to her eyes, and the dash of a startled rabbit emerging from a hole directly in front of her caught her unawares. Her toe caught in the hole and she stumbled, righting herself just in time, knowing as she did so that she was at the end of her tether. That if she did not sit down and rest at once disaster would befall her. The limestone outcrop was just large enough for her to lower herself carefully on to it. Then she sunk her head over her folded arms and waited for her heartbeats to slow down.

There was something immensely calming about the silence up here, where the only sound to be heard was that of the frozen heather being crushed by the grazing sheep. She did not hear the approach of the man who walked very carefully, very slowly, so as not to startle her. He was only a few feet away from her when he spoke to her.

'You'll find yourself with a bad back if you sit there for long in this temperature,' he warned quietly.

Andrea ignored him, keeping her head averted.

'I would have thought, since your work is so important to you, that you would have been more careful with your health.'

She would not be stung into making the sort of reply to this remark that she longed to hurl at him now that she had control of her breathing again. If she did not respond he would go away.

'Come on now, don't be stupid! This is a dangerous place to be in the dark when you are not used to walking in fell country.'

At that she swung round to answer him. 'I'm not stupid, and I am used to fell walking! Why don't you leave me alone?'

His sigh of resignation quivered on the frosty air. 'God knows! I've enough problems without having to worry about you as well.'

'I never asked you to worry about me!' she hit back.

'Since you came to my farm to help my mother that puts responsibility on to me to see that you don't come to any harm while you are on my land. So I'll see you safely back to your car, whether you like it or not.'

The tone of his voice made her realise that he meant what he said. It brought her to her feet so hastily and clumsily that he was forced to reach out a hand to steady her. For a long moment then they were close, too close for her peace of mind.

'I can manage,' she said sharply, twisting her shoulder to shake off his grip on her. 'I don't need any help.'

'Why have you been crying then?'

'I haven't!' she insisted.

He raised his hand from her shoulder and touched her cheek with one large finger. 'You're lying, Andrea. What's wrong?'

'I would have thought that was obvious, even to you,' she muttered. 'Especially to you.'

Dave kept his hand on her cheek where it was still damp from her tears. He let his breath go on a long sigh. 'Yes, it's bloody awful having to go on living on your own when there's nothing left to live for.'

Fury rose inside her at his words. 'Nothing left to live for? You have to be joking! You've got two nice children, a lovely mother and your home and your work in this marvellous place.'

'I've got two children I can't cope with, a mother who's about to leave me to manage as best I can, and a farm that brings me nothing but problems I can't solve.'

'We all have problems we can't solve right now, and some of our problems are ones we make for ourselves.'

'You can't say that about my problems,' he broke in.

'I can say it about some of them, the ones to do with your children.'

'What do you mean?' He dropped his hand from her cheek as though suddenly becoming aware of where he had left it.

'You don't have to be so hard on them, especially on Carla.'

'As I said before, you don't know what it's like being left to cope on your own with kids.'

'No, no, I don't. I only wish I did.'

With that she walked away from him, taking her anger with her before it spilled over again. He held his breath as she negotiated the steepest part of the sheeptrack then gathered speed to put distance between them as fast as she could.

Twenty-Two

Andrea found it impossible to banish from her mind the angry words she had exchanged with David Bramley, even though she spent a long time in Nyddbeck Church praying that she would be able to both forgive and forget the hurt he had inflicted on her, when all she had tried to do was to help him and his family. He needed help so badly. Why would he not let her help him? The thought of the man and his problems was never far away from her as she became more and more involved with preparations for her first Christmas as Minister of Nyddford with Nyddbeck. She mentioned him to Julie Craven, Jill Bramley's friend, when they met for coffee in Nyddford one day.

'I don't know what will happen when Dave has to cope without Dorothy,' Julie replied with a frown. 'Dorothy seems to think that Ben sending his own housekeeper over to Abbot's Fold for a couple of days a week will solve that problem, but I don't believe it will. Dave Bramley will fight every inch of the way to prevent Mrs Grainger setting a foot over his doorstep.'

'He's certainly got an attitude about accepting help, even from friends. I discovered that when I went up there to take Communion to Dorothy while he was away at the cattle market, and stayed to help with some cooking and cleaning,' Andrea told her. 'I knew he wouldn't like it, so I intended to be away before he got back. Only it didn't work out like that.'

'Was Dave very unpleasant to you?'

Andrea nodded. 'Yes, he was furious with me. He seemed to think that Carla ought to be able to do everything that needed doing when she came home from school, as well as getting her homework done.'

'If he's not careful he'll cause major problems for himself there,' Julie said, as she stirred cream into her coffee.

'What do you mean?' Andrea could guess what Julie meant, but she was anxious to find out whether Julie had any idea that Carla had been hanging around Bill Wyndham.

'I mean that because Dave can't find the time to talk to Carla, or to help her with her school work, she's taking herself more and more often to Bill Wyndham's place. I'm beginning to suspect that she's making a nuisance of herself to Bill. He's a bit too near to home for her. It's too easy for her to invite herself into his cottage when her father isn't around. I don't know whether Bill is aware of just how young she is, but when she's not wearing her school uniform she looks much older than fifteen.' Julie paused, frowning, then went on. 'When I was up at Abbot's Fold visiting Dorothy while she was ill, I saw Carla slip out through the old dairy door at the side of the house all tarted up as if she was just off to disco. Only she was heading for Jacob's Cottage to see Bill.'

'She won't find it so easy to do that now because Bill's left the cottage and moved into his new home in Nyddbeck,' Andrea told her.

Julie's face showed her surprise. 'Oh! I suppose that's why he wasn't around when I called to see Dorothy yesterday. I didn't realise he was planning on going so soon. He didn't mention it, the last time I saw him.'

Julie looked a bit put out as she said that, Andrea thought. Could it be that she had a fancy for Bill Wyndham herself? Was that why she had risked going to Abbot's Fold again, even though she knew that David resented her visits?

219

'Bill probably didn't know then how soon he was moving. There was still a lot of work to be done at Beckside.'

'They must have got things done quicker than he expected?'

'I don't think so. My guess is that Bill had begun to realise what was happening with Carla and decided to put some distance between them.'

Julie's face brightened when she heard that. 'Yes, that could be it. He's such a nice guy. He wouldn't want to cause trouble for anyone.'

'No, I don't think he would,' Andrea agreed. 'Though I don't know him very well.'

'Dorothy's told me quite a bit about him. She became very fond of him while he was living at the cottage and having some of his meals in the farmhouse. That's where I first met him. He's a very interesting guy. I like his pictures too. Do you?'

Andrea smiled. 'I don't know. I haven't seen them, except for part of one that he was painting near the bridge at Nyddbeck. I've been meaning to ask you to supper, Julie, and haven't got round to it yet. Could you come next Thursday?'

Julie fished out her diary and gave it a hasty scan. 'Yes, I'm sure I can. I'd love to! There's not much on my horizon just now except work. I'm here today because of work. I'm going for an interview this afternoon for a new job.'

'At the hospital here?'

'No. At the health centre. I'm ready for a change from Marksley Cottage Hospital.'

'Good luck then, Julie. I'll see you on Thursday, about seven thirty.'

She would invite Bill, Andrea decided, as she drove back from Nyddford. Perhaps that would stop him from asking her to go out for a meal with him again. Inviting him to supper at the manse at the same time as Julie Craven could be a good move since Julie obviously had a liking for him.

She met Bill the next morning as she was taking a short brisk walk to clear her brain before starting on all her paperwork, and he again broached the subject of their going out for a meal.

'I'm getting very tired of my own company, so do say yes this time,' he begged. His hazel eyes were warm as they met her own blue ones. Bill was nice; he was interesting, too. His admiration was good for her ego and she was honest enough to admit to herself that it would be good for her to have a man in her life again after the long desolate months when her faith and her work had been the only things worth living for.

'I'm up to my eyes in work just now, Bill, but perhaps you'd like to come to supper at the manse on Thursday?'

His face lit up, the auburn brows lifted and the wide mouth opened on a smile. 'Oh yes, I would Andrea. I certainly would!' he responded eagerly.

Maybe he was assuming that the meal would be just for the two of them. She must put him right about that. 'There'll be just a few of us, very informal, but I would like you to be there, Bill,' she said hurriedly. 'Half past seven. I must go now or I'll be running late all day.'

She was about to leave him and make her way back to the manse, when she experienced a strong feeling of being watched. As she turned her head to look beyond Bill to where Beck Lane merged with Church Lane she just managed to catch a glimpse of Carla Bramley making her way into Church Lane where Bill's home was situated. What was Carla up to, going to visit Bill at a time when she ought to have been at school? She ought to warn Bill. But there was no need; Bill had already seen the girl.

'What the devil is she doing here?' he said wearily. 'I thought the damn girl had come to her senses!'

'Evidently not,' Andrea said dryly. 'It looks as if you didn't put quite enough space between you when you decided to move down here.'

He sighed. 'Sorry, Andrea. About the language I mean. I'm afraid I get really uptight about the way that girl is behaving. I just don't know what to do about it. I've tried to talk sense into her but she won't listen. If her father finds out there'll be hell to pay.'

There certainly would be big trouble if David found out that his young daughter was chasing after Bill. Andrea felt a shiver of apprehension run down her spine when she recalled that the field behind the manse, the field which gave a wide view of the village from the rising ground at the topmost corner, belonged to Abbot's Fold Farm. What if David came down from Abbot's Fold to work in that field and saw his daughter looking for Bill?

'Would you like me to go after her? To have a word with her?' she found herself offering, against her better judgement.

Relief flooded his features. 'Would you really do that for me, Andrea? I know I shouldn't ask it of you because Carla's so unpredictable. She could give you an ear-roasting.'

Andrea laughed. 'It won't be anything I haven't heard before. We don't live in ivory towers because of our faith, Bill.'

'Shall I come with you? Or would you rather go alone?' he asked then.

'I'll go alone,' she decided. 'What will you do? You can't wait here in the cold.'

'There's always the church porch. I'll wait there for you. Good luck!'

She would need it, Andrea knew. Girls of Carla's age did not find it easy to listen to reason. They usually acted on blind instinct, really believing that disastrous things only happened to other people. Carla Bramley was like her father in one respect, in that she was living on a short fuse. So Andrea guessed that she could be in for a tough few minutes, and all because Dave Bramley would not give enough time, care and love to his children.

When she reached Beckside, Carla was nowhere to be seen. The beautiful old house stood back a little from the lane. Plain square stone gateposts led the way to a curving drive and a bed of winter-flowering heathers, with evergreen shrubs beyond. It was a pleasing picture, but there was no young blonde-haired girl waiting in either the garden or the porch. Perhaps Carla had gone round to the back garden to wait for Bill? Andrea decided to find out.

The large back garden was bordered by old trees. At the end of a flagged pathway was an unusual stone pagoda-style summerhouse. Honeysuckle smothered part of the front of this. Andrea set off down the path to take a closer look. It was probably locked up for the winter but she might do well to investigate whether someone was sheltering there from the icy wind. As she neared the building she noticed a robin sitting on a bird-bath close to the door. It did not move but watched her with bright eyes as she put out a hand to grasp the door knob. A moment later she was facing a red-faced scowling Carla, who greeted her with a torrent of angry words.

'Why can't you leave me alone? What have you come here for?'

'I was going to ask you that, Carla,' Andrea broke in. 'Aren't you supposed to be in school at this time?'

'I don't see what that has to do with you! I thought you were here to look after the church, not to go nosying round other people's private affairs!'

'What I'm afraid of, Carla, is that your father will find out you are here and think there's something going on between you and Bill.'

'There is,' the girl insisted. 'Only my dad isn't interested enough to notice.'

'Bill assures me that there definitely isn't anything between you, except friendship.'

'So you've been talking to Bill about me again!' Carla's voice rose hysterically. 'You're just making excuses to see

Bill by telling him you're worried about me. I know you are!'

'Don't be ridiculous, Carla,' Andrea said crisply, hanging on to her temper with a great effort.

'I'm not! It's true, I saw you talking to him just now. You stopped him as he was going to the post-box. You're always hanging around him.'

'You are quite wrong, Carla, if you think I have nothing better to do with my time than chase after Bill or any other man. I'm here to do a job. If trying to stop families from falling apart becomes part of that job I'll get involved, even though I'd much rather not do so. I don't enjoy confrontations like this, I can assure you. In fact I've had my fill of hard words from both you and your father since I came here.'

'Then you should keep away from both of us. We don't want you interfering in our lives.'

With that, Carla pushed past Andrea and ran through the back garden to take a left-hand turn at the open gate. Andrea stared after her with troubled eyes, wondering whether there was any point in racing after her. Better not to, she decided, since she was unsure where the left turn from Beckside would take her. She had been going to explore the path that led upwards via a flight of steep narrow steps to where the vast area of moorland began, but had just not found time yet to do that. Somewhere up there on the upper reaches of the moor there must be sheeptracks that would lead to Abbot's Fold. If she followed Carla in that direction she might find herself facing David Bramley again, and that was the last thing she wanted right now.

Instead she closed the door of the summerhouse and retraced her steps to the front gate. On the way she paused for a moment, attempting to calm herself before she joined Bill at her church. Dear Lord, where did I go wrong? she found herself praying. Am I getting too involved with the Bramleys and their problems? Isn't that what I'm supposed to do? How can I help them if I don't risk becoming too involved? Why don't You help me, Lord? Why don't You tell me what to do to stop this family from falling apart? Because if I don't manage to do something soon David will find out that Carla is pestering Bill. I dread to think what will happen then.

Her hands were icy cold and the piercing wind was cutting into her cheeks as she began to walk back along Church Lane, wondering as she went what she was going to say to Bill. She must not let him suspect that Carla was accusing her of wanting Bill herself. It would be too embarrassing for them both. When she reached the place where a drystone wall enclosed the churchyard on one side of the lane the first soft flakes of snow were beginning to fall, and she still had not made her mind up what to say to him.

She reached the church porch, expecting to find Bill waiting for her, but discovered it was empty. The heavy oak door of the church was open though, and from it issued the sound of music. Someone was playing the organ. Someone who was able to play a Bach toccata with skill. Slowly she moved forward, her eyes fixed on the organ screen. She was very close to it when the music stopped. A moment later Bill was standing only a few feet away from her. His face wore a rapt expression as though, still wrapped in the joy of creating music, he was unaware of her presence. She waited for him to speak.

'I do hope you don't mind, Andrea,' he began uncertainly. 'It was cold in the porch and I found the door open so I came inside to wait, and began to take a look round. When I came to the organ I just couldn't resist finding out whether or not I could still play Bach.'

Andrea smiled. 'You certainly can! We'll know where to look if our organist suddenly decides to go on strike, won't we?'

'I don't know about that! I mean, whether my playing

would be of the required standard. It's so long since I did play that I'm very unsure of myself.'

'You don't need to be. When did you learn?' she wanted to know.

'When I was quite young. My mother was a music teacher and a church organist. I used to go with her when my father was away, but I haven't played for a long time.'

'Why? Didn't you miss the music?'

'I suppose I just got out of the habit,' he said honestly. 'Both of playing the organ and going to church. There were other things to do. Things that seemed more exciting to me at the time.' He grinned at her before going on. 'Things like girls, and travel, and then ambition. Now I'm not so certain that I made the right sort of choices. In fact I'm almost certain that I didn't.'

'It isn't too late to make the right choices now, Bill, if you really want to,' she told him. The light from the north-facing window showed his expression to be uncertain.

'That's something I'd like to talk about with you, Andrea, but not yet. Not right now.'

'When you are ready, let me know,' she said quietly, not wishing to hurry him. Not even sure of what he was trying to say. 'I hope I'll be able to help you, though I'm afraid I haven't been of much help over Carla. I found her waiting for you in your summerhouse, but when I tried to talk to her she ran away.'

He shrugged, seeming with the gesture to throw aside the problem which had earlier given him cause for so much concern. 'Thanks for trying, anyway. What would I do without you?' he murmured quietly.

The softness of his tone, the gentle touch of his fingers as they brushed her cheek, warned Andrea that it was time for her to put distance between them. His words, and his touch, had begun to stir up a longing inside her that made her feel vaguely uneasy.

'I'll have to be going, Bill. I've got to drive over to Ravensdale this morning and I want to get back before the weather gets any worse,' she told him hurriedly.

'Would you like me to drive you over there?

'No, thanks. It's something I have to do alone,' she told him, moving towards the door of the church.

'I'll see you on Thursday then, if not before,' he answered as he followed closely behind her.

Andrea closed the door, wondering as she did so why it had been left unlocked the evening before. Wondering also about her sudden decision to drive to Ravensdale today. Had her decision anything to do with the unexpected emotions which had filled her when Bill spoke to her so tenderly and touched her cheek with gentle fingers?

It was too soon for her to give way to such feelings. She was here to give all of her mind to her job, and all of her heart to her faith.

Twenty-Three

By late morning, as Andrea brought her car to a halt in the car park of the Raven Falls Hotel, she found herself wondering whether she had been wise to set out on her journey on such a day. The snowflakes were whirling about her in a strengthening wind and already the car park was in a dangerously slippery condition. She would spend only a short time in the hotel, just long enough to have a bowl of soup and a sandwich before she started on her drive back to Nyddbeck.

The lounge bar was almost deserted on this day when the tourist season was long over and the weather had discouraged most of the week-day fell walkers. As on her previous visit, she was greeted by a blazing fire and a friendly welcome from the landlord.

'Have you come far?' Jeff Barclay asked her after handing her a menu.

'Too far for this sort of weather,' she told him.

'What were conditions like where you came from?'

'Not too bad when I started out from Yorkshire, but they began to deteriorate when I reached the Pennines.'

'It looks like we'll have a quiet day then, except for a few businessmen who'll have to keep their appointments.'

'I rather wish I hadn't set out, but it was a spur of the moment decision,' Andrea found herself telling him, because he was the sort of man who was easy to talk to and because she always talked too much when she was nervous. She was in a very edgy state of mind now that she was expecting the girl Beth to appear at any moment. The girl who had been Ian's lover. The girl who was the mother of Ian's child.

Jeff Barclay took her order and said they wouldn't keep her waiting long. 'You'll be anxious to be on your way before the weather gets any worse. The Ravensbridge road can be a dangerous road at the best of times,' he warned her.

She hardly needed any warning about that, after what had happened to Ian, she reflected. The landlord had gone through a door behind the bar and left her alone except for a couple of well-dressed men who were talking earnestly at one of the tables on the other side of the room. It took only five mintues for her food to arrive, brought to her by Beth.

'There you are! I'm sure you're ready for something nice and hot after driving in such awful weather,' Beth remarked.

Andrea looked into beautiful green eyes that were set in a heart-shaped face. The eyes were warm with concern, the smile that lifted the full pink mouth was friendly. She ought to hate this girl who had taken her place in Ian's life. Certainly the last time she had set eyes on Beth Barclay her mind had been full of bitterness and jealousy. That had been some weeks ago, when she had still been busy clearing out the home in Durham that held so many memories of her life with Ian. Now, to her amazement, Andrea felt no animosity towards Beth Barclay. Though she was still curious about her.

'Thank you,' she said. 'The soup smells nice.'

'It's homemade,' Beth told her. 'I hope you enjoy it.'

Andrea found she was able to enjoy both the soup and the ham sandwich before Beth returned with a cup of freshly brewed coffee and a small pot of cream.

'I really enjoyed the soup. It was delicious,' she told the younger woman. 'I don't ever seem to have time to make soup these days.'

Beth smiled. 'My father grows the vegetables and I make the soup. My mother taught me how to make it long before I went to catering college.'

'So you're a professional chef?' Andrea found she wanted to know more about the girl, much more. It might help her to understand how Ian had become involved with her.

'Yes. I had a job all arranged in a big London hotel for when I finished my college course. Only my mother died very suddenly at that time, so Dad needed me here.'

'Were you very disappointed about the London job?'

Beth nodded. 'I was at first, but it worked out for the best because I met someone here soon afterwards who became very special to me, and now we have a lovely son.'

'I think I saw him with you the last time I came here. Do you call him Jamie?'

Surprise widened Beth's eyes. 'Yes. Fancy you remembering his name!'

'It was probably because he reminded me of someone I used to know.' Andrea spoke carefully, thoughtfully, keeping her gaze fixed on the swirl of cream she was stirring slowly into her coffee.

'Was it . . . was it someone from Durham?' Beth asked the question with difficulty.

'Yes. Yes it was.' Still Andrea kept her gaze downcast.

'Jamie's father came from Durham.' The words were only just audible.

'Does he still live there?' Andrea held her breath, aware of her heart pounding and her hands beginning to tremble as she waited for the girl to answer.

'No,' the girl whispered. 'Not any more. He was killed six months ago, just a mile or so away from here.' There was a tremor in her voice that she was unable to control. 'We were going to get married next year.'

Andrea found herself reaching out a hand to comfort her. 'I'm so very sorry.' She meant it. She really was sorry that

Ian had not seen fit to tell her about his love for this girl, and for their child. If he had told her she would have released him from their marriage. Why had he not told her?

'I'll . . . I'll let you finish your coffee. You'll be wanting to be on your way.'

Beth hurried away into the back of the bar, leaving Andrea staring after her with troubled eyes. She came back as Andrea was paying for her food. With her was her baby son. Yes, the likeness to Ian was unmistakable. An aching sense of loss filled Andrea as she acknowledged that.

'Hello, Jamie,' she said, swallowing the lump that was filling her throat. The smile that dimpled the chubby baby face was all she needed to bring a rush of moisture to her eyes. Once, she herself had been the mother of a baby boy who had been the living image of this one. The living image of his father. So there was no doubt left in her mind. She must get away from here without delay. The pain of it was too much for her to bear.

'Don't bother about the change,' she muttered as she turned her back on the mother and baby.

'Are you all right? Have I upset you? If so, I'm sorry—' Beth was saying.

'I'm all right. It's just . . . I had a baby myself, once.'

Then she was outside in the car park, making her way with some difficulty to where her vehicle was waiting. Tears were pouring unchecked down her cheeks. The sooner she was away from this place the better. She ought not to have come, she told herself, as she sat behind the steering wheel trying to gain control of her feelings before she faced what was bound to be a hazardous journey back to Nyddbeck.

Yet in another way she was glad she had come to the Raven Falls Hotel, because now there was no doubt left in her mind that her marriage had been over long before Ian had been killed. His love had no longer belonged to her. It had all belonged to Beth and their baby son.

*　　*　　*

Carla's headlong dash over the moor towards her home came to an abrupt halt when one of her father's dogs caught sight of her and raced across the frozen heather to welcome her. A second collie followed the first one, and behind them came her father striding towards her at great speed with his whole body sending out vibes of fury. There was nowhere she could go to escape from him. All she could do was to stand there and stare at him defiantly.

'What the hell are you doing up here, girl?' he demanded.

'What do you think? Going back home!'

'Why? You're supposed to be in school at this time of day.'

'I didn't feel well.'

'You never said anything about that at breakfast this morning. You went off to the bus stop as usual. Why did you do that if you weren't well?'

'I was all right then.'

'What's wrong with you now?' He didn't believe her, Carla knew.

'I've got bad stomach ache.' That would do as well as any other excuse. Dad wouldn't be able to prove that she had nothing wrong with her, even if he suspected it.

David looked back over her shoulder, working out which way she had come across the moor, remembering perhaps that the sheep track his daughter had followed ended beside the long steep flight of steps which the monks of long ago had used to walk from the Abbey down to the little settlement of Nyddbeck.

'Why did you come this way if you weren't feeling well? It would have been nearer for you to come straight back up Abbot's Hill instead of up Abbot's Steps.'

She had to think fast, Carla knew, before her father guessed that her intention had been to visit Bill. 'I saw Mrs Cameron walking up Church Lane as I got off the school bus down in the village and I remembered Gran had given me a message for her about the wedding. So I went to talk to her.' It wasn't much of an excuse but it was the best she could do on the spur of the moment. Another glance at her father's glowering features told her that it had been a mistake.

'You were feeling too ill to go to school all of a sudden, but you were well enough to hang about down in the village gossiping with someone like her? If you were feeling so bad why didn't you ask her to bring you home in her car?'

That was all Carla needed to make her forget any sense of caution. 'How could I do that when every time you meet her you are rude to her? If I was her I wouldn't risk coming anywhere near our place at any price!'

Standing there like that, defying him with that same glint in her brilliant eyes that her mother used to have when she was thrashing out a problem with him, brought a stab of pain to David. If only Jill had been here still to help him cope with the girl! His mother did her best but she was far too easy on Carla. He pushed the thought away from him and set about denying what his daughter had accused him of.

'I don't know what you're talking about.'

'Of course you do! You can't resist shouting at Andrea Cameron as if she were some sort of ignorant slag, yet all she's trying to do is help us.'

'We don't need help.'

'Of course we do! She knows it, even if you don't.'

'What does she know about our sort of life? What does she know about bringing up children?'

'She's been a teacher. She told me so.'

'That doesn't mean she understands what it's like to be a parent.'

'She's been a parent too. She had a little boy, once. He died of meningitis when he was nearly three.'

Dave felt a wave of coldness wash over him which had

nothing to do with the large flakes of snow being blown across the moor.

'How do you know?' he said harshly.

'She told me!' Carla hurled the words at him as the snow battered her face.

'Oh God!'

Her father did not seem to be aware of her any more, Carla realised then. He did not even take any notice of his dogs as they raced after a hare. All he did was to stand there, utterly still, with the snow turning his black hair white. So she made her escape while the going was good.

By the time Andrea reached Nyddbeck, the lane leading to her manse was a carpet of white, with the overhanging branches of the trees around the village green and alongside the beck weighted down with their burden of snow. Underneath the wheels of her car, impacted snow made driving tricky. What would it be like when she reached the sloping drive that led to her front door and the garage? She might have to leave the car outside the gate. While this thought was still fresh in her mind she saw that a vehicle was already parked in front of the manse.

Was someone waiting for her because they needed help? She frowned as she cast her mind over the members of her two congregations who were seriously ill. Then, as she was bringing her own car to a slow and careful halt behind the parked vehicle, she caught her first glimpse of the two figures diligently shovelling the piled-up snow from the wide drive of her home. A moment later she was out of the driving seat and making her way towards them.

'Hello! How kind of you to help me . . .' her words died away as she half-recognised the boy and fully recognised his father.

'Dad said you might have to get your car out during the night if anyone was taken very ill so we ought to come down and clear the snow away.' Young Jack brushed the snowflakes from his nose and grinned at her as he spoke. 'We've nearly finished now.'

'So I see. I can't tell you how grateful I am to you. I'll go in and make you some coffee.'

The house was warm and welcoming as she went in through the front door and made her way to the kitchen at the back where she set the kettle to boil, put milk on to heat and got out mugs and a pack of chocolate biscuits for the boy. Had it really all been Dave's idea to come down and clear the snow from her drive? Or had he been prompted to do it by his mother? What did it matter, anyway? Maybe now that he had done something to help her Dave would find it easier to accept help from her. Dear God, please let it be so, she found herself praying as the steam began to emerge from the kettle. A moment later Jack was calling to tell her they had finished.

'Come through then, the coffee's ready,' she invited. Would Dave do that, she wondered, or would he say it was time they were going back to the farm?

'Our feet are in a mess,' was what he said.

'It doesn't matter, just come and have a hot drink. You've earned it,' she told him.

A moment or so later he was standing in the spacious kitchen, looking down awkwardly at his legs, which were clad in thick knee-high socks. 'I've left my boots in your porch,' was all he could say. Everything else was trapped inside him, needing to wait for the right moment. The moment when he managed to summon up enough courage.

'Where's Jack? Isn't he coming in for a drink?' Andrea asked.

Something that was almost a smile softened his bleak features. 'He'll be in shortly. He's making you a little snowman on your front lawn.'

Andrea laughed. 'That's nice of him. I'm far too tired to

make one for myself.' She poured hot water on the instant coffee and stirred it. 'Do you like milk? Or sugar?'

'Both, please.'

She placed the steaming mug on the worktop nearest to him. Frozen snow was melting from the front of his hair and dripping on to his shoulders, so she handed him a towel. 'You'd better dry your hair,' she suggested.

He was staring at her from only a pace or two away, the towel gripped in his fist. There was an expression in his eyes that she was unable to fathom. She waited for him to speak, aware all of a sudden that this was what he needed to do.

'I owe you an apology.' The words came out with a rush.

'Do you?' What was he going to apologise for, his rudeness to her on her last visit to his farm or the incident in the porch when he had so spontaneously embraced her because she reminded him so strongly of his late wife?

He sighed. 'I suppose I owe you several if it comes to that.'

She nodded. 'I do seem to have an adverse effect on your temper,' she admitted wryly. 'I wish I knew why.'

'I just wish I knew what to say to you, how to explain. Only I don't really know myself why I tend to be so unpleasant to you. The last time, when you ran away from me up on to the moor, what I said to you was inexcusable. Absolutely uncalled for. I spoke like a bloody idiot.' Hot colour crept down from his face into his neck. He sighed. 'There I go again! I beg your pardon, Mrs Cameron.'

She bit the inside of her lip to stop herself from chuckling. 'I have heard worse, and at least you were speaking out of turn to yourself this time.'

'All the same—'

'Forget it, please! Here comes Jack.'

The boy burst into the house with a great stamping of feet and shaking off of snowflakes.

'Leave your boots in the porch, lad,' his father ordered.

Then Jack was standing in the doorway of the kitchen, beaming at the sight of the chocolate biscuits and looking extraordinarily like his father. Or like his father must have looked when he was a carefree boy, Andrea decided.

'I've made you a snowman,' he announced. 'Just a small one because there isn't an awful lot of snow yet.'

'That's very good of you, because I don't think I'll have time to make one myself,' Andrea said, as she passed the biscuits to him and went to make him coffee.

'Did you make one last year?' he wanted to know.

'No. It's quite a long time since I made a snowman.'

'How long?' he asked as he bit joyfully into a chocolate biscuit.

How long? Five years, the last winter of Andrew's life. Andrew had been wearing a bright red padded jacket and a red and white woolly cap knitted by Ian's mother. His chubby cheeks had been bright red too, just like Jack's were.

She gulped away the lump in her throat. 'Five years.'

'You'll have forgotten how to make one after all that time,' Jack said, looking longingly at the biscuits.

'Have another biscuit, Jack.' Andrea turned away to stare out of the window at the dazzling whiteness of the sloping meadow which began where her garden wall ended. She was aware of the man watching her intently from across the room, the man who had told her in his anger that she did not know what it was like to be a parent. All she wanted now was for him to go, and to take the boy with him so that she could be alone with her memories of that other boy for whom she had made the snowman. Surely he would go soon? He must have things to do. There was a fox moving stealthily up the meadow alongside the drystone wall. She kept her eyes glued to it and her shoulders tensed as she waited for David and his son to leave.

'You'll never know how sorry I am,' David murmured from immediately behind her. 'I had no idea, when I said

237

those things to you. Will you forgive me, even if I don't deserve it?'

She nodded, but could not speak.

'Come on, Jack, it's time we went home. Mrs Cameron has things to do.' The boy ran out into the hall ahead of him. David turned back to speak again. 'Will you be coming to see Mother on Thursday?'

Andrea took a deep breath. 'Yes, I probably will.'

He smiled. 'I might see you then. Goodbye!'

'Goodbye, David.'

She listened as the Land Rover engine roared into life, taking the man and the boy back to their home on the snowbound moor. All was quiet then and she was alone with her memories. The memories sent her into the big living room to pick up the photograph her father had taken of Ian and herself with Andrew during their last holiday together in Scotland. As she stared down at it she was struck again by the strong likeness Andrew showed to Ian, and also to Jamie Barclay.

Then a new thought came leaping into her mind. A thought she found profoundly disturbing, yet one which had to be faced. The loss of her only grandchild had brought great sorrow to Ian's mother. Ought she to disclose the fact to Nancy that she now had this other small grandson? It was something she would have to give a great deal of thought to, and a great deal of prayer, too.

The prayer must begin at once, because in less than a month Nancy would be arriving to stay with her for Christmas. Only after the prayer would she feel able to reach a decision that could have such far-reaching consequences both for Nancy Cameron and for Beth Barclay and her baby son.

Twenty-Four

A s she drove up the long steep incline of Abbot's Hill on Thursday morning Andrea saw that there were still a few small patches of frozen snow lingering beneath the drystone walls which enclosed the road on both sides. This would be her last visit to the farm before the wedding and they were to discuss final details of the service. She wondered whether by now David had agreed to accept the help of Ben's housekeeper, Mrs Grainger.

When she parked her car in the lane beyond the farm gate and looked into the yard there was no sign of the Land Rover. So David would have already left for the cattle market at Nyddford. How beautiful was the picture made by the old grey stone farmhouse set against the towering fell on this December day, when the pale greens and silvery greys of the landscape seemed to sparkle in the bright light that streamed down from a cloudless pale blue sky. It was a day to give thanks for all the good things about her life here. All the things that were still here for her in spite of all that she had lost. Her friendship with Dorothy Bramley was one of those blessings.

Dorothy was coming out of the house now to greet her, looking well and happy in her bright rose-coloured sweater and dark grey slacks. 'Hello, my dear! Isn't it a lovely morning?'

'Yes. It feels good to be alive!' Andrea drank in deep breaths of the bracing moorland air as she went with the older woman across the yard to the back door of the farmhouse. As she did so she caught sight of the board hanging over the wall close to Jacob's Cottage. 'I see you're advertising your cottage for rent now that Bill's moved out.'

'I don't suppose we'll get any takers until nearer spring,' Dorothy told her. 'The people who like to come and spend Christmas around here will have booked their properties long ago. So, if you find yourself with more guests for Christmas than you have room for in the manse you're welcome to send them up here. As my guests, of course,' she added quickly.

'That's very kind of you, Dorothy, but I think there'll only be Ian's mother staying with me. My own mum and dad will be on duty over Christmas. I might ask Julie Craven if she'd like to join us for part of the time if she isn't working. She's coming for a meal tonight.'

'Julie will appreciate that, with her parents being so far away. She doesn't seem to have anyone really close to her now, and I know she still misses having Jill here. I do wish she could meet someone really nice and settle down,' Dorothy added wistfully.

Andrea smiled as they went into the farmhouse kitchen. Perhaps Julie Craven had met someone she fancied in Bill Wyndham? Though of course it took two to make a couple and she had a feeling that Bill was not the one to complete that partnership. She would see how things went at her party tonight.

'I've sometimes wondered whether she had her sights set on Bill,' Dorothy said, as though reading her thoughts. 'She's spoken to him often enough during his time here, but I've an idea he's had some sort of bad experience which has put him off marriage. Or what are known as relationships these days,' she added with a smile.

Andrea opened up her briefcase, wanting now to leave behind the discussion of other people's partnerships and concentrate on the one which would soon involve her in conducting her first marriage service at Nyddbeck Church. As soon as Ben arrived, there were hymns to be chosen, and organ music to be decided on without delay, so that she could give a list of their requirements to the organist. She took out a copy of *Songs of Praise*, trying to guess whether Dorothy and Ben would go for the traditional hymns or for something much newer and livelier.

An hour or so later it had all been done, with a fair amount of laughter and some more serious comment, and Dorothy was handing round mugs of coffee. Andrea raised hers to toast this couple who, while not in the first flush of youth, were showing obvious signs of their love for each other.

'There won't be any need for me to give you two the usual pep-talk that I give most young engaged couples, will there?' she asked with a laugh in her voice. 'You've both got plenty of experience behind you.'

'Yes, we both know what it's like to stick together for better or worse,' Ben said with an unexpected air of sadness about his handsome face. 'I fell in love with Dorothy very soon after she came here, but she chose Jacob then instead of me, and I remained faithful to my wife to the end of her days.'

Their glance met across the kitchen table. 'My last two years with Jacob were not easy, but it was in "sickness and health" as far as I was concerned, and Jacob was a very good man,' Dave's mother said quietly. 'I was lucky too, because Jill was a great help to us both, and David did everything he could for us.'

'Now it's a fresh start for us both, and you'll be the one to tie the knot for us, Andrea.' Ben beamed at her as he said that.

'I'm really looking forward to it.' Andrea got to her feet. 'Now, how can I help you today, Dorothy? Is it cooking, or housework?'

Dorothy had a surprise for her. 'It's neither, my dear. I've been feeling so well this last few days that I've got well ahead with the cooking, and Mrs Grainger is coming tomorrow to help with the housework. We are all going out to lunch today to celebrate your birthday.'

Andrea was startled. 'How did you know?'

'That would be telling!' Ben chuckled 'Get your coat on, it's time we were going.'

As they drove away from the farm to the country hotel where Ben had booked a table for lunch Andrea found herself wondering whether David would be surprised when he came back from his day at the cattle market to find that she had already left. Would he even remember that he had asked her if she would be going to the farm today?

When she arrived back at the manse in the middle of the afternoon, Andrea set about putting the finishing touches to the party food for that evening, washing salad, dicing melon to mix with prawns, whipping cream and setting the dining-room table to seat five. As well as Julie Craven and Bill Wyndham she had also invited Rob and Jan Scott to her supper party. Rob, formerly an accountant, had trained with her at college and was now a Methodist minister for three churches further up the dale. When everything had been done that could be done she decided to put her feet up on the sofa and enjoy a few minutes of relaxation with a cup of tea while she listened to some music.

It was a luxury to just leave everything and concentrate only on herself at this time of day, but her guess that it wouldn't last long proved to be correct. Her caller was Ian's mother, ringing from the antique gallery to wish her a happy birthday.

'I thought I'd ring you now instead of waiting until I get back home in case you're going out somewhere to celebrate,' Nancy said.

'I've already been out celebrating. I had lunch at a nice hotel with a couple whose wedding is to be at my church on

New Year's Eve,' Andrea told her. 'And a few people are coming for supper tonight.'

'My dear, I've been thinking about you such a lot. I know you can't put the clock back, but it does seem so unfair to me that you have to celebrate your birthday with strangers when you ought to have had Ian with you today. I hope I haven't upset you by saying that?' Nancy added hastily.

'No. We can't pretend that what has happened never did happen, Nancy. I've accepted it, and I'm coming to terms with it. The people who are coming tonight really have become friends, and I'm finding my work here very satisfying even if it isn't always quite what I expected.'

'It would have been so much easier for you if you'd still had Andrew.' Nancy's voice broke as she spoke of her adored little grandson. 'I don't know how you can still believe in God now. I don't think I'll ever be able to come to terms with going to church again after losing my only son and my only grandson. Life has been too cruel to me for me to be able to go on believing.'

There was a pause while Ian's mother struggled to gain control of herself. During that long moment of silence Andrea found she could not get her mind off the words Nancy had just uttered. 'My only grandson' she had said. But Andrew had not been her only grandson because there was now that other adorable little boy. The boy called Jamie Barclay, who should really have been called Jamie Cameron.

'Are you still there, Andrea? Forgive me, dear, please. I meant to cheer you up, to just say have a happy day, and now I've spoilt it all. I'm so sorry, but I do worry so much about you.'

'Please don't, Nancy,' Andrea begged. 'I really am able to cope, and I really do have some lovely people here to help me. You'll see for yourself when you come for Christmas. It won't be long now!'

'I'm looking forward to seeing you then. Enjoy your

birthday party. I hope the sweater I sent arrived safely and fits you.' Nancy sounded slightly more cheerful.

'It does. It's perfect! I was going to ring you tonight to thank you for it. I'll ring you on Monday next week to find out what time you'll be arriving.'

In the silence that followed Nancy's call Andrea found that she could not forget the despairing words the older woman had uttered. Nor could she banish from her mind the image of little Jamie Barclay. Should she find a way of revealing the truth to Nancy? Or ought she to pretend he did not exist; that Ian had been faithful to her and that there was no fatherless wee boy living in a country hotel with his mother and grandfather? If only she knew for certain what would be the best for everyone concerned: for Beth Barclay and her father, and for Nancy Cameron – most of all for Jamie.

The only way she could be absolutely sure of what she ought to do would be to spend a great deal of time in prayer. To ask for guidance. To ask and then listen for the answer, and when the answer came to act on it. That could be one of the most difficult things she had ever had to do, but do it she must. She would make a start on the prayer right now in the solitude of her study.

In his new home at Beckside, Bill found himself spending more time on his appearance than he had done since coming to live in North Yorkshire. Tonight he put on a well-cut charcoal-grey suit and a peacock-blue shirt with a colourful silk tie. Surveying himself in the hall mirror when it was time to set off for the short walk to the manse he grinned at his reflection, telling himself that he was acting like a lad in his teens going on a first date.

Yet it was important that he should get it right, because Andrea would have other guests there tonight and he did not want to let her down. After all, this was the first time he would be in her home as an invited guest, as a friend.

He was quite determined it would not be the last. His mind was full of the woman. In spite of the times he had tried to convince himself that she was not for him, Andrea Cameron had become an obsession. Sleeping or waking, she dominated his thoughts.

He saw Andrea's face beside his own in every mirror, he heard her voice breaking into every music session he enjoyed. Now he had stopped trying to fight against his feeling for her. All his energy was given instead to devising ways in which he could encounter her by accident so that he could learn more about her. Especially so that he could discover whether she was getting over the death of her husband. Perhaps the party tonight would provide him with a clue? If the time seemed right it would not be long before he invited her to share dinner with him, just the two of them, but he must be careful not to rush things. Already she had changed his whole world, altered his outlook on life in a way he had never expected.

Julie was the first to arrive at the manse. She had come twenty minutes early because she wanted to be there to help Andrea with any last minute tasks, she explained, when Andrea opened the front door and welcomed her.

'It looks like you've had a special delivery,' she said then, as she bent down to pick up a sheaf of tall, red spray carnations which had been left in the porch.

'I wonder who brought those?' Andrea saw that the flowers were not beribboned and gift wrapped in an expensive style but simply presented in floral paper. There was no card to give a clue to the donor. 'They're lovely!' she exclaimed.

'There was a Land Rover turning round in front of your drive as I came along the lane,' Julie told her. 'I'm not certain, but the driver looked a bit like Dave Bramley.'

'Oh! I wonder if Dorothy asked him to deliver them for her?'

'I wonder! They don't look much like her style though.

Dorothy is an expert flower arranger; these have a man's touch about them. How intriguing!' Julie finished dryly.

'Come inside out of the cold and have something to warm you,' Andrea broke in hastily.

The flowers were put into a vase without any further comment, but Andrea found herself giving them a puzzled glance several times during what turned out to be a very pleasant evening. The Scotts were both extroverts, and extremely entertaining with their talk of camping trips to far-away places and the trials of coping with three churches where the congregations were so different.

Bill was a great deal more reserved. He spoke briefly about the work for which he was already quite well known, not just in Yorkshire, but in some of the London galleries. They listened as he told them of favourite places which he loved to capture in oil or watercolours and which sold very well to visiting tourists.

'Do you have a studio where they can watch you at work?' Rob Scott wanted to know.

'I used to have, when I lived in York. I might open one in my new home here once I'm settled in properly,' Bill answered.

Julie had her own contribution to make towards the end of the evening when she told them about leaving the hospital where she had worked as a senior nurse for some years and taking a job as practice nurse at one of the village health centres.

'It'll be quite a big change for you, won't it?' Bill said thoughtfully. 'There's always so much activity, so much drama, around hospitals. Life in a rural health centre will probably be much quieter. Is that what you want, Julie? Is that the reason you're making the change?'

Bill sounded really interested, Andrea thought, watching Julie's face light up as she answered. 'In a way, I suppose it is. I want to be part of a small community like this; to put down roots. I want to settle down and maybe buy a home here. Do you understand what I mean?'

She spoke to them all, but it was on Bill's face that her glance lingered longest. So she was making her play for Bill, letting him know that it was up to him now to move on a step from their casual friendship. Andrea wondered whether he would take up her invitation. It would be interesting to see. When the evening was coming to an end and her guests were departing she found herself listening to what was said between them, but all Bill said to Julie was, 'Goodnight, Julie. It's been good to see you again.'

The Scotts had already left when Julie drove away from the manse. Only Bill remained to voice his thanks and his appreciation before he walked home to Beckside. In the front porch, with frost sharpening the air about them, he held out a hand. Andrea put her own slim fingers into it to be held firmly, and retained.

'Have you really enjoyed your birthday, Andrea?' he wanted to know. 'You haven't just been pretending, have you?'

She smiled radiantly as she replied. 'No, I haven't been pretending, Bill. I've really enjoyed myself very much. More than I expected to, in fact.' At the start of the evening she had felt burdened by the knowledge that she would have to come to a decision very soon about whether to tell Nancy about Jamie Barclay. Her first session of prayer, intense as it had been, had not brought her the answer she was seeking. She would have to go back to it, maybe many times. Yet as the hours had flown by her burden had lifted, and even been forgotten for a time, in the cheerful company of her friends.

'Does that mean that you are no longer as unhappy as you were a few months ago?' Bill wanted to know.

She nodded. 'Yes, I think it does.'

His hazel eyes were intent on her own. He was still holding

her hand. She did not attempt to withdraw it, because their friendship seemed to have progressed during the hours that had flown so swiftly that it was already midnight. It was good to share that warm handclasp with Bill. So absolutely right.

'Are you still glad you came to live and work here?' he asked then.

'Oh yes. Very glad.'

'You're not thinking of moving on because of what happened to you here?'

Andrea took her time about answering, wondering why he should put such a question to her. 'No. I'll be staying to get on with the job I came here to do.'

'So you haven't lost your faith?'

'Did you think I might?'

'I wondered about it. Because of what happened to Dave Bramley, I suppose. It isn't easy to hang on to everything you once believed in when your life goes badly wrong.'

Andrea frowned. 'Are you speaking from personal experience, Bill?'

'Not the same sort of experience as Dave, but certainly a testing time.'

'Have you come through it now? Or are you still struggling with it?'

It did not take him long to answer. 'You've helped me to come through it, Andrea. Don't you know that yet?'

She was conscious then that it would be wise for her to withdraw her hand. Yet she did not want to do that. She wanted to keep him close to her. She wanted to know more about him. Especially she wanted to know what she had helped him to come through.

'There's a lot I don't know about you, Bill,' she said quietly. 'So I'm not really sure how I can have helped you. I don't seem to have been able to do the only thing you asked me to do.'

'You'll have plenty of time to find out all you want to

248

know, because I won't be going away from here again. Not permanently anyway. Everything I've always wanted in my life is here. Including you, Andrea.'

With that he lifted her hand to his lips and kissed it. Then he walked away from her, striding at speed away from the manse and over the bridge, through the moonlit village until he came to the start of Church Lane and disappeared from her view. Not from her mind though. In her mind he was still there, a tall, muscular, bronze-haired man of immense interest to her. A man she wanted to know much better. A man who had just put the thought into her mind that her days of darkness and despair could soon be ending.

Twenty-Five

It was a long time before Andrea managed to get to sleep that night, as her thoughts ranged over the evening and the way she had suddenly seemed to be drawn to Bill. It was bewildering because, just a short time ago, she had thought she was attracted to David Bramley. She guessed now that it had been the feel of David's arms holding her close which had brought to life in her a longing to share love with someone. That someone must not be David, who needed a wife who would accept that the farm came first. For her, the Church would always come first. So she must take her time about falling in love, even with someone as wonderful as Bill. It was going to be so hard, taking her time about falling in love with Bill, because she could not erase from her mind the way their hands had met in the long clasp that was more like an embrace. She had waited for Bill to kiss her then, had longed for him to kiss her. Perhaps it was too late and she was already in love with him?

As she brushed those thoughts away, she was faced with what she had pushed aside during her supper party, the question of whether she ought to tell Nancy Cameron that she had a grandson called Jamie, whose existence had been kept a secret from her. Every time that particular worry returned to her she went back to praying about it. The praying did not get any easier for her in her tired, confused state of mind yet she would not give up. There had to be an answer to her prayer. She must be patient and wait until that answer was revealed to her.

When morning came the vase of red spray carnations had filled her living room with their fragrance. They were a reminder that she ought to be thanking someone for sending them. Could the sender have been Dorothy Bramley? There was only one way to find out. She went to the phone and rang Dorothy.

'No, my dear, your flowers were not from me,' Dorothy answered. 'What made you think they were?'

'Julie found them in the porch when she arrived, and she said she had seen a Land Rover being driven away by someone who looked rather like your David.'

The older woman chuckled. 'Perhaps they were from David. Maybe it was easier to say it with flowers.'

Amazement kept Andrea silent for some time. Dave coming down to clear the snow from her drive, and to apologise for his extremely bad behaviour, had been something of a shock to her, but Dave coming down to the manse to bring her flowers was really hard to believe. 'How did he know it was my birthday?' she managed to ask at last.

'I suppose I must have mentioned that we were taking you out to lunch,' Dorothy responded. Quite evidently she was not so surprised by her son's out-of-character behaviour. 'Did you enjoy your supper party?'

'Oh yes! Bill came, and Julie, and Robert and Jan Scott. We talked until almost midnight. Did you know that Julie is leaving the hospital?'

'She told me she was hoping to change her job, and would tell me more if it came off.'

'I don't suppose she'll mind me telling you then that she's coming to the village health centre as a practice nurse.'

'That'll mean a change of home for her as well as a change of work. Her present flat is near the hospital but she'll need to be closer to this area now. I wonder if she'd like to use Jacob's Cottage for a time, until she finds something else? I'd much rather she used it than the place stood empty. Julie has always been a favourite of mine.' Dorothy paused for breath, then went on. 'Carla and Jack are very fond of her too. I had hopes, at one time, that David might be drawn to her in time, but it worked the other way. He just couldn't stand the sight of her because he thought she had encouraged Jill to go back to nursing when he wanted her to be at home with him in the evenings. After Jill was killed he just wouldn't speak to her when she came to the farm to see me and the children.'

'How is Carla? I know Jack's fine because he came down with Dave and cleared the snow from my drive, and also made me a lovely little snowman.' Andrea was glad to change the subject as it so obviously upset Dorothy to discuss her son's unreasonable behaviour.

Dorothy sighed. 'I don't think Carla's fine these days. The sparks fly every time she and David are in the house at the same time. She's seems to be permanently in a black mood. I don't know what will happen when I'm not here to try and keep the peace between them.'

'I expect it will all sort itself out,' Andrea said with a confidence she could not feel.

'I wish I could be sure of that. I thought having Mrs Grainger come down to help was a good idea but now David says he can't afford her. Oh, there's something else I ought to mention at once, Andrea. We might have problems with the music for the wedding.'

'Why? I thought we worked all that out yesterday?'

'We did, but then I heard last night that Brendon May had fallen on the ice at the beginning of the week and broken his wrist. So what are we going to do?'

'That's bad news, for us as well as for him. Can you think of anyone else who might be able to help, Dorothy?'

'Not at such short notice. With so many services at this time of the year the organists get very booked up.'

'I'll ask my Methodist minister friend if he knows of anyone in his area who might be prepared to come here. In fact I'll do that right away and let you know what happens,' Andrea promised.

She was unable to contact Robert Scott immediately, and in any case was not too hopeful that he would be able to suggest anyone to help at this late date. It was as she walked through the village to the post-box that she remembered how she had heard Bill playing the organ while he waited for her. As soon as she had posted her letters she turned into Church Lane. A couple of minutes later she was ringing the doorbell at Beckside and waiting for Bill to answer it.

'Andrea! I was about to ring you to thank you for the great time I had last night. Come in!'

Bill was obviously pleased to see her, but would he be as pleased when she explained why she had come? Andrea followed him through a spacious hall and into a room which looked out over the back garden. She could see from the window the summerhouse where she had found Carla hiding. Was she still bothering him, she wondered?

'What brings you here, Andrea?' he asked. 'Not that I'm not very happy to see you, I certainly am, but I can guess how busy you must be these days with Christmas so close.'

She turned to face him. 'You might not be so happy to see me when you hear why I've come.'

The slight frown that came to his high forehead drew the bronze-haired eyebrows closer. A beam of brilliant winter sunshine pouring through the window brought a glow to his thick auburn hair. His face was long and lean. It was an interesting face, but Andrea knew she must not allow herself to dwell on it for too long. She was here to ask a favour of him.

'It's not problems with Carla again, is it? You were saying last night that you had been to the farm yesterday to talk to Dorothy and Ben about their wedding service. Did something come up then that I ought to know about?'

'Oh no! It's nothing like that. It's a problem about the

music for the service. Dorothy has just heard that Brendon May, who was to have played the organ for their wedding, fell on the ice at the beginning of this week and broke his wrist. So I wondered if you would be willing to help out, Bill?'

'You mean with the music? With playing the organ? Do you really think I'm good enough for that when I'm so out of practice?' Plainly, Bill was taken aback by her suggestion.

'Yes, I do, Bill, and I'd be so grateful if you would at least consider it because the chance of us getting any of the local organists to play on New Year's Eve at this late stage is almost nil. The ones that are any good will all have been booked up ages ago. Please say you'll help!'

There was a long moment of silence, during which Andrea watched uncertainty flicker across his face. All at once she became aware that her request, if granted, could bring problems for Bill, and maybe for herself. It was too late to change her mind now though.

'If I agree, it will mean me having to fit in quite a lot of practice. Will I be able to do that? It will mean being in the church for a time almost every day.' He still sounded dubious.

'I don't see any problem there, if you are willing to take it on.'

'Can I give you my answer tonight, when I've put in some practice? It's quite a long time, you know, since I played.'

'You were playing well enough the other morning when I heard you. When you were in the church waiting for me,' she reminded him. 'You were playing Bach, I think.'

'The Bach was probably the only piece I could remember without music. I'll need to look out some music. It's all still in boxes waiting to be unpacked, along with most of my books.'

'Thanks for offering, anyway,' she said as she made for the door.

'I didn't offer, you twisted my arm,' he reminded her with

a grin that wiped away the frown and made him look much younger. 'When you hear me play again you might regret doing that.'

'We'll see! I must be going. I'm on my way to the church right now.'

'I was hoping you'd stay for coffee.'

'Sorry, I can't, Bill. Some other time.'

She gave him a smile that made him forget that there were other things he had been going to do this morning instead of searching out music scores from the boxes of books which still waited to be unpacked. He held out a hand to her, but already she was hurrying out of the house and into the garden, pulling up the big collar of her fleece jacket to keep out the biting wind. Because the collar was so large and was pulled up so close to her eyes she missed seeing the girl who came down the Abbot's Steps, caught sight of her leaving Beckside, and waited in the shelter of a gorse bush until it was safe for her to walk confidently through the gates of Beckside and round to the back of the house.

As she entered the church she had already come to love, Andrea felt that surely here in this special place she would receive the guidance she needed so badly. Walking slowly towards the Communion table, she lifted her eyes to the plain oak cross above, and from there moved her glance up to the stained-glass window through which bright morning light illuminated the figure of her Lord. Children were grouped about His feet, looking up at Him with questioning eyes. 'Suffer the little children' said the text beneath.

For several long moments she kept all her concentration on that text. Then she began to pray about a small boy called Jamie, and the heartbroken grandmother who did not know of his existence. First she found herself using the words of the old psalms she had grown up with in her parents' Scottish church, then she used words from the present day. Words which had brought her comfort in her days of deepest shock and distress. Words which had brought her strength when her future seemed without hope. There must be hope for the wee boy who had lost his father, and for the woman who had lost both her son and her grandson. She knew that there would be hope if she was brave enough to take the right action.

All at once then she knew that she had found the answer to her prayers, knew that she must go back to the Raven Falls Hotel and talk to Beth Barclay. She would not be able to rest until she had done that. The decision made, a great sense of peace took possession of her. Her prayers then were of thanksgiving.

Bill was on his knees in the utility room using a knife to open up one of the stout cardboard cartons, inside which he hoped to find the music he needed if he was to become proficient enough within the next few days to play at the marriage service. Dorothy had shown him so much kindness during the time he had lived in her cottage he felt she deserved only the best from him on her special day. When Andrea had come to his home so unexpectedly and asked him to help his first reaction had been that he would not be able to do it. Then the pleading look in her wonderful eyes had banished all his doubts. He would play the organ at this wedding, and play it well.

So immersed was Bill in sorting the music that he was startled by the tapping that sounded on the window of the small room. A glance through the glass sent his spirits spiralling downwards. He shook his head at the young girl who was smiling at him. Was she never going to give up?

'What are you doing here? Shouldn't you be in school?' he said sharply, as he flung the window wide so he could speak to Carla without having to admit her to the house.

'No! It's Christmas holidays now, so I thought I'd come

and see you. Aren't you going to ask me in? I'm frozen out here,' the girl added plaintively.

'No, I'm not. I have work to do. Shouldn't you be helping your grandmother, Carla? She must be very busy just now with the wedding so near.'

'I hate being up there! That's why I've come down here.'

'Don't be silly, Carla. You've got a good home and you know it.'

'You don't know what you're talking about, Bill. My dad hates me.'

'Rubbish! Of course he doesn't hate you, just because he has to tick you off sometimes.'

'He does! We're always having rows. That's why I'll be leaving soon.'

A quiver of uneasiness descended on Bill. 'Where are you planning on going?' he asked. 'Away to college?'

'No, Dad wouldn't let me do that. I'm just going away, as soon as Gran has left. I'm not staying on at the farm without her.'

Now Bill was feeling seriously alarmed. 'I hope you're not thinking of doing anything stupid, Carla, because your gran, and your father, have had enough trouble without you adding to it.'

'You'll have to wait and see, won't you? I really wanted to come and live with you. I could help you with your work, I could cook for you. I know I could!'

'I don't need anyone to help me, Carla. Now be a good girl and go home. It's not the weather for hanging about in gardens.'

'Are you really not going to let me come in? Not even for a coffee?'

'No, I really am not! I've got to go out right now, so there's no point in you staying.' As he told her that, Bill slammed the window shut and turned his back on her. The sooner she found herself a boyfriend her own age the better.

She was a bloody nuisance. There she was, on the other side of the double-glazed window, still staring at him with wide, reproachful eyes as the icy wind whipped her long blonde hair about her chilled white face. Waiting no doubt for him to change his mind and ask her in. The girl was a disaster area. She was trouble waiting to happen. For someone, but not for him. He would put distance between them right now. Gathering up the entire pile of music scores in his arms, he strode out of the house and hurried at speed in the direction of the church. His first session at the organ would start right now, providing the church was open.

Andrea was turning slowly away from the altar as he came in. Her face wore a look of such radiance that he stood, transfixed, just inside the door. She did not seem to be aware of him even when she was walking towards him. The rapt expression was still there in her eyes when they met. A wave of emotion engulfed him. All thoughts left him except for the one thought that had total possession of him. It was the sure and certain knowledge that here at last was the only woman he wanted to spend the rest of his life with.

'Hello again,' she said quietly, as though she had only just seen him.

It took some time for him to conquer his longing to fling aside the pile of music and take her into his arms. The intensity of that longing shook him to the core. Words that he might have uttered, words that he longed to speak out loud, must remain inside him. All he could say to her was, 'I didn't realise you were here. I came to start practising.'

He knew that he must sound like an immature boy, very unsure of himself. It was the way he felt, right now. The immensity of his love for her had robbed him of his usual self-confidence. All he could do was stand there waiting for her to say something to him.

'So you're going to help! I'm so glad, Bill.'

'I'm going to try. I might not be good enough. You'll have to be the judge.'

'Are you always so modest?' She laughed, and the sound was like music as it echoed about the little church.

'I'm just afraid of letting you down. Of having people criticise you for asking me to play, if I don't get it right.'

Her face grew serious then. 'I have faith in you, Bill. I know you'll get it right. Will you bring the church key back to the manse when you've finished, please? We have to keep it locked when there's no one around. I don't like doing that, but we've had the occasional wino in, leaving broken glass behind. Then last week someone left a dog here, a nice cross-bred retriever-collie.'

'What happened to it?'

'It's still in the police kennels at Nyddford, but only for another couple of days if someone doesn't claim it by then. I was tempted to offer to have it myself, but I'm going up to my parents in Scotland on New Year's Day and it doesn't seem right to take it in then put it back into kennels for another week. The poor thing would be bewildered.'

'Would it help if I took it in?' he found himself asking. 'I was wondering about having a dog.'

'Won't you be going away for Christmas yourself?'

'No. I'll be here.'

'You could go to the kennels and introduce yourself. See how you get on with him. He hadn't been claimed up to yesterday. Why do people do such things? A dog asks for so little; it's unconditional love as far as they are concerned.'

'The best kind of love. Only you don't often find it, do you?' Bill said gravely.

Andrea's face took on radiance again as she answered. 'You can find it in places like this. It's here for anyone who is willing to take it on board. It isn't an easy thing to take on, though. I can't imagine my own life without that unconditional love. It means everything to me.'

Was that love enough for her now? Or was there room in her life for his own love? He had a burning need to know, but he knew it was too soon to ask her.

'I must go,' she was saying. 'Something urgent has come up. I have to deal with it today, and that means a forty-mile journey each way.'

'I'll let you know how I get on about the dog.'

'I'll be back by early evening because there's a meeting in the manse at seven.'

The heavy door closed behind her. Bill was alone then, with his mind full of questions about his own life and hers. The most important question, the one that he could find no answer for yet, was whether he could come to terms with the fact that he would need to share Andrea's strong faith if he was to gain her love. It was not that he did not believe. Perhaps it was just that he was as out of practice with faith as he was with playing the organ?

With that thought bringing a faint smile to his firm lips, he sat down at the instrument, opened one of the Handel scores, and sent the glorious sound of the 'Hallelujah Chorus' soaring upwards.

Twenty-Six

T he sight and scent of the red carnations when she got back to the manse reminded Andrea that she ought to thank David Bramley for them, since it seemed that both his mother and Julie Craven thought they had come from him. It would also give her the chance to ask him if he was going to escort his mother to meet her bridegroom at the altar. Dorothy had told her that David had not yet made his mind up whether he could do that.

'Could I speak to David, please,' she asked when Dorothy answered the phone. 'If he did send me these lovely flowers I must thank him.'

'I don't think there can be any doubt that David did send them. As they were not for me, I can't think who else they could have been bought for,' Dorothy told her with a chuckle. 'David was never really one for the girls, until he met up with Julie and Jill, and as you know he's not been at his most sociable since Jill died. It's good to see him coming to life again. I've been so worried about him, and scaring myself to death at times with wondering what will happen when I'm not here. I'll be very glad if Julie decides to take Jacob's Cottage. I know she'll keep an eye on things for me.' Pausing for breath, Dorothy added, 'David has just come in for his coffee break so I'll hand you over to him.'

Andrea waited, wondering what she would say if it turned out that the carnations were not from David after all. She would have to think of something.

He came straight to the point. 'Hello! Is it to do with the wedding?'

'Well, I was wondering if you had made your mind up yet about walking down the aisle with your mother?'

'She seems to have made her mind up that it will spoil her day if I don't, but I really don't want to do it, for obvious reasons.'

'She's come through a bad time, and now she has the chance to make a fresh start with Ben, so she wants you there with her.'

'I don't know what I'm going to do without her.'

'You'll manage, when you have to.'

'Will I? I wish I could be so certain.'

'You have to find a way, for your children's sake. At least you've got them.'

There was a long silence as her words hung between them, words which reminded him that for her there had been no such comfort.

He sighed deeply. 'Yes, at least I've got them. I'm very sorry I spoke out of turn to you that day, Andrea. I just didn't know, then, about your child—'

'Thank you for the lovely flowers,' she broke in. 'Was it you who left them for me?'

'Yes. I wasn't brave enough to face you with my apology.'

'Shall we forget about it? I have to go now, but I do hope I'll see you at the wedding.'

What would David's reaction be if Julie Craven decided to move into Jacob's Cottage, she found herself wondering as she drove out of the village and headed for the main road that would in forty or so miles bring her to Ravensbridge. Would there be open hostility between them? Or would David begin to appreciate that Julie was someone who had been a good friend to his wife, and also to his mother?

By the time she reached the Ravensbridge road these

thoughts had been left behind with the miles and her mind was racing ahead to her imminent encounter with Beth Barclay. She did not question any more whether she was doing the right thing in making this journey to see Ian's lover and her child. A feeling of certainly about this had come to her as an answer to her prayers. It was right that she should ask Beth if Ian's grieving mother could at least see her grandson. It was also necessary to her that she should make sure that Beth and her baby were not in any financial need. So far she had not been able to find out whether Ian had made any provision for them before his death.

Yet even with the certainty so strong inside her that she was doing the right thing, when she was at last walking towards the entrance to the Raven Falls Hotel she felt her hands beginning to tremble. She sent up yet another silent prayer that she would handle this meeting wisely. So much depended on that. At the last minute, when she entered the lounge bar and caught sight of Beth, she felt a strong compulsion to turn round and run away. To run back to her car and drive home to Nyddbeck, putting out of her mind and her life this girl who had loved Ian and given birth to his child.

'Hello, it's nice to see you again.' Beth greeted her with a smile as she reached the bar.

'How are you?' was all Andrea could find to say.

'Fine, thanks, and busy getting ready for Christmas. What can I get for you?'

'Oh . . . I think just a tonic water, please.' Her mouth felt dry with nerves. What was she going to say next to Beth? Nothing in her previous experience, nothing in her long training for ministry had prepared her for this. Dear God, please let me get it right, was the thought in her mind as Beth set before her a glass with a piece of lemon floating on top.

'Anything else? A sandwich or some soup?' Beth asked, as Andrea closed her fingers round the glass and took a gulp from the icy drink.

'No, thanks. What I wanted, really, was to talk to you in private. I need to do that.'

Now Beth's lovely green eyes were looking puzzled. 'Is anything wrong? I could bring my father to speak to you, he's only down in the cellar.'

Andrea swallowed. 'It doesn't concern your father, what I have to say.'

'What is it?' Anxiety was plain to be heard in Beth's voice.

'It's about Jamie.'

'Jamie! I don't understand—' Beth whispered.

'Could we go somewhere more private, please? Somewhere where we are not likely to be interrupted.'

'Why? Is there something wrong? Is it bad news about Jamie? Are you a doctor or a nurse?'

'No, it's nothing like that. I'm not a medical person, I'm a church minister,' Andrea told her.

'Oh, I see!' There was relief plain to be heard in the words. 'Are you wanting me to have Jamie christened? I have been wondering about it, but I've been so busy. We never have much free time in this business, you see. Though I'd like to do what Jamie's father would have wanted. Is that why you've come?'

'In a way, yes.'

'Did you know Jamie's father? You said you had come from Durham, last time you were here.'

'Yes, I did know him. That's why I need to talk to you.'

'I'll ask Dad to come and take my place.'

As she waited for the girl to come back Andrea stared down into her glass and prayed hard that it would be all right. It seemed ages before Beth was facing her again across the bar, with her father standing only a yard or two away from them. His face was creased with perplexity.

'Come this way, please. I'm sorry I don't know your name,'

Beth said as she led Andrea into a small sitting room at the back of the building. 'Won't you sit down?'

'In a moment. I have to tell you who I am first.'

'You said you were a minister. That's why you've come, isn't it?'

Andrea hesitated. 'It's partly the reason, but there is something else. I'm Andrea Cameron.'

She watched the colour drain from Beth's face, saw her sway momentarily then gain control of herself again. 'Are you Ian's—? He said your name was Andrea, and that it was your ordination service that day. The day of the accident, I mean.'

'Yes, I am, Beth.'

'Oh!' Beth put a hand to her mouth to stifle her shocked gasp. 'So that's why you are here! It isn't anything to do with a christening, is it?'

'No. I hope I haven't upset you by coming, but I do need you to help me, if you will.'

'Help you? How can I do that?'

'By allowing Ian's mother to see Jamie.'

Beth drew in her breath sharply. 'But she doesn't know about him, does she?'

Andrea shook her head. 'Not yet, but I'd like her to know. You see she's so terribly distressed still, so desperately unhappy because now she has no one of her own. Nancy's a widow, and she's still grieving for the little boy Ian and I lost five years ago.'

'Ian told me about him. I'm very sorry,' Beth said quietly. 'I just don't know how you managed to come to terms with that. I don't think Ian ever did, but maybe the church helped you?'

'The church, and the support of my parents.'

'Why didn't you want another child? Was it because of your career?'

The questions were so unexpected that Andrea found

herself lost for words. What could she say? To tell this girl who had borne Ian a child that he had refused to allow his wife to have another baby would more than likely not be believed by her. Besides, what good would it do now to disillusion her?

'I'm sorry. Very sorry! I had no right to ask that,' Beth broke into her anguished thoughts.

'I'd have loved another child, but it seemed it was not to be,' Andrea managed to say at last.

'I just thought, with your career being so important to you that perhaps—'

'I had not even thought, until after Andrew died, of training for the Church. That came later.'

'Ian told me how much that mattered to you. It was the reason why he wouldn't tell you about us, about Jamie and me, until after your ordination. He was afraid that any gossip would harm you when you were just starting at your new church. I didn't want him to leave us that weekend because Jamie wasn't well, but he was determined to be with you for your service. Only of course the accident happened when he was on his way to you.'

'Yes.' Andrea sighed as she remembered how she had waited for Ian that day. How she had wondered where he was. How she had begun in the end to be afraid that he might have had an accident – but there was no point in reminding herself of that now. The past was gone and could not be altered. It was the present, and the future, that were her only concern now.

'Do you mind my asking if Ian made any provision for Jamie?' she forced herself to ask. 'I have been a bit worried about that ever since I found out about him.'

'You don't need to worry about us,' Beth told her proudly. 'I'm a partner in this hotel with my father, and I'm an only child. So Jamie won't go without anything he needs.'

'Perhaps he needs more family members to love him, and for him to love too,' Andrea said.

Beth was obviously taken aback. 'I never thought about that! I just imagined that as he had me, and Dad, that we would be enough for him.'

Andrea felt it was time for her to leave; that it would be a mistake for her to stay too long. Beth would need to be alone to think about what she had said. 'Jamie is your child so it must be your choice, Beth, but if you'd like him to have a grandmother as well as a grandad Ian's mother would be a really nice one. She's such a lovely person. It hasn't been easy for me to come here today, but I knew I had to do it for her sake. Now I'll go and leave you to think about it.'

Beth bit hard on her trembling lip. 'I'll do that, when I've got used to the idea. You'd better leave me your phone number, hadn't you?'

Andrea took a card from her Filofax and handed it to her. 'Please try to understand why I felt I had to come, Beth.'

The younger girl smiled at her. 'I do understand, Andrea. I hope you haven't found it too distressing. I don't think I could have done what you've done today, I just wouldn't have had enough courage.'

Andrea held out her hand. 'I'm glad I came, no matter what you decide, because it's much easier for me to understand now why Ian didn't tell me about you.'

'How did you find out?' Beth asked as she put her own hand into Andrea's.

'I found a teddy bear, and a note that said "with love to Jamie" when I was clearing out our house in Durham, and later I found a card from this hotel, which I couldn't remember Ian ever mentioning. So I began to wonder. Then I wanted to know the truth.'

'Now you know the truth, do you hate us?'

Andrea shook her head. 'No, I don't. In fact I like you, that's why I've been able to come here and talk to you as I have. Now I really must go or I'll be late for my meeting this evening.'

Beth walked with her to the car park. 'I'll be in touch with you, whatever I decide,' she promised. 'Drive carefully, Andrea.'

Then Andrea was back on the Ravensbridge road again with the mid December afternoon already darkening about her. There were flowers on the grass in the place where Ian's car had come to rest in the drystone wall. Without intending to do so, Andrea found herself bringing her own car to a stop on the grass verge. She would say her final goodbye to Ian here, because she did not intend to come this way again.

Forty miles further on, as she drove along Beck Lane she saw that there was light filtering out through the church windows. Was there something on in the church that she had forgotten about with her mind being so full of her visit to Beth? She parked in the church car park, which was empty, then went to investigate. With her hand on the heavy oak door she hesitated before pushing it open. There was nobody about and it was quite dark now, rather silent and scary. Then she heard the music, the familiar melody of an old hymn tune being played confidently, faultlessly, on the church organ. 'The day Thou gavest Lord is ended' were the long-remembered words.

A moment later she was within the building, allowing the tranquillity of the place to flow over her. She was home. The day the Lord had given her, the day which had demanded so much of her, was indeed ending. Now she was exhausted, but she was home. Unexpectedly, tears of relief began to slide down her cheeks. They were slow, silent tears which she did not attempt to wipe away as she walked slowly towards the altar. It did not seem strange to her that someone should be playing the organ at that time. Even before the hymn had ended and the organist had come to stand close to her she had known who it would be.

'Andrea, what is it? What's wrong, my love?' Bill asked softly.

'Nothing, Bill,' she murmured, dropping her head so he might not see her tears.

'Then why are you crying? Has someone hurt you?'

She shook her head and a tear splashed on to the hand he was reaching out towards her face.

'Can't you tell me? Can't you trust me?' he asked, as he took out a large handkerchief and gently mopped the moisture from her face. 'You know I would do anything for you, anything to make things right for you.'

'I do know that, Bill. It's just that I've had to do something today that was terribly hard for me, and now I'm just sold out, exhausted, and not even sure that I've done the right thing. Even though it seemed to me at the time to be the right thing.' She was unable to think straight now.

'You could talk about it, and I could listen,' Bill suggested.

All at once she wanted to do just that: to talk and let him listen. Wanted to have someone to share it all with. Someone she could trust. Someone who cared about people. Someone like Bill.

'I'd like to do that. I'm so afraid, Bill, that I might have got it all wrong.'

'You're over-tired, and perhaps hungry too,' he suggested.

'Yes, maybe you're right and I'll feel better when I've had something to eat. I haven't eaten since breakfast.'

'Where have you been, to miss out on your lunch?'

She managed a smile. 'It's a long story, Bill, so it'll have to wait. Will you lock the church door when you've finished practising? Not that you sound as if you need much practice.'

'I've finished now, as far as the organ is concerned. As for the minister, I'm just about to make a start. There's a chicken casserole in my Aga that I'm going to share with her. So let's go!'

Andrea was too weary to protest. It was just so good to

269

leave it to someone else and go out to her car while Bill locked the church. She ought to go to the manse first and check if there were any calls on her answer-phone, but for once that would have to wait.

Where had Andrea been since he had spoken to her this morning? What had happened to leave her at such a low ebb, so drained and tearful? So unlike the strong and confident woman he had come to admire so much. Why was she so afraid that she had got things wrong? What things? Were these things she had spoken of to do with her work? Or were they concerned with her personal life?

The questions spun round and round in Bill's mind as he gathered up his music and strode out of the church, locking the heavy door behind him and then looking round for Andrea. There was no sign of her. She had gone. Disappointment hit him like a blow as he left the churchyard and began to walk up the lane towards his home.

When he reached the gates of Beckside and saw her car parked in front of his door a great surge of joy engulfed him. Andrea was here! She was waiting for him. Waiting for him to take care of her, waiting for him to listen to her, waiting for him to help her. Was there really something in this prayer business, he found himself wondering then? All he had said, back there in Andrea's church, was, 'Dear God, let me be good enough for her.'

Twenty-Seven

There was warmth from the Aga filling the spacious kitchen of Beckside as Bill went unhurriedly about the business of setting the pine table for two, opening a bottle of wine and putting bread rolls to warm. That was after they had both been given a rapturous welcome by the retriever-collie Bill had brought home from the Nyddford police kennels earlier in the day and left in the utility room while he was in the church.

'He seems to have settled in well,' Andrea remarked as she stroked the silky head of the animal. 'What are you going to call him? There was no name on his collar when the lady who cleans the church found him. So you'll have to start from scratch.'

Bill thought about it. 'What would you call him, Andrea?'

'I'd call him Lucky, I think. Because if he'd been dumped outside the church he could have been killed on the road, and perhaps brought disaster to someone else as well.'

'Lucky it is then.' Bill brought the casserole to the table and invited Andrea to help herself while he poured the wine.

'I can't help but think how lucky I am, Bill, to have your friendship. To have you taking me into your home just when I need someone to show concern for me.'

'Hush!' he ordered. 'You are here to eat, not to embarrass me.'

So they ate the delicious concoction of chicken, mushrooms and peppers and drank the red wine followed by

271

Wensleydale cheese and apple pie before taking a tray of coffee with them into the big living room where a log fire was burning.

'That was a lovely meal, Bill,' Andrea said as she poured the coffee into sturdy pottery mugs.

'My cooking does seem to be improving these days. We ate out quite a lot when we lived in London. Gina was not very domesticated,' he told her.

'Where's Gina now?' she asked.

'She's part of my past, and I've no regrets about that. We shared a home for a time. I thought we were going to marry and share a family, until Gina went to work in America and met someone else. She rang me then and told me she was not coming back to me.'

'At least you found out before it was too late,' Andrea said slowly. 'Though I can understand how hurt you must have been.'

'Can you? You with your happy marriage to a man you loved, a man who loved you to the end of his life.'

Andrea set down her mug with fingers which were not quite steady. 'He didn't, Bill. Ian didn't love me to the end of his life.'

Shock kept Bill silent for a long moment. Then, 'What are you saying, Andrea?'

'I'm telling you that my husband didn't love me right to the end of his life. He loved someone else. That's where I've been today, to see the woman he loved more than me.'

'Perhaps he didn't love her more than you, Andrea,' Bill tried to comfort her. 'Maybe it was just an affair, an infatuation.'

'It wasn't. It was much more than that. He was going to ask me for a divorce, once my ordination was over and I was settled in and accepted here.'

Bill frowned. 'How do you know that? How can you possibly know that for certain?'

'Because Ian wouldn't let me have another child, but he gave her one.'

The words were full of a bitterness that Bill had never heard Andrea express before. She was such a calm person, so sure of herself and her faith. The hurt must have gone very deep, and it had not yet healed. What could he say? How could he comfort her? There were no words coming into his mind that were anything like adequate.

'You said "another child". Does that mean you have a child already?'

'It means I did have a child, once. A boy, Andrew. He died five years ago from meningitis when he was nearly three.'

'Why didn't your husband want another child?'

'He said he just couldn't go through all the pain again. He adored Andrew. We both did.'

'How terrible for you,' was all Bill could find to say.

Andrea sighed. 'Looking back, I think that was what spoiled our marriage, losing Andrew. We couldn't seem to bring any comfort to one another. Ian threw himself more and more into his work, and into his golf. I had a small breakdown and went to stay with my parents in Scotland. They were very good to me but they didn't seem to understand what was happening. I haven't told them yet about Beth. I'll probably tell them when I go home for New Year. My problem now is that I may have to tell Ian's mother when she comes to stay with me at Christmas.'

'Why? Why will you have to do that? Does she really need to know? Surely it would be kinder not to tell her that her son was unfaithful to you?'

'Yes, it would in a way. Except that there's the baby grandson she would perhaps love to know about. A little boy who doesn't have a grandmother. My mother-in-law is heartbroken because after losing her grandson she's now also lost her only son. Nancy's a widow, and she's a lovely person. I'd like to tell her about little Jamie because it might help her.

Though only if his mother agrees. I went to see her today at the hotel she runs with her father. She agreed to think about what I suggested.' Andrea stopped speaking and gazed into the fire as she relived her visit to the Raven Falls Hotel.

'It was very brave of you to do that, Andrea,' Bill said into the silence. 'No wonder you were so upset when you got back. It must have been such an ordeal for you.'

'Yes,' she admitted on a long sigh. 'I only hope it works out right. That it doesn't cause any more pain for Beth, because I found that I liked her.'

Astonishment froze the words Bill had been about to utter.

'Beth told me that Ian was on his way to join me at my ordination service when he was killed, and that he was going to tell me afterwards about her and their baby.'

'Did you believe her?'

'Yes. Now I hope she'll let Nancy see her baby grandson.'

'I don't know what to say to you, Andrea, except that I'm glad you've felt able to share all this with me.'

Andrea smiled. 'I needed to share it with someone. Someone I could trust. I was desperate to do that. I'm so grateful that you were there for me when I needed you, Bill.'

'I always will be,' he told her.

The carriage clock chiming from the shelf above the stone fireplace reminded Andrea that she was due at a meeting in less than half an hour. She rose to her feet reluctantly.

'I'll have to be going. I've got a meeting in the manse at seven o'clock. A meeting I could do without. I'd much rather stay here,' she added with a sigh.

'There'll be other times for us, other long talks, Andrea,' he promised.

They went with her to the door, the tall, bronze-haired man and the tall golden retriever. The dog licked her hand when she gave him a farewell pat. The man put an arm about her shoulders and gave her a swift hug.

'Don't let your meeting go on too long, love. Tell them you are tired,' he said.

'I am tired, so tired, but much easier in my mind, thanks to you, Bill,' she told him.

'Take care, Andrea, and God bless,' he found himself saying.

He watched as she drove away. Then he walked with the dog to the end of Church Lane, to the place where from the village green he was able to see the lights come on in the manse. There was a longing inside him to be there with her. To make sure they did not put too much stress on her, these people who were meeting to talk about her churches. He did not have the right to do that yet, but if he had his way he would be there with Andrea, one day.

Mercifully, the meeting did not drag on for too long because the man who usually questioned everything at length had gone down with flu. By ten o'clock they had all gone, and Andrea was curled up on the sofa sipping from a mug of hot chocolate when the phone rang. She was tempted to let it go on ringing and allow a message to be left on the answer-machine, but the fact that a couple of her church members were in hospital stopped her from doing that. If they needed her she would go to them, however tired she was.

'Julie Craven here, Andrea! Hope you don't mind my ringing so late.'

'Hi, Julie! Of course I don't mind.' Her eyelids were drooping now.

'I just wanted to tell you my news. I've had a call from Dorothy Bramley tonight and she's offered to let me rent Jacob's Cottage until I find a place to buy. Isn't it great?'

Andrea hesitated. 'Yes, I suppose it is, as long as you don't keep coming face to face with David. That could make it difficult for you. Are you sure about it, Julie?'

Julie laughed. 'Oh yes, quite sure!'

Andrea was puzzled. 'I thought . . . I mean I had the impression that you and David were not on the best of terms.'

Julie laughed again. 'We certainly weren't a little while ago, but Dave seems to have softened up quite a lot recently when I've been to visit Dorothy.'

'I suppose he has.'

'Dave's much more like he used to be before the accident,' Julie told her now. 'Almost like he was when I first met him. He was so different then.'

'Just after he married your friend, you mean?'

Julie laughed again. She seemed to be in really good spirits, Andrea thought.

'No, when I first met him at the hospital. Long before he met Jill.'

'Oh, I didn't realise you knew him before she did.'

'Yes, I bandaged him up when he cut his hand quite badly. Then we started going out. It lasted for months, until he met Jill.'

'You stayed friends with Jill?' Andrea's voice betrayed her surprise at this.

'Yes. I was very hurt, but I didn't let it spoil our friendship when he married Jill so quickly. I knew why he did it, and I understood. Jill's faith was so strong that she would never even have considered a termination,' Julie finished quietly.

'It must have been quite hard for you, visiting Jill after they were married?'

'Yes, it was. It would have been easier for me if I'd met someone else, but I didn't.'

'It's not too late for you to do that,' Andrea reminded her.

There was a long silence before Julie spoke again. 'It is

too late for me to meet anyone else,' she said quietly. 'I've tried hard enough over the years. I've even tried hating Dave for the way he turned against me when Jill died, but it didn't work. There'll never be anyone else for me, Andrea. It always will be Dave, or no one, for me.'

'So that's why you're so excited about going up there to live?'

'Yes. If it doesn't work out, if I don't make him fall for me again, I'll buy a place of my own and settle for a cat and a dog instead of Dave and some kids. Wish me luck, because I move into Jacob's Cottage at the end of next week.'

'Of course I wish you luck, though I thought you had your sights set on someone else who used to live there?'

'Surely you can't mean Bill? Of course I like him, he's a very interesting guy, but I wouldn't have a cat in hell's chance with Bill. He's only ever had eyes for you.' Julie stopped, then went on with a rush. 'Sorry, Andrea, I shouldn't have said that. It's far too soon to say things like that to you. I'd better ring off before I make things worse—'

Andrea laughed. 'Please don't, Julie. We're friends now, and it's good to have your friendship. I'm glad you rang, and I'm glad you've told me how you feel about Dave because I'd have been doing quite a bit of worrying about you, and a fair bit of praying for you, if you hadn't.'

Julie sighed. 'I don't think you need to worry about me. I can look after myself, but I think I'll still need the prayers because Dave is more stiff-necked with pride than ever now that farming is in such a bad way. You'd better start praying right now!'

'I will,' Andrea promised. 'If you're not on duty on Christmas Day why don't you come here for Christmas dinner with Nancy and me?'

'I can't, Andrea. Because I'm on my own I've volunteered to work on Christmas Day, but I'd love to come another day.'

'Make it Boxing Day lunch then, and if it's fine we'll have a good walk first. Can you come about eleven?'

'Yes, I'd love to. Thanks a lot for asking me. I'll let you go to bed now. Goodnight!'

As Andrea locked up the house, her whole being felt suddenly free of the weariness and trauma that her journey to the Raven Falls Hotel had brought about. A single sentence from Julie's phone call would not be banished from her mind. A sentence that brought lightness to her step and a smile to her mouth. Was it really true that Bill had only ever had eyes for her? Did she want it to be true? Or was it all in Julie's imagination? Bill was certainly a good friend to her, but what if he wanted more of her than that? The thought kept her awake far into the night.

In the week that followed she scarcely had time to dwell on Julie's words, so full were her days with school Nativity plays, extra services to arrange, more sick visiting than usual and her own preparations for Christmas food and shopping plus a huge number of Christmas cards to write. So tired was she at the end of each exhausting day that sometimes she fell asleep over her meal. The only times of peace were those which were set aside for private prayer, and even then there were more people than ever in need of her prayers.

At the heart of them all were her mother-in-law Nancy, Beth, and baby Jamie. She had not heard from Beth, so it appeared that the girl had not decided whether she would allow her child to meet his grandmother. There was no doubt in Andrea's own mind that she had done the right thing in speaking to Beth, because she had only taken that step after a great deal of thought and prayer. Now she prayed on ceaselessly that it would turn out right, that new hope and joy would come to Nancy, and more love would be there for Jamie.

There was no pain left in her now. She had come to terms with the way things were, and accepted the fact that her marriage had been over long before Ian was killed. It had helped to hear Beth say that Ian had been on his way to her ordination service when he was killed and to know that he had cared enough to wait until after that service was over to ask her for a divorce.

When several days had passed and there had been no call from Beth she had to face the possibility that her prayers had not been answered in the way she had hoped. It was disappointing, but it was the way things happened sometimes. You just had to go on having faith that in the end things would happen for the best, even the very worst of things. Having no time to brood about it was a great help. If she could not present Nancy with the fact that there was a lovely baby grandson waiting to meet her she would at least give Ian's mother as pleasant a time over Christmas as was possible the first year that she could not celebrate the festival with her son.

Nyddbeck was already looking very festive, with a tall tree bedecked with fairy lights towering up on the village green, and with most of the cottages and larger houses displaying evergreen decorations. The air rang with the sound of carols being practised inside and outside the church and the greetings cards arrived at the manse every day in shoals. There were only two days to go now to Christmas Eve.

Andrea made a final shopping trip to Nyddford to buy a turkey and fresh fruit and vegetables. In her kitchen, waiting to be cut on Christmas Day was a beautiful iced cake sent by her mother. Alongside it were loaves of Yorkshire tea bread, miniature Wensleydale cheeses, pots of Christmas chutney and mincemeat all brought for her by members of her two churches. She was very touched by their gifts, and by the sentiments expressed as they were given to her.

'Nay, it'll be nobbut a poor Christmas for you this year, lass,' one old farmer from the outer reaches of her parish said as he handed her a box of eggs. 'Being on your own, like. If there's owt we can do you'll 'appen let us know?'

'Yes, I'll do that, Mr Swales,' Andrea promised when she had swallowed the lump in her throat.

'You'll be welcome to come and spend Christmas Day at Ford House with Dorothy and me,' Ben Harper told her.

Andrea explained that her mother-in-law was to be with her for a few days and that Julie would be joining them on Boxing Day. She had seen little of Bill since the evening when he had shared his supper with her, though she had heard him playing the organ in her church several times and been tempted to go in and see him. It was too soon, she told herself. She could not face him yet, while those words of Julie Craven's were still lingering in her mind. So she paused on her way to the post-box to listen to his music. To listen and to wonder. To listen and give thanks. Thanks for the music, and for Bill.

Then it was the morning of Christmas Eve and Andrea had overslept after working into the early hours of the night before, preparing food. There was another pile of cards falling through her letter box as she yawned her way round the manse, pulling aside curtains to let in the bright winter sunshine. She would open the post after she had finished preparing her address for the early evening service, when many children would fill the church with their excitement. She went to her desk and switched on the computer, after bowing her head in prayer. There had still been no phone call from Beth. Perhaps there never would be, now.

Twenty-Eight

Andrea switched off the computer and stretched her shoulders to ease out the tension. She must have some fresh air or she'd be forgetting something important. Coffee first though, since she had skipped breakfast, and while she drank it she would make sure there were only Christmas cards in the envelopes on the hall table and nothing that needed to be dealt with urgently.

A couple of minutes later she was standing gazing through the kitchen window, the mug of coffee forgotten, and in her hand a single sheet of notepaper bearing the heading 'Raven Falls Hotel'. The date at the top showed that the few words it contained had been written four days earlier. 'I'm willing to do as you ask, but I found it too difficult to phone you, Andrea. I'm sure you'll understand. It will be much quieter here after Christmas so perhaps you could bring Jamie's Gran to meet him then?' The message was signed Beth Barclay.

The paper shook in Andrea's hand. She wanted to cry, but she would not let herself do that. She wanted to give a shout of joy but she would not do that either. It was too soon. First there was the news to break to Nancy, and that was not going to be easy. When her fingers steadied she drained the coffee mug in one long gulp, then sped up the stairs to fetch her boots and a thick padded jacket.

There were children playing on the village green and along Beck Lane. Some of them were floating sticks and dry horse chestnut leaves along the beck and under the bridge. They waved to her and she caught their excitement as they all spoke at once telling her what they hoped to find in their Christmas parcels the next day. Then she heard the sound of the organ drifting on the still air as Bill practised the carols chosen by her for the candlelit carol service to be held in the church tonight. She ought to tell him about Beth's message, but there were women going into the church now to decorate it, so she would wait until later.

Crisp, cold air caught at her throat as she walked swiftly along Church Lane, passing Bill's house as she did so, and then leaving the last of the village dwellings behind her as the lane became narrower and steeper until it was only a footpath, ending where the ancient Abbot's Steps began. When she reached these Andrea hesitated, knowing that they would bring her in less than a mile to the grazing moorland that was part of Abbot's Fold Farm. It was possible that if she took the right-of-way footpath across the moor she would meet David Bramley.

A few weeks ago that thought would have been enough to send her in the opposite direction, but not now. Now she knew that there was another side to him, that he was not always morose and surly.

It was wonderful up there on the great beautiful roof of North Yorkshire. Overhead the sky was a canopy of brilliant blue, under her feet the heather sparkled beneath a thick covering of frost. Her head felt clear and her body felt full of energy. She could go on and on walking up here with the abbey ruins standing starkly white in the distance to draw her onwards, and with only the homely murmuring of the hundreds of Abbot's Fold sheep to break into the stillness.

Then she turned and looked back to where the village of Nyddbeck nestled in the lower land far below her and knew that it was time to go back because there were things to be done down there and in her other parish at Nyddford. It was then, as she made the decision, that she heard the sound of a powerful engine and the high-pitched bark of a collie. They were catching up with her rapidly, too quickly for her to be able to escape, so she turned and waited for them. It was the dog who jumped down from the vehicle first to greet her with a couple of excited barks, then an encircling movement that was full of speed and grace. David followed and the animal obeyed his command, lying prone at Andrea's feet and gazing up at her with laughing eyes.

'I'm glad I've seen you,' David began, then came to a halt, frowning.

Andrea held her breath as she waited for him to go on. Was he mad with her again? She watched his face relax into something like a smile. It made him look incredibly handsome. Perhaps he had looked like this often before tragedy entered his life. If so, she could understand why Julie Craven still wanted him and no one else.

'I wanted to tell you that I'll be at the church with my mother for her wedding,' he began. 'It seems to mean an awful lot to her.'

'Of course it does. We all want our loved ones close to us at times like that,' she told him with a smile.

'I didn't want to hurt her by refusing to be there,' he confessed. 'It was just that I thought I wouldn't be able to cope with being in the church again after the last time. At my wife's funeral, I mean. Do you understand?'

'Yes, I do. It takes time for most people to be able to come to terms with things like that.'

'I wondered if it had been any easier for you,' he went on slowly. 'I mean, because of the job you do?'

'Things still hurt terribly, but I've had my faith to support me. That's what has helped me most. Maybe you ought to give it a try? I'll be there to help you, if you do.'

'Do you really mean that, after the things I've said to you?'

'Yes.'

'I do know that I need help. I've caused my mother a lot of worry, and I know I've been far too hard on Carla. I couldn't seem to help myself. I just wanted to hit out at anybody who didn't have all my problems to deal with. I couldn't cope, and that's the truth.'

'At least you know now that you have to accept help. That you must accept it for the sake of your children.'

He sighed. 'I've been such a bloody fool, this last couple of years; so wrong right across the board. Some of the times when I've spoken out of turn to you and you've hit back at me you've reminded me so strongly of Jill that I've begun to wonder what Jill would have thought of me these days. I think she'd hate me the way I am now, when I keep on losing my temper with Carla and my mother, and when I can't exchange a civil word with Julie, who was her best friend.'

Andrea smiled. 'I think you ought to amend that now to the way you were, David. Don't be too hard on yourself, and do try to accept help when it's offered.' There would be plenty of help on offer for him once Julie had moved into Jacob's Cottage, she guessed.

It was as if he had read her thoughts. 'Did you know that Julie's moving into mother's cottage next week?'

'Yes. It will be a good base for her when she's working from the health centre.'

'Jill would have been pleased because Julie's always got on well with Carla and Jack.'

'I'd better be getting back,' Andrea decided. 'I've an awful lot to do before tonight, but I just needed to get some fresh air to clear my head.'

'I'll see you at the church on New Year's Eve.' Dave snapped his fingers at the dog as he prepared to get back into the Land Rover, and it jumped into the passenger seat.

'There's a service tonight at seven, and a short one tomorrow at ten if you feel like getting into practice for New Year's

Eve,' she told him with a smile. 'Have a happy Christmas, David.'

He did not answer, but as she began to walk back towards the Abbot's Steps he gave her a salute from his vehicle. She halted then and sent up a short prayer. 'Thanks a lot, Lord. We've made a start. Please help David to keep it going.'

David slowed down his vehicle and looked back at her still figure. She was probably praying for him right now, he guessed. He certainly needed her prayers because he had been behaving like a moron. It was going to have to stop though if he wanted to make a good job of bringing up Jill's children. Jack was certainly not much of a problem, except for getting him out of bed on a morning and into bed reasonably early in the evening, but Carla was something different. He had handled Carla all wrong and now he was seriously worried about her.

Carla thought he didn't know about the way she had been hanging around Bill. In the beginning he had been blind to it, and had thought she was simply asking Bill for help with her school artwork because he himself was not showing enough interest. Then he had caught a glimpse of her going into Beckside while the workmen were still there and assumed she must have taken a fancy to one of the young joiners or decorators. Soon afterwards he had heard gossip while he was at Nyddford market about the young girl who was hanging round the well-known artist who had bought a house in Nyddbeck. He had guessed that they were talking about Carla. Something had to be done about it, especially now that Carla had started her two weeks of school holiday and would have more time to seek out Bill.

Perhaps Julie would talk to the girl, try to reason with her? Maybe he should ask her if she would? Yes, he'd do that as soon as Julie moved into Jacob's Cottage. A moment later he was driving as fast as safety permitted down the long moorland slope that led to the farmhouse, sending dozens of his sheep scurrying out of the way.

Andrea glanced at her watch as she reached the bottom of the Abbot's Steps and turned into Church Lane. There wasn't time for her to go into the church and tell Bill that she had heard from Beth Barclay this morning. She would need to hurry back to the manse at once and finish her preparations for the meal she wanted to have ready before Nancy arrived. While she was doing that she would snatch a sandwich and some coffee before driving to Nyddford to take the service of nine lessons and carols that was due to start at four in her church there.

So involved was her mind with the dovetailing of all her tasks that she failed to see the girl who was hovering close to the gate of Beckside until Carla spoke to her, loudly and fiercely.

'If you're looking for Bill he's not here. Do you know where he is?'

Andrea was taken aback. 'No. Unless he's still in the church practising at the organ,' she said.

'So you've got him roped in for that job as well. Anything so you can get him away from me.'

'What on earth are you talking about, Carla?' Dismay crept into Andrea's mind as she stared into the girl's resentful face. She had begun to hope that Carla's crush on Bill had fizzled out.

'You know very well what I'm talking about. First you talked Bill into leaving Jacob's Cottage and buying this place so he'd be nearer to you. Then you got him to say he'd play the organ at Gran's wedding, and now he's hardly ever here when I come to see him. You'll be sorry though! You'll all be sorry when you find out what I'm going to do when Gran moves out of our place.'

Andrea felt more disturbed than ever when she heard that.

She must try to talk sense into her before it was too late and Carla did something stupid.

'I hope you're not thinking of doing anything that might spoil your gran's wedding, Carla,' she said quietly. 'I can't believe you would do anything to hurt her after all she's done for you.'

'No.' Carla broke in far too quickly. 'I won't do anything till after the wedding.'

'Why don't you just catch your dad at a time when he's not busy and talk to him about what you want to do. I'm sure he'll listen to you.'

Carla's laugh was scornful. 'You don't know my dad if you think that! He won't listen. He never does listen. All he ever does is grumble at me, and I've had enough!' Her voice cracked as she uttered the final few words. Then, before Andrea could say anything else, she had turned and was running away, fast, along Church Lane to the Abbot's Steps.

The concern she felt about Carla would not be banished from Andrea's mind as she prepared vegetables and a pudding for that evening. They would not eat until after the service so everything must be ready to go into the oven before she left for the church. It was at times like this that she knew she really ought to have someone to help her in the house for a few hours each week as her mother had suggested. Perhaps she would have done if Ian had not been killed, but somehow after his death she had not wanted to have anyone invading the more private areas of the manse.

This thought brought her to the decision she was going to have to make very soon about how she was going to reveal to Ian's mother that he had been unfaithful, and that there was a child living forty or so miles away who was Ian's son, and her own grandson. It would have to be done very carefully if she was not to bring further grief to Nancy. She would be relieved when it was done, she told herself as she cleared the worktops of rubbish and emptied the kitchen bin. There was no time to make a sandwich now, with the clock showing two thirty; a mug of coffee and a chocolate biscuit would have to do or she wouldn't have time to pick up fresh fruit and bread from the shops in Nyddford before the four o'clock service.

There wasn't even time to give just a few minutes to prayer about the things that were weighing so heavily on her mind today, as she ought to have done. Prayer time had been crowded out today by things domestic, and Andrea felt guilty about that.

'Sorry, Lord, please forgive me,' she said in her mind as she picked up her car keys and hurried out of the house.

Bill was striding back towards the village by mid afternoon at the end of a six-mile walk which had taken him away from Nyddbeck via several public footpaths through farmlands to Skellbeck, where there was an excellent village inn and also a garden centre. He had become a fairly regular customer at both the inn and the garden centre since buying Beckside but what he had bought there today, after he had disposed of a pint of beer and a hearty helping of local cheese, home-baked bread and pickles at the pub, was not meant for Beckside.

Would Andrea like the miniature garden that he had chosen for her? He was not sure. Perhaps he ought to have bought flowers after all, but there had been something about the low oval basket of heathers that had caught his imagination. Was it right for Andrea? Was he right for Andrea? They were at ease with one another in friendship. They were attracted to one another too, he was certain of that. It was just the church thing, her role as Minister of Nyddbeck with Nyddford that he was uncertain about.

How involved would she expect a life partner to be with her ministry? How involved had her husband been with the church? Would she find it impossible to share her life with a man who did not share her own absolute belief?

When he reached the stile over the drystone wall from

where it was possible to see the manse and the church, he halted, setting the miniature heather garden at rest on the top of the wall so that he could look downwards at the place which had become to him the best place in the world to be. What right did he have to even consider asking Andrea to be his life partner?

Her adult life had been one of service, as a teacher first, and a wife and mother, then as a minister of the church. His own life had been so different, always putting first his compulsion to paint. Living a very spartan life at first, teaching art once he was qualified and wanting nothing more than that. Then becoming successful and being able to command high fees for his pictures. His work had been his reason for living.

Now Andrea had become his reason for living. Did she care enough for him to share that living? Or was it just gratitude that had made her cling to him as he hugged her when she left his home on the night of the snowstorm? The stumbling block, the great unknown, was the area of faith, the part of her that he might never come to understand. If he were to share her life, and he was desperate to do that, he would need to understand.

Sometimes lately, sitting at the organ in the little church down below him, it had seemed to him that there was something there waiting for him. Something just out of his reach. Something he wanted to grasp and could not. It was not just the beauty of the music he played or the simple loveliness of the plain little church. Soon, after the Christmas and New Year services were over, he would not be the one sitting at the organ. Soon, Andrea Cameron would not be here, she would be in the Highlands of Scotland with her parents. How empty his life would be then.

Once the wedding of her gran and Mr Harper was over and Gran was living at Ford House, there would be no one to take her side when Dad was mad with her, Carla knew. So she would pack her things and go, slip out of the house when Dad was working well away from there and get a lift from one of the big lorries that sometimes cut across country to rejoin the main road a couple of miles away. She didn't really care which city she ended up in, there was sure to be casual work to be had there. The sort of casual work she had wanted to do at the Nyddford Arms, until Dad said she had enough to do at home without taking on weekend work. A week from now she would be away from the farm for good.

Twenty-Nine

T he little church was crowded with families from both Nyddbeck and Nyddford. A tree which was almost too tall for the building was ablaze with coloured lanterns, and above the oak pews a latticework of metal, constructed many years ago by the Nyddford blacksmith, held dozens of short white flickering candles. Andrea had planned the service in anticipation of having many very young children there with their parents and grandparents and this was certainly the case, but, glancing round the congregation as she stood at the lectern to welcome them, she could not find the Bramley children even though Dorothy and Ben were present.

In a little over an hour it was all over, they had sung the old familiar carols and one or two new ones with such enthusiasm that they were all ready to enjoy the cups of coffee and the warm mince pies which were served in the hall next to the church. The place hummed with the combined excitement of forty or so children and the cheerful conversation of their families, but for Andrea exhaustion was creeping in and she was longing for a quiet hour to herself before it was time for her to drive to Nyddford where her final service of the day would begin at eleven thirty.

She was not to get that quiet hour alone though because her mother-in-law was waiting for her at the manse. Nancy had opted out of coming to this service, saying she was tired after her long drive to Nyddbeck. She would stay in the manse and have the supper ready for when Andrea returned, she had said firmly.

'You look tired, Andrea,' Bill murmured as she made her way towards the door. 'Is there anything I can do to help you?'

She shook her head. 'I don't think so, Bill. The clearing up will be done by some of the ladies, and people are beginning to leave now. Thanks a lot for playing the organ again.'

'You don't need to thank me for that. I'm really enjoying it. In fact I'll probably miss it when your usual man comes back.'

Andrea smiled. 'I'm sure you'll be asked to step in again before long,' she told him.

'I'll be glad to.'

'The invitation to Christmas dinner with us still stands, Bill, if you're going to be on your own tomorrow,' she said then.

'Thanks, but I won't take you up on that. You need to ease up on company after your heavy work load this week, and you'll have such a lot to talk to your mother-in-law about. I'd like you to share a meal with me one evening next week, if you will. Come to Beckside and I'll cook for you. Let me know when you'll be free, and how things have gone for you.'

'Yes, I'd like to do that, Bill.' She put out a hand and he took it into both of his for a long clasp that neither of them wanted to end.

'I'll pick you up at eleven to drive you to Nyddford,' he murmured before he turned away to stride off into Church Lane.

Before he reached Beckside he turned back and retraced his steps to the place where he was able to see her clearly in the moonlight walking across the bridge to the manse. It was only when he had seen a strong beam of light pouring out from her front door to assure him that she was safely indoors that he hurried to his own home.

'Will you come with me to the midnight service at Nyddford, Nancy? Or are you still feeling tired?' Andrea asked the older woman an hour later as they finished their supper and took coffee into the firelit warmth of the living room.

Nancy's hair was expertly styled and her casual suit of purple jersey was elegant, but her expression as Andrea waited for her to reply was desolate. She was obviously making a valiant effort to be cheerful, and at the same time losing the battle for self-control.

'It's more than just tiredness, my dear,' she said in a low voice. 'I simply don't know how to face going into a church again, even though I know I will have to do that one day. I'm not sure that there's any belief left in me after what happened to Ian and Andrew. It's as if there isn't any point in life now, nothing to work for because there's no one who needs the money, and no young ones to look forward to. Why, Andrea? Why! That's what I want to know! I can't go into a church again until I know the answer to that. I have to tell you, even though I know it might hurt you, that I can't imagine how you can go on believing, after losing first Andrew and then Ian.'

There was a long silence while Andrea considered her mother-in-law's anguished statement, then she reached out a hand to place on Nancy's shaking shoulder while she sought for words, the right words to bring comfort.

'I can't explain it properly myself, Nancy,' she said at last. 'I only know that at first, after Andrew died, I wanted to die myself. Then, when I was feeling absolutely at rock bottom, I met a woman who was able to convince me that leaning on her faith had helped her to come to terms with an appalling tragedy. I went on from there to where I am now.'

'Surely your faith must have been shaken when you lost Ian as well?'

'Shaken, but not destroyed.' Andrea halted, and knew then

that this was the time to tell Nancy about Jamie and Beth. 'I needed my faith more than ever when I discovered that I had lost Ian long before he died.'

Nancy half rose from her seat. 'What do you mean?' she whispered.

Andrea eased her back into the chair. 'I'm trying to say that Ian didn't love me any more.'

'How can you say that? Just because he didn't understand why you wanted to go into the Church instead of having another child—'

Andrea swallowed. Had Ian really told his mother that her intention to train for ministry was more important to her than having another child?

'I don't think you quite understand, Nancy, how things were between us after Andrew died. It was certainly not that I didn't want to become pregnant again. I wanted another baby more than anything at that time, only Ian wouldn't agree. He said he couldn't risk losing a child again. Nothing I could say would change his mind about that. It was very hard for me to accept, and looking back I think it was what made us grow apart.'

'I'm quite sure Ian still loved you,' Nancy broke in. 'I expect he would have changed his mind about the baby if you hadn't decided to train for the Church.'

Andrea sighed. 'No, I don't think he would. I asked him often enough before I even started my training but he wouldn't even talk about it.'

'But he did still love you,' Nancy insisted. 'It wasn't his fault that he couldn't get here for your service that day. If it hadn't been for the accident . . .' Her lips quivered.

There was no way Andrea could save her from knowing the truth now. 'If it hadn't been for the accident, Ian would have asked me for a divorce long before now.'

'How can you know that?'

294

'Because he wanted to marry someone else. He was only waiting till I was settled in here.'

'I still can't believe that. You must be mistaken, my dear.'

Andrea took a deep breath. 'I'm not, Nancy. Ian needed me to divorce him so he could marry someone else.'

Nancy shook her head very slowly. 'Did he really tell you that? Why didn't he tell me?'

'No, he didn't tell me. I found out by accident that there was someone else when I was clearing out our house in Durham.'

Plainly Nancy was shocked. 'Oh, my dear, why didn't you tell me then?' she wanted to know.

Andrea sighed. 'I couldn't, Nancy. Not until I'd found out for certain if it was true.'

'And now you have! What can I say to you? Only that I'm most dreadfully sorry for the pain it must have caused you. It must have been a great shock—'

'Yes, it was. I had no idea, you see. I thought, when Ian said he was going away on business or to play golf, that was true. I didn't know then about the Raven Falls Hotel, and Beth Barclay.'

Tears were sliding down Nancy's cheeks now. 'You must hate him for that,' she said at last.

'No. Not now. I was very bewildered and hurt when I first discovered it, but I've been able to come to terms with it since then.'

Nancy wiped her eyes. 'I don't understand how you can say that. You can't really mean it?'

'Yes, I do. I've found it much easier to come to terms with since I met Beth, and Jamie. Once I'd seen Jamie I knew why Ian wanted a divorce.' Andrea paused, wondering how to go on and say the rest of what had to be said.

'Who is Jamie?' Nancy broke in.

'He's a lovely little boy who is almost a year old. He's your grandson, Nancy.'

'You don't mean—?'

'Yes, he's Ian's son.'

'But how do you know?'

'Because Beth told me, and because not only does he look like Ian he's also very much like Andrew was at the same age.'

'Oh, Andrea, what are we going to do?' Nancy whispered. She reached out to take Andrea's hand in her own. 'What are we going to do?'

'That's up to you, Nancy,' Andrea said after a long silence. 'His mother is willing for you to meet Jamie, if you would like to.'

Now the silence was even longer. 'How do you know?' Nancy murmured.

'I went to see her, and told her about you. She wrote back a few days ago. I'll show you the note she sent.'

Andrea went to the bureau and took out the few lines from Jamie's mother, which she handed to Nancy.

'I don't know what to say. I hardly know how to face you now, Andrea.'

'Why? It isn't your fault, Nancy. It isn't little Jamie's fault either. It's just something that's happened, something we can't change so we have to accept it. Whether you go to see Jamie is up to you, but he really is a lovely baby. I think you'll like his mother too.'

'Do you?' Nancy's eyes widened with surprise.

'Yes. I liked her.'

'What can I say to you—' Nancy's voice broke.

'Don't say anything more now. Wait until tomorrow when you've had time to think about it and to get used to the idea. I must get ready to go to Nyddford now for the midnight service.'

Andrea left the room then and went to prepare herself,

mentally and physically, for what was to come. In her bedroom she stood at the open window taking in great gulps of frosty air as she prayed silently that what happened after her revelation to Ian's mother would be the best for her and for Jamie, and for Beth.

'I've done my best, Lord. Now it's up to you,' were her final thoughts before she slipped the stiff white collar of office into the neck of her white silk shirt.

As she lifted her head she was able to see Bill striding across the bridge with Lucky on his last walk of the day. As though he sensed her presence there, Bill halted and looked up at her window. The sight of him brought immense comfort to her.

Had Andrea seen him down here with Lucky, Bill wondered, as he made his way back to Beckside with the dog trotting happily to heel on the frosty grass. Would she like the basket of heathers dressed with dark tartan ribbons which he had left in the porch of the manse? Had she disclosed yet the secret of her son's infidelity to her mother-in-law, and if she had, how distressing had it been for her?

If only he had the right to be there with her tonight when she was so tired and anxious, but he did not have that right, yet. Perhaps she would not need him? Perhaps her strong faith would provide her with all the support she needed?

He found himself longing now for that same support to lean on because he knew that if he could not have Andrea with him for the rest of his life his own existence would be no more than that. Just an existence spent with only his painting for company. Once, it had been enough for him. Now it was not. If he could have Andrea with him he would ask no more than to share with her here in this village the times like today, and all the other difficult days. Yet there would surely be days of great joy too. He felt absolutely certain of that as he went back to his home to collect his car and drive Andrea to Nyddford for the midnight service where he would be playing the organ. It was such a small way of being able to help her but it would have to be enough, for now.

All Andrea's weariness left her as the beautiful late night service took over her entire being. Some of the congregation had been celebrating at parties but they were reverent for all that, until the bells of midnight were ringing and everyone was streaming out of the church exchanging Christmas greetings. Some of those she knew best kissed her cheek, some who were more reserved tried to express their sorrow that she would be spending her first Christmas without her husband.

'You must find it hard to take at times, all these well-meant words of sympathy,' Bill said, as they headed back for Nyddbeck.

'Yes. I wonder what they'd say if they knew the truth?'

'I think they'd still feel sad for you.'

'I hope they never have to know the truth.'

'Does your mother-in-law know yet?'

'Yes, I told her tonight, just after she had apologised to me for not feeling able to come to any of the services this year.'

'How did she take it?'

'With disbelief at first. It seems to have been firmly in her mind that I preferred my career to having another child. She was quite unaware that it was Ian's decision, and that there was nothing I could do to change it.'

'Do you think she'll go and see this other girl's baby?'

'I don't know. I left her to think about it. I hope she'll go because I think she needs him to love, and I believe her love will be a blessing to Jamie.'

'Do you feel better for having told her?'

'Yes. It's as though I've handed over responsibility to her now and I can get on with my life.'

'Then you've done the right thing.' They were at the gate

of the manse now. He reached across to open the door of the car for her. 'Goodnight, Andrea, and happy Christmas,' he said.

'Happy Christmas, Bill.' She touched his hand, then was hurrying away, leaving him cursing himself for not kissing her when he had the chance.

Nancy was waiting for her with a tray of hot milky drinks and home-made biscuits. 'I thought you'd be ready for this after such a hectic day,' was all she said.

'Thanks, I am.' Andrea sipped the hot chocolate gratefully.

'I'm sorry I didn't come with you. I ought to have done. Please forgive me, dear?'

'Of course. You've had a lot to take on board tonight.'

'I'm ready to deal with it, now, and I'm so grateful to you for giving me the chance to do that. You must have been tempted to keep the knowledge to yourself.'

'Yes, I was. Until I realised how unhappy you were. I had to do something then.'

'I'd like to go and see Jamie,' Nancy said tentatively.

'I'll take you there, the day after tomorrow,' Andrea promised.

Long after she was in bed she found herself trying to look ahead, to envisage how that meeting would go. She knew it was not possible to predict. All she could do was to pray hard that it would turn out right, until utter exhaustion pushed her into a deep sleep.

At Abbot's Fold Farm Dorothy Bramley was placing parcels round the tree for the children to open on Christmas morning. David was watching her as he ate a late night snack after doing the final walk round the farm to check that all was well.

'You've been very good to us all, Mum, since I lost Jill,' he said quietly. 'I don't know what I'd have done without you. Ben Harper is a lucky man to be getting you.'

'I'm lucky to be getting him, too. He's a good man and a very generous man, Dave. That's why I'm able to give you a special gift this year, something that will make life easier for you, I think.' As she spoke Dorothy handed him a long parchment-coloured document.

'What is it?' he wanted to know.

'It's the deeds of Jacob's Cottage. I won't be needing it again so I want you to put it on the market now, while prices are buoyant, and use the money to invest in the farm.'

'I can't do that—' he began, as she had known he would.

'It's what your father would have wanted, and it's what Ben and me both want.'

'I thought Julie was going to live in the cottage?'

'Only until she finds a place to buy.'

'I don't know what to say, Mum—'

'Then don't say anything, son. Just accept it, and set about making a better life for you and the children. You're still young, David. You don't have to wait until you're my age to find a new partner you know.'

David grinned at her. 'I hope you're not matchmaking, Mum, but thanks. Thanks a lot.'

Julie Craven, coming back to her flat from a hospital staff party, found her thoughts going to Abbot's Fold, and Dave. By this time next week she would be living close to him. Very close. Dave would no longer have his mother always at hand. He would be vulnerable at times; in need at times. She would make sure she was there at those times.

If she had not made herself indispensable to him by the time Jacob's Cottage was sold she would give up. She knew she was attractive, other men had told her that, and she knew she was right for Dave and his children. Since there was no other man she was prepared to share her life with, it would have to be Dave Bramley or no one for her. Deep inside herself she was certain that it would be Dave.

By Faith Divided

*   *   *

Carla lay awake listening to the hooting of an owl in the great oak tree close to the farm gate. In her mind she was going over again the small number of things she would be able to get inside her backpack when she left the farm next Friday. She wouldn't be able to carry much if she was going to walk the best part of a mile to hitch a lift. That meant she wouldn't be able to take the new clothes that would be in the parcels waiting to be opened beneath the Christmas tree. They would have to be left behind, but she would be able to wear the new jacket Gran had bought her to wear for the wedding.

She was going to miss Gran, and Jack too, even though Jack could be a pain at times, but it couldn't be helped. It would have been different if Bill had let her go and live with him as she wanted to. Other girls of her age went to live with people they fell in love with. Perhaps she would ask Bill just once more before she left. It might be worth a try.

Thirty

Throughout the whole of Christmas Day there was an air of suppressed excitement about Nancy Cameron which seemed to have entirely banished, at least for a time, the pall of lingering grief which she had brought with her to the manse. Being a woman of kindly disposition she did her best to avoid asking questions about the grandson whose existence she had so recently been told of, but Andrea was aware that she was longing to know more about him. Several times Andrea found her mother-in-law gazing intently at one or other of the family photographs which featured Andrew as though she hoped to find there some clue as to what Jamie would look like.

'I thought Jamie looked very much like Andrew in that photo,' Andrea managed to say, just once, and saw Nancy's face fill with delight.

'I just can't wait . . .' Nancy began, then she broke off to say, 'Sorry, Andrea. It can't be easy for you to talk about this.'

'No, but I felt you had the right to know about Jamie. We'll go to see him on Monday. It'll be quiet then at the hotel.' Nancy was going back to Durham on the Tuesday, so it had to be then if they were to go to the Raven Falls Hotel together.

On Boxing Day, when Julie Craven came for lunch, the subject was not mentioned. Julie was simmering with anticipation about her move to Jacob's Cottage. She arrived in time to spend an hour walking with Andrea while Nancy finished cooking the late lunch they were all to share. Soon they were taking the right-of-way footpath that led from Church Lane via the Abbot's Steps to Abbot's Moor. It was Julie who decided on this route, but it was Andrea who slowed down as they neared Beckside. Though there was no sign of Bill or his dog.

'Where did Bill spend Christmas?' Julie wanted to know.

'He was here to play the organ for the midnight service at Nyddford and the short family service in Nyddbeck yesterday, then he was invited to relatives of his mother who farm near Richmond. I'm not sure where he is today.'

'What an asset he's been to you! So much talent! I've always liked his pictures, but I'd no idea he was an organist.'

'Neither had I, until I found him trying out the organ in the church when he was waiting for me one day,' Andrea told her.

'Waiting for you? Don't tell me you're converting Bill!' Julie laughed.

'He doesn't need converting,' Andrea smiled. 'He's just a little out of practice, that's all.'

They walked up the steep steps and on to the moor, by which time Andrea was wondering whether Julie was intending to walk in the direction of Abbot's Fold Farm or if they would go in the other direction to where the ruined abbey stood out starkly against the brilliant blue winter sky. The decision was made for them when they caught sight of David and young Jack taking a look at the sheep half a mile ahead of them. Jack soon spotted them and shouted, 'Hi, Julie!'

When they met it was evident that Julie and Jack were on good terms. 'It'll be great when you come and live with us,' Jack said, after thanking her for the football she had sent him.

Warm colour had deepened the pink of Julie's cheeks as she corrected him. 'I won't be living with you, Jack, I'll be across the yard in the cottage.'

'It's nearly the same. Gran says it'll be good for us.'

Julie bit her lip, embarrassed. Andrea tried to hide her amusement. David began to cough.

'If there's anything you need when you move in on Friday don't be afraid to ask,' he said as he bent to inspect another ewe.

'It looks like they'll be glad to see you settled in Jacob's Cottage,' Andrea remarked as they strode on swiftly towards the abbey.

'That's what I'm hoping,' Julie confessed. 'I intended to stay on in the flat and look for something to buy from there, until Dorothy offered me the cottage to rent very cheaply until she sells it. She seemed quite keen that I should live there until the place was sold. So I decided to do that and see if I can get close to Dave again.' When they reached the abbey, she turned to face Andrea with a serious expression. 'Will you pray for me, Andrea, please? Pray that it works out for all of us, I mean, not just for me. I love Dave, and I love his children, so I just have to try and get him to love me again, as he did before he met Jill.'

Andrea put a hand on her shoulder. 'Of course I'll pray for you. You'll be good for Dave. He needs you. So do his children. Especially Carla.'

They did not speak of it again but walked quickly back to the manse to do justice to the hearty meal that Nancy had ready for them. The day clouded in, and by late afternoon when Julie left to drive back to her flat, there was a threat of snow showers.

'I'll see you on Friday at the wedding,' she told Andrea. 'I'm looking forward to it.'

So was Andrea, but first there was the journey to the Raven Falls Hotel to be made with Nancy, and the meeting with

Jamie and his mother. Andrea lay awake for a long time that night, praying hard and trying not to worry about it. They would take the teddy bear with them that Ian had bought. That might help to break the ice, she decided.

By the next morning the threatened snow showers were already being driven in by a fierce east wind. Because of the weather, and because she had an early session with the church secretary the following morning, Andrea suggested that Nancy take her own car.

'If you decide to stay the night there, or if you want to be sure you can get back to Durham on Tuesday to open the business, you would be free to do that.'

Nancy agreed. 'We don't know what will happen, do we? Of course I'd like to spend some time with Jamie, but his mother might not want that,' she worried.

Because the roads were quieter now that Christmas was over, the two vehicles were able to stay close to one another throughout the journey and keep up a reasonable speed. It was only when they reached the Ravensbridge road that Andrea dropped her speed right down, then came to a halt when the roadside flowers came into view. They were chrysanthemums, huge and white, dressed with white ribbons, resting against the drystone wall where Ian's car had crashed. Nancy got out of her own vehicle to stand close to them for a few minutes. Andrea left her alone, until it began to snow. The she led her back to her car.

'We're nearly there,' she said.

Beth met them at the door of the small hotel when they had parked in the empty car park. In her arms was Jamie, rosy cheeked and smiling happily at the sight of the teddy bear which they had brought for him.

'This is Beth, Nancy. Beth, this is Ian's mother. And this is Jamie.' Andrea stepped back as pain, swift and unexpected pierced her. This adorable little boy should have been hers. Ian and hers, not Ian's and this other woman's. Her throat and eyes burned as she fought to remain calm, to accept something that she could not change. Then there was Beth's father, leading her away to his own small study where he poured her a brandy without asking and urged her into a chair.

'You'll feel better in a little while,' he said gruffly. 'I'll go and bring some coffee.'

The worst was over when he came back five minutes later and handed her a mug of coffee.

'Thanks. You're very kind,' she said.

'You are an exceptional woman, to be able to do what you've just done. It must have been very distressing for you.'

'Yes, but Nancy needed to meet Jamie. She had lost all hope for the future. Now she has something to live for again.'

His kind grey eyes were intent on her face. 'Do you have anything to live for now?'

She lifted her head, calm again, in control again. 'I have my work, and my faith,' she told him.

He smiled. 'Me too,' he said as he slipped into the only other chair in the room. He began to tell her then about the dark days after the loss of Beth's mother, and how Beth had given up her job to come and live with him. 'I'll admit I was very upset when Beth became pregnant, especially as she couldn't marry Ian, but the baby has been such a comfort to us both. A real blessing.'

'A real blessing, perhaps, for Nancy too?'

Suddenly then Andrea knew it was time for her to go; time to leave these people who had baby Jamie to bind them together. Because there was nothing here for her. Everything she wanted was back in the village of Nyddbeck. She got to her feet and held out her hand to Jeff Barclay.

'I'm sure you'll understand why I feel I must leave now. Will you explain to Nancy and your daughter for me, please? Thank you for your kindness to me.'

They shook hands. Then he led her to her car, gazing anxiously up at the snow-filled sky. 'Have a safe journey, and a happier future,' he said.

Squally snow showers accompanied her all the way back to Nyddbeck. She hoped that she would not be called out again that evening because she felt utterly exhausted by the trauma of the day. All she wanted was to relax by the fire and empty her mind of all the sadness, all the pain. She was about to do that, having put her car into the garage and checked the answer-phone, when the sound of the front door bell broke into the absolute silence brought by the snow.

Pushing strands of damp hair from her forehead she opened the door, mentally saying goodbye to her plan to rest for the remainder of the day. There was a thick covering of snow on Bill's rusty hair, and on the coat of his dog.

'I saw your lights were on when I was walking Lucky,' he told her. 'So I thought I'd check that you were all right. Are you all right, Andrea, after your journey and what you had to do there?'

She ought to have been able to say yes, to assure him that she had coped with the experience perfectly well. Only the words wouldn't come out of her mouth. They were trapped inside her by a strange mixture of pain and gladness. Pain because it still hurt so much to recall how much like her own beloved child baby Jamie was. Gladness because Bill was there, standing so near to her with his face full of concern for her.

'It was . . .' she began when the silence had lasted too long. 'It was so hard to do, Bill. It hurt so much, and I felt so alone.'

'You are not alone now, love,' Bill said, as he opened his arms so that she could weep on his shoulder.

He was in her kitchen heating a can of soup for her while she washed the tears from her face when the phone rang. It was the matron from the nursing home where her predecessor,

307

old Mr Bickerdike, was a patient. His condition was causing concern.

'I'll come at once,' Andrea said without hesitation.

'You'll go when you've had some hot soup,' Bill told her when she said she had to go out, 'and I'll be driving you there. I'll take Lucky home and come back with the car while you eat. I don't suppose you've had anything since breakfast?'

'No, but I don't want anything—'

'Sit down and eat, Andrea, or I won't be playing the organ for you on Friday.' He poured the soup into a bowl and placed bread and butter beside it on the kitchen table. Then he called his dog and departed.

She felt better when the soup was gone and her casual gear had been exchanged for a skirt, a shirt and her dog collar. By then Bill had pulled his car on to her drive. Apart from her telling him how to get there they did not speak. When they reached the place he did not go in with her but remained in his car listening to the radio.

The frail old clergyman took her hand and told her he was glad to see her. 'I've just heard that my daughter is coming from New Zealand tomorrow, Andrea,' he whispered.

'I'm so glad,' she responded, wondering if he would still be alive then.

A mischievous grin touched his ashen cheeks. 'I don't intend to depart till I've seen her.'

Andrea read some favourite passages from the Bible to him and they shared a prayer before she knew it was time for her to go.

'They tell me you're doing a good job at Nyddbeck and Nyddford. Keep it up, my dear,' he said quite clearly.

The snow had stopped and the plough had cleared the road .as Bill drove her back to the manse. When she got out of the car the landscape all about her was breathtakingly beautiful.

'Thanks for everything, Bill,' she said. 'I don't know why you're so good to me.'

He laughed softly. 'Don't you? I'll tell you one day, when the time is right.'

She stood in the porch and watched him drive carefully away, and all the time she was wishing he was not leaving her. Was she falling in love with Bill? Was he in love with her? Did she want to fall in love again, or would it be better for her work here if she remained celibate? The questions went with her into the manse, and by the end of the day she had still found no answers to them.

A call from Nancy the next day gave her the assurance that she had done the right thing. Nancy had stayed the night at the hotel and was to visit again the next weekend. Andrea felt easier in her mind once she knew that, and was able to give all her time and energy to preparing her short address for Dorothy and Ben's wedding service, clearing up a mass of paperwork, getting through more church meetings and making another visit to Mr Bickerdike. By Thursday night it was all done and there was only her packing to do for her visit to her parents, and the midday wedding ceremony to perform the next day.

If she was going to have one more attempt to try and get Bill to let her live with him and work for him it would have to be today while Dad was at the Nyddford cattle market, Carla decided on Thursday. Her bag was packed ready to go with her either to Bill's house or to hitch a lift on the main road. She put on the eye make-up that her father disapproved of and made her way across Abbot's Moor until she came to the Abbot's Steps. It was easier to reach Beckside from there without the chance that Andrea Cameron would see her.

She was there just before ten thirty, in time for coffee with Bill. Only there was no answer to her ring at the front door. Perhaps Bill was in his back garden or garage? As she walked round the side of the house she could see a tall figure and a long-legged dog at the bottom of the garden near the summerhouse. They hadn't heard her approach. Then the dog did hear her and began to bark, so the man turned round. It wasn't Bill at all.

'Hi there! Is this your dog?' he said in the sort of voice that you heard in American films.

'No. He belongs to Bill. Where did you get him from?' The man was much younger than Bill. Not many years older than she was, Carla decided.

'He came to my house, early this morning, and he wouldn't go away.'

'Where is your house?' Carla had never seen this guy before. She would have remembered him because of his vivid blue eyes and his thick blond hair. For his neat bum too. He was a dish!

'The big one that used to be a mill. Mill House, it's called. Do you live here?'

'No. I live up on Abbot's Moor. We have a farm there.'

'Well, what do you know! My Mom's folk have a farm in Connecticut.'

'Honest? What're you doing here then?' She had to know. This guy was so cool!

'Pop's here on a teaching exchange at a place called Nyddford High.'

'That's where I go,' she told him.

'I'll be seeing you then when I go there for my final year.'

'Honest? I thought . . .' She had thought him older than that.

'Now, what are we going to do about this dog? I can't just leave him out in the cold.'

Carla smiled. 'We could go and look for Bill. I expect he's out looking for Lucky.'

'OK! Let's do it. You lead the way – what did you say your name was?'

'Carla. Carla Bramley, like in apples you know.'

'Hi, Carla. I'm Josh Bolton.'

They met Bill half an hour later on his way back from searching the moor. He was obviously relieved to see Lucky, who gave him a rapturous welcome. 'I was afraid this fellow might chase the sheep, when he went missing early this morning. I'm glad you found him before he did that. Thanks a lot, both of you,' Bill told them.

'It was Josh who brought Lucky to your place,' Carla explained.

'It was Carla who said where we might find you,' Josh told him. 'We'd better go to my place now and tell Mom he's found his master. I guess she'll like to meet you, Carla.'

Bill watched them go, grinning. 'That could be the end of my little problem, Lucky,' he said.

Later in the day, much later, Carla accepted a lift back to the farm from Mrs Bolton. She also accepted an invitation to the American family's New Year Party for her and Jack. There was just time for her to unpack her backpack before Dad came home. It wasn't the right time for her to be leaving here, not with Josh Bolton just arriving. She was stowing the bag away at the back of her wardrobe when she heard the Land Rover return to the yard. Perhaps she ought to tell Dad about the party at Josh's place?

When she looked out of her bedroom window he was jumping down from the driving seat. He was not coming into the house, though, he was crossing the yard to Jacob's Cottage where Julie's car was parked and he was carrying a bright pink plant to the door of the cottage. She watched as Julie took the plant from him and reached up to kiss his cheek. When she looked again the plant was out of sight. All she could see then was the back of her dad as he stood in the porch of the cottage with his arms around Auntie Julie. He was kissing her, Carla was certain, and it was one of those long kisses like you saw in the movies.

If she stayed here would Josh Bolton kiss her like that one day?

There was a murmur of anticipation in the little church that was now almost full of family members and friends of Dorothy Bramley and Ben Harper. The men wore their best suits and most of the women wore hats with their smart outfits. Flowers were everywhere, filling the air with the fragrance of carnations and freesia. Ben was already in his place in the front pew with his best man beside him, awaiting the arrival of his bride. The organ was playing softly. Andrea waited, wearing her best white silk shirt and holding her prayer book.

Then Dorothy was walking slowly to the front of the church, with folds of soft violet silk drifting down from a matching embroidered jacket, and with a simple posy of violets and freesia in her hands. How lovely the violet-trimmed boater was with her silvery fair hair, Andrea thought, as David proudly escorted his mother to her bridegroom. How handsome he looked in his dark suit and dazzling white shirt worn with a brilliant silk tie.

The service which was to join these two people who had known one another as friends for so long moved serenely to its conclusion, the marriage register was signed in the vestry, and then Dorothy and Ben were leaving the church to a hail of confetti and a barrage of good wishes. Soon everyone had gone, the church was empty, and the only ones left there were Andrea and Bill, who was emerging from behind the curtain which screened the organ.

'You played beautifully, Bill,' she told him.

'You look beautiful,' he told her. 'I can't seem to take my eyes off you.'

She could feel the warmth of his gaze from where she was standing. She could feel the strength of his longing for her even though they were not close enough to touch. She knew then that he was in love with her. She knew it and was afraid of the knowledge because her own love for him made her vulnerable.

The love in her marriage to Ian had not been strong enough to survive the sorrow of losing a child. Neither had it been deep enough for Ian to accept her decision to become a minister. Was Bill's love for her great enough for him to be able to share her faith as well as her love? If it were not, there would be such harm, such pain, waiting for them both.

'I have to go to the manse and get changed before I go to the reception, Bill. I'll see you there,' she said as she almost ran out of the church.

They were never alone at the reception held in Ben's spacious house. Other people shared their time and their company. She would see him for the last time late tonight when the watchnight service was held in Nyddbeck Church. Then she would not see him again until she came back from Scotland. It would be safer if she did not meet him. When she came back, Brendon May might be fit enough to play the organ, and the closeness which she and Bill had shared would perhaps no longer be there. That thought left her feeling melancholy.

Everything was ready for her early departure the next morning when she walked across the bridge half an hour before midnight to lead the last service of the year, and the century. Already people were arriving and organ music was filling the air. There were new people walking along the church path, people she had not met before. People who greeted her with American accents. Andrea was surprised to see Carla and Jack with them. Right at the last minute there was Julie too, and David, still wearing his dark suit. Her heart lifted at the sight of them. Then she took a deep breath and sent her voice to the back of the church in the first prayer.

Just after midnight they were all out of the building welcoming in the millennium to the sound of church bells ringing and fireworks exploding. Andrea found herself hugged and kissed by many people. By everyone except Bill. Where was Bill, she wondered, when they had all drifted away to continue the celebrations in their own or other people's homes?

Bill had gone back into the church. He was standing before the two steps that led to the altar. There was a stillness about him, an air of waiting that made her footsteps halt and her heart give a lurch. His hair glowed red where the lamp above the altar shone down on it. He did not say anything until she was close enough to see his face clearly. Then he spoke, and the words he said echoed on the cold, quiet air. They were words she was to remember always.

'I've been wanting to tell you all day, Andrea, that one day, when you are ready, I'll be waiting here for you. I'll be waiting to share your work and your faith, as well as your love. Just don't keep me waiting for as long as Dorothy did Ben, will you, my darling?'

Andrea felt a great wave of joy begin somewhere deep inside her. Her face was radiant as she put out her hands to him and Bill lifted them to his lips.

'You won't have to wait long, Bill,' she promised.

They walked together out of the church. When they reached the lich-gate Bill stopped.

'Do you think there'll be a scandal in the parish if I kiss you now, Andrea?' he asked softly.

'I'm prepared to risk it if you are, Bill,' she said, as she lifted her mouth to meet his.